LUCA VESTE

BLOOD STREAM

SIMON &
SCHUSTER

London · New York · Sydney · Toronto · New Delhi

A CBS COMPANY

First published in Great Britain by Simon & Schuster UK Ltd, 2015
A CBS COMPANY

3 5 7 9 10 8 6 4

Simon & Schuster UK Ltd
1st Floor, 222 Gray's Inn Road
London
WC1X 8HB

www.simonandschuster.co.uk

Simon & Schuster Australia, Sydney
Simon & Schuster India, New Delhi

A CIP catalogue record for this book is available from the British Library

Paperback ISBN: 978-1-4711-4137-9
eBook ISBN: 978-1-4711-4138-6

Typeset in the UK by Hewer Text UK Ltd, Edinburgh
Printed and bound in Great Britain by CPI Group (UK) Ltd, Croydon, CR0 4YY

Simon & Schuster UK Ltd are committed to sourcing paper that is made
from wood grown in sustainable forests and supports the Forest Stewardship
Council, the leading international forest certification organisation. Our
books displaying the FSC logo are printed on FSC certified paper.

For my parents. All of them.

Thank you.

A flower cannot blossom without sunshine, and man cannot live without love

Max Muller

Love is composed of a single soul inhabiting two bodies

Aristotle

Even psychopaths have emotions if you dig deep enough. Then again, maybe not . . . I gave up on love and happiness a long time ago

Richard Ramirez

Chloe and Joe

She watched him die.

She did nothing, as the man she supposedly loved took his final breath. Knowing that she would have to live with that inaction for whatever time she had left.

She told herself there wasn't much she could have done anyway. She could only watch as the realisation hit him, filmy eyes locking with hers. A single word dropping from his mouth, before it dissolved into nothingness and he began to fade away.

She had simply stared at him, soft tears rolling down her cheeks as she watched him convulse. Saw him fight with a diminishing strength, his muscular, fit body amounting to little in the end. A growing horror building inside her as the final gurgles of breath left his body. The effort of keeping her eyes open exhausting her.

She didn't try to move, to try to help him. The desire to do so obliterated by his words.

The knowledge that she had wanted this was driven to the back of her mind. Only the thought of what was going to happen next. Whether she would die or be let go.

She was glad he went first.

She was glad he had died looking her in the eye, knowing she had wanted it to happen.

She was glad that he'd died knowing that she was happy that he was gone.

It hadn't started out like that.

They were famous, away from that room. Celebrities. Everything she'd ever wanted to be. Chloe Morrison. Famous for no reason other than for being famous.

Chloe was taken second, after Joe, and only because of what she had been shown. Joe, tied to a chair, beaten and bloodied. She hadn't thought of herself or her family. Only him and the danger he was in.

She knew what people thought of her – that she had an elevated sense of self-worth. She had a reputation for getting what she wanted, when she wanted it. That she believed she deserved the attention, based purely on who she was.

It wasn't completely true. Not all of it.

Joe had been central to her life. It didn't matter if she spent hours making herself look 'right', presenting the flawless version of herself to the world. The spray tans and endless hair and make-up sessions. The rumours of plastic surgery to explain the way her body looked in tight-fitting clothes. To Chloe, that was all just part of the celebrity game. One she had wilfully taken a role in.

She had sought fame. She had a need to be famous. To be noticed. Without the talent or skill for it to be in music or sports, or even a vile personality. There was only one way.

Reality TV.

Chloe had thought the only way to get on one of those programmes was to either turn posh and move to Chelsea, or pretend to be from Newcastle and become more willing to piss the bed in front of a camera. That was until she saw the advert on Twitter, asking for girls from Liverpool to audition for a new reality show that was being made. She'd slept in her rollers and turned up along with hundreds of others a few weeks later, prepared to be as glam and gorgeous as possible, knowing that she had to be more *real* to stand out in the crowd.

The first time they'd met was at the auditions. She'd thought he was good-looking, if a bit full of himself. It was clear the producers on the show had plans, pairing them off a few times before filming began. It had made them comfortable together, giving them better on-screen chemistry. She'd found out Joe played for a lower division football team she'd heard of in passing. Played on her side of the water, on the Wirral. Not that she was pretending to be anything other than a proper Scouser at that point.

That had been almost two years ago. Since then, her life had changed in every single way she could have dreamed of. She was *known*. People stopped her in the street, asking for a selfie – the new autograph. She'd become the queen of the fake smile. People would tell her how funny she was, how *real* she was. How they'd known from day one that she and Joe would end up together. How happy they were that Chloe and Joe had fallen in love. How they just knew ChloJoe were going to be together forever.

On the show, cameras had followed every move they'd made. The 'first' meeting in the house they'd all had to share. The first date. The first kiss. The first time they'd said the words 'I love you' to each other. Granted, that had been in the middle of a nightclub, shouted over music, which wasn't all that romantic. They'd had to go back and dub it over, so it could be heard properly on TV. Saying it over and over in a sound booth into a microphone had kind of stripped away the romance of it, but she'd tried her best. Even if it was the weirdest thing she'd ever done.

The sex was awful, but she had all the time in the world to make that better. The proposal episode of the show had millions of viewers. She'd known beforehand, of course, but had to act as if it was all a surprise to her. It wouldn't matter. She was going to be a bride.

Then, just like that, she was bound to a chair, on what had, at first, been just a normal Friday. Darkness and the smell of rotting wood. A room in a boarded-up house, somewhere she didn't know. Joe was opposite her, breathing in short bursts as he sobbed quietly. A man almost blending into the black, his voice a whisper in her ear.

'Secrets and lies. That's why we're here. They're wrong. Everyone knows that. So many relationships have these secrets and lies going on within them. And now here you both are. The ultimate celebrity couple ... until another one comes along to replace you. Even the two of you can't escape what is real. The veneer of celebrity, everyone looking up to you. All these impressionable young minds you pollute with your lies. I'm talking real lies. Real secrets. You disgust me.'

Chloe heard the words through a fog of confusion, aware of the voice speaking directly to her and Joe. She wasn't able to focus on form or being. Just the words and the puzzling mix of them.

'Say we have a relationship as public as yours. One that is in the news all the time, in every glossy magazine, every tabloid, every celebrity blog ... one would think there could be no secrets. No lies. Everything out in the open, for us all to enjoy.'

The man moved closer to Chloe. 'But we know that's not true, don't we?'

Chloe shook her head, slowly, the room spinning as she did so. She tried to speak, before remembering the duct tape plastered across her mouth.

'Don't worry, I'll be removing it soon,' the man said. 'This would be no fun if you couldn't speak to each other.'

Chloe looked across at Joe as his head slumped forward onto his chest. Tried to catch his eye, but he wasn't moving.

'Chloe,' the man said after a few more seconds of silence. 'I want you to tell each other everything. All the secrets you have kept from each other. Then we'll see how I feel. Do you understand?'

She began to feel a little more clear-headed; the mist lifted and her focus returned. She rocked her head side to side, almost losing it again.

'Oh, Chloe. From what little I know about you, I don't think you could hide a single thought in that thick little brain of yours. No, I'm guessing you're an open book with little old Joe here. I bet he knows everything you're about to say before you've said it. Probably because it'll be about shopping or exposing yourself in some magazine.'

Chloe could feel herself shaking, the duct tape binding her hands together straining against her wrists.

'Chloe, you have to listen now. Do you understand? I think Joe has something he wants to tell you.'

It wasn't quick in coming.

When it did, she had stopped shaking through fear. Forgotten about the man in the room, what he'd done to make Joe tell her the truth. There was only her and Joe.

And anger. For everything he'd said. Everything he'd done to her.

A few minutes later, she watched him die. Watched as the man curled a piece of rope around Joe's neck, and choked him to death.

Chloe had wanted it to happen.

She was pleased that it had. That he'd got what he deserved.

'Now, Chloe,' the man said, coming down to his haunches as he got close to her. She could feel his hot breath on her neck, as he whispered in her ear. 'It's time for you to go to sleep.'

Part One

@scousemum38
Have you heard about that Chloe and
Joe from that shit Liverpool show?

@kezza11990
Yeah. Just read it. Bet they've just
gone off on holiday somewhere.

@EchoNews
BREAKING – 'ChloJoe' missing. More
information here – bit.ly/576fb5 #ChloJoe

@Gizmod87
Waits for 'exclusive' beach pictures

@Insert_Name_Here_22
Ugh. I hope they are found in ditch
somewhere #realitytvisshit

@ScouseanProud_8
They give us a bad name anyway.
Hope they don't come back.

@ScouseanProud_8
Both wools anyway. Sod 'em.

@Fayz20
I reckon they've gone off and got
married. #fairytale #newshow

@HELsBELs98
Shes a slag anyway. Hope hes found
someone better. #Joeishot

Chapter One

He hadn't seen anything like this for a long time. An authentic confession to murder. No ifs and buts. No *I didn't really mean it, it was all just a terrible accident.* Simply a total and utter acceptance of the facts and what seemed like genuine remorse.

Detective Inspector David Murphy let his size thirteen shoes slide off his feet a little and scratched at the closely shorn beard on his face.

'I don't believe you.'

The man sitting in front of him didn't gasp in shock, but moved back in his chair a little.

'Wh . . . what do you mean? I'm telling you I killed her. Stabbed her right in the chest, here,' the man said, hitting his heart for effect.

'I'm not buying it,' Murphy said, letting his eyes drift round interview room two. It needed a new paint job. The white walls where now a faded, almost grey colour.

'I'm just trying to be helpful here,' the man said, almost pleading. 'I'm doing the right thing, aren't I? I mean, it must have been me who did it. It has to be. I hear her voice sometimes and I have to tell someone what I did so she'll stop. That's the right thing to do, isn't it?'

'Oh, it would be. If a word of it was true,' Murphy replied. 'The problem is I don't think any of what you've told us since you sat down in here is the truth. Is it, Keith?'

A long sigh came from beside Murphy. DS Laura Rossi becoming bored of the exchange, he guessed. 'Tell us again.'

Keith took a deep breath and began to speak.

'We were seeing each other, me and Amy. We're like boyfriend and girlfriend. We talk about everything. Spend loads of time with each other. Have been for a few months . . .'

'See, that's the first problem, Keith,' Murphy said, attempting to keep a smile from his face. 'Boyfriend and girlfriend?'

'That's right.'

Murphy shook his head and tried to hold the laughter in. That this guy could have any chance with Amy was ridiculous. Amy was just about to turn nineteen, a fresh-faced beauty with her pick of men. Keith was in his forties, with a pock-marked face scarred by teenage acne that had yet to disappear. The grease from his hair alone was enough to keep the local chippy in business for a good few weeks. That was before you considered other 'issues'.

'Go on,' Murphy said with a wave of his hand.

'We must have got into an argument, like, and I had hold of a knife. I did it. Stuck it right in her chest. Sometimes people argue with me and they won't stop. They just go on and on, so I have to stop them somehow. I see knives and I put them in their chest and they go away for a bit. Then they come back some time later and start up with me again. So, that'll be how it happened. I can see it, all in here.' He paused a second, but then pointed to his head.

'Go back a minute,' Rossi said, writing down notes as Keith spoke. 'Slower this time. You've been seeing Amy for a few months, right?'

'Yeah. I have, honest. I know it sounds weird, right, but she liked me. Always speaking to me nicely, smiling and saying sweet things to me.'

Murphy made a noise, somewhere between a snort and a laugh. Rossi ignored him and continued talking.

'Why do you think no one close to Amy would mention you, Keith? Because this is the first time we've heard your name mentioned.'

Keith looked off to his left. 'I . . . I don't know. Maybe she never told anyone about us.'

'You've been together for a few months in your words and she doesn't tell anyone?'

'Must be.'

Murphy pictured Amy walking hand in hand round town with this guy, laughing with him, gazing into his eyes . . . it was ridiculous.

'How did you meet her?'

'I went into the shop where she worked. It's over the road from my flat. It's on the ground floor, so I'm level with the street. I like that. I used to go in every morning for the paper and other stuff. Then, I'd wait until she was definitely on shift. Got to know her pattern and that. We hit it off straight away, honest. She was so nice to me. Always smiled as soon as I went in there. Then, I practised at home asking her out. Over and over again and she always said yes. So . . . so, I did it. I asked her. I definitely did. I think I did.'

Murphy shook his head and looked away. Muttered 'Christ' under his breath and checked the time.

'What happened after you say you stabbed her?'

Keith glanced at Rossi before averting his eyes from her stare. Murphy watched him, trying to work out why he thought he had done something like this.

'Well, when you stab someone, they bleed a lot. I've seen it on telly and that. In films, they stab people and there's blood everywhere. So, I wou . . . couldn't stop the bleeding, but she wouldn't be breathing anyway by then. If you stab someone in the chest, they die really quickly. It happens in loads of films and TV programmes. I have bin bags in my house, so I must've wrapped her up. I would have done it nicely though. Then I took her home. Carried her there all by myself. From the shop. There must have been a lot of blood there, so can you say sorry for me? I don't remember cleaning it up, so it must have been all over the place. I don't know. I haven't been in there since.'

'When was this?'

'About ten in the morning, I think on a Friday. Or a Tuesday. Few weeks ago. Or two. It was quiet, so no one saw me. She didn't weigh that much, so I could do it on my own all right.'

Murphy motioned with his hand to continue.

'After that, I reckon I took her out to the front past Speke Airport. Garston way, down by the docks there. Put her in the Mersey and watched her float away. That's what I probably did.'

'You didn't do anything to her other than wrap bin bags round her and just dump her in the river?'

Keith looked at Murphy and gave him a shrug of the shoulders.

Murphy allowed the snort from his nostrils to escape. Bodies didn't float down the Mersey for very long without being seen, even those at the tail end of the river where there were fewer tourists. Further up, near the Albert Dock, it wouldn't have lasted five minutes before being seen. It ... she ... would have been found by now.

That was just the practical element. There was also the fact that Keith seemed to have mental health issues, which made everything he was saying about what he may have done to Amy questionable to say the least.

Part of Murphy was thinking 'poor guy' ... the other part was complaining about the time that was being wasted.

'Are you ready to give us your surname yet, Keith?' Murphy said, attempting to be more professional and not the irritable detective he had been for the previous hour. 'So we can check into you, things like that?'

Keith didn't respond. Just stared at the table, finding the grooves scratched into its grey surface of unyielding interest.

Amy Maguire had been missing for over three weeks. Vanished, one Thursday night. Into thin air and everything that went with it. Murphy and Rossi had been helping the short-staffed F Division in Liverpool South investigate Amy's disappearance. Their division in North Liverpool had been almost overstaffed at that point. The newly created Major Crime Unit now in existence, following a few years of increasingly high-profile cases. Higher command hadn't spread resources widely or anything as logical as that. Instead, they had simply bulked up the numbers in Liverpool North.

The Amy Maguire case might have fallen through the cracks if it wasn't for the fact nothing major had come through their doors in almost a month. Liverpool South had a multitude of other cases to deal with, so the investigation had been shifted north and Murphy was about to hand it off to a detective constable to handle, when he'd seen something in the file which piqued his interest.

Amy's mother, Stacey. A name and an address he remembered well.

A few days after she had disappeared, Murphy and Rossi had gone down to the shop where she'd worked. Rain had been coming in bursts, threatening to soak the ground and anyone in its way. Rossi had struggled to hold an umbrella over them both while Murphy looked towards the shuttered-up shop as they stood in the last place CCTV had caught Amy's image. The camera only caught the area immediately outside the shop entrance. Amy had left the edge of the frame and disappeared into darkness. Police tape strewn almost randomly across the street, as uniformed constables struggled to keep order. A small number of angry voices with nothing better to do, snarling at the plain-clothed detectives, screaming for a justice the country didn't provide.

Murphy blinked and was back in the interview room.

'Interview terminated at ten fifteen a.m.'

Amy Maguire was still alive. She had to be.

Murphy walked ahead of Rossi as they left the quiet of the room and stepped out into the corridor. He pushed through into the stretch of corridor that led towards the main incident room, making an effort to keep the door open for Rossi, before letting it swing shut behind him. Calm to cacophony in a single walk.

'How long have we worked together for now? And don't you dare say "too long".'

'Must be over three years. Why?'

'Have we ever had someone come in and confess to a murder they haven't committed?'

'A few times. Usually they don't get this far though. Uniforms downstairs tend to see them coming. Obviously slipped through the cracks this time.'

'It's not like I'm averse to people confessing crimes to me – I've heard enough of them in the past – but it doesn't half piss me off when someone confesses to something that hasn't happened.'

'Wait up, will you . . . *Mannaggia.*'

Murphy slowed a little to allow Rossi to match his step, then carried on towards the new office near the back of the building. Their old incident room was now used by the Matrix team who focused on drugs and gangs, leaving domestic violence, trafficking and the occasional murder for Murphy and his team. He wasn't sure which was worse.

He threw open the door and walked to his desk at the back of the room past the array of staff now technically under his supervision. In his peripheral vision he saw his boss through the glass of her internal office, but he kept his gaze forward, unwilling to be beckoned within just yet.

Murphy slammed his fist into the back of his chair, instantly regretting it as it spun away and into the wall.

'I've told you not to hit it so hard,' Rossi said, sitting down at the desk opposite Murphy's. 'You'll end up breaking a bone. We'll have to get you a punchbag in here or something, if you're going to spit your dummy out every time you don't get your own way.'

Murphy made some sort of guttural noise at her and dragged his chair back. He sat down, shaking his right hand to rid himself of the low throb which had already set in.

'Why don't you start up boxing again,' Rossi said, leaning across the desk.

'Because I'm too old for all that now. Been almost twenty years since I was in a ring. I'd get flattened in a second. Plus, the pain in my hand says I've forgotten how to throw a punch properly.'

Rossi hummed and sat back in her chair. 'Who does that?'

'Does what?' Murphy replied, as he began to calm himself. 'Punch chairs? At least it wasn't a wall . . .'

'I meant confess to a murder which sounds not only improbable, but of which there is no evidence that it has actually happened.'

Murphy swept open palms across his cheeks. 'Attention seeker? Mental health patient . . . God knows. We know it's not true . . .'

'Possibly . . .'

Murphy went on as if Rossi hadn't spoken. 'We're still treating this as a missing person, not a murder enquiry. So, we send a report and see if there's anything anyone wants to do with Keith. That's not our problem.'

Rossi nodded slowly. 'Don't think we should dismiss it entirely though. It's not like he was confessing to killing JFK or something. It's possible that he could be telling the truth.'

'It was Amy on the video. Walking from the shop at eleven at night, not at nine in the morning like he said. Her mum was still awake at one in the morning and it's only a ten-minute walk from there. Amy would've been home well before then.'

Murphy had spoken a little harsher than he'd meant so wasn't exactly surprised when Rossi didn't answer at first, instead giving him a silent moment of contemplation.

'People don't just disappear ...' Rossi replied after allowing the silence to drag on for a few moments longer than was comfortable.

That was the only problem with trying to dismiss the thought that something had happened to Amy. Almost three weeks with no word. Nothing to say that she had run off of her own accord. Murphy scratched the back of his head and pulled himself closer to his desk. 'Sometimes, you just have a feeling, okay? Remember that girl we pulled out of that basement a few years back?'

'How could I forget? That was the first proper case we worked together on. It's burned on my memory. It was about that time I started seeing more lines on my face in the morning.'

'Well, I bet everyone thought she was dead or on some island somewhere. Turned out to be wrong, didn't it?'

'I think that was probably a one-off. I'm not sure how many people want to take young girls off the street then keep them alive in a dark basement for a year. Just for some kind of experiment. We have to be realistic here.'

'Yeah, well, maybe it's something else this time.'

'I'm all for positive thinking, Murph, but even I'm struggling with this one. Kick it back to Liverpool South and let them deal with it. Nothing more we can do now. We've spoken to all her friends, done the press thing, all that. Not a single lead, other than a possible mental health patient, confessing to a murder that we have no evidence for.'

Murphy didn't answer. He was remembering Stacey Maguire as she had been years earlier. Seventeen, almost the same age as Amy was now. Mid-nineties haircut and pale skin. He smiled without thinking.

He was broken from his thoughts by DC Michael Hale appearing next to his desk. 'Boss is calling us in.'

Murphy raised an eyebrow at Rossi before following her and DC Hale, catching up to them as they entered the boss's office. The boss being DCI Stephens, head of their not-so-little corner of E Division.

'I'll get straight to the point,' Stephens said. Murphy closed the door behind him, not for the first time bristling at the fact that there was enough room for four people to work comfortably in this room whereas everyone else was tripping over themselves.

'We've got a situation developing at the moment near Anfield ...'

'At the stadium? Someone nicked a footballer's car or something?' Hale said. Murphy gave him a withering look, which made Hale stiffen and turn away.

Stephens deigned to look at him for a second before switching her attention back to Murphy and Rossi. 'If you'll allow me to finish my sentence ... no, not at the stadium. Although not far from it. Two bodies found in a house in Anfield.' She rattled off an address which Murphy was pleased to see both Rossi and Hale noted down.

'Suspicious?' Murphy said, noting a harried look in Stephens's eyes and wondering what had caused it.

'Very. And that's not all. Early reports are that we've found our missing celebs. And that it's bad. Very fuc—'

Stephens stopped herself short. 'Let's just say if what I'm hearing is right, we're about to have a lot more company than usual.'

Murphy nodded and turned round, not waiting for Rossi and Hale to follow.

It always begins with a body. Or bodies, in this instance. Murphy thought of the cases over the years – the bodies he had seen in their last moments – and carried on walking.

That was what he was paid to do. To keep walking towards the bodies.

Chapter Two

They had arrived to a scrum of uniformed officers, all trying to look like they were being useful. Murphy guessed most were just hanging around in the hope of getting a glimpse of the scene. The opportunity to tell their friends and family later, that they had been involved in what was shaping up to be a much-discussed case over dinner – or 'tea' if you're from the north and correct – in the coming days.

Murphy had parked between a forensics van and a marked vehicle, squeezing the pool car into the tight space.

'Looks a bit different around here,' Rossi said, once out of the car. 'Thought they'd have got more done by now, though.'

'Yeah, sprucing it up isn't going to do much if the residents are still the same,' Murphy replied, looking down the street at Anfield Stadium in the distance. Regeneration projects and the expansion of the football stadium were transforming the area of Anfield, albeit slowly, and arguably not in the way most people had envisioned. 'Disenfranchised youth and a battle-hardened older generation aren't the best of mixes. Nice to see those boarded-up houses around the stadium finally go though. About bloody time. Might even move up the season ticket waiting list with the ground expansion. Just hope ticket prices don't keep increasing.'

'Like you'd go that much anyway.'

'You never know, Laura,' Murphy said with a grin. 'I could become a regular for all you know. Probably better than just Sky Plussing *Match of the Day* once a week and fast forwarding through that big-eared ex-bluenose. Bet it's murder round here on match days.'

Rossi didn't reply, just gave a slow nod of her head as she looked towards the row of houses that had been marked for demolition and rebuilding a number of months ago, all post-war brick and years of disregard.

Murphy knew the front facades only told part of the story. The steel coverings on the windows would have been broken into. Never at the front, always at the back – even squatters and robbers had sense. Armed with a crowbar or some other tool, they'd have easily pulled back the coverings and taken their fill of the leftovers or settled in and set up home. The security company in charge of keeping the houses empty would have made some attempts to clear squatters out, but Murphy knew that most of the time it was more trouble than it was worth.

Murphy brushed past the uniform standing outside the derelict house where all the attention was gathered. The PC acknowledged him with a nod.

'Have you noticed they never ask me for ID?'

'Let's see,' Rossi said, keeping in step with him. 'The two highest-profile murder cases we've had in the past decade, and you've managed to be involved with both investigations. On top of that, you've also successfully closed cases against a number of other people, and had your face in the *Liverpool Echo* more times than Ricky Tomlinson. And you wonder why you might be recognisable?'

'It's not like I was doing those things on my own. You were with me, remember?'

'I know when to hide from the cameras.'

'I wish I did.'

Forensic teams were already in place. Murphy was about to step inside the house when a voice shouted from within.

'Suit up.'

'Sorry,' Murphy called back, turning round to see a smirking Rossi behind him.

'How long have you been doing this again?'

'Obviously not long enough,' Murphy replied.

A few minutes later, looking like extras from a film about pandemics, they entered the final resting place of Chloe Morrison and Joe Hooper.

The smell attacked them as soon as they crossed the threshold. Decay and blood. Rotting meat and something Murphy could never put his finger on.

The house was long abandoned; gutted and ready to be pulled down and replaced by whatever the building group who now owned this part of Anfield decided. More houses, Murphy guessed. Only smaller, and using worse building materials, but with a nice modern finish to the kitchen and bathroom to con those buying or renting the properties. Walls as thin as paper, small rooms dressed up to look big enough for growing families. Similar developments were everywhere, popping up on disused parcels of land across Merseyside, making money for invisible directors on multiple boards.

'Together until the end. Kinda nice if you don't think about it too hard.'

Murphy didn't respond to Rossi, who was peering past people into the room in which the couple had been found.

The house may have felt abandoned, but Murphy walked through on the off-chance the person responsible had left behind something obvious. A three-bedroomed terrace, with nothing but damp in the walls and mould growing over old wallpaper. He walked upstairs, the smell above almost as wretched as the one below. The main bedroom which overlooked the road outside was bare, its wooden floorboards broken in places, newspaper pushing its way through cracks to the surface. The second bedroom was no different apart from an airing cupboard in the corner which had once housed the boiler, now taken apart and capped off.

The box bedroom was different.

At first, Murphy was surprised that only one officer was taking pictures of the walls carefully, methodically. Then he realised the space within the room was really only big enough for one person. There was no natural light due to the boarded up window so a small beam from a stand-up light had to suffice.

Magazine covers, articles and newspaper clippings covered most of one wall inside the room. From his position by the doorway, Murphy could just about see the other walls were bare. The forensic tech took photographs from all angles to capture the entire spectrum of pictures.

Murphy spied the headlines nearest to the room entrance, taking note of the names displayed in black capitals.

CHLOE AND JOE'S TICKET TO PARADISE
CHLOE AND JOE REVEAL ALL
CHLOJOE – WE WANT A FAMILY

'Looks like a stalker's collage,' Rossi said, looking over his shoulder. 'Some of these are from when they first started going out. They go back a long time. Must have been collecting them.'

'I didn't keep up, to be honest,' Murphy replied. 'Not my sort of thing.'

'You didn't watch the show?' Rossi said, a sceptical look plastered across her Mediterranean features. 'Everyone did.'

Murphy shook his head. 'Couldn't bring myself to. You know I can't stand hearing Scouse accents on TV. Not even my own.'

'You missed out then. You wouldn't believe some of the things these people got up to. Made my uni days look like I was in a nunnery. Not those two though. They were a bit different. Found each other quite early on and that changed them I suppose . . .'

Murphy held up a gloved hand to stop Rossi talking. 'There'll be plenty of time to catch me up. Right now, I think we should concentrate on the scene at hand, yeah?'

Rossi grunted and stepped back as Murphy asked the forensics officer if he could come into the room.

The wall came into view, giving him the chance to see

the message scrawled across the pictures. Red ink, bleeding into the walls.

NOTHING STAYS SECRET

Murphy blinked and the message was different. A different house, a different time. He blinked again and was back in the box room.

He was aware of Rossi on the edge of his vision. He looked at the words again, realising they weren't red, but black.

It wasn't that place. Not the same. Different house, different time.

'Christ, thought I was somewhere else then for a second,' Murphy said, turning away from the wall.

'*Merda,* your mum and dad's house after . . . after they were, you know.'

Murphy didn't answer. He looked out towards the hall and shrugged off the memory. 'Let's get back downstairs.'

Murphy passed by her as she let him go. Rossi took in the wall once more before following. At the bottom of the stairs, he took a proffered mask from a tech and kept walking.

That's just what you do.

'In the back of the room, not the front. That's interesting,' Murphy said, standing in the doorway as Rossi joined him. A through lounge and dining room, the entrance in the middle. The bodies were to Murphy's right. 'Hidden away from the street just in case, I suppose. Not that it matters with those covers over the windows. Weird.'

'The whole thing is a bit weird,' Rossi said, looking towards the front of the house as she went past Murphy and into the room. 'You all right, Mike?'

DC Hale held up a hand towards them, standing near the front window. As far away as he could possibly get without drawing attention to himself, Murphy thought.

'How long do you reckon?'

Rossi shook her head. 'Smelled worse. Can't be that long. Couple of days maybe?'

The smell of ammonia and decomposition was overpowering, sticking in the air so it felt thick and tangible, but Rossi was right. They had experienced much worse.

Two bodies sitting upright on the chairs. Bound and gagged, their faces dropped into their chests. What was once life, now something indefinable, imperceptible. Empty. Murphy could just about make out the duct tape which had been used to keep them fastened to the chairs, frayed in places, pulled tight in others.

'How long have they been missing now?'

Murphy turned towards the voice of Dr Stuart Houghton, the pathologist who delighted Murphy ever so much.

'Two, three days?' Murphy replied, moving towards where Houghton was crouched. 'I forget which. How can you tell it's them?'

'If it's not, someone has gone to a lot of trouble to make us believe it is. Wallet found next to him with his ID in. The tattoos covering him are pretty much exactly what I've seen every time I visit a newsagent and peruse the magazine shelf. He's wearing ripped jeans and I believe that's a black T-shirt on the floor next to him. That'll match what he was last seen in. She's wearing black joggers and a red vest-top, which is yet another thing I've read in the paper the last couple of days more than once.'

'Still . . . could be anyone.'

Houghton sighed and raised himself from his haunches. 'Yes, of course. I know that, you know that, even those idiots outside know that. But, I'm just trying to save you a bit of time. Look at his body. Look at the things he's etched across himself. Do you think anyone else would be stupid enough to do that to themselves, David?'

Murphy shuddered at the use of his first name. Very few people used it outside of his own home and it still rattled.

'Okay, okay,' Murphy said, raising his hands in defeat. 'I understand. Hard to look past . . . well, this scene, to start recognising faces.'

Houghton shrugged and went back to whatever he was doing, leaving Murphy to move closer to the chairs.

'At least a couple of days . . .' Murphy said, under his breath.

The bodies had taken on the pale pallor of death, the victims showing signs of discolouring as the process of breaking down began. The male victim was more marked than the female, but there was no doubt that both were decaying into obscurity.

Murphy couldn't see any obvious signs of violence on the female, but imagined it lurking beneath the surface of decomposition. The male was different. Bloodspots, illuminated by the beams of lights set up in the corners of the room, had dried dark brown in places.

'Who called it in?' Murphy asked, not turning round to face anyone in particular.

'Their agent,' came the response from DC Hale who had come closer to the edge of the back room.

'Agent?' Murphy replied.

'Yeah,' Hale said, hovering in the space where living room became dining room once upon a long time ago. 'Looks after these celebrities and that. He got an anonymous phone call earlier this morning with this address. He came down but when he couldn't get in, he rang the local station. They gained access through the back.'

'They broke in?' Murphy said, raising himself up now and backing away towards the doorway.

'No, the panel on this window was only hanging by a thread. They saw the bodies through the window.'

Murphy looked towards the window at the back of the room. Easy enough to see directly into the room and see what was inside once the steel covering was removed. 'Uniforms must have shit themselves. Where's the agent now?'

Hale shouted over towards the front entrance to the constable in uniform still standing guard there. 'Where's our man?'

Murphy didn't hear the response, but followed as Hale left the open doorway. Rossi lingered a moment longer before following.

'You ever get the feeling this sort of thing follows you round, Murphy?' Rossi said as she caught up with him in the hallway.

Murphy suppressed a laugh and smiled thinly down at her.

'All the time,' he replied looking towards where DC Hale was heading. 'But then ... I chose this bloody job, didn't I? Let's see what Mr Agent has to say and go from there. For all we know we'll be done by the end of the day.'

'Murder and then suicide?'

Murphy shook off his coveralls as they left the house and didn't reply at first. 'They were both bound to those chairs, Laura.'

'I know, but I've seen that kind of thing before. Guy doesn't want to be known as a murderer – even after he's gone – so he makes it look like someone else was there. It's definitely happened in the past.'

Murphy stared down at her, giving her the look he had to every now and again.

'I know, I know,' Rossi said, holding her palms up. 'I'm just saying we shouldn't rule anything out, that's all I'm saying.'

'We won't,' Murphy said, making his way to the end of the path which led onto the street. 'Let's cross our fingers and hope that's the case, shall we?'

Chapter Three

DC Hale was leaning on the side of the van, one dark shoe raised against it. Marked and unmarked cars were scattered across the road, some still blinking blue lights across the street. It was becoming busier. Hastily strung-up crime-scene tape was marshalled by constables in heavy uniform, their only job to keep a growing number of onlookers away from the scene as they held on to smartphones, updating Facebook and Twitter. Embellishing the nothingness of what they could actually see into something more tangible and interesting.

Murphy was becoming used to the latest way news spread. Didn't like it, but he assumed not many on his side of the tape did. He looked both ways as he crossed the road, before realising such an action was redundant.

'How is he?' Murphy said as he reached Hale. 'Sounds quiet.'

'Not sure,' Hale replied, looking past Murphy towards the house. 'I haven't spoken to him.'

Rossi shaped as if to say something, then stopped as Murphy gave her a look.

'Don't just stand there,' Murphy said, drawing himself into Hale's line of vision. 'Find out what you can. See if anything else has been found out. If anyone saw anything. That kind of thing, yeah?'

Hale stood up to his full height but failed to reach Murphy's towering figure by a good few inches. 'Yes, boss.'

Murphy allowed Rossi to enter the van first, then let the uniform who had been sitting inside slip past him and leave. He stepped up into the van and sat next to the man.

'I'm Detective Inspector David Murphy, this is Detective Sergeant Laura Rossi . . .' Murphy realised he hadn't even asked the man's name. 'And you are . . .?'

'Thomas Parker,' came the muted response. Parker's head hung low, almost touching his knees in the cramped seats of the van. An almost perfectly round bald patch winked back at them as Parker slightly turned his back to the window. His shoulders looked bulky on his slight frame, solid as if he worked out, Murphy thought.

'Is it them?'

Murphy cleared his throat and let the pause grow a little longer. 'We're not sure yet,' he said after a few moments more. 'We're still making enquiries . . .'

'I think it is. I don't want it to be but Joe's tattoos . . .' Parker raised a hand to caress his own upper body, before letting it drop down to be clasped by the other.

'We'll know for certain soon enough, Mr Parker,' Rossi said, leaning forward towards him from across the small aisle which separated them. 'For now, we're just going to ask you some questions, okay?'

A slight nod but still no raised head.

'Can you tell us what happened this morning?'

'I got a phone call around six, maybe just after.' Parker's voice was monotone, no life to it. 'It was from Chloe's phone, so I answered. A man on the other end said I could find Chloe and Joe at this house, that they were waiting for me. I thought it was a wind-up at first, but he was . . . he wouldn't let me talk.'

'What else was he saying?' Murphy cut in.

'I don't know really, it was all a bit strange. He said I had to go and see what their love had created, what lies had been told, that they needed me to be there. Just a stream of stuff that I didn't really understand. He was insistent that it was no joke, that I had no time to mess about.'

'Then what?'

'I didn't go straight away. Took me about five or ten minutes of lying there deciding what to do before I moved. I was waiting for Chloe to ring me back and say it was all a joke. When she didn't, I came straight down. I got here around seven and tried knocking on the front door.' Parker paused, lifted his head for a second before letting it drop to his chest again. 'I got a feeling something was bad, you know. Nothing looked right, not in the whole street. I was worried . . .'

Murphy glanced out of the window of the van, wondering how quiet it would have been there at that time of morning. 'You were alone at this point?'

Parker nodded slowly. 'I walked round to the back of the house, to see if I could look through a window or something. I realised the houses were all empty here, so I wasn't expecting there to be any problems. The back gate looked locked, so I just rang you lot . . . the police.'

'And they just came down? Like, straight away?' Rossi asked, a hint of incredulity in her tone, causing Murphy to give her a glance before looking back at the top of Parker's head.

'Well . . . I know a few people, if you know what I mean. Only had to mention a couple of names and I didn't have to wait long.'

Murphy shook his head slightly. The wonders of knowing the right people, moving in the right circles. 'So, you waited until uniformed officers arrived. Did you see anything out of the ordinary at that point?'

Parker shook his head. 'I felt something though. Like . . . I was being watched or whatever. Couldn't see anyone and there were only the empty houses around anyway.'

Murphy looked towards Rossi who gave a nod in return, which he hoped meant that the other houses in the street were being searched.

'They turned up and took over really. I hung back a little, but my curiosity got the better of me. When they got into the back garden, I followed them and saw what they . . . found.'

Murphy looked for tissues as Parker finally dissolved into the sobs that had been threatening to appear since they had entered the van. He found nothing.

'Take your time,' Rossi said, shrugging her shoulders at Murphy as he came up empty-handed.

'I'm . . . I'm sorry. She was just such a sweet girl. She didn't deserve this.'

'Of course she didn't,' Murphy said, thankful the crying had subsided a little. 'That's why we need to know as much as possible at this point, so we can find out who did this.'

'Yeah . . . yes,' Parker replied, wiping a sleeve across his eyes, drying them for a split second before they became wet again. 'I'll do anything.'

Rossi cut in, changing tack. 'When did you know they had gone missing?'

'Two . . . well, three days ago now. They were supposed to be at an event for the opening of some local film on Friday. They didn't show up and the PR in charge of the event called me. I tried getting in touch with Chloe, but didn't get an answer. I gave her a few hours, but started to get a little worried.'

'So you called us?'

'Well . . . not you specifically, but yes, the police. Not straight away, though. I called the cleaning firm who looks after the apartment.'

Murphy asked for the name of the firm and wrote down the answer before allowing Parker to continue.

'They went over there and found an empty apartment. The doorman there hadn't seen them since Friday morning . . . I'm sure you already know all this.'

Rossi held up a hand before realising the futility of the motion as Parker still sat with his head bowed. 'For now we just want to hear what happened before this morning. Gives us more of a complete picture from your side of it.'

'Fine . . . fine. That's it though. Police came over, found nothing to suggest anything untoward had happened and left. Said they'd probably gone away for a holiday or something without telling anyone.'

'You didn't think that was possible?' Murphy said, wondering exactly how close this agent was to his client.

'Not at all. Chloe knew not to do anything like that. She had to be ready at a moment's notice to attend events, openings, things like that. She has . . . had . . . to be on call at all times. If Michelle Keegan, or Charlotte Crosby, or any of those reality TV celeb types backs out of some PR, Chloe has to be straight in there to get her face seen. If she wanted to go on holiday, she knew to tell me. She trusted me.'

'So,' Murphy said, attempting to bring a close to the conversation. 'Chloe and Joe go missing at some point on Friday. No signs of a struggle at their home, then a phone call this morning, telling you to come to this house where they're . . . found.'

Parker's voice grew almost inaudible. 'Yes . . . that's about it.'

'What did the voice on the phone sound like? Familiar, someone you recognised maybe?'

'I've never heard that voice in my life. It was gruff, like someone was trying to sound older than they were. A weird, put-on accent as well. A Welshman trying to do a Geordie kind of thing.'

Murphy sat back a little, crossing his arms. 'Tell us more about them. They had been together for almost two years? Since that TV show?'

Murphy watched Parker shift in his seat. The first time he had noticed a distinct change in his demeanour. 'It would have been two years this coming July. All starting with that show. Didn't think it would last this long, but it seems they knew what was best.'

'You didn't like him, did you?' Murphy said, happy to finally be able to make eye contact with Parker as he fixed them with a watery gaze.

'Not really, no. He wasn't right for Chloe. I didn't like the way he was with her.'

'What way?'

Parker exhaled, his breath a long, drawn-out sigh. 'I think she was more invested in that relationship than he ever was. He . . . There were rumours. That's all.'

'What kind of rumours?' Rossi said, her pen flying across her notebook as she made the notes Murphy never did.

'That he *enjoyed* himself a little too much when she wasn't around. In my line of work, that's usual though. No one seems to have any kind of loyalty in this game.'

Murphy listened as Parker went into a little more detail, thinking about the reasons murder usually occurred. Domestic issues was still number one. Although the last couple of years had shown him that there were always more reasons to kill.

'Did they have any enemies?' Murphy heard Rossi ask as he paid more attention to what was being said.

A short laugh from Parker. 'Tons of them. There are thousands . . . maybe millions of people who hate reality stars. Just go on the internet and search for their names . . . Hell, just read any newspaper. There's always someone saying nasty things about them. Social media is the worst, of course. Some of the tweets Chloe used to receive . . . Christ.'

'Anyone specific,' Murphy said, mentally crossing his fingers for an easy ride.

'Not that I can think of. I will of course pass on the hate mail.'

'Hate mail?' Murphy replied, surprised that sort of thing still happened. 'Didn't think anyone sent letters these days . . .'

'Oh, it's all emails. We've really moved on as a society.' Parker shook his head and looked on the verge of tears again. 'Is that it for now? Only I'm going to be quite busy today. There'll be a lot of interest in this.'

Murphy looked at Rossi who narrowed her eyes at him.

Always suspicious.

*   *   *

'There wasn't anything we could keep him on for now, you know that.'

Murphy and Rossi were standing in the cordoned-off street, keeping their voices low as more onlookers crowded round the crime-scene tape a hundred yards or so further up the road.

'Yeah . . . just seemed shifty to me. All that crying . . .'

'He was upset.'

'Okay, maybe I wasn't expecting that. I thought he'd be more of a loudmouth. Like those ones you see on telly. What was that bloke called?'

'Which one?' Murphy said, staring across towards the crowd of faces, all trying to get a better look at what was going on.

'You know, the one who was always on *Sky News* and that. Turned out to be a paedo rapist or whatever . . .'

'Max Clifford?'

Rossi clapped her hands together. 'That's the one. Would have annoyed me all day that.'

'What about him?' Murphy said, after waiting a few seconds for her to speak first.

'That's what I was expecting. Bit more gregarious, you know what I mean?'

'Not really,' Murphy replied, looking back towards the house. 'Anyway, I think we've got work to do. We start now. Suggestions?'

'Two things. The house and the victims.'

'Good.' Murphy nodded, wondering how infamous the house was about to become. 'But that's actually three things. Plus, you've forgotten about witnesses.'

Rossi tutted then shook her head. 'There's no one here really. All these houses are being pulled down.'

'Maybe,' Murphy replied. 'But I guarantee there'll be at least someone who hasn't left yet. Always is. And it's usually the one person who takes notice most of what happens around them.'

'Fiver says you're wrong,' Rossi said, extending her hand. 'Bet you there's no one here.'

'You're on,' Murphy said, gripping Rossi's hand in his and shaking once. 'A fiver on someone being here, who saw something suspicious.'

He lost the bet.

Chapter Four

Murphy and Rossi left DC Hale at the scene, along with a number of other officers, to finish up as much as was possible at that point. The scene would be cordoned off for a while yet, but most of the work would be down to forensics – the detectives' work now focused on a multitude of different lines of enquiry. Most turning out to be dead ends, but requiring investigation all the same.

The familiar building on St Anne Street loomed into view as Murphy drove towards the station, wiper blades swishing across the windscreen as rain battered down on the car. Rossi was silent beside him, fingers flying across her phone screen.

'Do you ever stop texting him?'

'Of course I do,' Rossi replied, turning a shade of embarrassed red, despite her angry tone. 'I've got to sleep some time.'

'This could be The One . . .'

'Do you want there to be three murders for the team to deal with today?'

'All right, all right, I'll let you get back to the modern version of whispering sweet nothings to each other.'

'Anyway, I had to put up with it when you got back with Sarah and she's your wife. Surely once you're married that sort of thing stops.'

'Don't worry,' Murphy said, slowing down as they approached the entrance to the car park. 'I won't tell you any of the text messages she sends me now ... far too racy for such a young woman to hear.'

Rossi made a sound like she was going to throw up. Murphy snorted and slowed the wipers down as the heavy rain subsided a little. He went back to letting his mind wander. In his head, he began delegating jobs to the team, hoping the restructure was going to work as well as had been intended.

The team. Murphy was still trying to get used to the new set-up. The Murder Squad as they were known collo-quially – although their official title was the Major Crime Unit – had been established in the wake of a busy couple of years in the city of Liverpool. A serial killer, then a mass murderer months later, had finally had an effect on those with their hands on the purse strings. A specialised section had been created to meet a seemingly growing demand – with a public outcry helping it along. It allowed the Matrix team to concentrate on what they were good at, leaving the detectives in the Liverpool North division to focus on what seemed to be a never-ending parade of serious crimes.

'You know, for a team nicknamed the Murder Squad, we've had very little murder. It's been all domestics, assaults, robberies ... that sort of thing lately.'

'It was only a matter of time,' Rossi replied, not look-ing up from her phone screen. 'You're a bloody death magnet usually.'

'Shut it, you,' Murphy said, hiding a smile. 'I could still throw you over the water to work with our mate Tony Brannon.'

'I'll shut up,' Rossi said, miming a zip going across her mouth.

Murphy smirked, thinking of Brannon briefly. The misogynistic, opinionated ball-ache, who had made his life a misery on a daily basis. Right up until Murphy had him transferred to Wirral CID.

Murphy indicated right and waited for a van to pass before pulling into the car park. St Anne Street station looked like a retro office building from the eighties at first glance. It didn't get much better on the second either. It wasn't one of the glass-fronted modern structures which were seemingly being built every week in the city, but distinctly old-fashioned-looking.

Murphy liked it that way.

Leaving Rossi talking to a new DC outside, Murphy was in the office within a few minutes. Might have been sooner if he hadn't paused at the top of the stairs to catch his breath. He could have used the lift, but he was forcing himself to do a little more exercise. Anything to slow his march towards the dreaded age of forty and the increasing threat of a middle-age spread. He drank occasionally, but it wasn't alcohol he was worried about. It was the takeaways and bacon sarnies that were going to catch up with him. His rapidly thinning hair was made palatable only by the fact he'd never known what to do with it anyway – but its loss compounded the feeling of *getting on*. Sarah said it was his beard that made him look older, but he thought it was life which was doing a fine job of things.

The office, with its bank of desks, would look indistinguishable from any call centre in town, if it wasn't for the murder boards which headed the room. Pictures of victims and lists of places, people, things – information they hoped would bring a close to the cases. Not that it mattered of course. Justice was supposed to be the most important part of getting past a death. You got that and moved on. It didn't happen that way, of course. Not with the thankfully rare cases of serial killing and mass murder. Nor the domestic cases that happened almost constantly. Over one hundred deaths per year; people murdered by partners or exes. People gone in an instant, but for those left behind, the deaths would linger for an interminable amount of time.

He knew that only too well.

Murphy shook his jacket off, placed it on the back of his chair and sat down, switching his computer on as he did so. He looked round for someone he knew the name of to ask them to make him a cup of coffee, but saw only strangers in smart clothes. The few detective constables left behind to deal with the other cases the team had on consisted of an interchangeable cast of faces. Rotating in and out of the squad, leaving Murphy with no one he could remember the name of.

He settled for the warm, half-empty bottle of water left from the previous day, swigging back most of what was left before instantly regretting it.

The house would be easy. All records for those on the street would be held by the council, along with a list of previous occupiers, he hoped.

'What are you betting then?'

Murphy tore his eyes away from the screen on his computer and looked towards an approaching Rossi. 'At the moment, I'm betting there was someone else in the room.'

'Well, if it's not murder–suicide, I reckon a spurned ex. Of his, I mean.'

'Really? Something that simple?'

'Yeah,' Rossi replied, retying her hair back up into a ponytail. 'If this Joe was playing away from home, it wouldn't take long until he was found out. Or, to meet some bunny-boiler type. Imagine having to see pictures of them both out there all the time. They're in the papers constantly. It wouldn't surprise me if he's had a bit on the side and it's come back to haunt him.'

'And her?' Murphy said, not buying the theory.

'Chloe? That's just simple jealousy. Whoever it was couldn't handle the fact that Chloe was the one who got all the attention.'

Murphy pursed his lips, then scratched at his beard. 'It's a leap. It just doesn't feel right. Could be a murder–suicide as you said. She kills him or vice versa.'

'I'm not so sure of that now. How do they end up in that house?'

'I think we need to actually spend a bit of time on this before trying to solve it. We're quite obviously not frigging Sherlock Holmes.'

'You'd be Watson anyway ...' Rossi said, under her breath.

'I heard that.'

The start of every case was much the same. Called to a scene, have a look at a dead body or two. Interview whoever found them and then start to build a picture. Murphy liked to see the whole thing laid out before him and then he could view it as a complete story. To be able to look at what fit and discard what didn't. He enjoyed talking to people – or rather it wasn't so much the people he liked but the actual talking, teasing out details and information. Rossi was different. They had been working together a few years, but the differences were still stark to Murphy. He saw her as more analytical, looking for reasons and meanings behind everything.

They worked well together, he thought. The two most high-profile cases the city had seen in the past few years had shown him that.

The Sherlock Holmes jibe had been correct though. The resolution of a case never seemed to happen like magic, as it did in those stories. It was solved by relentless investigation and hopefully a mistake made by a perpetrator. Asking questions until you found an answer that made sense. Or a killer who left behind clues to their identity.

'Start drawing up a list.'

'Of what?' Rossi replied, her eyes not leaving her own computer screen as she did so.

'People we need to speak to. Family, friends, that cleaner who went in the house . . . the usual.'

Rossi gave him a half-hearted thumbs-up and got to work, leaving Murphy to get up from his desk and cross to the murder boards. He lifted the marker pen and began afresh.

*   *   *

'I knew he'd be the death of her. I knew it.'

As introductions went, Murphy thought it was solid. Chloe's mother had ushered them in, showing two women around the same age as her out of the living room as she did so.

'I always said he'd do something to her. Never liked him. I said that to her. Why didn't she listen?'

They'd had to travel to the other side of the water to visit Chloe's mother – the water in question being the River Mersey. A mile wide, separating Liverpool from the peninsula on the other side of the Wirral, the two sides bonded together by tunnels which ran underneath the river bed.

'Where did you use to live again?' Rossi had asked as they drove through the Wallasey tunnel which ran from just outside the city centre into the east side of the Wirral.

'Moreton. Nice enough place. Well, where I was living was anyway. Gets a bit rougher the closer you get to the old estates.'

'Never fancied it myself. What's that place over here where all those footballers live?'

'Caldy, I think.'

'If I had that kinda money I'd still be looking at Formby and the like. Something about the Wirral just puts me off.'

Murphy laughed and wagged his finger at Rossi. 'You're an old-school Scouser. Next thing you'll be moaning about woollybacks and posh gets.'

'*Vaffanculo,*' Rossi said, shaping to give him a smack on the arm before thankfully realising he was driving.

'It's not that bad over here. Once you get used to it, it's just like anywhere really. It's not Liverpool, but then, where is? Liverpool isn't like anywhere else really.'

'I'm not convinced I want to find out if that's true.'

'What was the name of this road again?'

Rossi took her notebook out. 'Broadway Avenue. You've told me to write down *Off Belvedere*. Don't know why we don't just use the satnav . . .'

'Don't need it,' Murphy said before Rossi could moan any further. 'It's a straight run from here.'

A stretch of main road led from the tunnel exit, once Murphy had navigated a somewhat confusing roundabout. Houses lined the widened roads, with buses and traffic passing almost constantly.

Broadway Avenue was in the more expensive part of Wallasey. The road was dominated by large semi-detached houses, almost all with their own drives, many with new, expensive cars parked on them. Trees beginning to finally accept that spring had begun, almost blocked the view of the homes behind them.

'Okay,' Rossi had said as they'd left the car parked outside. 'I'd live in a place like this if we got a pay rise. Would have to be a big raise, but I could have one of these places.'

Then they were inside. The smell of leather and some type of air freshener emanating from seemingly every corner of the room. The black of the armchair Murphy had perched himself on was darker and richer than he'd ever seen.

A glamour shot of Chloe, tasteful, almost fully clothed, adorned the wall over the modern marble fireplace to one side of the room. An obscenely sized television overpowered the corner.

'I'm telling you now, if he wasn't already dead I'd have done it myself.'

Murphy allowed Chloe's mother to talk herself out. Karen Morrison was the epitome of someone who *looked good for her age* as he'd heard Sarah say often about someone on TV. Murphy knew she was in her forties at least, but would have put her as younger than himself.

The only betrayal was in her eyes, which even without the puffiness of crying, were dark with age and life.

'She should never have gone on that show . . . my poor baby.'

Rossi leaned over and patted at Karen's hands, now clasped on her knees as her head bowed forward. 'We're really sorry, Karen. We're going to do everything we can to find out what happened to Chloe, okay? We just need to know as much as possible at this point. Can you tell us a bit more about her?'

As Karen Morrison began to talk about Chloe's childhood, Murphy's attention moved from the woman's words to the room around them. Aside from the large picture above the fireplace, the room was dotted with more photographs of Chloe. A couple of pictures stood on a sideboard in an alcove. More were displayed on a bureau which held a range of alcohol within.

It was almost a shrine.

'She wanted to be famous,' Karen said, shaking her head. 'That was her goal and nothing was going to stop her. When that show came up, she auditioned again and again for it. Honestly, I didn't think she'd do it when they picked her but she was determined. Told us that it was what she wanted, so we went along with it.'

'After the show finished,' Rossi said, her voice still low. 'What was it like for her?'

A breath from Karen. 'She changed. Not that most people noticed, of course, just people who knew her. Little things. The way she talked, the things she said. That kind of stuff.'

'Like what?'

'Her accent, for one. She was brought up over here, on the Wirral, but all of a sudden she had this broad Scouse accent, like she was from one of those council estates over there. I suppose if you're on a show about Liverpool it's required, but I never liked it. She went to nice schools over here, we made sure of it. Not that she ever did very well academically. Always had her head in the clouds.'

Murphy had become bored of looking round the room. 'What did you think of her relationship with Joe?'

There was a change in the atmosphere then as the temperature dropped a degree or two.

'That one,' Karen said, her voice different to the soft, lyrical one she used when she spoke of Chloe. 'He was never right for her. I'm telling you now . . . it's his fault. He will have done this to her.'

Love

Here's the thing they don't tell you about love.

It kills you.

The death which follows love around, as if it's a constant companion, it is the worst of them all. It hurts the most. The feeling of utter desolation, the loneliness that follows. When love dies, a piece of you goes with it.

He used to wallow in that feeling. Every relationship he had, destined to end in the same way. Bitter acrimony and regret. The endless days which stretched out into his future, alone and isolated.

Livid. A growing sense of irritation which became anger, acidic as it became bile in his throat.

Love is violent.

It was never his fault.

'Have you seen the way they're falling over themselves to talk about this shit? You would think it was Kate and Prince bloody William that had been murdered.'

He turned the laptop screen towards her, shaking his head as she turned away with a sniff.

'Do you think they really loved one another ... you know, deep down? Or were they just stuck with each other. In it for the money.'

He didn't get an answer. Just a pathetic look. The one she gave him more and more these days.

She was Number Four on his list of great loves. He numbered them, wanting to make them something more than just simple names. They deserved more. They deserved their own significance.

The first one, she had been his favourite. His first love. Number One. Two decades later and he still remembered the way she smiled, white teeth glittering back at him. The front two jutting forward just a little. You never forget your first love, that's what they say.

Alison King. The name came forward in his mind, jarring him. He erased it and thought of Number One. That's all she was now. A number.

They had met in high school, the first day, eleven years of age and weary of the new environment. She was small in stature but big in everything else. Loud, funny, popular.

He had loved her before he even knew what the feeling was.

For three years she had no idea of his intentions. He engineered time to be spent together, lesson projects that he could work on with her, made friends with people who could get him closer to her. Found out all the things she liked and mirrored them.

He played the game.

At fourteen, they were almost on speaking terms.

He pined for her, a yearning deep inside he couldn't get over. Would think of nothing but her for endless hours. At first, it was just to spend time with her, to be in her company, her presence and nothing else. As his voice began to break and hair began to grow in new places, he thought of other things. What it would be like to brush her lips with his own, to run his fingers through her hair. To stroke her back softly, gently, with his fingertips.

To see her close her eyes.

At fifteen, there were meetings. The school were worried about things they were being told about. That he was scaring one of their pupils. One of their female pupils. And they weren't going to allow it to continue. His father had been called in to be made aware of it. He was to change classes, no longer with *her* any more. No contact. They wouldn't hesitate to call the *police* if they had to.

The disappointment etched across his father's face was enough for him. The beating he'd received later the final nail.

It was her fault. She hadn't accepted his love. Had chosen others ahead of him. It didn't matter that he had exposed their lies to her, that he had pleaded with her to open her eyes to the things that went on behind her back. That it was he who would be the right *man* for her. He'd watched as she flicked her long brown hair over her shoulder and looked at him with pity. Not love. It didn't matter how many times he followed her, sitting outside her house for hours. She didn't understand. Didn't care that the *boy* who she so loved did terrible, disgusting things when not around her.

The boy had been his revenge. And he'd liked it.

An accident. It's so easy to make it look like an accident. Something that couldn't be helped. Wrong place, wrong time.

He remembered the *boy's* face as he'd gone under the water of the River Mersey for the final time. The knowledge that he had lost. That the better *man* had won. The sun still shining down on them, as the evening began in that end of July heat.

BOY DROWNS IN MERSEY ACCIDENT

The *boy* had been known to do stupid things. Swimming alone off the prom and getting into trouble wasn't out of the norm.

No one had ever known.

He left her alone after that. The love had died. Withered away by her betrayal. The anger dissipated by the knowledge he had taken a piece of her without her ever knowing.

He had never really thought about the fleeting nature of his feelings back then. When he was in that moment, it felt like everything in his life was geared towards that first love. He thought about her constantly. The first thing he thought about when he woke up, the last thing before he fell asleep. Her face, her body. The thought of being next to her. Just breathing in her scent. The warmth of her, near him.

He moved on. Once that love had died, he grew up a little more. Met someone who had an interest in him. She was Number Two. Lost his virginity to her in a fumble of teenage limbs and disappointment. That love began to die when she moved away to a different city for university. He thought about how close they had been, driven apart by distance and jealousy. The new guy she met there had got rid of him. Killed that love he had.

Number Three – Jane – was someone he now didn't need to think of. Gone, after months of planning and courage. Best forgotten, given how it had ended.

Number Four ... Number Four could be the one. It was early in their relationship, but he could sense something. It was different from the other three, of course. He was a changed man.

He had a mission.

He had to show her what happened when you took that love and destroyed it. Show her – Number Four – that everything could be different.

He had to show Number Four what real love was.

It all went back to Number One. He had tried to find her recently, but couldn't trace her at all. She had been everything to him. He could have been everything to her, but she threw it back in his face.

He had still wanted her.

'Are you not talking to me tonight?' he said, his voice breaking into the silence between him and Number Four. He smiled and breathed in a few times. 'You know I'm doing it for you. It's all for you. These people ... they don't deserve what we have.'

He leaned closer, ignoring the fact that she cowered away from him. He placed a kiss on her cheek, ran his fingers through her hair. 'You're so beautiful. You do know that, don't you?'

He moved back, away from Number Four, leaving her to attempt to crawl into a ball, away from him, the chains holding her to the radiator limiting her movement. She looked past him, a pleading look coming to her face as she spied the bucket in the corner. He slid it closer to her with his foot, unlocked one of her arms, then turned away.

'I'll be everything to you. Once I've finished, there will be no doubt. You will love me, the way it's supposed to be. You'll never leave me, never want anyone else.'

He crinkled his nose and stepped closer to the window, looking at the empty street outside. He spied a couple walking in the distance, the gap between them closing as they moved away. He imagined an arm slipping around a shoulder, a hand slipping into another, a stolen kiss under a flickering street light.

'You will be mine. Forever.'

Chapter Five

Murphy was tired. Damn tired. He waited until Karen left the room – excusing herself to go to the bathroom – before talking quietly to Rossi.

'Same thing. It's always the same bloody thing.'

'We don't know that yet,' Rossi said, standing up and going over to look at the large picture of Chloe above the mantelpiece. 'Could just be that she didn't like the relationship between them and is now just venting.'

'There'll be something. I reckon it's what you suggested. Spurned ex or bit on the side. This knobhead has been playing away from home and got them both killed. We see stuff like this all the time.'

'Not sure about that . . .'

'Domestic issues turning violent. We see it all the time. Arguments over petty, small things boiling over and becoming all about power.'

'I'm not really following your logic here.' Rossi picked up a small photo frame from the mantelpiece, inspected it then placed it back.

'I don't know the whole thing yet,' Murphy said, throwing his hands up. 'Joe is just another one, I bet. The dominant one in the relationship . . . every relationship he has. Always in control . . .'

Murphy stared off past Rossi to the more tasteful shot of Chloe in the far alcove, pretending he saw only innocence in the eyes looking back at him. He thought about the endless parade of destroyed relationships, people desperately clinging on, unwilling to give up. Those changed forever by domination, all the women he had come into contact with during his time on the job. The scared, the lost, all terrified to speak out because they knew he couldn't stop it.

'It's something for us to look at,' Murphy said, fixing Rossi with a stare.

Murphy could see the familiar darkening of the eyes in Rossi – the slight dip in the shoulders at the possibility of another woman becoming yet another statistic. Someone who couldn't get away, couldn't fight back, couldn't save her life. Wasn't allowed to.

The familiar story.

'Let's see if we can get any more out of her,' Rossi said, pointing towards the door which had been left ajar – hearing footsteps descending down the stairs towards them.

'Why do you say that about Joe, Karen?' Murphy said, once they had settled back down into their previous positions.

'The way he was. He was never right for her, I knew that . . . we all bloody did. She changed with him. Was totally different. I brought her up to be independent. To never make the same mistakes I made and become the trophy wife. I have a job now, but for years my life revolved round my kids. I didn't do anything for myself, everything was about this house, my husband and kids. He never forced me into it, understand that. It was just the way I allowed things to happen. My husband is a good man – not Chloe's real dad, but he always treated her as his own. Chloe was going to be different. She was going to be her own woman.'

'What happened to Chloe's father?' Murphy said, ticking off the possibility.

'Died when Chloe was two. Got drunk and drove into a tree in the lanes near Frankby. She doesn't remember him at all.'

'And she was different?' Rossi said, now looking towards the woman and not writing in her notebook.

'Yes. With the few boyfriends she had before, she was in control, always. They'd swap and change all the time.' Karen gave a small laugh, cut off before it had time to have any effect. 'Chloe would drop boys for the smallest things. The tiniest issues and they were gone. Not this one. He walked all over her. Treated her terribly. You must have heard some of the rumours?'

Murphy shook his head, whilst Rossi gave no response. Karen shrugged her shoulders and waved a hand as if it didn't matter.

'They were all true,' Karen continued. 'He was off out on his own all the time. Left her at home, crying down the phone to me. I tried, at first, to get her to see sense, but that wasn't going to work.'

Silence grew for a few seconds. Murphy opened his mouth to speak, before Karen continued in a voice so low and angry.

'He hit her once. Well, once I know of, anyway. When he'd come in drunk and had been due home hours earlier.

Didn't even bother calling her, just turned up in the early hours. They argued, and he slapped her. Broke down immediately, of course, saying he'd never do it again and all that *shit* they always say. She believed him, in the end. I told her to get out there and then. That it would never be just one time, but she didn't listen. She needs him. Needed him. I don't know why.'

'When was this?' Rossi said, Murphy not for the first time impressed at how she could swallow the fire back and ask the right questions.

'About six months ago. Chloe has never mentioned it since. The bastard got her, didn't he?'

'We don't know that yet,' Murphy said, leaning forward to close the distance between them. 'But we're going to find out, OK? We're going to find out what happened to Chloe.'

And he believed it.

They left Karen with the family liaison officer. Rossi checked in with the station as Murphy wrote down a few notes he would probably never read. The DC who Rossi spoke to sounded harassed from what Murphy could hear over the radio.

'Media?'

'Of course,' Rossi replied, pulling her seat belt on. 'This'll be big.'

Murphy's teeth tugged on his bottom lip. He allowed himself a small jot of sharp pain before snapping his own seat belt on and starting the car. 'We'll deal with it.'

'You think it was him then?' Rossi said once Murphy had turned round in the road and headed back towards the Wallasey tunnel.

'Wouldn't be the first time, would it?'

'Not the last either,' Rossi answered with a sigh, her face turned towards the window. 'I don't think this is murder–suicide.'

'It definitely doesn't look like that. Could be something related to him, though. The "bunny boiler" angle?' Murphy slowed down for traffic lights as they turned from amber to red.

'Just ... that scene doesn't fit. Domestics are almost always in the home. Away from public view. This, in some derelict house, miles from where they live, I can't see it. If Joe did it, why is he the one injured? If someone else did it, why do it in that house, rather than in their one?'

'Stranger things have happened. I once worked a case where the guy did it in a hotel. Called his wife, told her to meet him there, then did it in plain view of everyone at reception. Didn't give a shit. She died, he survived the carving knife he took to his own wrists.'

'He pleaded not guilty, right?'

'You know the case?' Murphy said, realising the lights had changed to green a second too late, earning him a beep from the car behind him.

'No. I just know the way these things go.'

They fell into silence as they made the five-minute trip back towards the tunnel entrance, down the slip road off Gorsey Lane and back towards the city. Traffic was lighter than Murphy was familiar with; his trips when he had lived across the water had always taken place early morn ing, when it seemed the whole of the Wirral escaped like rats from a sinking ship into the proper city. Only a smattering of cars were taking the trip now.

'You didn't answer my question,' Rossi said as they entered the tunnel. 'Do you think it's him?'

Murphy took one hand off the steering wheel to scratch at his beard. 'No, I didn't answer that question.'

'Well, do you think it's him? You got angry enough back at the house about him and now you're going all "introspective" on me.'

'I don't know. I'm just bloody tired of hearing the same story, that's all. We've had too many domestics lately.'

'Can't disagree with you there.'

'It would probably be easier in a way if it was something like that. I'd be just making stuff up and guessing at the moment though.'

'Doesn't usually stop you.'

He couldn't argue with that. 'I suppose not. Gut feeling?'

'Always.'

'I think there's something more to this one. Something I really don't want to consider.'

'That there's more?'

'Maybe. In the past and to come.'

Silence grew in the car once more. Murphy turned on the stereo, the sound of Pink Floyd filling the car a few seconds later.

'Do we have to listen to this?' Rossi said, reaching over and turning the volume down.

'What, you want to listen to the shite that's around these days?'

'This is old music. Older than you, I would bet.'

'That's beside the point. This is classic stuff.'

Rossi sighed, then reached over and turned the volume down even further. 'Can you still hear it?'

Murphy couldn't really, not over the noise of the traffic as they travelled through the tunnel, but decided against any further argument.

'I don't know how to best broach this . . .' Rossi said, the change in subject abrupt enough for Murphy to notice. 'Only, I know it's coming up to two years since Peter died.'

Murphy didn't respond at first. He thought back to that night, his godson tied up and helpless. A man with a gun to the eighteen-year-old's head, ranting at Murphy as he stood there watching.

The smell of gunpowder and blood.

'What about it?'

'We haven't spoken about it in a while, that's all. I was just wondering if there's anything I should be wary of saying.'

'I'm doing all right. Better than I thought I would be. The counselling helped a bit. Things with Sarah are sorted. I wish I could speak to Jess, but she still won't speak to me.'

Jess – Peter's mother, and Murphy's friend of twenty years. Still blaming Murphy for not doing enough to save his life.

'Good. I'm glad you're doing okay.'

'I have to. He wouldn't want me to wallow in self-pity. He looked up to me. I've got to keep going, otherwise I sully that.'

'Sully?'

'Word-of-the-day calendar at home. You missed the day I used "discombobulate".'

Rossi laughed, then turned back to her phone. Ten minutes later they were pulling into the car park behind the station. There was already a significant media presence gathered, waiting to hear more news. Murphy knew – had too much experience to not know – that there would be more TV crews up at the crime scene itself. Battling against each other to report the same news. Repeating similar information on an hourly basis, desperately waiting for something more.

Murphy had a feeling it would be him giving it to them before too long.

He parked up and the pair entered the drab building, nodding to the harassed-looking receptionist and passing their ID cards over the security scanner. Murphy gave a longing look towards the lifts before ascending the stairs behind Rossi, taking two at a time to catch up with her.

As Murphy and Rossi walked past the normally quiet offices they could hear conversations between small groups as they discussed the morning's events. Continuing down the corridor, Murphy ignored the surreptitious looks he and Rossi received. He held up a hand to someone he knew in the drugs squad when they called out his name, but carried on walking.

Eventually they made it to the sanctuary of their own corner of St Anne Street.

'Wondered when you were getting back,' a voice said from behind one of the computers. 'Interview with the mother go okay?'

'As well as they always do,' Murphy replied, taking off his suit jacket and loosening his tie a little. 'I trust you're doing the necessary.'

DC Graham Harris manoeuvred himself round and stopped his wheelchair at the end of Murphy's desk. 'CCTV, witness statements, home owners contacted, brief press release signed off saying the usual. All in hand.'

Murphy gave Harris a nod and switched his computer on. He glanced towards Harris as he turned to speak to

Rossi. Felt that familiar twinge of guilt as he allowed his eyes to settle on his chair before turning away.

Harris had been injured on the night of Peter's death. Murphy had taken Harris with him to chase up a loose end, which had ended for Harris with the blast of a shotgun. A knock at an uninspiring door and the world turns, spewing out a random series of events which can change lives in an instant. Murphy had survived without a scratch, but Harris couldn't say the same. He had been peppered with shotgun pellets, which had resulted in a severed spinal cord, making his legs as useless as Murphy in the moments following the shooting. Doctors had saved Harris's life, but not his full mobility.

Harris had returned to the job as soon as he'd been able to, determination overruling any word from a girlfriend who hadn't lasted much longer. Murphy had asked for him to be on the team before anyone else ... even Rossi, though he would never tell her that. He wanted that reminder of what his poor planning had cost, sitting there day after day, to drive the point home into his thick skull. Harris had turned out to be a great desk jockey as things had turned out, relishing the minute details better than Murphy or Rossi could arguably have done.

He never once blamed Murphy. Wouldn't even allow him to apologise.

Just doing my job. Our job. Could have been either one of us.

'Where are we then at' – Murphy checked his watch – 'six hours in?'

Rossi crossed the floor to the murder boards at the rear of the office. Soon, Murphy knew, they would be full of information, but at that moment it was sparse. His own handwriting staring back at him, a few details added near the bottom of the board by Harris.

'Chloe Morrison and Joe Hooper,' Rossi said, notebook in one hand, marker pen in the other as she wrote on the board. 'Two victims found in an abandoned house in Anfield, cause of death unknown. Possible asphyxiation on male. Bodies found by agent who had received a phone call this morning at around six a.m., to go to the house. Local uniforms were called once he couldn't gain access to the property. They broke in, finding the victims.'

'That phone call,' Murphy said, turning towards Harris and allowing Rossi to write more details on the board. 'Any way of tracing it or something? Seeing where it was made from? Not sure if they've found Chloe's phone yet.'

'We're on that,' Harris said, shuffling loose papers across his desk. 'Should have some info soon. We'll also be able to find out if it's still turned on if we haven't got it.'

Murphy nodded. 'Good. Shouldn't take them too long.'

Rossi continued talking as she wrote. 'Interview with mother of female victim. She'll be doing formal ID, with informal provided by Thomas Parker. Mother didn't know of anything that could help, but told us of issues within the relationship . . .'

'Another domestic,' Harris said under his breath.

'Which may prove significant.' Rossi carried on, ignoring Harris's interruption. 'Mother – Karen Morrison – provided a list of Chloe's friends.'

'We'll start getting people on the phones then, organising interviews and so on. We've got another set of parents to visit.'

Rossi's shoulders slumped. 'Damn. Forgot about the other one.'

'Come on,' Murphy said, checking his email and shutting down his computer once he'd decided there wasn't anything he deemed to be urgent. 'Shouldn't take us long. At least it's this side of the water this time.'

Murphy grabbed his jacket from the back of his chair and nodded towards DCI Stephens's private office and held up a finger to Rossi. 'Just give me a minute.'

Murphy walked off towards his boss's office, smirking as he heard Rossi start complaining to Harris.

Murphy gave a short rap on the door, waited a few moments for a reply and then entered the office.

'David,' DCI Stephens said, picking up the telephone on her desk, staring at it for a second before replacing it. 'Sorry, my head's up my arse this morning. Glad you've dropped in. Want to tell me what's going on?'

Murphy drew a chair towards him and sat down. 'Looks like we've got a tricky one,' he began.

Chapter Six

There are parts of Liverpool that look entirely different from what some people might expect. Leafy suburbs, newly built detached houses, mansions even. Streets kept clean, well looked after. You could drop some parts of Liverpool into more affluent areas of the country and no one would think they looked out of place.

And other parts of the city looked much as an outsider might expect.

'Well ... this is different from Chloe's parents' house.'

Murphy turned towards Rossi, raised his eyebrows then opened the car door. Passenger side this time. Rossi had made it clear it was her turn to drive, so he'd had to squeeze himself into her car. She was still refusing to drive one provided from the pool at the station, even though Murphy had relented and begun picking one up for most journeys.

Rossi was right though. It was different. The terrace house in front of them had seen better days and was a direct contrast to the well-kept, large, semi-detached house owned by Chloe's parents. Even for Walton the street wasn't in the best condition – the main attraction being a tired string of England flags blowing in the breeze high above them, tied from lamp posts and strung across the road. Wheelie bins were dotted about the place, house numbers daubed across them in magnolia paint.

'It's got character,' Rossi said, joining Murphy outside Joe Hooper's father's house. 'I'll give it that. Bet they'll even say they have a sense of community.'

Murphy ignored the comment and instead basked in nostalgia. He felt more comfortable on streets like these than the one they had spent time in that morning.

'This is where proper people live, Laura.'

'Oh, I know that. Six kids in a three-bedroom house, remember?'

Murphy smirked, recalling the time he had tried to work out the logistics of Rossi's upbringing.

'Come on,' he said after a few more seconds. 'Let's get this done.'

Murphy began to walk towards the metal gate which was hanging on only one hinge, and sidestepped a smear of what he hoped was only dog shit on the pavement. He managed to place one hand on the gate before the voices rang out. Not from inside the house, but from behind him.

'Are you from the police?'

'What's happened to Joe Hooper, Detective?'

'Is it true he was found in a drugs den with Chloe?'

Two journalists crossed the road with purpose, both had obviously been camped in separate cars waiting for them to arrive. Murphy turned and shook his head, allowing Rossi to step in between them as he reached through

the gate and pulled up the handle, scraping the metal
against the doorstep.

'We'll be making a full statement later. For now, we'll
neither confirm nor deny anything. Thank you.' Rossi
turned away.

The journalists followed Rossi, still shouting questions
as if they were part of a media scrum, rather than two
middle-aged blokes in clothes that would have looked
fresh on three days earlier.

'Keep your voices down,' Murphy said, unable to keep
his mouth shut as the noise level went up another notch.
'Have a bit of decency. We'll speak to you later. Down the
station, not here.'

Murphy wasn't sure if it was because a six foot four
bloke had said it, or whether they had actually dredged
up a sense of decorum, but the journalists stopped talking. He assumed the reason for their sudden silence was
the third option – they had simply run out of questions to
ask. The voices of the two men died down as they moved
back towards their cars.

'You're always more polite than I am with them.'

'Well, you have to remember the camera thing,'
Rossi said. 'Could be one filming at any point. Last
thing we need right now is one of us giving hell to a
journo.'

'Still, it's always nice to give them a bit of agro back.
Bane of our bloody lives most of the time.'

Murphy stepped forward and knocked on the door. It
was opened a few seconds later by the family liaison
officer, sent to the house ahead of them. Murphy went
first, ushered into the living room. The walls felt like
they were closing in on him as he stepped inside; the

smell of damp and nicotine mixing together, creating something he struggled to imagine living in. Yellowing paper on the walls, peeling in places. Black mould in the corners of the room. A rhythmic cough coming from the only occupant. A man in his forties, who could have passed for late fifties if Murphy hadn't already known the guy. The coughs coming each side of drags on a rolled cigarette, the can of lager not doing anything to stop them.

'The cavalry's arrived then,' the man said, purposefully not making eye contact with Murphy or Rossi. 'What kept youse?'

'Hello, Chris,' Murphy said, waving away the family liaison officer who, judging by the speed of his departure, was relieved to escape the confines of the room. 'Long time no see.'

Chris Hooper looked up, appraised him with a weaving head and sniffed. 'I remember you,' he said, placing his can of lager on the threadbare carpet at his feet and replacing it with a lighter. 'How the fuck could I forget a big fucking lummox like you though, eh?'

Murphy looked at the stained couch behind him and decided against sitting down. Mainly for his own health. Rossi had likely made the same decision, leaning against the now closed wood-panelled door.

'Keeping yourself out of trouble?'

'Better than my boy by the sounds of things.'

Murphy didn't remember many faces from his uniform days, but Chris Hooper's was one of them. Not the name, not at first. And definitely not the familial connection to that morning's victim. He didn't keep tabs on the family members of men he'd arrested countless times back in those days. He remembered Chris Hooper though. The amount of times he'd had to battle with him, drunk and endlessly violent.

A regular.

Murphy nodded towards Chris. 'Nothing confirmed as yet, of course, until you ID him. But we think it's him, Chris.'

Chris's head dropped to his chest, the rolled cigarette between his fingers burning out, waiting to be relit. 'Yeah, I know.'

'When was the last time you saw Joe?'

'Years ago,' came the slurred reply. 'Not interested in his auld fella once he'd become famous. Embarrassed about me probably. Can't believe he went over and played for those fucking wools anyway. Tranmere bloody Rovers? Hardly Anfield or Wembley, is it? Still looked down his nose at us, though, didn't he?'

'Spoke to him recently?'

'Tried to. Wondered if he'd see his way to giving us some money to get out of here and that. Brought him up, didn't we? Deserved a bit of payback. Never got back to us though. Now . . . now he'll never get the chance. And we're stuck here forever. Poor kid.'

Murphy waited for Chris to light his cigarette, and for another coughing fit to finish, before speaking again. 'You never met Chloe then, I gather?'

'That bint he was in the papers with all the time? Nah. He wouldn't bring her here, would he? Ashamed of us. Didn't even see his brothers and sisters either. Cut himself off. What good's that done him? Christ.'

'So, when did you actually speak to him last?'

'Years ago,' Chris said, sniffing and choking on whatever came up. He swallowed and then took another drag on his cigarette. 'Don't know anything about his life now. Never sold our story though. Tried to tell him that, but he didn't care. Not even now, to those two dickheads out there. I'm better than that.'

Murphy looked towards Rossi, raising an eyebrow which indicated a dead end.

'We're going to be speaking again, okay, Chris? But for now, the family liaison officer will be here to answer any questions and to take you down the Royal to ID the body.'

A slow nod was the only response.

'Chris, look at me,' Murphy said, his voice a little louder in the small room. Chris lifted his head slowly, looked at Murphy with bloodshot eyes.

Murphy bent down a little. 'I'm going to find out what happened to your son. Understand?'

Chris stared at Murphy for a few seconds before taking a drag on his cigarette. 'You were always one of the good ones,' he replied.

* * *

'We were never going to get anything from him anyway,' Murphy said, sitting back in the passenger seat and forgoing the opportunity to stick a middle finger up at the two journos who were now sitting on a car bonnet on the opposite side of the road. 'He hasn't seen any of his kids for years.'

Rossi started the car and fiddled with the satnav on the dashboard before giving up on it. 'Guess not. Had to be done though.'

'One of the perks we have on this job.'

'*Vaffanculo.*'

Murphy let out a short laugh at Rossi's response and took out his phone as the police radio crackled into life, looking up to make sure Rossi turned it down. He scrolled down his mobile phone screen looking for Sarah's name in his contacts list, before giving up and going back to recent messages instead. He sent her a short text to tell her he'd be late home and not to fall asleep on the sofa. She replied instantly.

Had a feeling you would be late. Heard the news. Don't worry, I've got plans. Hope you don't come home too tired ;-) xx

Murphy smirked and put his phone back in his pocket.

'Ring the office while you've got that out,' Rossi said, indicating to turn right, onto Rice Lane. 'Find out when the PM is scheduled for.'

'PMs, Laura,' Murphy replied, trying to find DC Harris's number on his phone. 'Plural.'

'You know what I mean.'

Murphy called Harris as Rossi made the trip back to the station, the drab houses of Walton becoming the drab houses of Kirkdale and Everton, as County Road became Walton Road.

'Not until tomorrow morning,' Murphy said, ending the call. 'Chloe's mum has come over to ID her, though, so I imagine Chris Hooper won't be far behind.'

'Why the wait?' Rossi replied.

'I don't know. Maybe Houghton is getting too old? Probably has a few in the queue ahead of them or something. Nothing can be rushed with him.'

'Suppose. Would have thought with the shit storm that's about to rain down on us he would have got the word to sort it sooner.'

'I'm sure that'll come in time.'

They fell into an easy silence as the five mile trip back to St Anne Street passed quickly. Murphy rubbed the bridge of his nose with his thumb and forefinger, and allowed his eyes to close briefly. He opened them as he felt the car slow down and turn off, seeing the station loom into blurred view.

'More of them now,' Rossi said, waiting for the barrier to lift before driving on. '*Parassiti.*'

'Can't argue with that,' Murphy replied.

The office was even busier now, a few detective constables had returned from the crime scene and were back at commandeered desks. Murphy started considering the future of the case. Although they all answered to people of higher ranks, essentially the team of detectives and officers was under his command; it would be him they would come to. To be told what to do, how to *proceed*.

If he had an ego, he would be dangerous. As it was, he was barely interested in telling himself what to do, never mind a whole load of other people.

'Quiet down,' Murphy shouted over the din of raised voices. 'Meeting room, five minutes. I want to know everything we have so far and update you on what's been going on here.'

A few 'Yes, boss' and 'yes, Sir's could be heard before the conversations started up again. Murphy checked the murder board for any updates, saw only Rossi's sloped handwriting and carried on to DCI Stephens's office.

'Back so soon, David?' Stephens said once he was sitting down opposite her.

'Yeah,' Murphy replied, stretching his already tired legs out in front of him. 'Father hadn't seen the victim in a while. Wasn't a good relationship, but we knew that anyway. I know the guy from old—'

'Your days in uniform?'

'Of course,' Murphy said, accepting the interruption. 'Low-level stuff. Alcoholic, so always fuelled by drink. Violence mostly. Pub fights and so on.'

'The mother?'

'Dead a couple of years. Alcohol got to her a lot sooner than it'll get to him. Joe – the victim – moved on pretty quick by the looks of things. Still a lot to work out on that side.'

DCI Stephens pushed a few grey strands of hair behind her ear where they had come loose from her tight bun of a hairdo. 'Possible suspect?'

Murphy shook his head. 'I'm not ruling it out, but I think we need to look at their personal lives outside of family at the moment. That room in the house, all the magazine cuttings and that? That's saying something to me.'

DCI Stephens raised an eyebrow. 'Enlighten me, Poirot. What's it saying?'

Murphy took a second, tried to work out what he wanted to say but failed. 'Honestly, I'm not sure yet. There's just something about it that isn't right. It was like a shrine to them, but . . .' Murphy struggled to find the words to describe what it was that was niggling at him.

'It's a bad one, that's what you're saying?'

'Not just bad,' Murphy replied. 'Something we've come across before.'

DCI Stephens waited for him to continue, but Murphy didn't have any more. Except one thing.

'Obsession,' he said after a few seconds. 'This is someone who was obsessed with them or what they represent. That's my feeling. Not some domestic murder–suicide ridiculous situation. This is something worse.'

Fate

There was a question he thought of often, never receiving an answer that placated him. It niggled at him late at night, when he slept fitfully in the adjacent room to the one he stood in now. He asked Number Four, not waiting for an answer.

'Do you believe in fate? Some guiding force which brings us all together? Loads of people do. I've noticed that over the years, talking to people in work and other places. In pubs, betting shops, supermarkets. You hear them all the time, talking about karma and saying things like *It was written in the stars*. Millions of people read horoscopes in newspapers, believing the things they say, as if they could apply to hundreds of millions of people simultaneously.'

Did he believe in fate?

'It's what people say in new relationships all the time, you know. Circumstance had driven them together, but they believed they were always *meant* to be together.'

His voice went up an octave, a mocking tone to it. 'It was fate that he missed his bus. That she decided not to eat her lunch in the same place she always did that day.' He ignored the fact Number Four shrank back from him as he laid the palm of his hand on the top of her head. He stroked her hair, and she whimpered from behind the duct tape across her mouth.

His voice went back to normal. 'Fate supposedly made sure they were pushed together, so they would meet and get married and have kids and grow old and have grandchildren and then die a few months apart. Blah, blah, blah, life, blah.'

He sniffed and shook his head. Lifted Number Four's face by her chin, staring directly into her eyes. 'I don't think I believe in it. But I sometimes wonder if fate brought you to me. To give me purpose. To make someone see what true love is. To make you understand that what I feel is more than what you think could be possible. Without that, I wouldn't be making them see that what they're doing isn't right. That their love is wrong.'

He was almost sure that fate didn't exist. However, the way he had met Number Three was almost too coincidental. It was that meeting that had set him on the course he was on now.

'I'd only been working there a few weeks when I met Number Three. Still learning people's names, making sense of the layout. Just a normal evening shift. Jane. Simple name, for a simple girl. I've told you this before, haven't I?'

Number Four closed her eyes as he traced a finger down her cheek. The noise of the chains against the radiator echoed in the almost empty room.

'When I fall in love, I want to devour them, immerse myself within them and take total control. Become one and the same person. She wasn't overly attractive. Just plain Jane. If people passed her on the street, they wouldn't look twice. Not like you, Number Four. It was easy for me to see past the imperfections, though. I noticed other things about her. The way her mousy-brown hair flicked up slightly near the ends. The pear-shaped curves, which only accentuated her best feature. Her face in pale light, clear and line free.'

He stood above Number Four, watching her chest move up and down, then turned away and moved over to the window. He shivered against the cold coming through the single glazing. 'I watched her during breaks in work, reading a book or eating a sandwich. Her lips parting to reveal off-white teeth, a small gap between the front two. I had to have her.'

He pursed his lips at the memory of the days it had taken to work up the courage to speak to her. The memories of too many wrong paths taken. Bad things said, which had almost stopped him.

'She was more than willing to speak to me. I'd say she was excited. Meeting me on breaks and discussing whatever book she was reading at the time, or the state of politics in the country, the latest news in the world. She was from over the water, so we would talk about the differences between the loudmouth, Boris Johnson-wannabe Mayor of Liverpool and the invisible Wirral mayor. I pretended to listen and be the normal person. I really tried to do things the "right" way.'

He shook his head at his own stupidity. Slammed a closed fist onto the window ledge, causing flakes of paint to drift to the floor. 'I tried being direct this time. I didn't flirt, I was much less subtle. So stupid of me.'

He turned back to Number Four. She was still slumped against the radiator, her shoulders juddering up and down. He moved across the room to her, his bare feet feeling the cold from the floorboards.

'She had someone. His name was Stuart. Twenty-eight years old, worked in an accountancy firm. He'd proposed a year earlier. She didn't wear the ring to work as she was worried about losing it. Her parents loved him, thought he was a good guy.'

The pulsing in his head was growing as he spoke. His palms glistened with sweat as he imagined this Stuart and the things he and Jane had done together. He placed his hand on Number Four's arm, squeezing it slightly, so he could remember she was still real.

'Yet another barricade put down between me and happiness. What could he have that I didn't? They'll think Stuart and Jane were the first. When they start putting things together. But, we know that's not the truth, don't we? We know this didn't start with them. Or those stupid *celebrities*.'

He breathed deeply, once, closing his eyes, and he caught her scent. It was still there, faint now, battling with the sweat and tears which emanated from her more often now. He had bought the perfume she wore, spraying her down once a day, but it was already running out.

'I became obsessed with this Stuart's life. I wanted to know why he had Number Three and I couldn't. All these questions running through my mind. I wanted his life to end and become my own. You know what I learned though. Stuart wasn't Stuart. What was known wasn't real.'

He hesitated before speaking into the silence once more. He knew that he hadn't told Number Four everything. He found it hard to admit to himself, but he had also wanted to destroy Number Three and her *Stuart*. To put them in the same situation he was in. Alone, no one to care for him.

'You became Number Four after that. That's when I knew I had to start from the beginning. Break you down and make you mine. To show you what real love was. I'd watched you for a long time. Your age put me off. I didn't think you'd be interested in me. But, the heart wants what the heart wants.' He smiled at her, as she opened her eyes and glanced at him. She averted her gaze so he took a fistful of her hair in his hand and pulled her closer to him.

'That's what you'll be, isn't it? When I've shown you everything I can do for you. To prove that our love is different. That it will be different. You'll be mine, forever.'

His dad used to say they were all the same. One woman was no different to any other. Drummed into him, the same things over and over. Keeping him up late just so he had some company as he drank and shouted at mute images on the television.

He was going to prove him wrong.

He let go of Number Four, ignoring the muffled cry which came back at him as he stood. 'My first instinct was to tell Jane, but it wouldn't have helped. She wouldn't run to me for care and protection. It just makes them angry and resentful towards me for opening their eyes to the truth. I become as much to blame as the bloke, as if I am somehow complicit in the betrayal.'

He blinked and looked down at Number Four, imagining a time when she wouldn't cower from him. When she would be glad to see him. Once he had shown her every-thing he could do.

'Maybe if I had never spoken to Number Three, I would have meandered throughout life with no purpose. I may never have discovered the joy, the satisfaction, the power I felt over them in that room. The moments as they finally accepted their fate, as I tightened a length of cord around the liar's throat. Saw the hatred in their supposed loved one's eyes as they watched them die. It's what I was made for.'

Fate or coincidence, it didn't really matter. It only mattered that he did things correctly. Discovered the secrets and lies and then exposed them. To make them see the light, to see what was right.

'I'll never be lonely again. Not now I have you. Because you're going to be mine, no matter what anyone says. I'll change you. You'll be something more. Soon, you won't be just a number. You'll be a living, breathing epitome of everything that I know to be right and just. You will know what love really is. You'll love me with everything you have. Your life will be mine.'

He breathed in and out and faced the window again. The street lights outside cast a long shadow across the bare floor inside the room, providing just enough illumi-nation to keep out total darkness. He ignored the noise coming from behind him and closed his eyes.

'Everyone is going to see what I did to them. The third couple. I know who they are and what they've done. Everyone will see my work and they will see what I have done is right. But that won't matter. All that will matter is that you understand what love is really all about.'

That was the way it had to be.

'I just need to show you again, don't I? I need to prove myself worthy of your love.'

He ignored the shake of her head and the screams behind the gag across her mouth.

'I'll be back soon, my love. With more tales to tell you.'

Chapter Seven

Murphy heard the low whistle from beside him and had to stop himself from matching it. The waterfront lay behind them, Albert Dock in all its resplendent glory, the Liver Buildings just a little further up the road on the same side as the docks. The road which ran alongside them was busy with rush-hour traffic, which would begin to quieten as the evening drew on. Murphy shielded his eyes as the evening sun slipped from behind clouds.

'Now, this is a nice place,' Murphy heard Rossi say beside him.

He looked up, giving a non-committal shrug. The top of the apartment building reached towards white drifting clouds, rising up in an odd shape and finishing in a sharp, wide point at its tip, dwarfing them and everything around it.

'Did you know it was an Argentinian architect who designed this?'

'I'm surprised you know it,' Rossi said, smirking at Murphy. 'Never mind me.'

'Read about it in the *Echo* ages ago. Bet it doesn't come cheap.'

DC Hale piped up behind them. 'Amazing what getting your baps out for some lads' mags can buy you.'

Murphy turned to watch Rossi smack DC Hale on the arm and say something in Italian to him.

'Now, now,' Murphy said, trying to imitate a school teacher and failing. 'None of that here, kids.'

'Tell *him* that,' Rossi replied, walking ahead of them. 'Are youse coming or what?'

The apartment building was one of the new glass-fronted monstrosities that had appeared near the water-front in the past few years. Money dribbling down from the Capital of Culture days meant property developers were now getting involved, building bespoke two-bed flats for those with more money than sense.

'Who wants a view of the Wirral anyway?' Murphy said to no one in particular. 'Everyone knows the best view is from the other side.'

One Park West was a fairly new residential develop-ment. A communal entrance guarded by a 24/7 security team gave its occupants a sense of safety and superiority.

'How much is the rent for one of these places?' Murphy said, as he, Rossi and DC Hale waited for the lift to take them to the higher levels where the apartments lay. 'A grand?'

'Probably more,' Rossi said. 'I know they're at least a couple of hundred grand to buy.'

'For a tiny two-bedroom flat . . . we're becoming more and more like that London every day.'

There was a uniform outside the apartment, standing to attention and trying not to fall asleep on his feet.

'Anyone else inside yet?' Murphy asked him as they reached the door.

'Few forensic guys, but that's it.'

Murphy led the way inside. A small hall led into the open-plan living and kitchen area. He could smell the expense. A large sofa in the middle of the room was plonked in front of one of the largest flat screen televisions he'd ever seen. It wasn't that which drew his attention, however. It was the floor-to-ceiling windows which wrapped around the room, giving a panoramic view of the Albert Dock and, in the distance, the River Mersey, the ferry almost visible on its way home.

'Wow,' DC Hale said from beside him. 'How the other half live.'

'You can say that again,' Rossi said, standing near one of the windows and looking out. 'Think I can see Bidston Hill from here. Bloody telly is blocking most of the view though.'

'Michael,' Murphy said, gaining DC Hale's attention. He lowered his voice so the two forensic officers in the room couldn't hear. 'You start going through personal effects. See if they've found anything suspicious hidden away in the other rooms. Check everywhere, just in case they haven't. The bedroom is a good place to start – under the mattress, the bed, back of the wardrobe, that sort of thing.'

'Sir.'

DC Hale toddled off like a good little boy, leaving Rossi and Murphy in the living area, along with the two officers who were waiting for Murphy to speak again. 'Don't let us stop you,' Murphy said. 'We're wearing gloves and everything.'

Murphy joined Rossi at the window, gazing out onto the waterfront. 'I think you could get bored of this view. You know, after seeing it everyday.'

'I'm not so sure about that,' Rossi replied, tearing her stare away from the window. 'Long way from where Joe came from.'

'Laptops and phones?'

'On it,' Rossi said, pacing round the room and leaving Murphy to stand at the window.

'Nice life if you can hold on to it,' he said quietly to himself.

*   *   *

The light outside had finally faded by the time they'd got back to the office, the visit to Chloe and Joe's apartment coming to an end just as the night began to take over.

Once the positive IDs had been given for Chloe Morrison and Joe Hooper, things could really start for Murphy. As the day wound down and jobs were given out to an expanding team, Murphy began to formulate a list of everything that could have resulted in the two victims being found dead in an abandoned house.

It could have been longer.

'Laura, get yourself off. Another long one tomorrow and there's nothing more we can do now.'

'Five more minutes. Just finding out one more name for interview.'

Murphy had left the task of tracking down the friends and other close family members of the victims to Rossi. DC Harris had been helping her, but had left an hour earlier, a long day having more of an effect on him than it once had.

'Fine, but I want you fresh tomorrow.'

Murphy, receiving an Italian slur under Rossi's breath in response, left her to it. The day had stretched out now into a slow, meandering end, as investigations tended to do.

Not that you would believe it from watching the twenty-four-hour news channels. Someone had made the decision to have the TV playing in the background; there was no volume, just many excitable faces changing every few minutes as coverage of the deaths of Chloe Morrison and Joe Hooper reached national level. A never-ending yellow ticker across the bottom of the screen announcing the news on a loop.

REALITY STARS 'CHLOJOE' FOUND DEAD IN LIVERPOOL

Murphy had been spared the first press conference – a professional media spokesperson taking control. It seemed as if every station had their own press and media consultant now, someone to keep the police's profile in check.

Less crime, more news.

He knew it wouldn't last though. At some point Murphy would be forced to sit in front of a bank of cameras and pretend the investigation was moving forward. Give platitudes and reassure the public. Feed the masses.

Murphy had been surprised at the level of interest. He'd barely heard of the pair, but it seemed as if everyone in the country was suddenly interested in Chloe and Joe's fate.

Domestic Violence – Murder–suicide
Drugs
Sexual Motives
Revenge – Person/s known to victims
Stranger

It was the last item on his list which gave him pause. A stranger coming into the lives of Chloe and Joe, taking them to that place and killing them ... that was the worst-case scenario. Thankfully, it was also the least likely.

Murphy would play the odds, but the pictures cut out of magazines and stuck to the wall bothered him. That would have taken time. Effort.

It would be just his bloody luck.

'Done,' Rossi said, closing her laptop with a bang. She passed a piece of paper to one of the night-shift DCs and shared a few words as Murphy waited. 'Last one ticked off. Have to say, it's a short list of people who were actually close to them.'

'You'd think those famous types would have tons of friends,' Murphy replied, leaning back in his chair and stretching his long legs out under his desk.

'Turns out most are just friends in name only. I've spoken to the agent a few times today and it seems like he was really the only close one.'

'Don't ignore him either. Nothing to say he doesn't know more at this point.'

Rossi grabbed her coat from the back of her chair and placed one arm inside. 'Of course not. Just using what we have so far. Most of them are going to be prepared though, you know that?'

Murphy nodded. 'Nothing we can do about that,' he said, pointing towards the TV on the wall.

'Suppose not. What happened with that guy from this morning? Our confessor?'

'Whole case is going back to Liverpool South. They're dealing with it all now. Which means ...'

'She'll be listed as missing and forgotten about. She is eighteen, I suppose. Not much we can do, especially if it does turn out that our man from this morning had nothing to do with it.'

Murphy gripped the side of his chair a little harder. 'Suppose so.'

'Shame about the girl though. If Amy Maguire's disappearance got half the coverage this thing has got . . .'

Murphy bit his tongue and simply nodded. He wanted to say more, but decided it wasn't the time.

'Right, I'm gone,' Rossi said, when Murphy didn't say anything more. 'See you first thing, unless anything happens overnight.'

Murphy watched Rossi leave, working out how much longer he would have to stay to show himself willing.

Ten minutes was enough.

He made his way out of the station and was on the road leaving the city centre within minutes. Checking the clock on the dashboard of his car, he turned the volume up on the stereo. Pink Floyd had switched places with David Bowie. Murphy banged his hand on the steering wheel in time to 'The Jean Genie' in spite of himself.

He spared the inside of his car his tuneless voice.

It was a straight run along the waterfront and past the Festival Gardens, through Otterspool. It was probably quicker going through the city, but Murphy preferred the route he was on, taking in the sights of the River Mersey at night, as the docks were left behind and became the promenade.

Murphy was pulling off Western Avenue and onto the road he'd grown up on within half an hour. The differences from his childhood were laid bare before him. Everything changing in a blink of an eye. The pub where his dad had used to drink was now a hotel, convenient for the airport. The small row of shops – where he had been sent by his parents with a quid for a loaf of bread and a pint of milk and told to keep the change more times than he could remember – were still there. Under new ownership, of course, but still hanging on. The chippy, which did the best savouries, but the worst fish, was now neighboured by a funeral director's. Murphy imagined they did good business in Speke, given the average life expectancy.

Damwood Road, where Murphy had lived for the first twenty years of his life, was lined with homes set back from the road. The houses had massive back gardens, and the Venny was only up the road. Jess had lived five minutes' walk away, off Damwood on Marton Green – her house one of a bunch which surrounded a patch of grass no one ever kept trim.

Murphy turned left before reaching his old home. Now forever tainted by the memory of what had happened there three years previously. His parents murdered in their own living room by a bitter, jealous man. A man who had torn not only Murphy apart, but almost his marriage to Sarah too.

He felt a pang of guilt as he remembered Sarah back then. Trying to make sense of what that man had done. A man she had once shared a bed, even a home, with, before Murphy had come along.

Now, on a quiet street round the corner from that house, Murphy sat in his car wondering if he was about to do something very stupid.

Murphy got out of the car, leaving it parked up on the kerb. Keying the lock he heard the familiar beep accompanied by a spray of lights. He walked up a short path and knocked on the glazed front door, remembering a time when it had been blue, splintered wood.

'Hey, thanks for coming,' Stacey Maguire said, moving aside so Murphy could get past her.

'No problem,' Murphy said, waiting for her to show him the way in. 'Can't stay long. Got to get back home and that.'

'Course you have,' Stacey replied. 'Do you want a brew or anything?'

Murphy shook his head. 'I've only come to let you know the latest.'

'I can't believe the case landed on you like that. What's that word . . . serendipiddy?'

'Close enough,' Murphy said, sitting on a two-seater sofa that had seen better days. He noticed the threadbare carpet beneath his feet, and he was sure he recognised the wallpaper on the walls from the last time he'd visited, almost twenty years earlier. She'd taken the house over, her parents now living in a smaller place elsewhere in Speke. 'I've got some bad news though.'

'Oh no . . .'

Murphy realised his mistake as soon as the words were out of his mouth. 'Shit, no, not that. We still haven't found her, Stace. The guy who came in this morning, looks like he didn't have anything to do with it.'

'You scared the shit out of me then.'

Murphy held his hands up. 'I'm crap at picking my words, remember?'

'Of course I do. I remember everything from when we were kids. We all used to fancy you rotten, all the girls around here.'

'Wish I'd known back then,' Murphy replied, remembering his lack of luck with the opposite gender. 'Might have been a happier teenager.'

'All of us made it as clear as we could. Except Jess White, of course. How is she after . . . you know?'

Murphy paused, not wanting to say anything about Jess. 'From what I hear, she's doing okay.'

Stacey seemed to sense that it wasn't ground he wanted to go over and left the subject. 'What's going on then?'

Murphy looked at the picture which took up a significant part of one wall. A large canvas photograph of Amy Maguire – the resemblance to Stacey at that age incredible – sitting beside her two younger brothers. 'Did you hear about the murders earlier this morning?'

'The ChloJoe thing? It's all anyone is talking about. I'm telling you, if Amy's face had been in the news this much, she would have been found by now. Shit sells, I suppose.'

'Thing is, I'm on that case . . .'

'Oh, for fuck's sake . . .'

'So, they've sent Amy's case back here, to Liverpool South. I'm sorry.'

Stacey paced alongside the old, varnish-stained mantelpiece. 'You've got to do something, David. Can't you tell them why you need to be looking into it?'

'I definitely can't do that,' Murphy said, standing up. Suddenly wanting to be anywhere but there, in that house. 'I will keep an eye on things, put as much pressure on them as possible, but for now, I can't do anything about it.'

'She could be your daughter. Think about that.'

Murphy stopped on the opposite side of the room. The reason he was there in the first place, sounding ridiculous when said out loud.

One drunken fumble and your whole life can change. In Murphy's case, he hadn't even known about it until recently.

'We don't know that for sure though, do we, Stacey? She *might* be mine. That's what you said to me.'

'I just want you to find her,' Stacey said, tears springing to her eyes. 'Please. She's a good girl. Honest. Then, we can find out for sure.'

He looked at the picture again, looking for anything that reminded him of himself in Amy's face. Could see only an eighteen-year-old Stacey, the girl from round the corner. Everything about the situation felt wrong. The way Stacey was acting towards him, the fact it had taken eighteen years for her to even tell him about Amy's existence. The way she was suddenly so interested in him being in her life.

It wasn't real. That's what he knew. That's what his head told him. Still, there was doubt. Enough to keep him there, for now.

'I'll do my best, Stacc,' Murphy said, walking to the doorway. 'That's all I can do.'

*   *   *

Murphy left, checking his phone on the way down the path back to his car. Swore when he saw the time. He quickened his pace, wanting to be away from the place he'd left behind.

Amy Maguire was alive. He was sure of it. She would be found and then the whole mess could be put behind him, putting a stop to his worries about missing out on a child's life he hadn't known existed until now. Still, Murphy knew what would happen now. Amy's face would join a myriad of others. Lost loved ones, gone without a trace. If she didn't turn up in the Mersey, or somewhere else, then Stacey Maguire would still be looking in years to come. Keith – the confessor from that morning – would be forgotten, just another man with mental health issues, who had claimed responsibility for something he hadn't done.

It wouldn't save her.

Chapter Eight

On his drive home, Murphy allowed himself to forget the victims of the day. The two from that morning, the eighteen-year-old girl who was still missing. He drove the faces of them out of his mind, attempting to clear it.

As he travelled back home through the streets of Liverpool it was as if the car were driving itself; the roads so familiar he barely acknowledged the journey. His home appeared in front of him as if by magic. Murphy listened to the radio for a few seconds more before another advert came on. He switched off the engine and got out of the latest attempt he'd made to bring some joy into his life. Barely a year old, a Citroën C5. Red, to match his favourite football team.

'You still up?'

'Living room,' came the response.

Normality. That's the effect a voice can have on a person.

'You had your tea?' Sarah said as Murphy walked into the living room, kissed her on the top of her head and sat down in his chair.

'Had a sarnie earlier,' Murphy replied, slipping off his shoes and moving them out of his way with one foot. 'I'll grab something in a bit.'

'Kettle's just boiled if you want a drink.'

'No, I'm fine. Just want to sit for a bit.'

Murphy focused on the TV, smiling as Sarah switched from the news to his least favourite channel. The one she watched constantly, Comedy Channel or whatever. The *Friends* channel he called it. No matter what time of day, that damn programme always seemed to be on.

He became aware of her waiting for him to speak. Murphy's smile fell little by little. He stared at the screen as canned laughter accompanied another unfunny line.

'You've been watching the news then,' he said, giving in earlier than he wanted to.

'Only bits,' Sarah replied, pulling on the bottom of her blonde hair, placing a few strands in her mouth. 'How's it going?'

'Slow,' Murphy said, turning away from the TV and meeting her gaze finally. She could still give him a jolt, warmth and love radiating from her in a simple glance.

'Doesn't it always at the beginning?'

'Not always.'

'Well,' Sarah began, turning away from him and facing the TV again. 'I'm sure you'll sort it all out. That's what you always do.'

Murphy averted his stare and focused on the side of her head, rather than her eyes. 'Not always. We still haven't caught a few people, you know. Still trying to track down who keeps nicking my bloody HobNobs in work. You offer them out one time—'

'I get the point, you sarcastic git,' Sarah said, turning back to him with a smile. 'You need to eat. I'm knackered, though, so order in if you want something.'

'I'll have a look in a minute. Just want to sit for a bit. How was your day?'

Sarah rolled her eyes at him. 'The usual. I'm basically a children's entertainer. Trying to teach a class of five- and six-year-olds anything is more difficult than it sounded. I miss my year fives.'

'You were the one who wanted a change. Only a few months left in the school year now anyway.'

'Four months,' Sarah said with a sigh. 'Not sure the head would let me go back to the older ones anyway. There's this kid in my class, cute little thing with glasses, who just wants to read. That's all she wants to do. Her reading level is about three or four years ahead of everyone else's. So bright, really clever. Uses the most incredible words for a five-year-old. And I'm supposed to stop her doing that and teach her the times tables and make her copy out stupid bloody royal family trees instead. It's heartbreaking.'

Murphy smiled at Sarah, feeling the warmth exude from her as she spoke. 'Maybe you care too much?'

'You're joking, aren't you?' Sarah replied, snorting as she spoke. 'There's a fair few of them I wouldn't mind pitching into the bloody Mersey, I'll tell you that. Even at that age you can tell which ones are going to be little bastards as they grow up. You can tell just by standing in the playground at home time and listening to the parents. And the names of some of them . . .'

'Careful. You're beginning to sound like that attention-seeking bint who's always on *This Morning*.'

Murphy received a cushion flung at his head in response.

'Sorry,' he said, laughing as he picked up the cushion from beside him. 'That was probably too far.'

'Damn right it was,' Sarah said, crossing her arms and frowning at him. 'Anyway, those are my days. Corralling a bunch of kids together, with the help of a teaching assistant who I'm pretty sure doesn't want to be there any longer. All the while making them do things they don't want to do, because someone who probably hasn't met a six-year-old in their life has decided what's best to teach them.'

'Could be worse,' Murphy said, smirking. 'Could be four-year-olds.'

Sarah grinned back at him, running a hand through her hair and pushing it back from her face. 'Go and get something to eat. I don't want to hear your stomach growling all night. There'll be something in the fridge, I imagine, if you don't want to order in.'

'I'm sure I'll find something,' Murphy replied, standing up and banging the living-room door open.

'You know, Sarah,' he shouted back from the kitchen. 'Used to be that the wife would have her husband's tea ready on the table for him when he got home.'

Murphy opened the fridge, looked over its contents, shut the door. Did the same with the freezer and stood up to look through the cupboards instead. He was aware of Sarah standing in the doorway, but pretended to ignore her presence.

'Used to be that the wife wouldn't have anything else to do but tend to the house and kids. But we have no children and I have a full-time job. So you can sort yourself out, you cheeky get.'

Murphy grinned back at her and placed his hands in front of him as if in prayer and bowed to her.

'We need to sort these cupboards out,' Murphy said. 'A tin of oxtail soup, a few tins of chopped tomatoes, and some mixed fruit.' He took the latter out and held the browning can towards Sarah. 'Think I won this in a raffle years ago.'

'I saw Jess today . . .'

'Yeah,' Murphy continued, as if Sarah hadn't spoken, 'that one at that church thing you made me go to at Christmas. Never been back since, but you convinced me it was something that would become tradition. Us going to the church fair at Christmas time. Then lighting candles on Christmas Eve at midnight.'

'Did you hear what I said?'

Murphy turned the tinned fruit over in his hand, walked over to the pedal bin in the corner of the kitchen and dropped it in. 'This is ages past its sell by date.'

'Two year anniversary is coming up . . .'

'And let me guess . . . I'm not to show my face?'

'Something like that. Although she is softening. She actually asked how you were this time.'

'What did you tell her?'

'The truth. That you're still carrying it, but that you've managed to get better over time. That the nightmares seemed to have calmed down a lot now. That you haven't forgotten what happened, but at least your life is in a better place.'

'I still think it's weird that she speaks to you and not me. I've known her for over twenty years.'

'It's still hard for her, you know that. Peter dying in the way he did, it changed her. She's not the same person any more. She'll come around eventually. Just takes time.'

Murphy closed the cupboards, rubbed his stomach and tried to decide if he was actually hungry or not.

'Well, I'll be here when she's ready. Now, shall we stop this charade where we pretend to have a proper conversation first and just go upstairs?'

Sarah lowered her head as she suppressed a grin. 'I thought you'd never ask.'

*　　*　　*

Rossi decided her timing couldn't be worse; the start of what promised to be a major investigation colliding with the start of what could be her first proper relationship.

Not a drunken one-night stand, or an affair with a married man. An actual relationship in a life of failed ones. A myriad of non-starters.

A few years earlier, there had been promise of a romance with a man who had been a murder suspect in her first case with Murphy. That had fallen at the first hurdle of reality a few weeks later. The pointed barbs from her mother – Mama Rossi – were becoming more explicit by the visit. Rossi's lack of interest in being part of a couple was not shared by her old-school mother. It was the *done* thing. She was supposed to be married off by now, according to Mama Rossi. Happily supplying her mother with grandchildren to fuss over.

Two bodies found in her division, minutes after a guy walks into her station and confesses to a murder her boss doesn't believe has happened. All in one day. Her reaction was not to go home and lie in her bathtub for an hour before getting an early night.

No. She was going out.

She had met Darren Logan through a friend weeks earlier. It had been a pity set-up, by someone who could no longer hide their disappointment at a single friend in a group of couples.

Who the hell had blind dates in 2015 anyway?

Rossi thought back to that night those few weeks before as she sat in front of her mirrored wardrobe and applied a third different shade of lipstick. She had made little effort, jumping in the shower once she'd made it home then changing into her most casual of going out outfits. Jumper dress, black tights and boots.

Darren Logan. She remembered being told about him and deciding he sounded too good to be true. Good job, good education. According to Christina – the friend in question who had set them up – he was also good-looking. She hadn't used the words tall, dark and handsome, but from her description it sounded as if the cliché would fit.

She wouldn't have been far wrong.

Since that initial first date, they had seen each other more than a few times. Rossi wasn't a wait-and-see kind of girl, so she'd slept with him on the second night out. She had been suitably impressed to agree to a third night. Other than that, they'd spoken mostly by text. Flirty messages becoming gradually more filthy. He had been funny, even if he did sometimes overuse those emoticons she had yet to decide if she liked or not. Nothing that screamed BAD GUY or anything as ridiculous as that.

Maybe too normal.

Now she was dressing up again. Deciding what to wear then discarding her choices. Checking the time and swearing as the clock conspired against her. Rossi dried her hair, taking a minute to decide if she wanted to straighten it as well, before checking the clock again and deciding to leave it to curl.

She sent him a text to let him know she was running late but she would be there soon. Knowing that she had an early morning, she decided against a taxi into town and picked up her car keys.

Checking the mirror image of herself in the hallway of her flat, she nodded and said, 'That'll do,' under her breath.

Timing. It was all down to timing. Get that right and things will go perfectly. It was the way things worked, she'd found. She had made sure to tell Mama of her burgeoning relationship, just to keep her quiet for a week or so. Rossi thought of Murphy and shook her head as she recalled the almost constant ribbing he was giving her for the relationship.

Darren Logan. She had found herself putting her first name with his last and had almost decided to end it all that moment. Laura Logan sounded like a news reporter or a comic book character. He lived near Crosby, in an apartment . . . which wouldn't work in the future. She didn't want to live that far north in Liverpool. She thought about a bright future together, knowing his job as an anaesthetist at the Royal Hospital was secure enough financially.

She was annoyed with herself for thinking about these practical things. It had only been a few weeks, but she was already considering a future. It was so far away from her normal thoughts that it continued to jar her every time her mind drifted that way.

It was already too much effort, she thought. Having to wonder if this was The One, as if everyone only ever had a single 'one'. She left her little house, unlocking her car before reaching it. The street was quiet, the evening almost in total darkness.

A couple of hours, a meal and no alcohol. Then, back to her home for an early night. That was her intention.

When she walked into the restaurant fifteen minutes later – seeing Darren sitting there, hair flicked back, designer stubble and eyes lighting up at the sight of her – all thoughts of that went out the window.

Sometimes she just needed the comfort of normality. Darren stood up and brushed her cheek with his lips, the stubble on his jawline rubbing against her face a little.

Rossi smiled back at him. Decided it didn't really matter if she was late the next morning.

Chapter Nine

Murphy listened as the overnight staff updated him on the few things which had occurred during the late shift. He sighed, the sum total amounted to bugger all. Almost twenty-four hours since they had found Chloe and Joe, and the layout was already beginning to rely on two things – people who knew the couple and the post-mortem.

'CCTV doesn't cover anywhere near there really,' DC Hale said, looking suitably haggard from being out at crime scenes most of the previous day. 'Could go further out, but I'm not sure how useful that would be.'

'No,' Murphy replied, eyeing his chair, knowing he wouldn't get a chance to sit down and relax much that day. 'Unless he's wearing a big sign announcing himself, I suppose not. Still, won't hurt to check. I'll let you know the timeframe after the PM this morning. Anything from the neighbours?'

'There really wasn't any. Closest one was at least a few minutes' walk away. Didn't even know we'd closed the road off.'

'I owe Laura a fiver then. Keep an eye on any reports from Crimestoppers coming in. Hopefully someone somewhere noticed something.'

DC Hale nodded and walked off, slower than usual. Someone else who hadn't slept all that much the previous night, Murphy thought.

'Anyone seen Laura about?' Murphy asked the few people milling about the desks. The negative response only lasted a second as the doors behind him banged open.

'I'm not late,' Rossi said as she hurried towards him.

'Didn't say you were.'

'Before you do then,' Rossi replied, a hand self-consciously sweeping through her hair, 'what time are we going to the Royal?'

'Now,' Murphy said, buttoning his jacket up. 'Ready?'

'Of course.'

The Royal Hospital was situated just outside the city centre, the largest in the county of Merseyside by some stretch and about to become even larger. Building work had been going on for the previous few years, providing another reason for Liverpool to be proud of itself. Rossi had bored Murphy with the details on another trip there previously, the links to the nearby university and its medical students something she was proud of. As if her attendance at that university – studying something entirely different – meant she was a part of it.

All Murphy knew about the place was that it housed arguably his most visited scene outside the station.

There was something they'd never told Murphy about all those years before in training. Post-mortems are boring, painstakingly slow and protracted. Only made worse by the fact his favourite doctor carried them out.

Dr Stuart Houghton, rotund purveyor of death, who Murphy had a difficult time getting along with for seemingly no reason at all. Not one that Murphy could fathom anyway. The good doctor had taken an instant dislike to him years earlier and Murphy wasn't really interested in changing that perception.

Maybe it was the beard, Murphy thought.

'You're here then,' Houghton said as they passed through to his office – cluttered with every box file and piece of paper in the hospital in Murphy's eyes. The doctor greeted Rossi with a warm smile. Murphy not even receiving a cold one. 'Come on then. Let's get down to it.'

Murphy bounced lightly on his feet as he watched Houghton and his assistant get to work, two bodies doubling the workload but not the number of workers.

'Cutbacks,' Houghton had said as way of explanation. 'Can't even claim for petrol on call-outs at the moment.'

'I bet it's a real strain on your wallet,' Murphy replied, his acerbic tone earning a withering look from the doctor.

'We'll do the girl first,' Houghton said.

Murphy never understood the need to be there, not when Houghton could just print up his report and send it on. Yet, it was the done thing for a DI in Liverpool North division. You gave press conferences for no reason and watched a portly doctor dissect a corpse for the same.

It's the habits passed down generation by generation that get you through life.

'There is nothing to suggest she was beaten,' Houghton said, a digital recorder capturing his voice in the silent theatre, 'other than some minor contusions on her wrists and legs. From the restraints, I would deduce at this point. Some reddening to her face, evidence of tackiness.'

Duct tape, Murphy thought. Bound and gagged. No need to *deduce* anything there.

'Puncture marks on her left forearm. Two in total. Evidence of bruising.'

A while later, organs removed and checked, Houghton made a sound like he was agreeing with himself and began to move on.

'Rush on tests,' Murphy said to Rossi.

She nodded back at him and noted it down.

The morning was getting away from them by the time Joe Hooper was in the spotlight. Murphy could see the condition of his body was very different from the pale glow of Chloe's.

'Multiple contusions to the head, caused by a blunt instrument. Possibly a hammer, the claw part.'

Rossi winced beside Murphy, earning her a look from him.

'*Mannaggia*,' Rossi said, turning away. 'I hate the claw end.'

Murphy let out a soft laugh, turning back to the table and Houghton's work.

'Slash marks to the torso. Seven in total. Caused by a sharp instrument. Strangulation, with a ligature, to the neck. Possible cause of death.'

Murphy's phone was buzzing in his pocket with text messages every few minutes as he received details of the interviews currently occurring. Chloe and Joe's friends going over what they knew, which appeared to be very little. He showed Rossi the more interesting ones. The detective constables were being made to feel useful though, so every cloud . . .

'Two very different bodies, David,' Houghton said, once he had finished. 'The lovely Chloe's death will be drugs related – an overdose of some type of opioid possibly – but we won't know until the report comes back on that one. Mr Hooper was not so fortunate.'

'How long were they dead in that house?'

'Around forty-eight hours, I'd say. Approximate time of death is between nine p.m. and six a.m. on Friday night, Saturday morning for both of them.'

Murphy thought of the murder–suicide theory and how stupid it seemed now. The discovery of what lay beneath the clothes of Joe Hooper had ended that theory for him.

'Who went first?'

Houghton dried his hands on some paper towels, before squirting some alcohol from a pump dispenser onto them for added effect. 'Sorry?'

Murphy shook his head. 'Which victim died first, Doctor?'

Houghton matched Murphy's shake of the head. 'Not sure. That'll require much more investigation and even then we'd likely still not know for sure. If their deaths occurred within minutes of each other, it's unlikely we'll be able to tell.'

Murphy looked at Rossi, waiting to see if she had any questions, then, when she didn't, they exited the theatre before Houghton and his assistant had a chance to leave them in there alone.

'What are you thinking?' Rossi said as they left the hospital and walked towards the car.

'That this case just got a little bit more interesting,' Murphy said, unlocking the car from a few feet away. 'And annoying.'

*   *   *

The media presence outside the station on St Anne Street had grown overnight, the waiting press attempting to get any kind of word from them as they drove in. The car was surrounded by people as soon as they'd pulled up to the gate, word spreading quickly that they were of importance to the case. Murphy knew his face had become more recognisable to the local media over the years, but it seemed the nationals had also been tipped off to his notoriety. His name hadn't been shouted in public so much since his ill-fated return to Sunday league football a few months earlier.

At least it wasn't accompanied by shouts about his uselessness this time.

Inside the office, the number of detectives on the team had increased. DCI Stephens was standing silently at her office door, coming to life as Murphy and Rossi entered.

'Meeting, two minutes.'

Murphy mocked a salute and slipped his coat and jacket off. He stood near the radiator and placed a hand on it. 'Christ, this thing's barely warm.'

'No one is going to complain,' Rossi said to him, cupping a hand conspiratorially in front of her mouth. 'Winter finished in February according to those holding the purse strings. And everyone here is scared they'll take something away if they move money in the budget for heating.'

Murphy laughed and hung his coat back on his chair after it fell off again. 'Bit pointless having lukewarm radiators on, though. Bloody freezing out there and not really any better in here. We'll be wearing a vest and long johns by the end of the week.'

'I'm sure that's a good look on you.'

Murphy shrugged and made his way over to DCI Stephens's office.

'Tell me we have good news from the PM, David,' Stephens said as he closed her office door behind him.

'Only in the sense that no news is good news,' he replied, standing behind his usual seat. 'Joe Hooper was beaten and strangled by the looks of it, but we're not sure on Chloe as yet. Drug overdose is the likeliest option at the moment.'

'That's all we'd need. Plan of action, David? Make it a good one.'

'I assume the meeting is to keep everyone up to date?' Murphy waited for the nod, and went on. 'Once that's out the way, we finish up with family and friends and see where that gets us. We still have a number of different things here.'

'Press conference in a little while. Give them something before they shut our phone system down or finally come up with a good enough price for someone out there.'

'Boss . . .'

'Don't want to hear it. Platitudes will do, but we need to get out there and show ourselves. So far, we've given them that scrawny tit from media relations and that's it. It's not keeping any of them happy. They want us out there.'

Murphy sighed, gripping the back of the chair a little tighter. 'Right, course, boss. Just that there's not much we can tell them right now.'

'That doesn't matter. I had no idea how bloody famous these two were. Everyone is talking about it and we're doing nothing to calm that down. We've got to get a handle on things now.'

Murphy let go of the chair. 'Got it.' He turned and left the room, following the other detectives to the large meeting room at the other end of the office. Rossi fell into step with him as he walked.

'Let's just do the usual,' Murphy said as he stood at the door into the room and waited for a couple of stragglers. 'Not much else we can do.'

'You never know,' Rossi replied, fiddling with the bottle cap on the sports drink she was holding. 'One of them might have solved it already for us.'

Murphy looked at the back of the heads of the people within the room. 'I doubt it.'

The meeting room was a little larger than the one they'd had in the past, with windows on one side from floor to ceiling and blinds running down the length. Someone had placed a few plants in the room, trying to spruce the place up a little. The browning leaves on them suggested they weren't going to help.

'Settle down,' Murphy said, standing at the front as faces turned towards him one by one. 'Okay, here's where we are. Two victims, found in an abandoned house in Anfield. Post-mortem is inconclusive, but Chloe Morrison's death is possibly drug related, but the male victim – Joe Hooper – was badly beaten and then asphyxiated.'

A snigger caused by Murphy's pronunciation of the word, his Scouse accent having trouble with the middle syllables, was quickly snuffed out. Murphy aimed a stare in the general direction of the noise before continuing.

'We don't know who died first, so we're not concentrating on that aspect just now. What we need to know is how these two people ended up in that house and whether anyone else was there with them. Who's been doing interviews?'

A few hands shot up.

'Anyone get any kind of usable information?'

One hand remained in the air. 'Couple of things, one from a close friend of Chloe. From the circuit.'

'Circuit?'

The DC who had left his hand in the air shifted in his seat. 'The celebrity circuit. Apparently there's a group of them who all do the same events, clubs and that sort of thing. One of them was in *Hollyoaks* or something, done some reality shows since. I'd never heard of any of them though—'

'Right, that's great,' Murphy said, cutting in. 'Stay behind. The rest of you, I want double the effort on the private lives of the two of them. Anything that comes up, no matter how small and insignificant you think it is, I want to know. There has to be something which explains how they ended up in that house. Go through bank accounts, receipts, everything. We're going back to their apartment now, so Laura here will let you know which of you is coming with us.'

Rossi started scanning faces; Murphy imagined her checklist of who in the room she liked and disliked was being put to use.

'That'll do for now,' Murphy said, dismissing the meeting and leaning on the desk behind him. 'And I hope I don't have to remind you not to talk to the media. I don't care how much they offer. It won't replace that nice pension you're going to get in a few years. Which I'll make sure disappears faster than you can say "brown envelope".'

A few muted laughs, but otherwise silence. Murphy wondered if the weight of the situation, the case, was beginning to make itself clear.

'DC Kirkham,' Murphy said to the lone figure left behind – late twenties, early thirties, he guessed. 'That's right, isn't it?'

He got an eager nod in response. 'Yes, sir. It wasn't the *Hollyoaks* girl I wanted to tell you about . . .'

Another of those university graduates, fast-tracked into CID and moved up the ranks. This one was different from DC Hale, however. More old-school looking, with closely cropped hair and sharp features. Apart from the nose which had been broken at some point and not set properly, so now there was a slight deviation to it.

'Tell me on the way to the house,' Murphy said, smirking at Rossi as her shoulders slumped at him taking the decision away from her. 'I trust you haven't got anything better to do?'

'Course not, sir,' Kirkham said, jumping to his feet. He was tall, almost reaching Murphy's height but falling a couple of inches short.

'Good,' Murphy replied, trying not to yawn. 'Bloody knackered already. I hope you've got more life in you.'

'Yes, sir,' Kirkham replied, standing a little straighter as if to show he did.

Murphy gave him a little shake of his head. Tried to remember a time he had been so eager to please. Realised it wasn't that long ago.

'Come on then,' Murphy said, extending an arm towards the door. 'Lead the way.'

Murphy yawned again, then thought back to the reason

for his tiredness. He smiled and pulled out his phone to text Sarah.

They were like newlyweds lately, Murphy thought. He hoped it lasted a bit longer.

Greg

Greg had gone his whole life without getting into fights, not even so much as a scuffle in a playground. He'd shied away from violence with other men, never wanting to experience it. It was violent enough in his head without wanting that in reality. He would raise his voice but then hate himself for it. Would see women he supposedly loved cowering below him and he'd run to the bathroom and step into a cold shower.

Some part of him wished he was one of those big guys he saw walking around, conflict and war etched into their expressions. Just waiting for the wrong person to look at them. He wanted to be that kind of man. The kind who didn't worry about groups of teenagers hanging around street corners. The kind who protected his woman and did the right thing at the right time.

The type who wouldn't have frozen. Who wouldn't have let himself be led into his own back room and tied to a chair.

Listening to words which on the surface made sense.

Hannah had been there already. She was the one the man had wanted him to see. The relief in her eyes as he'd entered the room turning to desperation as he hadn't rushed to her rescue, instead allowing himself to be bound to the chair opposite her.

There was a song Greg always loved playing before he met Hannah. An old one, but still relevant. Couldn't even remember the band's name most of the time, but he knew every word of those lyrics.

'Love Will Tear Us Apart'.

He'd believed that was true until he'd met her. Every relationship he'd had until that point had ended badly. Not just arguments and the usual bullshit, but with complete and utter heartbreak in most cases.

When Greg fell in love, he fell hard. Off-a-cliff-onto-jagged-rocks hard. Devotion was too slight a word to describe how he would feel during a relationship.

He needed someone, always. Couldn't be alone. He had an overwhelming desire to be in a relationship. To have someone in his life. And that had led to situations he would never allow himself to think about. Blurred images fleetingly entered his mind – tears and blood – before he shut them down.

Hannah was different. He'd been different. Too often he'd been told he'd come on too strong and scared women with his attentiveness and dedication at the beginning of a relationship – as if that were really a bad thing. He'd decided with Hannah to dial that part of himself back a little. An experiment of sorts.

Try being Normal Greg. Never revealing his true feelings. Bottling everything up.

It had worked.

He wasn't aloof, or disinterested. He just hadn't turned up to her house at three in the morning with flowers and a shit-eating grin. He hadn't talked of joint bank accounts after a couple of dates. Named their future children. Greg fell in love with Hannah naturally, over a proper time period, and only when he felt sure she returned his feelings.

Four years together. That's what they had managed. Keeping down the old feelings of wanting to control everything was a constant battle. When Hannah wanted to go out with friends, or didn't respond to texts or emails instantly, he wouldn't snap or sulk. Instead, he'd breathe in and out, close his eyes, and calm himself.

If she talked about going out clubbing, he'd actively encourage it. He would spend all night wondering what she was getting up to, but would welcome her home with a 'How was your night?' and a smile. Two hen weekends abroad and he'd pretended to be excited for her. Asked if she needed any spending money and helped her pack.

Then he'd spent the three days she was away drinking and staring at his phone. Pacing the small flat they then shared, throwing accusations about her infidelity at the wall. Never receiving an answer. When she'd arrived back, he'd smiled and asked if she'd had a good time.

Now, it didn't matter. A man in dark clothing had taken over the show. Normal Greg was a memory. Now he was shit-scared Greg.

Greg wondered if there was anything that could have made him fight back. At least try to save himself, save her.

'We're surrounded by lies. We live with them every day, don't we?'

The hairs on Greg's arms stood on end as the cool air within the room settled on his skin. What was once so familiar – his own bloody dining room – now so alien. He shivered, once, remembering his mother saying *Someone's just walked over my grave.*

The man talked in a flat monotone, ignoring Hannah's cries behind the duct tape covering her mouth. Directing his words towards Greg, facing him as he stood between them. The man shifted to his right, a step aside, leaving Greg with a clear view.

Greg dropped his head and thought of Millie.

She had turned two years old already. A walking, somewhat talking, little person that Greg was supposed to be the protector of. To always be there for her, that was his job as her father. He pictured her, the blonde curls, the round cheeks which always had a rose of red in them. The absolute spit of Hannah. The smile that came naturally and easily. The personality which was developing, the way she would talk to her toys, bringing them to life.

They were parents. A family. Greg Bowlby and Hannah Flynn. An engagement ring lay in a box at the back of Greg's wardrobe, waiting for the right time.

Now, he didn't know if there was ever going to be a time.

'You don't know me, Hannah. Not really. But I know you. I know your kind. I've seen your type everywhere I've been. Always looking down your nose at others, as if your life, your decisions, are better. As if you have never done anything to regret.'

The man slithered round in front of Greg, moving through the darkness and almost sitting on his lap. He spoke into Greg's ear, the whisper invading him. 'She has a problem with living honestly, Greg. Hannah can't keep her stories straight. There are things she hasn't told you, things that need to be said.'

The man moved behind Greg, resting a hand on his shoulder and tapping his fingers. 'He deserves to know what he's doing, doesn't he Hannah? What he has been responsible for? We all need to know the truth. We all just need a little more honesty.'

Greg lifted his head, the face of his daughter fading as the man's words played with him. Honesty. That was all he wanted. Now, this man was bringing the doubt to the surface.

Hannah was no longer looking at Greg. Wouldn't look at him, he decided. As if she was ignoring him, had forgotten he was there. There was something in her eyes as she looked at the man standing to the side of them.

She was pleading with him.

'Wh ... what are you talking about?' Greg said, his voice catching at the back of his throat as he fought the urge to vomit. 'If you want money, we've got some, haven't we, Hannah?'

The man laughed softly, mocking him, Greg thought. His presence still hanging behind him, the tap of his fingers on Greg's shoulder incessant. 'Hannah is going to tell you her secrets, Greg. Or you're both going to die. She has a choice now. I hope she chooses the right one.'

The man came round and crossed the room towards Hannah. He tore off the duct tape that covered her mouth, a short scream escaping her as he did so. He placed a gloved hand across her face and shushed her, pushing her head back.

'Scream again and I'll cut your daughter's throat, you understand?'

Hannah didn't move. Greg watched as the man gripped her face tighter.

'Do you understand?'

Hannah nodded slowly, pushing against the man's hand to do so. 'Good,' he said. He dropped the tape to the floor and turned away from them both.

'Let us go,' Hannah said through gritted teeth. Spittle flew from her mouth and almost reached Greg. 'Now, you fucking bastard. We haven't done anything wrong.'

The man didn't reply, simply walked away and out of Greg's line of sight. A door closed behind him, leaving Hannah to curse in a low voice at no one.

'Greg,' Hannah said once she'd stopped. 'What's going on? Is Millie okay? Is she still at my mum's house? Are you okay? I don't know what's happening.'

Greg tried looking at Hannah, but couldn't. He had to look away, towards the shadows.

'Greg . . . talk to me. We need to get out of here.'

The breathing wasn't helping. She had ignored the man's words, so maybe they didn't mean anything. Maybe he was just a madman, someone who didn't know what he was talking about. But Greg didn't know. Not for sure. And he couldn't have that.

He blocked out Hannah's voice as it started up again. The whispers and low shouts for attention fading into the background as he breathed in and out.

The duct tape holding his right hand to the back of the chair was looser than the left. With a little effort, he could probably get it all the way out. That wasn't what he was thinking about though.

His voice started as a whisper, but became louder as he repeated himself.

'Tell me what you're hiding, Hannah. Tell me. Tell me now. Tell me, now.'

Chapter Ten

The apartment was quieter than the previous day. Fewer people milling about now forensics had finished their work. Items had been removed, sent away to be examined further. Every computing device – of which there had been a fair few – and mobile phone would be scrutinised for more evidence.

Policing had changed greatly since Murphy had started back in the late nineties. Now, it seemed as if everyone kept their entire lives on a tablet, phone or laptop.

'So, we think he was playing away from home?' Rossi said, snapping on gloves and picking through the mail which had arrived that morning.

'Looks that way,' Murphy replied, trying to stretch out his gloves a little more to make them fit. 'Kirkham here spoke to one of Joe's friends. Plays on the same team as him.'

'You mean . . .'

'No, not that. Football team.'

Murphy motioned to Kirkham for him to carry on with what he had been telling him on the way over. The eagerness had dissipated, replaced with an almost too-professional air.

He would get there, Murphy thought. He was already making a better impression on him than most of the new batch of detective constables they had been lumbered with.

'His name is Charlie Smith,' Kirkham said with no preamble. 'Hasn't played for a while due to a knee ligament issue. Had surgery a few months back. He has known Joe for a number of years. Before the TV show. He told me he was surprised Joe had agreed to the wedding, given the way he had been recently.'

'And how's that?' Rossi said, setting aside a couple of letters and dumping the obvious bills on the coffee table.

'He's been out with him a few times. Said he was with a different girl every night. Charlie enjoyed going out with him, said they would get into all the VIP parts of the clubs in town. Girls throwing themselves at them and Joe Hooper never turned that down. He would talk about Chloe, but it was always in a really nasty way. He called her the "Trophy Slut". '

'*Bastardo . . .*'

'Quite. Anyway, he asked Joe about it all one night – why he was getting married to her when it was obvious he didn't want to be with her – and didn't really get a good response. Joe told him that he was making more from the wedding to Chloe than he would make in three years playing for whatever lower league club would take him on.'

'Looks like it was about the money for him then,' Rossi said, turning towards Murphy who had been half listening in.

'Joe had offers to go to a bigger club – Reading, or some championship club – but had to turn them down to keep the relationship going. It was made clear to them that they had to stay up here. So, Charlie reckons that's what sparked him going to clubs and meeting girls. That sort of thing.'

'Money and not wanting to be in a relationship,' Rossi said, narrowing her eyes at Murphy. 'Seems like there was trouble in paradise for certain then.'

'Looks that way,' Murphy replied. 'Not sure how that fits into this whole thing though. Unless we're going with the angle that it's someone Joe has hurt with his actions. Of course, if Chloe was more into this relationship than he was and she found out about it, there's no telling how bad she took it.'

'Strapped herself to a chair before killing herself? Not buying it.'

'Exactly. This could all be just more celeb gossip and have nothing to do with their murders at all. Could be something else entirely.'

Rossi turned to Kirkham. 'What about drugs? Did you ask about them?'

Kirkham nodded. 'Told me they were totally clean. Joe and him just liked a drink. The FA have really clamped down on drugs testing and positive results. Neither of them wanted to get caught with anything in their system and get banned for life. Playing at that level of football, they don't really have anything else.'

Murphy turned over an ornament, tested the base and found no give. Went to the next one. 'Money then? Ransom gone wrong, possibly.'

'Well, they were killed hours after being taken on the Friday,' Rossi said, perching on the edge of the white sofa. 'Possible something went wrong and they never got round to the ransom part. Still doesn't explain the scene, or the collage of pictures on the wall.'

Murphy replaced the final ornament on the sideboard. 'We need to find something, anything, here. I'm in front of the press in two hours and so far I've got nothing. We need to find something fast.'

They didn't.

* * *

Murphy tried to rub some life into his eyes, failed, and settled for splashing his face with water instead. He dried off with paper towels, bringing roughness to his features anew, checked himself in the mirror a final time and left the toilets.

He hated this part.

It wasn't that he didn't know the media had a role to play – he knew that only too well – it was just something he'd never prepared for. When he'd imagined life in the police force – or service, as it now was – it hadn't involved sitting in front of a load of journalists, who were all just waiting for you to say the wrong thing.

In and out. That's what he wanted.

'Ready?' the press liaison officer asked as he met him at the doors leading into the press room. Murphy could remember his first name – Adrian – and that he was a scrawny git, as DCI Stephens had put it earlier. Another anonymous thirty-year-old man in an expensive suit, a hair full of products and a clean-shaven, unmarked face. They were becoming more prevalent within the station, each as interchangeable as the last.

DCI Stephens was a little behind them, talking to another anonymous guy in a suit.

'Yeah,' Murphy replied, giving his suit jacket one last swipe with the back of his hand. 'Let's get this done.'

They entered the room, DCI Stephens hurrying to catch up as Murphy held the door open for her. As Murphy walked to the front the room broke out into a cacophony of camera clicks, a few brave journos shouting out questions before being told to quiet down by their colleagues.

Keen.

Murphy had a statement prepared, a litany of bullshit words which said nothing when carefully examined. Words he'd used repeatedly, in a variety of different cases, but all of which amounted to the same thing.

We don't know what the hell is going on.

'Thank you,' Adrian said, silencing the voices in the room. He gave a brief introduction explaining why they were there, but glossed over any details. Murphy waited, drumming his fingers on one knee underneath the desk. 'I'm going to hand you over to Detective Inspector David Murphy now.'

Murphy cleared his throat, pulled the microphone a little closer and started his speech. 'Thank you. And thank you all for attending.' Murphy looked up, hoping he sounded genuine. 'Yesterday morning the bodies of two people were found at an address in Anfield. They were subsequently identified as being Chloe Morrison and Joe Hooper. Both deaths are being treated as suspicious. Enquiries are ongoing and are robust and intensive at this early stage.'

Murphy gave some further platitudes, feeling the life pour out of him as he sat there, speaking whilst his mind wandered.

'If anyone was in the area of Anfield, and noticed a vehicle parked up by abandoned houses, or anything of that sort, in the past week, please get in touch. If anyone has any information, please call either Crimestoppers or Liverpool North CID . . .'

Murphy reeled off phone numbers and websites he had given far too many times before. It was difficult not to see the pointless nature of the whole game, but he knew he was being broadcast into living rooms around the country at that point. Chloe and Joe murders were big news in a slow news week.

'We have time for some very brief questions . . .' Adrian had no sooner got the words out of his mouth before there was a clamour of voices wanting to be heard. Murphy gave him a glance, waiting to see if he was going to quieten them down and make them take turns. Happy to stay patient and waste a little more time doing nothing so he could get out of there.

Instead it was a voice from the other side of him which broke through. 'Enough,' DCI Stephens said, rising from her seat and holding her hands up for quiet. 'One at a time. You, there.' She pointed to someone on the front row.

'Damien Lomax, *Sky News*. Can you tell us how they died?'

Murphy waited a second or two to see if DCI Stephens had taken over completely, before deciding it was still on him. 'Details related to cause of death are not being released at this time.'

'Is it true that only one of them was strangled?'

Murphy nodded his head slightly, before catching himself. 'I cannot give you that information at this time.'

A hand shot up behind the *Sky News* guy. Murphy pointed to them and leaned forward to take a drink of water. 'Alice from the *Liverpool Echo*. Are the public being warned to be on the lookout for anything suspicious? Can you give more details about what they should be looking for?'

'I'd ask the public to always be willing to report anything suspicious, Alice.' That earned a titter amongst some of the journalists in the room. Murphy remained stony-faced. 'At this time, there is nothing in particular I want to convey to the public to be on the lookout for, but this may change in the future. However, I do want to make sure that the people of Liverpool go about their daily lives as normal. We believe there is no direct threat to anyone else at this time.'

A couple more questions were batted away with non-answers as easily as those which preceded them, earning a pat on the back from DCI Stephens once they had left the room minutes later.

'You're becoming a pro at this, David,' she said, checking her phone. 'You've come a long way.'

Murphy remembered the incident which had made him infamous a few years previously – a screaming match in a press conference with a particularly annoying local journalist. He hid a smile as he thought of that man's now-dead career and even deader newspaper. 'Easy when you know how.'

'Good. I have to go meet the superintendent now. Everything as it was earlier?'

Murphy nodded. He had appraised her of the current situation once they had returned from Chloe and Joe's apartment. 'Nothing more until forensics get back to me.

We had that info from Joe's friend, which we'll confirm. Not sure it'll be of any use though.'

Murphy watched DCI Stephens walk away, wondering if it was ever better to be away from the front line of policing. You had the responsibility for the cases which passed through the station, but were not directly involved with them.

He wasn't sure he could ever give up that attachment.

There had been a shift in mood whilst he was away from the office. He could sense it. Nothing tangible, just the feeling something had changed since he'd left.

Murphy made his way towards Rossi. She was sitting with her back to him, the desk phone cradled between her ear and shoulder as she wrote in her notepad.

'Great . . . No, really, that's a big help . . . We'll see you soon . . . okay, bye.'

DC Harris and DC Hale were sitting and standing respectively opposite Rossi, their attention on her rather than Murphy as he waited for them to acknowledge his presence.

'Sounds spot on,' Rossi said once she'd dropped the phone back into its cradle. 'Over the water, but close enough.'

'Shit,' Hale replied. 'Not a one-off then?'

Murphy leaned against Rossi's desk making her jump slightly. 'What's going on?'

'Did it go okay?' Rossi said, flipping pages back on her notebook.

'Yeah, yeah. Come on, what's happened?'

'We got a call from Wirral CID . . .'

'Not bloody him . . .'

Rossi sat back in her chair, rocking it a little. 'Unfortunately, yes. DS Brannon. And it wasn't for a friendly chat.'

Murphy swore under his breath. DS Tony Brannon. The last name he wanted to hear. 'Not angling to come back, I hope.'

'No, nothing like that. We could be seeing more of him, though.'

'Why?' Murphy said, already feeling his stomach sink.

'Because I don't think Chloe and Joe are our first victims.'

Chapter Eleven

There's always one person you can never stand working with. Having to walk the same bit of carpet as each other every day, thrown together by coincidence or a practical joke planned by a vengeful God. Someone who – either by design or accident – is the antithesis of everything you hold dear.

For Murphy, that man was DS Tony Brannon.

He had worked with Brannon in Liverpool North division for almost four years, before Brannon was quietly shifted to the other side of the River Mersey, to Wirral CID. Murphy had been asked outright near the end of Brannon's tenure at his station whether he could work side by side with him any longer.

He'd said no.

Murphy wasn't sure if Brannon knew of his role in his relocation. Didn't much care, if he was honest.

'Not much changed around here.'

Now Brannon was back.

'It's not been that long, Tony,' Murphy replied, closing the door of the meeting room. 'Only a year or so. Let's go through this from the beginning.'

'Happy to,' Brannon replied, producing a bag of cheese and onion crisps. Not much had changed at all. 'So, we found out about your case like everyone else. On TV. Spoke to some people over here I'm still in contact with and got the juicy bits.'

'When did you put things together,' Rossi said, her nose wrinkling as the smell of Brannon's snack began to assail her nostrils.

'Overnight. This case we had was a tough one, but not out of the ordinary, sadly. Some right little scrotes over on the Wirral.'

'What is the case, Tony?'

Brannon stopped eating for a few seconds, sucking remnants of crisps off his fingers before wiping them on his trousers and picking up his bag. He took out a folder and began emptying it on the desk between them.

'Jane Piper and Stuart Carter. Found dead just over three weeks ago now. They were discovered in their home, near Moreton. Not far from where you lived, Murphy, when you ... went off your head for that year.'

Murphy bristled, then let it go. 'How were they found?'

'Jane's mother. She had a key, hadn't heard from her daughter for a few days and was worried. Out of character apparently. Went round to the house, let herself in, and found them in the living room.'

Brannon produced a photograph from the folder and slid it over to Murphy and Rossi. 'This is what she walked into.'

The similarities struck Murphy instantly. Two victims facing each other, hands and legs bound to the chairs. The male victim's face puffed up and marked. The female victim seemingly untouched.

'This is almost exactly like our crime scene.'

Brannon grinned and crunched through another few crisps from the packet. 'Almost. I asked, but this one with the reality show idiots you've got now wasn't in their home. Plus, the rest of the house was a wreck at our scene. Everything turned over, proper thorough job done on the place.'

Rossi flicked through the other photographs from the folder. 'You were thinking robbery or something?'

Brannon tilted the packet and emptied the crumbs down his throat. Murphy averted his eyes at the sight.

'Something like that, yeah. It looked like a burglary gone really, really wrong. We thought there may have been, or had been, a large quantity of cash in the house as none of the electrical items had been taken. Not that they would have got much for them anyway. Just some old cheap shit from Tesco or whatever. That was until we started looking into the male victim a little more.'

Murphy looked up, the sight of Brannon's joker-like grin reminding him why he was so pleased not to have to work with him on a daily basis. 'Go on,' he said once it became clear Brannon was waiting. 'What about the male victim?'

'Well,' Brannon said, leaning back in his chair, his growing paunch protruding over his trousers as he widened his legs a little more. 'Turns out he was hiding something. A big something. His name wasn't Stuart. It was James. James Lynch.'

Murphy looked towards Rossi, the name ringing a bell for him somewhere.

'Paedo,' Rossi said without pause.

'One and the same. Got done for statutory rape years ago. Two thirteen-year-old girls. He was twenty-one and they were coming on to him—'

'Don't,' Murphy said, laying a hand on the table between Rossi and Brannon as he saw Rossi begin to rise out of her chair. 'He's a tool. Not worth it.'

Brannon seemed to enjoy the reaction, shooting Murphy a rolled-eyes look. 'As I was saying, he got two years in prison, suspended, and was on the sex offenders register. Lucky bastard didn't get his face plastered everywhere because it was the same week as Liverpool fluking that Champions League when he got sentenced. Anyway, he somehow got a job that didn't need background checks, changed his name, and was going by Stuart Carter.'

'So,' Murphy said, seeing where this was going, 'you think someone found out about him, his history, and got some revenge?'

'Something like that. We've had both of those girls in and their families, but no evidence yet. Been nearly a month and we've not got much further than that. Looks like it could be something else entirely now.'

'Maybe.' Murphy was thinking, turning things over in his mind. Two couples killed in a similar manner, one in their own home, one in an abandoned house. They were missing something.

'Leave the file,' Rossi said, interrupting his thoughts. 'We'll let you know if we're going to link them.'

'Course,' Brannon said, making no move. 'I'll stick around a while if you like.'

'Like we would . . .' Rossi said, a little too loudly under her breath.

'Got nothing much else going on,' Brannon continued as if he hadn't heard Rossi speak. 'Would be good to catch up with the boys out there.'

'Do what you want,' Murphy said, grabbing the folder, checking the front to make sure the case number was attached. 'Just don't get in our way, if you can help it.'

'It'll be like I'm not even here.'

Murphy waited for Brannon to leave before speaking to Rossi. 'I feel like I need a shower after that.'

'You forget how much of a prick he is,' Rossi said as they began gathering their files together. 'Then he reminds you within seconds.'

'It's been nice around here without him. Won't argue with that. But, for now, he could be useful.'

'You think it's the same case then?' Rossi said as they left the meeting room. Murphy spied Brannon on the other side of the room and dropped the folder onto his desk, opening it up and going through its contents. 'I'd say it'd be a massive coincidence if not. But there's also a lot that's different about the two scenes.'

'*Dio* . . . I hope they're not connected. I wouldn't even know where we'd start on that if they were.'

Murphy smiled thinly, before returning to the contents of the folder. He tutted and shook his head as he attempted to make sense of Brannon's handwriting. He fired up his computer and waited to log into HOLMES, hoping that would be easier to navigate.

He was reading through the case notes on his computer screen when DC Harris wheeled himself round the desk, DC Kirkham behind him, looking down in order not to inadvertently kick or trip over the back of Harris's wheelchair. Murphy recognised the stance from his own fears.

'Your man is here,' Harris said. 'The one Kirkham here spoke to.'

'Great,' Murphy said, minimising the HOLMES programme on his computer and switching off the monitor. 'Be there in a sec. Laura? You coming?'

Rossi tore her attention away from what Murphy guessed was the same reading he himself had been doing. 'Yeah, coming now.' Murphy waited as she made a few more notes on her notepad.

'Kirkham, you stick with Harris. Laura and I will speak to him this time. See if they've pulled anything from the laptops or phones of the two victims yet. They've been taking their time over it.'

'Got it, sir.'

Murphy followed Rossi out of the office, walking beside her as they headed down the corridor leading to the interview rooms.

'Media went well then?' Rossi said, giving him a quick glance.

'Yeah, usual stuff. Doubt it'll be the last one. If every case had the same spotlight on them . . .'

'I know, I know,' Rossi replied, holding the door open for Murphy as they reached the end of the corridor. 'Just doesn't happen like that though. I was thinking about that girl who's gone missing . . .'

'Amy Maguire,' Murphy said, wondering if Rossi had forgotten her name already.

'Yeah. I mean, it's not even about being famous like Chloe Morrison, or anything like that. Sometimes, it's just about what you look like, or where you're from. Amy is from a small area of south Liverpool, from a deprived background. Didn't do well in school, worked in a shop. She was good-looking, but no different to a thousand other girls out there. So, she gets left behind.

No one is going to run appeals for just another lost adult.'

Murphy listened, taking it all in and becoming more incensed by the second. 'It shouldn't matter. They should care about every single person who goes missing.'

'Quarter of a million a year? There's not enough time in the day to cover them all.'

Murphy grunted in response. He knew all this, but it still rankled. Amy's disappearance had barely made a dent when it had first occurred. A few paragraphs in the *Liverpool Echo* and some social media interest, but that would all be forgotten now.

'It's a shame,' Rossi continued, unaware of Murphy's internal monologue. 'But we have bigger priorities right now. I'm sure they can deal with it in Liverpool South.'

Murphy agreed, still thinking about Amy, a young woman who might share his DNA. Who could be his daughter. Who was currently lost, out there waiting to be found.

Thinking about all the things he wasn't doing to help find her.

Hannah

It wasn't supposed to happen like this. Not forced upon her, without a chance to prepare.

In fact, it wasn't supposed to happen at all.

Everyone who had known the truth was sworn to secrecy. Only a few people knew her secret – and she didn't think any of them would reveal it – so how the hell had this crazy prick found out?

There would be a way out of it. She knew that. It was just a case of sitting there and thinking things through logically. Working out the best course of action, cool and calm. Everything she was struggling to be at that moment.

She had thought better of Greg. He could have at least put up a fight. She bloody had, so why couldn't he? He was quick enough to be angry with her if she was a minute late somewhere, or said the wrong thing. He made a good show of pretending that everything was fine as he sulked on the sofa or in the restaurant, but she knew it. Enjoyed winding him up sometimes, just to get back at him for something wrong he'd done to her. Watching him squirm as he held back the things he wanted to shout and scream at her.

He was angry in that room. Finally, after years together, she was seeing the real him.

She'd thought things were different at the beginning. The way he'd treated her had been better than any guy she'd been with before. Attentive and caring. Listening to every bullshit thing she'd had to say, as if it was of high interest to him. It grew tiring after a while though. She knew there was something else there, something suppressed, which she hadn't witnessed before.

It was as if he kept a lid over everything within himself so she never saw what was lurking there. Frightened to show the good in case the bad revealed itself.

She was happy, that was for certain. He was a convenience for a long time, but she really did fall in love with him after a while. Couldn't imagine her life without him. He was part of it now. There would be a missing piece if he wasn't around.

That's why she couldn't believe what had happened. Had refused to for so long. Didn't want to think of one stupid decision affecting her for not just one night, but for an entire life.

When it had happened, she had barely felt any guilt. They hadn't been together properly for that long and it wasn't as if Greg's demeanour suggested he was committed to her either. It was just a stupid decision on the wrong night. Something which had lasted no time at all. A throwback to her younger years, when she would go out and not care what she did, or what people thought of her. She could do what she liked, screw what others would say. If she wanted to do something, she would just do it.

Alcohol lowers the inhibitions and brings more of yourself to the fore; the things you bury to seem *normal* and *good* in sober reality.

She'd lied to herself for so long it almost became truth. Deep down, she knew the facts though.

Hannah had sat down at seven months gone and worked out dates, times, acts, contraception used. It was clear to her then.

She hadn't panicked. Instead she'd weighed up possibilities and made a decision as to what she would do. Then she'd talked things over with the few people she trusted, checked her judgement and got universal agreement.

Never tell him.

Hannah couldn't really remember what the bloke in that alleyway had looked like, but from a blurred memory she'd thought there was enough similarity for things never to be certain from sight alone. Thankfully, when her daughter had been born, she looked like any other newborn. As she'd grown older, she'd taken more of her physical attributes from her mother than from whoever her father was.

From time to time, she felt guilty for what she'd done. The lie she was living. It didn't seem to matter all that much though. Greg had bonded with Millie, never questioning things, never treating his supposed daughter with anything other than paternal worship.

They were almost normal.

Now, the seeds of doubt had been placed in his head. If she could just get out of there, escape into a more relaxed situation where she could answer his questions patiently and with a hint of sadness that he was even worried about things, it would all be okay. She didn't have that luxury.

What she did have was an increasingly agitated Greg, sitting no more than six feet away, straining to get closer so he could lay his hands on her and shake the truth out of her.

She waited for him to stop, not lowering her eyes from his, willing her stare to portray what she wanted so much to be the truth.

They could have been happy. He would have eventually relaxed and revealed more of himself over the years. It wasn't like she couldn't take any character flaws he had and mould them into something she could live with. She'd done it before. Every man had some kind of issue to deal with.

'Tell me the truth, Hannah.'

Over and over. Waiting for something she could never say. Would never say. Hoped never to say.

The man who had strapped them to the chairs – dangerously close to toppling over in Greg's case – had been gone for at least half an hour by that point, Hannah guessed.

'There's nothing to tell,' Hannah said, the same answer she had given more than twice already. 'Seriously, this guy is just trying to mess with you. Mess with us. Don't let him.'

It was almost as if Greg had been waiting for someone to say something. That's what she was beginning to suspect. He'd had his own doubts but had never voiced them. Now someone had said something, Greg was going to get to the truth and wouldn't stop until he got it.

She wouldn't say. Not for anything. No one could prove it without some kind of test. Hannah felt a prick of nervousness as she imagined the man outside the room running a DNA test in her kitchen, or something equally ridiculous. She quietened down that side of her with logic.

He was just crazy, wanted to rob the house, or do something else. He didn't know. Couldn't tell.

'He knows you've done something. This is to punish us. Maybe he'll let us go if you just tell me the truth. Tell me the truth, Hannah.'

The last sentence hadn't matched the almost calm volume of those preceding it. Instead it was spat with venom and loud enough that she hoped her neighbours heard it.

The door opened softly, Greg ignoring it and continuing to fire questions at her. Hannah finally tore her gaze away from Greg and waited for the man to appear behind him, hoping this was going to be the end of it.

Knowing somehow it wouldn't be.

When she'd walked into her home, closing the door behind her, he'd been standing in the hallway waiting. Dressed all in black, a ski mask covering almost his entire face. Her first instinct had been to fight, but he'd overpowered her easily. Not that she let that be the end of it. She'd used everything in her arsenal to attempt to escape from his heavy grip. Her scream had been cut off quickly and with a practised ease, she'd thought. Gagged with duct tape across her mouth, she'd fallen to the floor when he'd tackled her. He had ignored her scratches, attempted headbutts and kicks, and had dragged her into the living room. Getting her into the chair had proved difficult for him, giving her a chance to escape. He had stopped, releasing her for a second, giving her no time to run before delivering a short, sharp blow to the side of her head, knocking her to the floor again.

Things had become blurry for some time after that. When her senses had come back to her, she couldn't move her arms or legs. Strapped to a chair which she couldn't rock over without hurting herself. Made to wait in silence, her shouts and screams muffled. Only audible in her own mind.

The man now stood behind Greg, Hannah's eyes locked on his position in the darkness. She couldn't see features, only his form, guessing that even if there were light in the room she still wouldn't be able to make out what he really looked like behind that mask.

Greg stopped talking, finally sensing the presence behind him. He tried to crane his neck to see, but he was too fixed in place to do so.

'Well, this was disappointing,' the man said. 'I was hoping you would have saved all this bother and told Greg the truth, Hannah.'

'I knew it . . .'

'Be quiet, Greg.' The man spat out the name with a disgust that shook Hannah. 'You're just like the others. You don't know what love is. There is no truth in this room, only lies. You could be better people, but you're not listening to me. You don't believe what I can do.'

It wasn't just her he was angry with. She should have guessed that, otherwise only she would be the one who was strapped down and unable to move.

'I think it's time we played a game,' the man said moving between them. He settled on his haunches between them, Hannah saw the flash of a grin in the darkness. 'It's called, how long can I hurt Hannah before she tells you the truth, Greg.'

Chapter Twelve

Murphy read the report on Chloe and Joe in silence, waiting for answers to appear as if by magic from the page. Forensics. Not as useful as they make out on TV, but usually useful all the same.

In this instance, not really useful at all.

It was the afternoon of the second day, already coming up to the thirty-hour mark of that magical forty-eight-hour period when the case was supposed to stand or fall. Not that Murphy ever bought into that kind of thinking. If anyone wanted to see a police service who didn't give up because they hadn't solved a case within the first few days, it was Merseyside Police. Sometimes a few months wouldn't even be a cause for worry. Two high-profile cases in the previous decade had taken more than a year before a charge was made.

Murphy focused on the forensics report once more, trying to discover the key thing that he may have missed in his first three reads. It hadn't taken him long to read it, it was mainly a list of items from which no usable information could be gleaned.

'Laura, you got anything from this?' Murphy said, giving in and throwing it open.

'Not really,' Rossi replied.

'That's not a no. What are you thinking?'

Rossi was still staring at the report across from him, one foot raised up on her chair, an arm casually strung around her knee. 'Just how clean it is.'

'I got that too. Could just mean we have someone who knows about forensics? They'd only have to watch any cop show on TV these days.'

'Guess so. Still, all that preparation with the magazine covers, the newspaper articles, and not one bit of DNA at all? That's strange. Not a fresh fingerprint in that room, or the area we found the victims? It feels ... I don't know ... prepared in some way.'

Murphy thought about it for a second, decided there was something he'd been considering himself.

'A kill site?'

'Yeah,' Rossi replied, letting her foot fall to the floor and pulling herself closer to her desk. 'Which could mean knobhead's case from over the water isn't linked to this one at all.'

'Killed in their own home, whilst our guy kills in a specific place outside of it? Unless there's another reason we're not seeing?'

'Possibly.'

'The set-up is too similar though. Bound to chairs facing each other. One killed by asphyxiation, the other by overdose of unknown origin. No, there's something else there. The security at their apartment, CCTV and the like. Bet that could put off someone ...'

'Bet you're right. That could be why it was a different location. The killer scouts out his victims, decides it's too risky killing them in their own home.'

'Let's speak to that agent again,' Murphy said, standing up and grabbing his jacket from the back of his chair. 'See if there's anything he's not told us yet. Or that we just haven't found out.'

*   *   *

The media presence outside the station had dispersed. Murphy had heard the house in Anfield was still attracting a few ghouls who wanted to stand by police tape and look at a couple of bored uniformed coppers. Outside Thomas Parker's house, it was different. A cavalcade of journalists descended on them as Murphy and Rossi pulled up to the driveway of Parker's house, flashes going off in the afternoon light.

It was the questions which always struck Murphy as odd.

'Are you here to arrest Thomas Parker?'

'Is Thomas Parker a murder suspect?'

'Did Thomas Parker kill Chloe?'

Murphy wondered if they actually expected an answer. It was as if they were hoping there would be a slip and the two detectives would suddenly give up all their information. It must have worked at some point, as what type of person tries the same thing over and over, expecting different results?

Murphy waited for the gates to open, spying the CCTV affixed to the pillar on the driver's side of the car, and angled towards them. They had phoned ahead, so Murphy hadn't expected too long a wait to gain entry, but thirty seconds was beginning to feel like thirty minutes.

Murphy had known from the address that they weren't going to be visiting a three-bedroomed terraced house. Or even the nice semi-detached where Chloe's mother lived. He knew where the money was located within the city, the houses kept for footballers, local celebs and people with much better-paid jobs than a detective inspector.

Formby.

'Not far from the professor's house this,' Murphy said as they waited. 'Not been back here since.'

'I'm not surprised. You were almost killed that time. Lucky that you had Jemma Barnes on your side. Wonder how she's doing . . .'

Murphy thought of the young woman who had been held in captivity for almost a year. How she had emerged from a dark basement and killed her captor, saving Murphy's life in the process. His thoughts turned to Amy Maguire and whether she was safe somewhere or in trouble like Jemma Barnes had been, without anyone suspecting.

Or, whether she was dead already. Her body waiting to be found.

'From what little I hear, she's doing well,' Murphy said, nosing the car onto the drive as the gates finally opened. 'She's kept out of public life as much as she can. Three years ago that was now.'

'Time flies and all that.'

The house was concealed within high, red-bricked walls. The house itself eventually revealed itself, the car's tyres crunching on gravel stones as they drove the short distance to the entrance. It wasn't palatial but it still screamed money. Built from dark red brick, with large windows, trimmed in a deep brown colour. Murphy could see a multitude of outhouses to one side and a front entrance framed by large pillars of brick masquerading as marble.

'There's even a bloody fountain,' Murphy said, pointing to Rossi's side window.

'Honestly,' Rossi said, taking in the grounds and shaking her head. 'You would never think places like this exist only a short drive from some of the shite we see on a regular basis. Like a different world. It's still in Liverpool and not bloody Southport though. No matter how hard they try to make it so.'

Murphy pulled to a stop near the entrance, gave Rossi a look. 'Don't let the money intimidate you,' he said, earning himself a muttered response from Rossi. 'I'm just saying, we treat him like any other guy.'

They were greeted at the door by a woman in an old-fashioned tabard apron – the hired help, Murphy assumed. She was the epitome of old English maid, with silver hair in a bun, wrinkled skin and thick gold-framed glasses. She ushered them through to the main living area, where Parker stood with his back to them, speaking on his mobile and gesticulating with one hand towards an ornate mantelpiece.

'Real marble that,' Murphy said pointing towards the fireplace. 'Classy.'

'And you're telling me not to be intimidated . . .'

Parker turned as they spoke, covering the mouthpiece of the phone.

'Thanks, darling,' Parker said to the woman who had shown them in before speaking into the phone again.

Rossi nudged Murphy as she turned to watch the woman leave. 'Bet she came free with the house,' she said covering her mouth slightly with one hand.

Murphy waited patiently for a second or two before clearing his throat and speaking louder. 'When you're finished.'

Parker turned, almost bowing with apology, before going back to his phone call. 'Course, course. I'll call you back . . . I don't know when, just don't say anything until I tell you to.'

Murphy decided to cross the room to get closer to Parker, drawing himself up to his full height in the vast space of the living area.

Parker stabbed at his phone, shaking his head as he turned to face Murphy and Rossi once more. His eyes widened as he took in Murphy's size directly in front of him.

'S . . . sorry about that,' Parker said, a slight shake to his hands as he returned the phone to his trouser pocket. 'Is, erm, everything okay? I mean . . . obviously not, but . . . erm . . . what's going on?'

Murphy fought against the temptation to grin madly and get even closer. 'Well, things are progressing, Mr Parker,' he replied, his voice flat and non-committal. 'We're here about Chloe and Joe, of course.'

'Yes, of course . . . sorry again about that,' Parker said, pointing to his empty hand before realising he'd already replaced his phone. 'It's all gone very mad around here, as you can imagine.'

'No, actually. Tell us what's been going on?'

Parker frowned. 'In what way?'

'Who you've spoken to, that sort of thing.'

Murphy allowed Parker a few seconds to think before sighing and checking his watch.

'Well, there's all the press of course. They all want to speak to me. Trying to get access to the families and that. I've been putting them off for now, but eventually it'll get to the point where we'll have to say something.'

Murphy shook his head. 'How about – just for once – we concentrate on things other than stories in newspapers and magazines, Mr Parker? Leave dealing with the press to us.'

Parker let out a nervous laugh, before realising the gravity of the situation. 'I didn't mean that ... I understand, but these people won't stop until they get something they can write, tweet, or blog about. That's just the way things are.'

Rossi stepped up in line with Murphy. 'Let's leave this conversation for now, what do you reckon? Talk about dead Chloe Morrison and dead Joe Hooper. You know ... important things?'

Murphy bowed his head, took a step back and leaned on the arm of one of the large sofas. Parker raised his hands in mock surrender but didn't move. 'I want to help. I'll do anything I can, of course.'

'Good,' Rossi replied, flipping through pages in her notebook. 'Then we're going to ask a few questions and let you get back to whatever it is you were doing. Sound fair?'

Parker nodded, his eyes still wide enough for Murphy to see the red streaks of blood in the whites. Coupled with the dark rings underneath his eyes, Murphy guessed sleep had evaded Parker since seeing the bodies of his two clients.

'What was the state of the relationship between Chloe and Joe?'

'I ... in what way?'

Rossi didn't look up, still standing with pen in hand. 'How were things between them? To the best of your knowledge.'

Murphy watched Parker clasp his hands together lightly. One hand massaging the other.

'Things were good, I think.'

'No arguments or disagreements?'

'Everyone has those,' Parker replied, his hands still wringing together. 'I hadn't heard anything out of the ordinary.'

'What about Joe?'

Parker's face darkened a little, his expression becoming even more drawn in on itself. 'What about him?'

'How was he taking to the celebrity lifestyle?'

Hesitation. Murphy could see words being discarded, chosen carefully.

'It's a shock to the system for those who have no experience of it. Everything is scrutinised. Your whole life is there to be commented on. They build you up, then spend all their time trying to knock you down. Joe . . . he enjoyed that. He didn't get anywhere near the scrutiny Chloe got, of course, but he loved it all the same. Couldn't believe the money they were getting for doing events, interviews, that sort of thing. I know he was earning a tidy sum playing football, but even at that level, he was earning a month's wages just for turning up at a restaurant or a club, being photographed next to the sign, then going back home.'

'Explain that to me,' Murphy said, losing track of what was being said.

Parker looked towards Murphy then back to the relative safety of Rossi's pen on her notepad as she scribbled notes. 'He could get five, sometimes ten grand from a restaurant in town, just for pretending he was going for a meal there. Papped – photographed

– outside, the restaurant sign all lit up, then five minutes inside with the owner. Few more photos for their walls, then back home. Didn't even have to eat there. Five grand for an hour's work. Tops. Next day, photos are in all the local papers and sometimes a few nationals. Same thing with clubs, shops. All that sort of thing. The news websites lap that sort of thing up. Five hundred words on what they were wearing, all that stuff. Chloe and Joe get their faces out there, keep in the spotlight, everyone's happy.'

Murphy looked away, tugged on his bottom lip with his teeth to stop himself saying something he would regret. 'Five grand . . .' he said under his breath.

Parker shrugged his shoulders. 'That's just the way things are.'

'Chloe would be with him when he did this sort of thing?'

'Of course,' Parker replied, the pitch of his voice higher now. 'The story was always about them. It was Joe who pushed those things, though. Always wanted to know when the next one was coming along.'

'And Chloe wasn't always happy to go along with that?' Rossi said, looking up at Parker finally.

Another hesitation. Murphy tried to catch Parker's eyes to make him aware that he wasn't happy at that, but they were fixed firmly on his own shoes.

'She wanted to do other things,' Parker said. 'Didn't want to be known for turning up to the opening of an envelope. Joe didn't care. He just wanted to make money.'

'Do you think they were in love, Mr Parker?' Murphy asked, seeing the answer already.

'I think . . . yes. I think Chloe loved Joe.'

'We know he was stopped from making a move to a bigger football club.'

Parker looked up, glancing at Murphy now. 'That wasn't her,' Parker said, his voice quivering a little, but attempting to be firm. 'That was me. Not that I thought he listened. He was still in talks until the end of that transfer window thing they have in January. I think Chloe convinced him she wouldn't be going with him if he moved. He knew that would bring an end to the way things had been. No wedding either, so the whole lead-up to that would be lost. Took a while though.'

Murphy went back over what Parker had said in the previous minute, trying to work out what it was that was niggling him.

Rossi got there before him.

'You said Chloe loved Joe,' she said, removing the pen that had been nestled on the corner of her mouth as she'd waited. 'You don't think he loved her, do you? You think the wedding was a sham. That he was just in it for the money, the fame.'

Parker sighed, the weight on his shoulders becoming harder and harder to bear, Murphy thought.

'I don't think he ever felt anything for her,' Parker said, his voice almost lost in the space between them. 'Nothing at all. Not from the start. She was a meal ticket and he got lucky.'

Chapter Thirteen

Murphy had moved to the sofa once the drinks which hadn't been offered arrived. He sipped on too hot coffee, enjoying the taste alongside the burning sensation on his lips. He chanced another sip before placing the cup down. 'They were having issues. I think we can say that much about Chloe and Joe.'

Parker nodded. 'I guess so. They always do, these types of couples. Everything starts out as a whirlwind romance, but it all calms down and reality hits. And not the distorted one we see on TV. It's when it's just the two of them alone, with no cameras, or other people watching, that things change. Then, you get to know the real person. How many times has it happened?'

'Loads,' Rossi said. 'I don't know this particular story, but there's Peter Andre and Jordan. TOWIE shite. Any *Big Brother* couple . . .'

'You could go on and on,' Parker said, a smile disappearing as quickly as it appeared. 'I've repped a lot of them. It's my job to make sure they make as much as possible before the bubble bursts and we're on to the next lot.'

'Did they keep in touch with any of the other people on the show?'

'I don't think so. They were nothing but friendly, but I never met them. I took Chloe and Joe on, but they were the only two of interest to me. The others have done bits here and there, but they don't have anywhere near the kind of pulling power Chloe and Joe had.'

'How did we get here, though? To the point where they're both gone?'

'I just don't know,' Parker said, his head in his hands. 'I mean, the stuff that is said to them on all that social media is bad. Really disgusting stuff that taken at face value could be threatening. But, this . . . I never thought it could lead to this.'

'That's what you think then?' Murphy said, eyeing the coffee and, taking the chance that it had cooled a little, picking it back up. 'Someone from Twitter or the like has had it in for them and taken it further?'

'Let me read you some of things that were said to them,' Parker said, producing the phone from his pocket and bringing it to life. 'I have an email saved that Chloe sent me a while back with some of the worst ones.'

Murphy waited, looking round the place once more, a new piece of grand furniture catching his attention with each passing glance. 'The word opulent was invented to describe this kind of room.'

'I'd be scared to touch anything,' Rossi said, looking up quickly then back to her notepad. 'I prefer to have easily replaced stuff in my house.'

'Here we go,' Parker said, breaking into Murphy's thoughts on interior design. 'This one is from a few months back. *Chloe Morrison is a fucking whore. She needs to fuck off and die* – that's actually one of the nicer ones. Here's one from a well-known troll. *You're a*

*fucking slut who needs to wake up and realise we are
laughing at you. Die bitch*. Oh, here's a good one – *I'll cut
your cunt head off and rape your neck you fucking slag*.
Apologies for the language.'

Murphy listened as Parker went on to read four or five
increasingly sickening messages before holding up his
hands for him to stop. 'We get the picture,' he said, his
coffee left to go cold as his stomach churned. He turned
to Rossi. 'If I ever think about signing up for that thing,
you have my permission to give me a smack.'

'Noted.'

'See what I mean, though?' Parker said, placing his
phone on the side table. 'They get abuse like this all the
time, celebrities. It's constant. I get it as well, but nothing
like the level they get. People just can't help themselves.'

'Jealousy, I imagine,' Murphy said.

'Partly,' Parker replied. 'But it's not just that. It can't be.
This is disgusting stuff they're saying about real people.
Who knows how far a person who writes things like that
could go . . .'

*   *   *

'It's about wanting to have an effect,' Rossi said, as
Murphy drove the car back through the gates and into
the waiting throng of people outside. 'They want a reaction to make themselves feel better. To know that they've
had an effect on someone they think is untouchable. A
celebrity – to these types of people – is rich, successful,
everyone knows who they are. They forget they're just
normal people with families and that. They just want to
hurt them in any way possible, just to give themselves
meaning. It's sickening to us, as we know Chloe a little,

and Joe, of course, but how many times have we sneered at someone on TV or in films? I mean, look at something like *The X Factor* or whatever. We like to laugh at people. We enjoy being nasty about each other. Social media is just another avenue for people to do that. Get a reaction and feel good about themselves for a few minutes. People like Katie Hopkins have built a career on it.'

Murphy guided the car round a few straggling photographers, finally picking up some speed as they passed them and made it onto the road proper. 'You think it could get worse than a few words on a computer screen, though? That someone out there could actually follow through with the type of things they were saying?'

Rossi allowed a few seconds to pass before answering. 'It wouldn't be the first time. Look at any famous assassination in history. It has its roots in the same feelings. Mark Chapman killed John Lennon because he thought he was a phony—'

'He kinda was . . .'

'That's heresy in this city, Murphy. You know that. You're just pissed off they renamed the airport.'

'It's still Speke Airport to me and loads of others.'

'Anyway, that's not my point. One of the reasons Chapman killed Lennon was because he didn't think he was deserving of his celebrity status. Now, that's a common thought to have. How many times do you hear people say this person or that person doesn't deserve to be famous?'

They reached a red light and Murphy scratched at his beard with one hand as the other rested on the steering wheel. 'True, but I think there's more to it than just that.'

'Of course,' Rossi replied, fiddling with the electric windows until she'd opened a gap that she was happy with. 'But that's all part of it now. The way society reveres its famous people and then wants to tear them down. It's an element of a whole way of thinking, and it's all about people who have no idea what it's actually like to have that level of fame.'

Murphy glanced up, realised the lights had changed and moved off before the car behind had a chance to complain. 'I'm not sure how that helps us though. If that Wirral couple turn out to have had the same killer, then it's probably got nothing to do with fame at all.'

'I guess not,' Rossi said, her head turned away from Murphy so he couldn't see her face when he risked a glance towards her.

Murphy broke the silence that followed. 'How's the fella?'

Rossi turned and smiled, then squirmed a little. 'Good. Saw him last night. He was asking about the case. Apparently I was in the background during one of the news bits at the house.'

'Sarah has learned not to ask me anything specific these days.'

'So will he. Especially after he didn't get anything out of me last night. Once we'd got past that, we had a good time.'

'It's good that you're seeing someone. Keeps your mind occupied when you're away from the job. Just . . .'

'Be careful?'

'Exactly. Maybe I should meet him some time. Just to make sure he realises what would happen if he hurt you.'

'I have five brothers, Murphy,' Rossi replied with a laugh. 'I think you'd have to join a queue.'

Murphy returned the laugh, deciding it was probably easier if he let five Italian Scousers loose, instead of him going it alone. It took them twenty minutes to get back to the station, the radio inside the car crackling into life just as they were parking up and about to get out of the car. 'Go ahead,' Rossi said, lifting the handset out of its cradle.

'We've got results on HP vics one and two,' DC Harris's voice came back to them. 'And something else coming in that may be connected. How long until you can get here?'

'We're in the car park as it happens. Be there in less than five.'

Murphy turned the engine off and grabbed his jacket from the back seat, almost headbutting Rossi as she reached to do the same for her own.

'What do you think the second thing is?' Murphy said slightly breathlessly as they walked briskly towards the station entrance.

'I have my theories,' Rossi replied, grasping the door handle and pushing forward, the door banging against the rubber stopper on the floor and almost hitting Murphy as it rebounded. 'Not saying them out loud though.'

Murphy let Rossi steam ahead of him, guessing that was the best course of action. Of course, she was right. The dreaded jinx of being a copper. It was always best not to say anything out loud in case the worst happened.

Not that it mattered, most of the time.

'The Wirral couple,' DC Harris said as they entered the office, Rossi a fair few steps ahead of Murphy. 'Looks like they're the same guy.'

Murphy closed his eyes for a few seconds and screamed a few obscenities in his head to a deity he didn't believe in most of the time.

'How do we know this?' Murphy said, once he'd finished his mental admonishment.

'Same type of drug killed both female victims,' DC Harris replied. 'An opiate-based drug of some sort apparently. Possibly one used as an anaesthetic in hospitals. They can't say for certain what the actual drug used was, but I think it's too much of a coincidence . . .'

'Same layout of scene, same cause of death, two victims, an intimate couple ... *merda*.' Rossi looked round, Murphy took a step back, not wanting to get in the way of what he thought she was about to do. He breathed again when she appeared to settle and sit down instead.

'Why can't we get the actual drug name?'

'Apparently it doesn't stay in the body long enough after death,' DC Harris replied, itching at stubble which was beginning to rival Murphy's own beard length. 'All they can say is the drug group it came from and that's about it.'

'Well, it's still something we need to look into. Get a list together of the types of drugs we're talking about and where they may have come from.'

'That's not all,' said DC Hale, appearing from the corridor behind DC Harris. 'I went over the file that DS Brannon gave us. Turns out there was another collage left there. It was in one of the photographs near the back of the folder, a picture of the spare room. They didn't mention it in the main report as they thought it was the victims that did it. Obviously, with what we found at the ChloJoe house, it might mean something else now.'

Murphy wanted to close his eyes again, but shook off the feeling. 'ChloJoe?'

'Erm ... that's, sorry. It's just what they call them on the news and that.'

'Well, let's try and not do that here maybe?'

'Course, sir.'

'Right, here's what we do,' Murphy said, loud enough that a few more heads looked up from various desks. 'I can guarantee that the previous scene won't have been gone over as carefully as ours has so, Hale and Kirkham, you go over the details as closely as possible with the idea it's linked to ours. I don't care how little or insignificant anything is, we need to investigate it. Rossi, you find out more about this drug that killed both victims. See if there's something we can use there. I'll speak to the boss.'

Murphy waited for everyone to start moving, DC Harris returning to his own desk once people had moved out of his way. 'Harris,' Murphy said, moving closer and speaking low. 'Get me the name of the detective in Liverpool South who's looking into the confession we got yesterday.'

'Sir?'

'The Amy Maguire case. Just do it. And keep it to yourself, okay?'

Murphy waited for Harris to nod acceptance and then turned towards DCI Stephens's office.

He hoped that the most he was going to get was a frosty reception and no more.

Chapter Fourteen

The process of taking the case over from Wirral CID had run more smoothly than Murphy had thought it would. It was as if they were happy to have one less thing to do, something else not to worry about. DS Brannon left the station not long after handing over the paperwork to Murphy, the fetid air he had brought with him disappearing from the office soon after.

'I hope we don't have to see him again too soon,' Rossi said to Murphy once he'd gone. 'Not sure I can take even small doses of him these days.'

'Forget about him,' Murphy replied, picking up a crisp packet left on one of the desks like it contained some sort of plague. 'Pass me the bin over.'

Rossi duly obliged, Murphy wiping his hands on his trousers. 'What's your plan then?'

'The drug we're looking for belongs to a group of opiates used during surgical procedures for anaesthetics . . .'

'So, we're thinking about a doctor or something?'

'Maybe, but it could be anyone working at a hospital. And then it's working out which hospital it is. We've asked all the local ones to report any missing drugs, of course.'

'What's your thinking then?'

'Well, we need to know more about them. If there's a way we can narrow it down, that sort of thing. I thought we could ask Darren as obviously he'd know more. He's working late today.'

'Are you sure this isn't just a way of nipping off during work hours, so you can go see lover boy?'

Rossi didn't blush, but Murphy was worried for a second that his own health was in danger. 'No. Of course not. I just think it's a good idea to find out as much as possible. And I'm not reading any more Wikipedia articles. They're boring the life out of me and I'm learning nothing.'

'It's also doing wonders for your grasp of grammar. What's he do?'

'He's an anaesthetist, working in the Royal. I didn't really listen to the details when he was telling me. Load of boring medical stuff, I imagine.'

'Sounds classy,' Murphy said, raising his hands in mock surrender as Rossi turned on him. 'Not that you're not a classy bird yourself or anything.'

'Bird?'

'I'm sorry. Sometimes the Scouse slips out. So, he'll help us out?'

Rossi nodded, leaning against his desk. 'Happy to. Texted him earlier and he's in work at the moment. Said we could meet him there.'

Murphy checked the time. 'Well then. Let's go see the man who has stolen my DS's heart.'

Murphy drove them to the hospital, the traffic beginning to build as rush hour took hold. Whilst the Royal was only a mile away from the station, the five-minute journey took treble that; every light was against them and cars were backed up in every direction.

Once parked up next to the hospital, Murphy followed Rossi through the reception area. The building looked more run-down by the day, he thought. He hoped the new premises being constructed a few hundred yards away would be more impressive than the dingy-looking block that was currently being used.

'Do you know which floor?' Murphy said, looking towards the information desk situated in the middle of the vast reception area.

'Second, I think he said.'

They used the lift, eventually getting out on the eleventh floor after checking the list of departments. Drab corridors stretched ahead of them, yellow signs pointing the way to different areas of the hospital. Murphy took the lead, reaching the surgical unit within a few minutes. The double doors were locked; Rossi pushed a green call button on the wall after Murphy had given up trying to pull the doors open.

'Hi, we're here to see Darren ... Darren Logan. It's Lau— Detectives Rossi and Murphy.'

They were buzzed through a few seconds later, Murphy walking after Rossi as she pushed through the doors.

'Hey, come in, come in,' a voice called from further down the corridor. 'Great to see you.'

There was an awkward moment, when Rossi and Darren Logan met, not knowing how to greet each other. They settled for a lingering handshake. Rossi scowled at Murphy as she turned round to see him smirking at her.

'This is DI Murphy,' Rossi said. Darren stepped forward, shaking Murphy's proffered hand.

'Is there somewhere we can talk?'

'I've got an office of sorts up here,' Darren replied, glancing at Murphy but turning back to Rossi. 'Have to share it with a few people, but it's better than nothing.'

'Lead the way.'

Murphy stayed a little behind Rossi and Darren as they walked, seeing the chemistry between them even in their current environment. There was a frisson between them; the fact they weren't able to touch each other noticeable. Murphy took in Darren's appearance, deciding the younger man was about what he'd expected. A few inches smaller than himself, but over six foot tall. Athletic, but not overly bulked up. There was a slight wideness to his mouth, which looked a little odd on someone with such a sculptured face, but Murphy supposed it all added to the charm.

'Ah, here we are,' Darren said, a hand guiding them into a room. 'Do you want me to get rid of these two reprobates?'

Murphy walked inside to see two other men sitting inside. 'Well . . .'

'I'm sure it's fine,' Rossi said, cutting off Murphy before he had a chance to finish his sentence. 'Maybe they'll be of use as well.'

'Excellent,' Darren said, introducing Murphy and Rossi. 'This is Ben, he's a fellow anaesthetist, and this is Sam, our resident nurse who is visiting us.'

Murphy settled for raising a hand at the pair. Sam barely looked up at them before returning to whatever he was reading. He was the older of the two, and by some margin, Murphy guessed.

'You're wondering if I'm old enough, aren't you?' Ben said with a smile. 'Honestly, I am. Got my boyish good looks from my dad.'

'I wasn't,' Murphy began to protest. 'I assumed it was me. Everyone looks a lot younger than they used to.'

'What's going on then? Not often we have the police drop in.'

Darren stepped forward, cutting in between Ben and Rossi. 'You said it was about anaesthetics . . .?'

Murphy realised Darren had noticed the lingering look Ben had given Rossi when she'd walked in. Protective or jealous . . . Murphy wasn't sure.

'Yes, that's right,' Rossi said, either unaware or ignoring Darren's reaction. 'We're dealing with a case at the moment that is proving a little difficult with regard to which drug was present in the victim's body. We know some sort of opiate linked to anaesthetics was used, but we can't find out which one.'

'Well, that'll be because they don't hang around for very long,' Darren said, leaning against a filing cabinet and staring at Rossi. 'They flush through the system very quickly.'

'What kind of drugs are we talking about here?' Murphy said, moving round to stand opposite the two.

'Well, for general anaesthetics we use Propofol and Fentanyl, which are highly effective drugs. Keeps the patient under and maintains the sedation.'

'Propofol? Isn't that the drug that killed Michael Jackson?' Rossi said, staring up at Darren. 'Think I remember that was what it was called . . .'

'That's the one,' Darren replied, flashing a wide grin at Rossi. 'He needed it to sleep at night, according to the doctor who was "looking" after him. Apparently Night Nurse just isn't enough for some people. Not only is it highly effective, it's also highly volatile if used incorrectly.'

'So, easy to overdose on then?'

Darren nodded at Murphy before turning back to Rossi. 'It wouldn't take much at all. It's a powerful drug, which slows down all the processes to do with respiration, things of that nature. Once you up that dosage, it would be just like going to sleep.'

'It's not easy to get a hold of, though,' Ben said from the other side of the room. 'You can't just walk into a chemist and buy it.'

'You'd be surprised what you can get if you really need it,' Sam said, flicking over a page and not looking up.

'Quite,' Darren said, frowning at the two men and then turning back to Rossi.

Murphy began to wonder what they were doing there, checking the time on his phone as Rossi continued to talk to Darren. As he went to put his phone back in his pocket, it began buzzing in his hand.

'Excuse me a minute,' Murphy said after looking at the incoming caller. He left the office, answering the phone as he did.

'Hey, Murphy, it's Nick Ayris from Liverpool South.'

Murphy looked up and down the corridor outside, and began walking away from the office. 'Thanks for calling me back. What's the latest on that Amy Maguire case?'

'Not much to tell you. Solicitor has come in for that Keith bloke who confessed to killing her. Turns out he's well known in the area to the uniforms. Guy has some mental health issues or something.'

'Twenty-four hours is up, isn't it?'

'We got an extension, but I don't think it's going to make a difference anyway. The guy is obviously confused. We have no evidence whatsoever and everything he said about how he supposedly killed her doesn't make any sense . . .'

'He knows everything about her,' Murphy said, stopping at the end of the corridor and leaning against the wall. 'It's clear he has some knowledge of her at least.'

'Well, yeah, he lives very close to the shop. My thinking . . . he did see and speak to her every day. We know she was good with the customers, just from the reaction locally since she went missing.'

'And that can't turn into something more? She rejected him and something else happens?'

'It's a big leap,' Ayris said with a heavy sigh. 'Nothing he says about the supposed murder makes sense. We've got nothing and his solicitor is pushing for a release.'

'Who's his solicitor?'

Murphy heard a hesitation on the phone, then silence. 'What?'

'Well . . . it's just that I'm not supposed to tell you. We were asked to keep the information away.'

'It's Jess White, isn't it?' Murphy said, thinking about his damned luck again. The conversation with Sarah from the previous night had not really convinced him that their relationship was on its way to being repaired, no matter what Sarah thought. Murphy knew Jess better than that.

'I didn't say anything,' Ayris replied, stuttering a little. 'He'll be out by the morning, I imagine.'

'There must be something more that can be done here, Nick? He knows something about Amy's disappearance.'

'I'm sorry, my hands are tied here. I wouldn't worry about it anyway. She's probably living it up somewhere or in some dosshouse doing God knows what. She'll turn up at some point, I reckon. They always do.'

Murphy sighed and thanked him. He ended the call and looked back down the corridor to see Rossi waiting outside Darren Logan's office. She was staring at him, lines creasing her forehead.

He headed towards her, fixing a normal expression on his face and preparing to pretend.

*   *   *

They were back across the Wirral again, the tunnel journey more difficult at that time of day. Constant traffic slowing them to a crawling pace at some points, as they navigated their way back over as the rush hour still kept hold.

'How far away are we?'

'Not long,' Murphy said, glancing over at Rossi and smiling. 'Only a short drive once we get away from the tunnel. Traffic will be easier then.'

He was right, in that it took just a few minutes to reach the house, but that was only if you knew where you were going. Murphy got lost at two roundabouts and the trip took twenty minutes longer than it should have. Eventually, he found the right address and parked up outside the house where Jane Piper's parents lived.

One of the first victims.

'Quiet around here,' Rossi said, getting out of the car. 'Where are we again?'

'Just outside Birkenhead,' Murphy replied, looking down the street and crossing the road. 'Bit nicer round here than it is as you get closer to the centre of the town.'

'Think I've only been to Birkenhead once.'

'That's usually the right amount of times to visit.'

The house was set back from the road and had a small front garden of paving stones surrounding a patch of grass. A large potted plant stood in the middle, leaves spreading across onto the stones.

'At least it's not a death knock,' Rossi said, standing to one side as Murphy rang the doorbell. The family liaison officer – sent over as soon as the connection to the Chloe and Joe case had been made – let them in, excusing himself once they were sitting in the dining room.

'We won't keep you long,' Murphy said, resting the file on his knee. 'We just want to update you on what's been happening.'

Simon and Carole Piper were sitting opposite them, their hands on the table almost touching. 'Thank you for coming so soon,' Simon said, nodding to himself as he spoke. 'We're a bit shocked, as you might guess.'

They were older than Murphy had expected, in their early sixties, he guessed. Simon had grey hair, but only round the sides. The rest of his head was devoid of anything other than a few brown spots. The dark wood furniture in the room matched nicely with Simon's skin pigment, which was the colour of leather; brown and rusty. Murphy glanced at the photographs on the walls; a montage of different holiday destinations surrounded him. Carole was meeker than her husband, her hair darker, almost as short. Murphy thought if he'd known her a few weeks earlier, he wouldn't have been able to guess her age. Now, she was beginning to wear down.

Losing a child – no matter what age you are – will probably have that effect.

'We're looking into your daughter's murder as part of a larger investigation . . .'

'The ChloJoe one,' Simon said, waving a dismissive hand in the air. 'We've seen the news.'

'Yes,' Rossi replied, from the end of the dining table. 'We've heard what Stuart – or James as we now know he was called – was keeping secret.'

'We never knew,' Simon said, almost banging his fist down on the table, 'if that's what you're thinking. If we had, we never would have accepted him.'

'We're not for one minute suggesting you did,' Murphy said, fixing a stare on the older man. 'We think it may be a reason they were targeted, however. Do you think Jane knew?'

'She had no idea,' Carole said, speaking for the first time. Her accent was harsher than her husband's. Murphy had her pegged as someone who had grown up in Liverpool, then moved across the water. 'She was too proper for anything like that. Very into her feminism as well. She wouldn't have been able to be with someone who had raped a child.'

'Rape is a strong term for it—' Simon began, before stopping as his wife glared at him. 'It's not important though. What's important is that he kept something away from Jane.'

'Tell us about her,' Rossi said, leaning forward and speaking to Carole directly.

'She was a good child, went to university and excelled. Always wanted to learn. Jane always cared about others, before herself even. That's why she wanted to work at the hospital. She wanted to be a part of making people better. I can't believe she's gone.'

Rossi continued talking, as Carole's breath began to hitch. 'Jane worked at the Royal in Liverpool, right?'

'Yes,' Carole said, looking at Rossi and Murphy in turn, before looking back down at the table. 'She was a nurse there. A damn good one as well, I bet.'

Murphy listened as Rossi and Jane's mother continued to discuss the person missing from the room. That weight of loss evident from every corner. There wasn't much else they could do to help the couple, other than hope that the fact their daughter's death was now being investigated as part of something bigger might result in a conviction.

'I hope that means you'll find the . . . thing that did this to our daughter.'

'We'll do everything we can,' Murphy said, holding on to Simon's proffered hand. 'We know your daughter deserves that.'

There was a shared look between the two men, standing there with hands still grasped.

'I believe you,' Simon said, letting go of Murphy's hand. 'She was a good woman. An exceptional one. She never had us worried or disappointed. Jane was one in a million.'

They all were, Murphy thought. Everyone's child, or parent. Always exceptional or different from everyone else. Placed on a pedestal in premature death, forever treated as something more than the norm.

He knew only too well how that worked. It was also what made him work that little bit harder to deliver justice.

Even if it made little difference to how those families would survive after.

Greg and Hannah

Greg had known all along. Deep down. The truth had been there from the beginning. It was nothing to do with him. It wasn't his fault. Nothing to do with the way he was, or the way he had been with Hannah. It was her. All her.

'Would you have ever told me if it wasn't for this?'

She still wasn't speaking to him. Stopped answering his questions once the man had begun hurting her. At first, Greg had been disgusted. Tried to stop it happening. Then, he'd heard two words which told him everything he needed to know.

'I can't.'

Two words that made the bottom of his world drop out. Now he knew there was something. That it was something she didn't want him to know badly enough that she was willing to go through pain not to tell him.

The man stopped, moving away from Hannah and allowing Greg to see what had happened to her. Greg ignored the blood, the bruises already rising up on her skin. The shaking of her body. 'Tell me, Hannah. He's going to hurt you again if you don't tell me.'

'You should listen to Greg,' the man said, moving in front of Greg, his back to him. 'He knows what he's talking about. I'm just trying to help you. Can't you see that? I'm stopping your lies.'

Hannah's words were almost quiet enough to miss. 'Don't. Please.'

Greg could see everything now. His eyes had become accustomed to the dark, enough so he could see the man move forward and slap Hannah across the face with an open palm. The crack in the silence making Greg jump in the chair a little.

His right hand slipping further out of the bonds which tied them.

Hannah screamed again, cut off by the stretch of duct tape placed across her face.

'You're good, Hannah,' the man said, grabbing a fistful of her hair and pulling her head up. 'I really didn't think you would hold out this long.'

Greg was done crying. Tears no longer springing forth as he watched the woman he loved in pain. It had gone too far. There was something she was keeping from him. And he wanted to know what it was.

He watched as the man hit Hannah across the face again. This time with the back of his hand, snapping her head backwards with force as he struck her. Clumps of Hannah's hair fell to the floor as he grabbed at it again, producing something Greg hadn't seen up to that point.

The blade was silver, catching the light as it shone through a gap in the almost closed curtains; almost sparkling as the man held the knife in front of Greg, before turning and showing Hannah.

Greg lowered his head as he heard the noises behind Hannah's gag grow in volume, pleading and crying.

'Stop, please. Let her talk.'

The man stepped back and turned towards Greg. 'You think she'll talk now?' He revealed Hannah again as he moved away unblocking Greg's line of sight.

A line of blood, rapidly growing and criss-crossing with others, stretched out across one side of Hannah's face. Greg imagined the blood hitting the ground in droplets, disappearing into the darkness and pooling at her feet, the gashes across her face widening around a mess of tears and red.

'Please, Hannah,' Greg said, tears finally beginning to form once more. 'Just tell me so he stops hurting you.'

There was nothing for a few seconds then Hannah's shoulders slumped further still and she began to nod.

'Good, good,' the man said, the glee in his voice causing Greg's stomach to flip. 'Let's see if you can get through this. If I take this off and you scream, Hannah, I'm going to find and kill your child. She might not be here right now, but I'll find her. Do you understand?'

The man and Greg waited for her to nod again. Greg breathed in deep, as he watched the man rip the duct tape off Hannah's mouth, a cry escaping as he did so.

'Now,' the man said, throwing the duct tape to one side and standing between them. 'This is how things are going to go. Hannah, you are going to tell him what we both know you've been keeping from him. No big explanations. No pleading forgiveness, or going all round the houses before slipping in the truth. You have ten seconds to say your piece, and if you haven't in that time, I'm going to take this little knife here and slice right into your legs, your hands, then finally your throat. Are we clear?'

'Yes.'

Greg almost didn't recognise her voice. In a single word, he heard the difference such a short amount of time spent in extreme fear could have on a person. Hannah was broken, wrecked. Scared.

'Excellent,' the man said. 'Are you ready, Greg?'

Greg swallowed, his mouth dry. He tried to speak, but the growing lump of bile at the back of his throat wouldn't allow it. He nodded instead.

'Then, Hannah, talk.'

There were a few moments of silence before Greg's life as he'd known it ended. His previous existence hadn't been blissful, but it was still preferable to what came next.

'Millie isn't yours,' Hannah said, her voice still betraying her. 'I . . . I slept with someone else. I didn't want to hurt you. I'm . . . I'm sorry.'

Greg had known it was coming. But the shock of the words spilling from Hannah's mouth still made him recoil despite being strapped to the chair.

'No. No, no, no. Not that. Not my daughter.'

'I'm so sorry, Greg. I'm so sorry.'

He didn't want to hear it. Not the apologies, not the continuing lies.

'I can't . . . why would you do this to me? I gave you everything. I loved you. Our little girl . . . how could you do that to me?'

'It was a mistake.'

Greg shook in the chair, every hair standing on end as the realisation hit him – everything had transformed in an instant. His life was irreparably changed with just a few words of truth.

'You fucking bitch.'

Once the words were out of his mouth – the way they hit Hannah and made her look even smaller in the chair opposite – he had a sudden realisation.

He wanted the man to hurt her more.

'I can't believe you did this to us. Was it worth it? Did he fuck you good enough to make up for what's happening now?'

Hannah didn't answer him. Greg thought of every instance he'd held what he'd thought of as his daughter in his arms and felt overwhelming love for her. Gone. The idea was alien to him now. The thought of loving another man's child, caring for it, cuddling and kissing it, allowing it to become his world, all of it repulsed him.

Greg leaned over to one side as the bile came to the surface finally, splattering over the carpet. A new stain added to go along with the rest. His throat burned as he retched, tears streaming from his eyes as he choked and spluttered onto the ground. He lifted his head slowly, unable to wipe his mouth or face. Desperately wanting to.

'Fucking whore,' Greg said, his voice not as strong as he wanted it to be. 'That's what you are. You've destroyed me. You know that? Do you care?'

'Of course I do,' Hannah replied through tears. 'I never wanted to hurt you.'

'Well you fucking have.'

The man stepped between them, facing Greg. 'That'll do, you two. Now, what happens next?'

'Hit her again,' Greg said, saliva and bile spraying from his mouth. 'She deserves it.'

'Can you forgive her?'

'No, not for this.'

'What am I supposed to do here, Greg? I have exposed her lies and it means nothing to you? Can you not move on from this?'

Greg shook his head, rocking the chair with the violence of the movement. 'I want her gone.'

The man sighed and turned away. 'This is what lies can do, Hannah. This is what happens when love isn't done correctly. You don't deserve it. I'm going to have finish it, aren't I, Greg?'

Greg shook in the chair. 'She's a fucking slut bitch who deserves all she gets.'

The man nodded once, then moved quicker than Greg had seen before. In one swift movement there was duct tape across Hannah's face again, her eyes straining out of their sockets as she screamed behind the tape. Her stare locked with Greg's as the blade reappeared.

He wanted her dead. She deserved it. That was all he felt. He wanted her to feel more pain than he was experiencing.

'You've taken my life,' Greg said. 'You deserve this.'

It wasn't until the blade of the knife went into her neck that he realised his mistake.

Chapter Fifteen

He is dreaming, he knows that. He can understand the unreality of it all, the broken images, the distorted scenery, the blurriness of his surroundings.

It feels real though. The anxious, nausea-inducing feeling in the pit of his dream form stomach is real.

He's entering the house again. The silence overpowering him once more. There is something else though, a different quality to it. The presence of people within, silent, hushed.

DC Graham Harris is outside on the pavement. Blood surrounding him as it exits his body. The thought is just there, in his head, all at once.

He doesn't remember leaving him there.

It's as if he is trying to walk through water, something pulling him back from entering the room ahead.

The door opens, independently, as he floats through it in his dream state. At first, the scene is different from what he remembers, and he feels confusion. There are words on the wall, dripping red onto the floor below it. He can't make out what they say, no matter how many times he tries to read them.

A second later, the scene shifts. The man is there, as he

was in reality. Standing over an unoccupied chair, holding a shotgun towards the empty space.

He doesn't want to see this again. He wants to wake up, turn back and run away.

Instead, he watches as the empty chair is replaced with one in which a young man is sitting down, his head lowered against his chest so he can't make out who it is.

He knows, of course, who sits there.

He hears Jess's voice. His friend of two decades. Best friend. One he shared his life with. One who shared her life with him.

He hears Sarah's voice, his wife, the other half of him. Take her away and he becomes less than whole.

Jess's voice overpowers Sarah's. She screams, but he doesn't move. He watches as the man holding the shotgun begins to shake with the exertion. He's mouthing words at him, but he doesn't know what they mean.

He remembers a name. Alan Bimpson. Only that wasn't real. Thornhill. That was what he was really called. Alpha. A killer.

The boy in the chair has become younger. He remembers his name, who he is, but tries to forget it.

He remembers holding him hours after he'd been born. Watching him grow into a toddler. Into a schoolboy.

Into a teenager.

'An eye for an eye . . .'

He doesn't want to hear this. He knows what comes next.

'I want you to see this.'

He looks down at his legs, willing them to move, but they won't comply. He bunches his fists, banging them against his thighs.

He turns his hands over, staring at them as they leave trails through the air as he moves them. They shake, he can't keep them still.

He's scared. He's shaking, and he can't move his legs. He can't run away, he can't hide. He buries his head in the crook of his arm. He doesn't want to watch. Not again.

Peter looks at him. He can't see this, but knows the boy's eyes are on him.

'Why can't you save me?'

He raises his head, slowly, afraid of what he'll see. This didn't happen. Not in reality.

The man finishes, his white T-shirt now drenched in splashes of blood. He stands back and admires his creation.

And he begins to laugh, quietly at first. Then louder, a crescendo of laughter erupting from him. He whispers, his voice slurred.

'You can't save them.'

There is another noise, a banging sound.

Bang.

The man turns, the laughter subsides, changing to a sadistic grin.

Bang.

He looks down at the shotgun in his hand, and moves purposefully towards Murphy.

Bang. Bang. Bang.

*   *   *

Murphy woke slowly, not like they do on TV or in movies. There wasn't a sudden moment when he sat up in bed, breathing heavily. There was just a moment when he was asleep, then over a period of a few seconds, he realised he was awake. The images of his dream beginning to slip away, joining the long line of similar dreams which had preceded it.

'You okay?'

Murphy turned to Sarah's side of the bed, as he propped herself up on one elbow.

'Did I wake you again?'

Sarah didn't reply, swiping a hand over her eyes. 'Don't worry about it. Same dream?'

'Yeah,' Murphy said, whispering into the darkened room. 'It's been nearly two years, you'd think they'd go by now.'

'You should go back to that CBT guy . . .'

'I don't think a dream is enough for that.'

'They're not as frequent as they used to be,' Sarah said, sitting up in bed and turning on the light on her bedside table. 'But they're still coming.'

'It's a small price to pay. Considering what Jess has to go through. I could have done something . . .'

'No, you couldn't . . .'

'You don't know that,' Murphy said, sitting up and swinging his legs over to the floor. 'I watched her son die in front of me. And I couldn't help him.'

Murphy heard Sarah shift across behind him. Felt her arms come around his bare shoulders and hold him. Breath on his back as she sat there, her naked skin against his.

He closed his eyes and remembered that night. A man who had called himself Alan Bimpson, determined to rid the street of what he thought was destroying them. Teenage boys, left dead in a farmhouse, before he took to the streets of Liverpool, exterminating everyone who got in his way.

Ending in an ordinary house in West Derby, with the death of the last teenage boy. Peter. Jess's son.

Murphy's godson.

'Let's go back to sleep,' Sarah said into his shoulder. 'You need your rest.'

Murphy allowed himself to be pulled back into bed. Sarah hooked her arm across his chest, her head snuggled into him.

The repeat of a scene which had replayed itself frequently over the first year following Peter's death. Less common in the following year. Almost two years since that night. Murphy could barely believe the time had gone so quickly. How he had carried on, become almost better.

He looked down towards the top of Sarah's head, her blonde hair looking grey as his eyes became more accustomed to the darkness. He leant down and kissed her crown.

She was the reason he carried on. It was all for her.

*   *   *

Sarah lay in the darkness, listening as her husband's breathing slowed and became more rhythmic. The gentle snore as he became comfortable, falling asleep within a few minutes.

She stared at the ceiling, the room around her settling back down. She thought of David's nightmare. She'd allowed herself to believe that he was finally coming to terms with what happened in that house almost two years earlier. It had been a while since she'd been awoken by his quickening breathing, the small noises and movements as he came back to consciousness. Dreaming horrific images.

She hadn't been fully asleep anyway. She'd been only dozing, her eyes closed and time slipping by, but on the edge of wakefulness for the hours they had been lying there.

Sarah considered slipping out of bed and going downstairs, maybe having a sly cigarette from the stash she kept for emergencies. She didn't really want to lie awake, waiting for the light to start coming through the curtains, sweeping the darkness away. Lie there with only her thoughts for company.

There was a letter next to the place where she kept her cigarettes, hidden behind the false panel at the bottom of the display unit in the back room. Up until a few weeks previously, it had hidden only smoking paraphernalia, a few old photos and poems she had written back in high school. Stuff that she didn't want him to see, if at all possible, but nothing she kept hidden with any malice.

Now there was the letter with its return address of HMP Manchester. She knew her husband well enough to anticipate his reaction if he found it. The hurt and recriminations it would cause. Sarah unable to say why she had kept it, or what she was going to do with it.

The man who had killed her husband's parents was currently serving a minimum of thirty years in HMP Manchester. A man Sarah knew only too well.

She continued to lie in bed, listening to David's breathing become softer, the occasional snore emanating from his side of the bed.

Sarah already knew what she was going to do with the letter and its contents. She would burn it, one day when David wasn't around.

But not before she'd used the invitation inside it.

Chapter Sixteen

Murphy pulled his car to a stop, checked he was within the parking bay then, realising he wasn't, reversed out and drove back in again. His hands were shaking on the wheel a little, so he left them there for a few moments longer once he'd parked. The fog which had spread over town that morning was beginning to lift, leaving behind tendrils of mist in the air, which dissipated the longer you looked at them.

He hadn't spoken to her in almost two years.

Murphy got out, walking away before stopping, turning back and pressing his fob to lock his car. The café was situated a few shops down from where he'd been able to get a parking space, but the short walk wasn't far enough for him to gather his thoughts coherently.

What was he supposed to say?

Almost two years since a shared word between them. Over twenty years of non-stop conversations grinding to a halt after what had happened on a dark and bitter evening all that time ago.

He picked an empty table off to the side. Only a couple of other people were sitting in there at that time of morning – a few hours before the lunchtime rush would start.

He asked for coffee and promised to look at the food menu when the waitress brought it over, but he wasn't expecting his appetite to show up at any point.

Jess came into the café. She spotted him immediately but made no move to greet him. She called the waitress at the till over as she headed towards the table and sat down.

'Hey,' Murphy said, trying to make eye contact with her, but failing as she looked back towards the waitress. 'Thanks for coming.'

'Don't thank me. Sarah asked me to come and meet, mentioned it was a work thing. That's the only reason I'm here.'

Murphy opened up another sugar packet and emptied it into his half-empty cup. 'Okay.'

'I can't stop for long. Got a lot on, you know.'

The waitress arrived, a tired smile on her face and a notepad in her hand. Jess ordered a cup of coffee and refused a menu.

'I don't know where to start . . .'

'Then don't,' Jess replied, finally looking towards him before turning away again.

'Look, you know I'm not good with this sort of situation.'

'Situation?'

'Whatever you want to call it. I've tried to get in contact before, but Sarah made it clear you weren't interested in seeing me.'

Jess took a packet of sugar from the bowl between them and shook it a few times. 'I'm still not. Not right now.'

'It can't go on like this forever, Jess. How long are you thinking about punishing me for?'

'About as long as it takes for my son to magically reappear.'

Murphy dropped his head into his chest. 'I tried everything to save him,' he said, his voice barely above a whisper.

'It wasn't enough, though, was it? And you know it isn't just about that. It was your case, David. You didn't do things right. If you had been doing your fucking job properly, none of this would have happened.'

Murphy let the words sink in and fester. There was nothing new in what Jess was saying; everything she was throwing at him was just a repeat of things she'd said back then.

What hurt was the fact that even after so much time had passed, the words were still so easy to say.

'I never meant for this to happen,' Murphy said once he thought enough time had gone by. 'You have to believe that. Peter was family to me.'

'And we all know what happens to your family, don't we?'

'Really, Jess? You're going after how my parents died now? Come on . . .'

'I knew this was a mistake . . .'

Murphy held his hands palm up. 'I'm sorry, really. We're not here to talk about that.'

'Fine,' Jess said, accepting the cup of coffee from an eavesdropping waitress. 'Were we talking loud enough for you, love?'

The waitress went the colour of LFC and scurried off without a word. Murphy allowed himself a small grin.

'You've not lost your common touch.'

'What can I say,' Jess replied, stirring sugar into the cup. 'I'm happy not to disappoint.'

'Amy Maguire. I heard you were brought in for the guy who confessed?'

Jess banged her spoon against the rim of the cup a few times. Then a few more times.

'Stop stalling, Jess. I know you can't go into specifics. I just want to know if you're the one getting him to recant?'

'Keith Hudson's confession was given at a time when he had many personal issues going on. He wanted attention, you gave it to him.'

'I know he didn't do it, Jess. I just want to know how he came to be in my station, my interview rooms, telling me he killed Amy.'

'I'm sorry, I can't help you any more than that. He doesn't know anything.'

'That's not true,' Murphy said, his grip tightening round his coffee mug. 'He knew some details. Not enough for me to believe he killed her, but enough for me to believe he knows something.'

Jess shook her head and picked up her coffee with a steady hand. 'You've been wrong plenty of times in the past, David. Not least in that case two years ago, when my eighteen-year-old son was shot and killed. You'll forgive me if I don't put much stock in your instincts.'

This was all it was ever going to be, Murphy thought. Going round in circles, always coming back to that one night.

'It wasn't all my fault, Jess. Sometimes, there's just nothing we can do. Other people are still grieving, and as a division we have had to take that hit. But we tried, honestly we did. We're human, we made mistakes and paid for them. Not as much as you and so many other families did, but we paid and still do.'

Jess banged her cup back onto the table. 'You were there, David,' she replied, her voice no longer loud, but a hiss. 'I couldn't give two shites about everyone else. You were in that house with that fucker and my son. You could have done something. You've been trained for those situations, for fuck's sake. Why didn't you save him? Tell me that. Why couldn't you save my son?'

Murphy waited for tears that were never going to appear. Jess's face had gone as red as the waitress's had earlier, but there was no upset there. Only anger.

'I tried.'

'Well, you didn't try hard enough. I'm going.' Jess rose from her seat, throwing a five-pound note on the table. 'Tell that nosy cow to keep the change.'

'Wait,' Murphy said, getting out of his seat. 'I need to tell you something. This Amy Maguire thing ... you know who her mother is?'

'I'm not interested—'

'Stacey Maguire. Remember from when we were kids? There's something she told me,' Murphy said, walking round the table towards Jess. He could feel the eyes and ears of the three other patrons in the café focused on the two of them. He dropped his voice to a whisper. 'I don't know if it's true, but there was one night when we ... you know ...'

Jess shook her head, laid a hand on Murphy's elbow and forced him back. 'You're a soft shite, but not an idiot.'

'There is ...'

'And she is supposed to have got up the duff eighteen years ago and is only now getting in touch? It's because her daughter has gone missing and she doesn't know what to do. She's using you, David.' Jess lifted her bag onto her shoulder and began to turn away. 'Stacey Maguire wouldn't know the truth if it smacked her in the face. Don't be stupid. You know why she's doing this now.'

'What if it is true, though? I've got to do something, haven't I?'

'Have you told Sarah?'

Murphy looked away and hesitated.

'Fucking hell, David. You're going to hurt that girl.'

'If Amy is my daughter and I haven't done everything I can, what do you think that'll do to me, never mind Sarah?'

Jess looked Murphy in the eyes for the first time since arriving at the café. 'Then maybe you'll know what it's like for me.' She half turned, then faced him again. 'You need to tell Sarah.'

'I will . . . eventually.'

'She doesn't deserve this. None of this. Stop believing idiots from back when we were kids and sort yourself out. Tell Sarah. All she talks about is how good things arc between you two now. Don't fuck that up.'

Jess turned away fully this time and left the café. Murphy watched her go. He went back to his coffee, stirred more sugar into it and gulped it down.

*   *   *

Rossi was daring to dream. A normal bloke, with a good sense of humour and a tidy body. Not footballer or boxer fit, but tidy enough. He was no Alessandro Del Piero, but he would do nicely.

'He's fallen head over heels, Laura. I think this is "The One".'

It was this that she didn't want, though: people asking questions, making assumptions.

'Christina, it's not about that. It's the fact that I'm busy at the moment and I'm sure he is . . .'

'Oh, don't give me that,' Christina replied, her voice almost at a squeal, making Rossi hold the phone away from her ear for a second. 'Don't try and ruin it now by over-thinking it. You're always bloody busy. It's plain to all of us that you both like each other a lot. This is the perfect guy for you. He works in the same type of job—'

'Hardly.'

'In the same *type* of job. None of us do what you do, Laura. That's not the point. He'll understand the pressures and all that. There'll be no surprises. You can't tell me you're not into him.'

'Well, yeah,' Rossi said, squirming in the driver's seat of her car, wishing she hadn't answered the phone at all. 'It's going well. But that's not really . . .'

'There you go then. And you can't tell me he's not good-looking enough for you.'

'Chris, just let me talk.'

A huff over the phone, Rossi squirming harder in her seat.

'Fine, go on.'

'I'm . . . I'm just not in the right place for this. You understand that, right?'

'No.'

It was Rossi's turn to huff. 'Come on . . .'

'You come on, Laura. Who knows what'll happen if you sack him off now. Someone else comes along and you'll be left on your own with a Pot Noodle and a box set on a Friday night. Just go with it, girl. Embrace the falling head over heels for each other part, before it turns into putting up with each other.'

Rossi placed her forehead on the steering wheel and closed her eyes. 'Okay, okay, I will. But I really don't think it's going to work out.'

'That's the spirit, girl. I've got to go. I'll speak to you later, yeah?'

Rossi murmured her agreement and ended the call. She wondered how she'd been talked into the whole thing in the first place. She was a walking contradiction. Arguing against something she was quite happy with, for no reason other than timing.

She checked the clock on her phone and swore loudly at the windscreen.

A few minutes later she was taking the stairs two at a time and bursting into the office. 'Where is everyone?' Rossi said, looking around and seeing only a smattering of people. She shook her jacket off and placed it on the back of her chair. 'Usually bustling in here by now.'

'No idea.' DC Harris shrugged. 'And as I keep saying, you shouldn't put your coat on the back of the chair, remember? Health and safety regs and that.'

'Yeah, yeah. I'll move it. Murphy called in?'

'Half an hour ago. He, erm ... has some meeting or something arranged first thing. Will he in soon.'

'Amy Maguire?'

DC Harris wheeled his chair back and away from his desk and Rossi. 'Amy ...?'

'The missing girl from Speke.'

'No idea.'

'Course you don't,' Rossi replied, tucking a strand of hair behind her ear. 'Never mind. Have we got anything from the CCTV at Chloe and Joe's apartment yet?'

DC Harris wheeled back to the desk, a couple of pieces of paper fresh from the printer under one arm. 'Nothing that jumps out for the Friday afternoon they went missing, but I've got the final sweep of the house contents and forensics report here.'

'Throw it over.'

Rossi reached for where the papers fell, a few feet from their intended target. She sat back in her chair and read through. 'This is shite. Loads of partials, nothing that matches on system . . .'

'Good for ruling out though . . .'

'*Grazie*, Harris. I know the score. Just would have been easier to rule people in at this point. Anyone would have done.'

'We're only on day three. Forty-eight hours. Could be a long wait yet.'

Rossi ignored DC Harris and continued to read. 'Pritt Stick used to attach the magazine covers to the walls. What adult uses that?'

'One who knows about DNA and fingerprints?'

'Suppose so,' Rossi said, not looking up. 'There's bugger all else on here though. Nothing we can use at all. What about over the water? Have we got their reports handy?'

'More of the same, I think,' DC Harris replied, rooting through paperwork on his desk. 'They have the same drug type as was found in Chloe's system, but . . .'

'It's been flushed from her system too quick to find an exact drug. Yeah, we know that score as well.'

'We're still waiting on a few hospitals to let us know about missing drugs.' Rossi tapped the Biro she'd picked up against her teeth. 'You know what these people are like. It'll probably take a couple of days to get all that info. Can you hurry them up?'

DC Harris nodded and returned to his desk.

Rossi continued to think, clicking on a few pages on the internet before closing the browser.

'Thank God you're here!'

Rossi spun in her chair as the voice landed on her back. *'Bastardo!* You scared the shit out of me . . .'

'Really sorry,' a red-faced DC Hale said, hands on his knees, trying to catch his breath. 'But something's going on. I think we've found another couple.'

Chapter Seventeen

Murphy checked his phone again and, deciding three missed calls during a murder case constituted urgent, thumbed the call button to ring Rossi.

'We think we've got another couple,' Rossi said, without saying hello. 'If reports we're getting are right, it's pretty much the exact same scene. Two people, found dead in their own home . . .'

'Where?' Murphy replied, fiddling with his car keys, cradling the phone on his shoulder and attempting to put on his seat belt at the same time.

'Osborne Road in Tuebrook.'

'Whereabouts is that?'

'Off the West Derby Road. Just before St John's if you're coming from town.'

'Got it,' Murphy said, giving up on the seat belt and settling for starting the car. 'I'll meet you there. What number is it?'

Rossi gave him the house number then ended the call.

Murphy cursed the fact he wasn't in a pool car, but he picked up speed anyway. He made it through a pedestrian crossing only a second or two late.

'Probably not the best time to be meeting someone about a completely different case, dickhead,' Murphy murmured to himself, as he beat another set of lights.

It didn't take him long to reach the new murder scene. The amount of traffic on nearby streets was building up as gawkers slowed down to look at the closed-off road, their attention caught by the blue flashing lights of marked cars entering and exiting the cordoned-off area. Murphy was surprised to see the crowd of onlookers was currently limited to the usual *concerned* neighbours and a few other waifs and strays. It wouldn't be long before some loudmouth let it slip to the press that there was a possible link to their favourite story of the week, and a thousand and one journalists and TV personalities descended on the quiet street.

Small mercies and all that.

He parked his car and walked up the street, taking in the number of uniforms and tech officers already in the area.

Murphy stopped outside the house, watching as forensic teams walked in and out, passing each other without much greeting or camaraderie. He looked towards the roof covered in old slate and at the dark-brown brick facade then noted the modern double-glazed windows – an old house, being forced into a new century. It was in a block of four detached houses, but the gaps between them were barely worth it.

Rossi spotted him. She raised a hand and, breaking off from the conversation she was having, walked over. Murphy looked across the road to the surrounding houses and back to the scene once more.

'It's a mess in there,' Rossi said as she reached him. 'Looks like he cut the throat this time, rather than strangulation. Pretty bloody scene.'

'Female victim untouched again, except for a needle mark?'

Rossi smirked and slowly shook her head. 'Not this time. The other way round.'

Murphy frowned, scratched at his beard and began to walk towards the forensic tent which had been erected around the entrance to the house. 'Interesting. You have names and that?'

'Greg Bowlby and Hannah Flynn. They lived here together. Bought the property a year or so ago. They have a daughter, almost two years old . . .'

'Don't tell me . . .'

'No, no,' Rossi said, her voice rising up a pitch. 'She was with a grandparent at the time.'

'Who found them?' Murphy said, breathing a sigh of relief that there wasn't an even worse scene than the one he was already imagining.

'The same grandparent. Hannah's mother, Emily Flynn. Hannah was supposed to pick up her daughter early this morning, but didn't show up. Emily was having her overnight as she does every week, but the kid is usually picked up around half seven in the morning by either parent. She left it quarter of an hour before trying to ring. Thought maybe they'd overslept so decided to drop the child off herself around nine a.m. Both of the victims' cars were parked outside but she got no answer when she knocked on the door. Let herself in with a key she had. Only took one step into the room before bolting back out.'

'Before the kid saw anything?'

'That's what she's saying. Not that we can get much sense out of her at the moment. Poor woman has gone almost catatonic with shock.'

Murphy grabbed a forensic suit and began putting it on. 'You been inside yet?'

'No,' Rossi said, pulling on her own suit. 'But someone took a picture and showed me, just to make sure we're dealing with a similar set-up. It's not good.'

Murphy nodded. He cleared their entrance to the scene with the head of the forensics team before stepping inside. The smell of blood assailed him as he walked through the hallway – old coins and bitterness – the odour becoming more apparent as they approached the living room.

The doorway opened into the middle of a through lounge. One side looked like a normal living room – two sofas, a large TV, a small, pine-coloured coffee table and some pictures adorning the walls.

The other side was very different.

What little furniture existed, in what Murphy assumed was normally a dining area, was pushed back against one wall. In the centre of the room, two chairs sat facing each other, but they weren't what his attention was drawn to.

It was the two people strapped to them.

'Christ . . .' Murphy said, the words escaping on a breath, barely audible.

'Looks worse in reality.'

Various techs and SOCOs faded into the background, giving them a proper look at what had been left behind. The male victim had his back to them. His head had slumped forward onto his chest, so the nape of his neck was on show.

'Must have happened pretty much when he got back from work,' Rossi said, taking a couple of steps forward. 'Still got a shirt and tie on.'

Murphy murmured an agreement, taking a closer look at the victim's now crumpled shirt and loosened tie. 'Stained as well,' he said as he moved closer.

'Sweat or something? Can't smell petrol or anything like that.'

'God forbid.'

'She came off much worse,' Rossi said, turning her back on the male and looking at Hannah Flynn.

Murphy took a breath and turned with her, the blood-stained tableau of the woman's death almost too much to take in with one look.

'Lot of blood here.'

Murphy didn't respond, just stared at the jagged pattern of flesh and blood on the right side of the female victim's bare neck. The injuries continued underneath her chin, but were masked from view by the position of her head. Blood had dripped down her shirt, pooling around the bottom of the chair.

'This isn't good.' Dr Houghton's voice broke the silence from behind them. 'Although, if it's the same guy, he's made my job a bit easier.'

'I'm sure that was his intention,' Murphy said, unable to take his eyes off Hannah Flynn's broken body, strapped to the chair.

'A minor convenience, I'm sure,' Houghton replied, moving towards Murphy and Rossi. He looked over the bodies, humming and whistling as he did so. 'Won't be able to tell you much here. We'll know more when we get them back to the hospital. They haven't been moved from this place, that much is sure. Not been here longer than twelve hours, I would guess.'

'That would fit with what we know so far.'

'Not sure you're going to get much more from these two at the moment. Think they're telling you everything they have for now.'

Murphy stood a little longer before turning away and walking towards the kitchen which ran off the back of the dining room. More SOCOs worked away, but nothing of interest leaped out at him. He headed back past a waiting Rossi and stepped into the hallway.

'People upstairs?' Murphy said, pulling his mask down.

'Yeah,' Rossi said, making an attempt to write in her notebook whilst wearing oversized gloves. 'Think they've found something similar to the other two scenes in one of the rooms up there.'

'Let's go look.'

Murphy took the stairs two at a time, looking in two bedrooms and a bathroom before finding two officers in the smallest room, taking pictures of the wall.

'Another collage,' Murphy said, shifting his bulk round the working officers and taking in what was on the wall.

'What's it say?' Rossi replied from outside the room.

Murphy stepped aside so Rossi could look past him.

NEVER HIS - NEVER HERS TO KEEP SECRET

'What the hell does that mean?'

Murphy looked at the array of photographs on the wall. 'What's the Italian for I have no bloody idea?'

'Tricky one. We usually just say *boh*. Covers you for the most part.'

'Well this is all very *boh*. There are the words and then pictures of just the two of them together and then pictures of them with the daughter. Not sure what it means.'

'Got me,' Rossi said, bouncing from one foot to the other in the doorway. 'Why is it always the smallest room?'

'I'm going with our new Italian word for the day. I think these pictures have just been collected from round the house.' Murphy searched the room, spotting what he thought he would find in a corner of the box room. 'Picture frames in here on the floor.'

'He's removed the pictures, stuck them to the wall, and left his message. Why?'

Murphy slipped past the SOCO lifting fingerprints off the wall and walked back out onto the landing, Rossi stepping backwards to allow him past. 'He wants to explain what he's doing? Usually the case, isn't it?'

'For some, yes. I've read a bit more about serial killers in the last few years. You know, since they started turning up more often in our fair city.'

'A little light reading before bedtime, Laura? I bet that was fun.'

Rossi headed into the main bedroom, standing at the foot of the bed as Murphy followed her in. 'It was, actually. The American ones are really interesting, as it happens. The various methods, motives, psychopathology–'

'I believe you,' Murphy said, interrupting her. 'I think I'll stick to just catching them for now.'

'Doesn't seem to be anything in here,' Rossi said, opening the bedside drawers. 'Not even a sex toy to make us giggle.'

Murphy looked around the room. 'A couple of photographs will have come from here. I'll get them to sweep the whole place. He must have left something behind this time, surely?'

'Beginning to think that's what we're going to need.'

'A mistake?'

Rossi stood up and faced Murphy. 'Isn't that usually the way we catch these people?'

Murphy hesitated, then closed his mouth.

He didn't want anyone to hear him agreeing with her.

Violence

He tried to be as still as he possibly could. Standing on the stripped floorboards, flakes of wood poking into the soles of his bare feet. When he stood like that, breathing slow and steady, he could almost be somewhere else.

When he spoke, he did so in almost a whisper. Loud enough for Number Four to hear, giving himself the comfort of knowing there was someone to listen to him speak.

'Some people think there's no reason for anger to play any role in a loving relationship. Those people have never been part of something real. I know different. I've seen it. You only have to walk the streets on a Friday or Saturday night in town to see that. The anger caused by love. Spilled tears, spilled blood. The guy who becomes so incensed by another bloke daring to look at his missus for longer than a split second that he decides to do something about it – the endless tales of deaths occurring from a single punch not acting as a deterrent. The alpha male showing his dominance. The women fighting each other over perceived slights, over men who will forget their names by the next morning. The couples who scream and shout at each other in the middle of town, walking past Primark and Burton, where they'd shopped with smiles on their faces only hours earlier. Wearing the outfits they'd bought as they tear into each other. Saying words they can never take back. Insults and viciousness spewing forth with every syllable.'

His breathing rate increased. He tried to slow it before he spoke again.

'And no one cares about the people who see them do this. About the strangers silently judging them as they pass them by at three in the morning. Couples who are on their way for the night bus, both wordlessly thanking their lucky stars that it isn't their turn to be the ones stared at.'

He crouched down, his weight shifting to the balls of his feet. He rubbed his hands together, generating some warmth in them. Number Four was already shivering in the coolness of the room, as spring refused to bring with it any warm weather.

He could see her, reflected in the remnants of a broken mirror propped against the wall. The ghost of wallpaper surrounding it. Peeling and coming away.

There was a story he told when he was in 'normal' mode. When discussions at work or somewhere else became political or such like. It was well rehearsed, one he felt comfortable telling.

He had been driving down Scottie Road, just as it turned off and became Stanley Road and faded off into the distance towards Everton. Keeping to the speed limit, watching for police with nothing better to do on a Thursday night at one a.m. than pull him over for doing a few miles an hour over thirty. The roads were almost dead – a couple of other cars dotted around here and there as town was left behind him, but the streets otherwise quiet. It had been a warm summer evening, and he'd had the windows down in his car, rather than wasting petrol on air conditioning. A warm breeze entered the car, cooling him as he drove.

Over the low voice of Pete Price's radio show, he'd heard the shouting before he saw the people doing it. He had begun to search out where the noise was coming from as the lights ahead turned to amber too soon for him to speed up and through them.

The couple were young. That had been his first thought. The girl possibly not even eighteen – her shaven-headed companion had the look of someone who had left school early and recently.

He'd watched with bemusement for a few seconds, not really paying them much attention as their words drifted around him. Mostly coarse and uneducated. Both of them unable to profess their anger in any other way than to scream and swear. He had been unable to work out what they had been arguing about, but the lad had been the angrier of the pair, so he'd begun to concoct a story in his head: infidelity or a slight on his character.

When the smack came, it took a moment or two to realise what had happened. The lad reeled back as the girl had gone for another slap. Then the lad raised a hand and punched her on the side of her head. Only a low wall had stopped her from falling. The lad was in her face by the time she'd stumbled, his words lost as he raised his fist and smacked it into her head again and again. She wasn't on her feet long before she slid down the wall onto the floor.

He remembered the feeling as his stomach flipped, watching as conflict had turned to violence in front of him. He'd got out of his car on instinct, leaving it idling as he approached the pair.

By the time he'd got to them, the girl was lying on the ground – the lad about to volley her in the legs for a second time, his face a blank mask, droplets of sweat cascading down it as he prepared to inflict even more damage. The girl was crying, sobbing, curled into the foetal position.

He remembered the feeling of disgust at the sight.

As the lad had drawn back his foot, he had tackled him to the ground. Pinned the lad's arms behind his back before he'd had a chance to react, pushing his face into the concrete. Used his whole weight on him, forcing him further and further down. The lad tried to kick out, but was outmatched and didn't have the strength he possessed. He'd given the lad a swift dig to the kidneys and side of the head to stop him struggling.

It had been almost too easy.

He had turned to see if the girl was able to get up, his mind working away as he prepared to tell her to ring the police, to get help. Get this lad who was underneath him away from her.

As he'd turned, he'd felt a stinging blow to the back of his head which sent him dizzy. His head turned to fog for a few seconds, causing him to relax his grip on the lad underneath him.

He'd staggered a little, looking to see where the blow had come from.

'Get off him, get off him.'

The girl was on him, hands on his shoulders as his head cleared, pulling at him and making his balance fail more.

He'd ended up on his side looking confusedly back at the girl, as she helped the lad to his feet.

'*I was trying to help you.*'

'*You've hurt him, you fucking prick. Look what you've done.*'

He'd stood up, feeling the back of his head as he stared at the girl who by now had the lad on his feet, a dazed look on his zit-scarred face.

'*Fuck off now, or we'll call the bizzies. His family will fucking do you.*'

He'd walked back to his car, which was still standing alone at the lights, got in and driven away, passing the couple as they limped home arm in arm.

When he told the story, it was always greeted with the same shocked expressions and shaking of heads and the silent agreement that there was nothing you could do for someone in that situation. That she loved him more than she loved herself. Endless platitudes excusing the violence the lad had displayed, or the bleeding hearts of defence for the girl and her reaction to the man trying to help her.

He told the story again, the endless shadows listening along, as the well-rehearsed story came forth from him. Number Four closed her eyes as she listened, holding on to the radiator for a warmth that wasn't there.

'That was their relationship. That was the way they showed love for each other. There's no other explanation for it. Love is just too close to anger and conflict. Why can't we change this? What can I do to make this different? Better?'

Love and anger go hand in hand.

Violence was just the outcome.

'Everyone uses violence now. It's everywhere. It surrounds me. Surrounds everyone. We live in violence, so it's only right that it has become a part of the most intimate aspect of our lives. Love. We consume anger and conflict, and violence is the result. Cruelty and sadism are used as a form of entertainment. War and terror are beamed into our living rooms, to be commented on and devoured.'

His words didn't comfort him. Spoken into the darkness, louder than a whisper now, they echoed back at him.

He was sick of it all. Wanted to make it stop, but didn't know how.

'That's my mission now. I have to stop it all. I have to use violence against them, when there is nothing else that can be done. I want it to end. I have to make you see that violence can be a force for good.'

He made her watch the video he had produced. Turned her face towards the screen, so she could see what his love for her had created.

'It's easy,' he said, wiping away the tears which fell down her cheek, onto her jawline. 'A dummy email account, a dummy Twitter account. Fake details, a fake persona. That's what all those *trolls* do, isn't it? Hiding behind anonymity. I'm just using the same process.'

He closed the lid on his computer and put it to one side. Tiredness swept over him, his eyes threatening to close of their own accord. Return him to normality.

He walked back into the other room, lay down on the mattress there and slept. Waiting for tomorrow to come, when he could be someone else instead for a few hours.

Whilst the world around him changed.

*   *   *

She waited for him to leave before she began to breathe normally. The smell of him, it stuck at the back of her throat. The sickly sweet smell of his fading aftershave disgusted her.

She couldn't move that much, could sleep upright only in short bursts, the pain in her arms when she awoke worse than ever. Pins and needles, needles and pins. Everything hurt. Everything felt wrong.

The duct tape across her mouth would need replacing soon. He hadn't let her drink since that morning and now there was pain in her stomach from hunger and thirst.

Her thoughts no longer made much sense. She knew why she was there, what he wanted. He wanted her. She just didn't understand why she was being shown videos of people being murdered. Why he would rant at her about love, as if it would make a difference.

She hated him.

He had never called her by her name. She wasn't even sure he knew what it was. She recognized him, of course: a regular from the shop where she'd worked. Someone she had thought of as normal.

How wrong you can be.

Now, she was just a number to him. Number Four. She knew Numbers One and Two were still alive, as he couldn't find them. She knew Number Three had been dead at least two weeks or three.

It could be days . . . she had no idea any more.

She was waiting for him to kill her now. Number Four. Then, there'd be a Number Five, a Number Six. Because no one could give him what he wanted.

She wasn't a number. That's what she held on to. She was a real person, with real feelings and thoughts.

She couldn't be reduced to a single digit. She wasn't a number.

She was Amy Maguire.

Part Two

@EchoNews
BREAKING – Couple found dead in Tuebrook
home. More news here – bit.ly #BreakingNews

@LiverpoolLid82
First #ChloJoe, now there's another couple.
What's going on in Liverpool??!

@Smithy_Says18
I was fine with it just being those two off the telly.
Don't want us normal ones getting it. #serialkiller

@RedAndProudWayne
Bet it's get nothin to do with #ChloJoe.
Someone tryin get attention. #RIPChloJoe

@ScouseNotEnglish1
Scared to leave the house now. People
gettin killed everywhere. #Liverpool

@EvaDunning30
It's like something on telly this. Police
everywhere in Tuebrook.

@TuebrookGuyKev
Just asked police when I can get back in
my house. Told me 'when we're finished'.
#Ipayyourwages #Wannagohome

@FitzyPatrick1
I hope they catch whoever did this soon. #Scary

Chapter Eighteen

Emily Flynn had come out of catatonia and into pragmatism. There were things that needed to be done, things that needed to be sorted out. There were arrangements to be made. It hadn't been long since she'd had to do the same thing for her mother, so she knew the things that would fall upon her to organise.

She was still Hannah's mother. Whether she was gone or not.

The big bear of a detective, who had his best *we're really sorry* face on, was beginning to annoy her. All po-faced and concerned. Scratching at his beard every time she asked him a difficult question.

It had all been too easy lately. No issues or crisis to sort out. All three of her children happy and settled at the same time for once. Now . . . there was this.

'When can you let me see her?'

Another hem and haw from the large detective. No set time, or straight answer. Just more obscuring of the facts.

At least Millie was being spared this part, Emily thought. She'd been picked up by Hannah's sister and ferried away to safety.

She put the conversation she would eventually have with her granddaughter to the back of her mind. How do you tell a two-year-old that her mum and dad aren't coming back? No, she thought. Another time, another place. Another worry. Right now, there were other things she needed to think about.

Not the room and how her daughter had looked as she walked into it. Not the blood, or the smell. Anything but that.

'I know how these things work, Detective. I just want to see my daughter. Properly this time.'

'We know that, Mrs Flynn. We'll make that happen as soon as we possibly can. We just need to ask a few questions, okay?'

Emily just wanted them to leave. Not that she wanted to be alone. Not with the way thoughts were flying round her head at that moment. She just didn't want to have to deal with any of these stupid things at that moment. Questions and suspicions. She knew how those things worked. She'd seen it on TV enough.

'I have no idea what's happened. I imagine it's burglary by some evil little thug, who your lot have let out onto the streets. What was taken from the house?'

'We're not sure about that right now, Mrs Flynn,' the brunette with the dark complexion said. Bit foreign, Emily decided. The olive skin, the vowel at the end of her surname. Definitely not totally English. Even if she spoke with a flawless Scouse accent.

'Well, they didn't have much. Worked hard and paid their bills. Hannah had only recently gone back to work. Just part-time. Greg works in a solicitor's. Low down on the ladder, but he's getting up there. They . . . they've done nothing wrong.'

Emily could feel the tears coming; she tried swallowing them back down, but failed to dislodge the lump at the back of her throat. She didn't want to cry in front of these two police detectives. She hadn't cried in front of anyone in a very long time and wasn't about to do it in front of strangers.

'Have there been any incidents in the past few weeks, Mrs Flynn? Something that may have worried or scared either of them?'

Emily hesitated, wondering if the impossible had happened. Decided it didn't have anything to do with what had happened. 'Nothing at all, as far as I was aware. They're a normal couple.'

What would she say to Millie?

'Do you give out those books,' Emily said, before either of the detectives could jump in with more questions. 'The ones where you explain ... this kind of thing ... to a child? Only, I don't really know what I'm going to say to Millie. I'm not used to that type of thing. Hannah's dad died young, but she was a teenager. I have no clue what to say to a two-year-old about her parents. I just ... don't.'

She could feel the tears now, falling in single file down her cheek. She choked back a sob and turned away from the pair.

'Please ... can I have a minute. I can't do this now.'

*   *   *

'She held it back well.'

'So unhealthy and bloody British to keep it in.'

Murphy and Rossi waited outside by the police van as a family liaison officer took over inside with Emily Flynn. A low morning sun, which had made a brief appearance, dipped behind dark clouds once more. A smattering of raindrops soon appeared above them.

'Sit in my car?' Murphy asked, turning to Rossi who already had a hand above her head.

'Better than out here.'

Murphy led the way, passing miserable-looking uniformed officers. It was the one thing most coppers could agree on – there was almost nothing worse than having to stand in the rain and look professional.

'That's better,' Murphy said once they were both sitting in his car. He turned the engine on and flicked the heater on. 'Hopefully it's just a shower.'

'From the look of those clouds, I'm not so sure.'

'What are you thinking then? Serial killer going after couples for reasons unknown?'

Rossi slipped off her jacket as the car heated up, ran a hand through her hair and shook the moisture out. 'Looks about right. Although there does seem to be something about all the messages he's leaving behind.'

'It could be a woman doing it.'

'You're always so quick with that one,' Rossi replied, fiddling with the heater controls. 'You're desperate for a female serial killer.'

'Well, we've seen most other types. Always good to have a bit of variety in your life.'

'I think you'll be waiting for a while yet. They're hard to come by.'

Murphy hummed agreement, watching the uniforms outside scramble for cover as the rain came down harder, the gentle swipe of his wiper blades clearing the view every few seconds. 'Talking about variety, I didn't get a chance to give you my opinion on the latest bloke in your life.'

Rossi shifted in her seat. 'Go on then. Give me the bad news.'

'There isn't any. I've done a full background check on him and he's clean—'

'No you bloody haven't . . .'

'Of course I haven't,' Murphy said behind a smile, dodging out of the way of one of Rossi's backhands. 'He seems all right. He's proper into you, though.'

'What makes you say that?'

'The way he looks at you. It's all in the eyes. I've seen that look far too many times not to recognise it. He even got a bit jealous, back at the hospital, when that other guy looked at you. You're feeling the same way, I hope?'

Rossi relaxed back into her seat. 'I don't know. It's nice to have a distraction, but it's a bad time for it, though, don't you think?'

'Is there ever a good time for it in our job?'

Rossi shrugged and turned away from him, looking through a rain-splattered window. Murphy faced forwards again, the road ahead now almost clear, save for a few hardened uniforms braving the now-slowing rain. 'I reckon you should just go for it. I can see you're feeling the same way as him. What's the worst that can happen?'

'That's the problem, isn't it?' Rossi replied, still turned away from him. 'I know what the worst is, don't I? Working this job lets you know that pretty quick.'

Murphy decided an answer or opinion wasn't what was wanted in that moment and kept his mouth shut. Waited a minute or two before speaking again.

'You think there's something more to this?' Murphy said, pointing towards the house and what lay within. 'Something we're not considering?'

'Oh, definitely. There'll be a reason for it, whatever that might be.' Rossi turned in her seat. 'A link between all three couples so far. The messages at both of our scenes seem to be saying something about secrets. Maybe he's targeting couples hiding things from each other.'

Murphy thought about Sarah, about the things she didn't know. 'Then he's going to be a very busy boy.'

'Why do you say that?'

Murphy switched the now-redundant windscreen wipers off, turned the key and began to open his door. 'Because we all have secrets. All relationships do. It's the only way they work.'

*　　*　　*

He hadn't meant to go there. Not then. He did like to visit the old places from time to time. See what had changed since he'd been there. Not for a sense of reflection, but more curiosity. He liked to know if what he had done had changed anything.

He was Working Man right then. Normal. Dressed up in another disguise. There were a few other people standing at the end of the street, peering past the police to try and get a better look. All gawping at the same nothingness. He was one of them, that was all. Nothing out of the ordinary there. Someone walking past who had taken a slight interest in what was going on. Who wanted to know what the commotion was. If there was anything to see.

He knew there wouldn't be. Not from where they were standing. Everything that would satisfy their curiosity was behind the closed door of a house they could barely see in the distance. They would read all the grisly details of what lay behind that door on their phones and tablets later. The words deadening the impact of what it was they were reading about. The deaths of two people, a couple who could be any one of them.

This couple would eventually give up their secret, so the public could judge and evaluate. Decide if they deserved their fate or not. Talking with their own partners and friends about every detail and passing criticism.

As if their own lives would stand up to the same scrutiny.

He thought of the girl in his life now. Number Four. How he wanted to show her how things could be so different. How this was all for her.

How it would all be worth it.

He watched as the big detective, Murphy, scurried back to his car, the rain now coming down harder, Laura Rossi following close behind. He began to shift things into focus, working through problems and the possible downfalls to his plan.

Decided that he had come so far in his life that there was no sense in giving up. That he had a job to do.

That nothing was going to stop him.

He had everything prepared, ready to go at the click of a button. All secure and untraceable to him.

It wasn't the time to be nervous.

It was time to show them all.

Chapter Nineteen

The meeting had been scheduled before Murphy and Rossi had even returned to the station. The Major Crime Unit was now in full swing; doing what needed to be done, and all that management speak Murphy so hated.

It was a chance for some important people to feel important. To feel like their job title meant they really mattered.

'It's not them who have to see these places close up,' Murphy said, Rossi an ear to unload on, as they arrived back at the station. 'Just a load of bullshit to justify the money they're on.'

'I'm sure they had their own fill of bad crime scenes on the way up.'

'Too busy sucking up to be dealing with that sort of thing. That's how these things work. You know that.'

Rossi elbowed him as his voice grew too loud. 'You're such a cynic. Just be quiet and take it all in. We need all the help we can get, don't you think?'

Murphy opened his mouth to moan further, but decided against it. Instead, he gathered up what information they had about the cases so far and walked over to the meeting room.

'Catch up with Hale and Kirkham,' Murphy said as he was about to enter the meeting room. 'See if they've finished up with the neighbours yet. And find out if they've had any hits from CCTV.'

Rossi gave him a thumbs-up and turned to talk to DC Harris. Murphy breathed in and pushed open the door.

He was the last one to turn up. Always a great first impression, he thought. Professional to the end.

'Ah, David, there you are,' DCI Stephens said as Murphy sat down without a word. 'I gather there's a lot still going on at the newest crime scene?'

Murphy relaxed a little. She was already making his life easier, which meant there was at least one person in the room on his side. 'Yes. We've only just got back now.'

'Well, you know everyone round the table,' DCI Stephens said, her outstretched palm sweeping across the room as if it were full to the brim with people. In reality, there were five faces peering back at him. All suited and booted, looking polished and pristine. Murphy looked up and attempted a welcoming smile, which he wasn't sure came off as genuine.

Stephens continued. 'DSI Butler, I'll let you take over.'

Detective Superintendent Gareth Butler made as if he were going to stand, before deciding against the action. Murphy had taken an instant dislike to the DSI a few years earlier and hadn't really altered his thinking in the time since then. He couldn't argue against the presence he had, however. It was as if George Clooney – or whoever the latest famous old-bloke crush was now – had walked through the offices, if the reaction from some of the female staff was anything to go by.

'Thank you,' said Butler, clearing his throat once. 'I understand this is the third case in the last few days, David?'

Murphy stopped himself from rolling his eyes. 'Not exactly, sir. The first case – the one brought to our attention by colleagues over the water – those murders occurred almost a month ago. Our case – the Chloe Morrison and Joe Hooper murders – began on Monday, but they were dead and missing for a couple of days before that. This new scene from this morning looks to have happened overnight.'

'Ah,' DSI Butler said, taking a sip of water from a glass in front of him. Murphy looked round for any other glasses and saw none. 'Our man is escalating. That's the term they use, isn't it?'

Murphy nodded, the beginnings of a headache starting to appear as he held his tongue. 'It looks that way, sir.'

'Then we need to give your command all the support we can in order to stop this in its tracks.'

'That would be nice,' Murphy said, earning himself a look from DCI Stephens, which he took as a warning not to finish his sentence.

'This is also a chance to see if this new command set-up works well in these situations,' DSI Butler said, as if Murphy hadn't spoken. 'Really test things out. We have a press conference scheduled for later today. David, you should be there, but don't worry, you won't have to speak. From now on, myself and DCI Stephens will be the faces of this investigation. I understand the second couple … what were they called again?'

'Chloe Morrison and Joe Hooper,' Murphy said, fighting to keep the steel out of his answer.

'Right, those two. I understand they were some kind of celeb couple type of thing?'

'ChloJoe,' one of the other suits said. Murphy remembered the name of the guy as soon as he heard the high-pitched voice: Sergeant Unsworth, from the uniformed side of things.

Murphy had to cough to hide a laugh as he remembered the nickname the man had. High-Pitched Harry – the thin-faced sergeant's voice having a tendency to sound like someone going through puberty.

'Yes,' DSI Butler said, breaking into Murphy's thinking. 'Quite. Well, I gather we've had quite the media interest over the past couple of days, due to the profile of those two. We'll be getting more of a handle on that from now on. I don't want the public thinking we're ignoring the fact that this could be three couples dead in one month. All by the same person or persons. We'll be up to our necks in outrage before we know it.'

Murphy tuned out as DSI Butler's voice droned on, waiting until he could leave the room and actually do some proper work. He thought – not for the first time – that promotion wasn't something he wanted at that moment. Possibly never.

He just couldn't pull off the power suit and management speak.

After another twenty minutes of almost interminable talking, Murphy escaped from the meeting room, motioning Rossi away from her desk and to the corridor.

'Any excuse to visit the vending machine,' Rossi said, lifting herself off the desk of DC Harris where she'd been perched. 'Want anything?'

DC Harris shook his head and continued to stare at his computer screen as Murphy waited. He gave Rossi another two seconds and began walking away.

'Hang on.'

'I did,' Murphy replied, waiting at the door and holding it open. 'You were starting to take the piss.'

'Meeting was fun then?'

'Aren't they always?' Murphy said, letting the door close as Rossi passed him. They walked side by side down the short corridor into the main lobby on their floor of the station. Rossi made straight for the machine holding the drinks captive, plugging money in and waiting for an energy drink to fall.

'What's going on then? I'm guessing we're to keep going?'

Murphy leaned against the vending machine. 'That's about the gist of it. They want to see how this new command unit works with something as big as this.'

'See if we're up to the job,' Rossi said, snapping the top off the bottle and draining a third in one long swig.

'Which we will be,' Murphy said, eyeing the chocolate bars in the vending machine opposite. He attempted to keep control of himself, despite the jangle of change in his pocket. 'Our friend DSI Butler will be in front of the media from now on, of course.'

'Glory hunter,' Rossi muttered under her breath. 'Takes some of the heat off us, though, I suppose.'

'There is that. What's the latest then? Any further with neighbours?'

Rossi shook her head. 'Most had no clue anything had happened overnight at all. Next door to one side were out until late at a family thing over in West Derby. The other side were a bit more cagey, according to Hale and Kirkham. Older couple, in their fifties or something. Eventually, they admitted they heard shouts, but thought they were arguing or something.'

'Was that something they heard often?'

'Apparently not. But the couple who lived there before Greg and Hannah had screamed blue murder at each other almost every night. They were used to that sort of thing, so just left them to it. Kirkham said they got very upset when they realised what had really been going on.'

Murphy pulled on his lower lip with his teeth. 'Interesting.'

'What is?' Rossi said, staring at her drink and shaking her head at its lowered contents.

'Our guy lets them shout out. Not worried about being interrupted and caught. Odd behaviour.'

'He probably just knows that screaming and shouting coming from a house next door is about as useful as a car alarm these days. We're all so used to it, we don't go running for the phone any more. Just try and block it out and get on with our own lives.'

'True,' Murphy replied, his faith in humanity struck down a little further still. 'Still happens though. I bet if you ask most uniforms the majority of their domestic call-outs come from concerned neighbours.'

'Yeah, but they're the ones we hear about. There's bloody loads more we don't.'

Murphy considered the number that did pass through the police's hands, then the many more that didn't. He shuddered at the thought of it.

'We've got Emily Flynn here, by the way,' Rossi said, picking at the label on her drinks bottle. 'Family liaison have calmed her down somewhat. She's waiting to speak to us.'

Murphy pushed himself away, straightened up and brushed off his jacket. 'Oh, good. Let's see if she's a bit more forthcoming this time around.'

*　　*　　*

Fifteen minutes later, they were sitting in the family room opposite a more composed version of Emily Flynn. Murphy had watched the woman that morning, seen the way she'd held back her emotions as her mind raced, remembered the time it had been him in that position some years earlier, as his parents lay in their living room, murdered by the hand of someone he'd been unable to stop.

He understood what Emily was going through.

'Thank you for speaking to us again,' Murphy said, using his concerned voice. Sarah had got a few laughs when he'd practised his different voices for different situations, but they did come in handy. 'We won't keep you for too long. I know you're eager to get back to your granddaughter.'

'Yes, of course,' Emily said, a flatness to her tone now. Nothing practised there, Murphy thought. 'Have you got any news yet?'

'We're working through everything as fast and as diligently as possible, Mrs Flynn.'

'I think you can call me Emily now, Detective.'

'Thank you, Emily. We just have a few more questions and then we can move forwards, OK?'

Emily raised a hand, motioning for him to go on.

Murphy asked a few questions just to ease Emily into things, not wanting to go in too hard straight away. Rossi

chipped in every now and again, just to keep things
straight. Murphy paused after a few minutes, preparing
for the more difficult questions. Those which could lead
to difficulties for them as well as Emily.

'Do you know if Greg and Hannah had any friends
outside of those you've already told us about . . . maybe
more high-profile ones?'

'High-profile friends? I don't understand . . .'

'Well, such as more well-known figures. People who
may have been in the public eye in the past couple of years.'

Emily narrowed her eyes at Murphy as he continued to
dance round the subject. 'No, they're just a normal couple.
I keep saying this.'

'Okay, not a problem. How about people over the
water, on the Wirral? Did they have any friends over
there?'

'Not that I know of,' Emily replied, rubbing her forehead with one hand. 'I don't understand what these questions are about. What do they have to do with Greg and
Hannah?'

'We're just looking into every possibility at the moment.'

Murphy hoped he'd placated her, but he could already
see the cogs turning in the woman's mind. It wouldn't be
long before she realised why he was asking about 'high-
profile' people.

'This might be a bit more difficult, Mrs Flynn,' Rossi
said, taking over from Murphy. 'But we want to know
more about their personal lives, if that's okay?'

'There's nothing really to say about that.'

'I'm sure there isn't, but it's important we ask anyway.
We don't want to miss a vital piece of information at this
point.'

Emily didn't answer. Just waved the creased hand again.

'Were they going through any financial trouble at all?'

'Nothing out of the ordinary. Hannah had to go back to work part-time, just to make sure they were still comfortable. They bought the house a year or so ago, but they were doing okay.'

'Neither of them ever spoke to you about borrowing money, or anything like that?'

Emily shook her head. 'Nothing like that at all. They would have come to me if they needed anything and they never did.'

'How about personally, did they get on well together?'

Murphy watched as Emily hesitated a touch before answering. He poked Rossi under the table out of sight.

'They're great together. No arguments or anything like that.'

'Was there anything Hannah may have come to you about,' Murphy said, glad Rossi had recognised his signal to allow him to speak next. 'Something she was worried about perhaps?'

Another hesitation. 'I'm her mother, so she would always speak to me. But there's nothing that could have led to this, I don't think.'

Murphy could sense a hesitation. 'There is something, though, isn't there, Emily?'

'I'm not sure what you mean . . .'

'This is very important, Emily. We need to know everything, because then we can discount anything we believe to be unrelated. We don't judge here. We've heard it all. Nothing will take away from the fact that we want to find the person who has done this to Hannah and Greg. If there's something Hannah was worried about, we need to know that.'

'I . . . I don't know,' Emily said, her voice faltering as her hands began to shake.

'Please, Emily. We need to know what it is.'

'There is something, but please, I don't want this being told to everyone. I don't want to read about this or . . . see it on the news or anything. If people found out, they would only say bad things about Hannah and it's not like that.'

Murphy knew better than to speak in absolutes or make promises. He'd been burned too often in the past.

'We'll do everything we can to make sure this stays private, Emily,' Murphy said, hoping that would be enough.

'Okay, but please, understand that this wasn't the way Hannah was. She was a good girl. She just made a mistake.'

'What was the mistake, Emily,' Rossi said. 'What happened?'

Emily began to speak, faltering at first, then resigned to telling them the whole story.

As she spoke, Murphy felt as if the air within the room became thicker. He listened, thoughts flying through his head, muddled and disorderly. Close to an answer, before it was stripped away.

Chapter Twenty

The video appeared on his timeline with little fanfare. A minute and a half of darkness, waiting to be clicked on and played. Retweeted by someone he didn't know, but who must have followed him at some point, prompting a follow back instead of an actual reply. An unknown Twitter account, forcing the video into his world.

He clicked on it, of course. Scrolling through hundreds of boring tweets, reading an *Echo* article, which had talked about two more people found dead earlier that morning. He hadn't been surprised that there was some kind of link to those two celebs who'd been murdered. He had his own theory about those two. Drugs deal gone bad or something like that. Good riddance, he thought. Like the world would miss those two oxygen stealers. Famous for doing fuck all, whilst people like him struggled along in life. Sod them.

He had gone back to Twitter, when something had caught his eye.

The video was titled 'The Third Couple – Why They Died'. Enough for him to stop and check it out.

It wasn't like he was some kind of weirdo who trawled

the web for disgusting videos to watch. He hadn't Googled beheadings or sought out anything equally shocking. He thought he was normal. Just a bloke called Andy, on a bus, on the way to work for an afternoon shift at a fast-food place in town. Making minimum wage, which barely covered the contract for the new smartphone he was holding.

He almost closed the video after a few seconds. If he hadn't had his headphones plugged into his phone, he probably would have done. The screen remained black, no sound or movement. His finger moved towards the back button on his phone screen.

Then the noise started. Crying, shouts. An argument of some sort. Begging. The video cut ahead: he was now able to make out two figures facing each other, sitting in chairs.

No, he thought, not just sitting. Tied to the chairs.

The words they were saying didn't make much sense. Some garbled noises, the bloke shouting, 'Tell me,' at one point. It was becoming boring. Andy's finger hovered over the button again.

Then the view changed to a close-up of the girl's face. Streaked with tears and fear. Marked, slashed on one side. Good special effects, Andy thought, although the lighting guy needed shooting. Could barely make her out most of the time.

'Millie isn't yours . . . I slept with someone else . . . I'm . . . I'm sorry.'

Andy clicked off the video, bored. He expanded the original tweet, to see what other people had commented. Then looked out the window and realised his stop was coming up soon.

@LiverpoolVids1 @themaninblack80
What is this? Don't get it.

@ScouseLad1983 @themaninblack80
Dunno, just got sent to me and I shared.

@LiverpoolVids1 @ScouseLad1983 @themaninblack80
That bloke looks like that fat one who does
the impressions of footballers.

@LiverpoolVids1 @ScouseLad1983 @themaninblack80
It's those two people who were killed in
Tuebrook. Bet ya any money.

Andy locked his phone, grabbed his bag and shifted across the seat. He waited until the bus turned the corner into Liverpool One bus station and then walked down the stairs.

He forgot about the video and how he came to watch it until later that day.

When everyone was talking about it.

*   *   *

Sarah Murphy was driving as the video was shared around – oblivious as Heart FM blared from the radio. The same songs repeated over and over.

She was barely listening, travelling down the East Lancs Road, heading towards the M62, and Manchester which lay at its end. Every now and again, she considered turning off and going back home, but shook the thought away each time.

She needed to do this.

There was a little voice in her head, telling her it was a mistake. That if David found out about her visit, he would never forgive her. There was a louder voice, though, which remembered everything that had happened all those years ago, a voice that wouldn't be silenced. She needed to know, to find out why.

Why did he do it?

Why them?

Why her?

She'd phoned the school that morning, feigning sickness, something that she'd never done before. She hoped it would be worth it.

Sarah's hands began to shake as she got closer, the signs on the motorway starting to include her destination. The reality of what she was doing beginning to hit. The thought of the man she had known so well, and everything he had done, turning her stomach.

Still she drove forward. The hour-long journey from Liverpool dragging out, but almost at an end.

Sarah thought about David, and what he was currently investigating. More death, as if he hadn't already had enough of it. She glanced at the mobile in its holder on the dashboard as it came to life, cutting over the radio. She hoped for a second it would be David, telling her to come home, that everything was finished and she had him back properly again.

'Hi, Jess,' she said, trying to hide the disappointment in her voice. 'Just driving at the moment.'

'You decided to go then?'

'Yeah,' Sarah replied, slowing as she took the exit from the motorway. 'Just something I've got to do.'

'Did you tell him?'

Sarah knew she meant David and not the other *him*. 'No. I don't think he needs to know. Yet.'

Jess's huff echoed round the car as it came through the

speakers. 'The pair of you need your heads banging together. Well . . . take care of yourself, okay?'

Sarah said she would and then ended the call. Within a few minutes she was pulling into the car park.

She passed the silver sign which filled her with dread. The dread of things that had happened years before, and of what lay behind those gates.

HMP MANCHESTER

*   *   *

Murphy was trying to get his head round what was being explained to him. The world of social media was an alien one to him; he had missed the whole explosion in the previous years, preferring instead to stay out of it all.

'Look, just tell me how we get rid of it.'

'It's not that easy,' Rossi said, rolling her eyes at DC Harris, who was struggling to keep a serious look on his face. 'Once it's out there and goes viral, we can't just stop it. That's just the way these things work.'

'Well, get in touch with the website. Tell them to take it down. And find out who posted it in the first place. Surely we can do that.'

'We can try, but this could have come from anywhere.'

Murphy rubbed a hand across his forehead. 'Just do something. We can't have this out there.'

Rossi turned back to DC Harris and began talking through options, leaving Murphy to work out how he was going to explain the latest development to DCI Stephens.

'The video appeared an hour ago,' Murphy said, once he was in her office. The harassed look on her face had increased in the time since their meeting with the higher-ups. 'One of the media team drew our attention to it when the Merseyside Police Twitter account was linked to it or something. The *Echo* have been on the phone non-stop since, but have been talked out of posting it on their site. Won't be long until national press link it to the Chloe and Joe murders.'

'This is a mess, David,' DCI Stephens said, removing her glasses and pinching her nose. 'Are we in the process of removing the video?'

'Well, that's the plan. It's not easy, I've been told, but they're working on it.'

'This is the last thing we need right now. There's already enough pressure on us from the media without this type of thing getting out there. What's on the video?'

Murphy hesitated. 'Do you want to see it for yourself?'

'Just give me the gist for now,' DCI Stephens said, placing her glasses back on. 'I'll watch it later.'

Murphy knew she was putting it off. It was all well and good sitting behind a desk and coordinating things but actually witnessing the things her detectives had seen was something she quite plainly wanted to avoid. 'We think it's the couple found this morning – Greg and Hannah – taken last night. Greg is asking Hannah to tell him something, tell him the truth. Then it cuts to a closer view of Hannah ...'

'Does she have the facial injuries at this point?'

'Yes,' Murphy said, trying not to think of the nasty gashes across her face. 'She then admits to Greg the same information her mother provided us with earlier. That the daughter wasn't his, she'd had a one-night stand, etc., etc. The video then goes back to Greg ...'

'And?'

'He . . . It sounds as if he's saying he wants her to be hurt. To be killed. He calls her some names and says she deserves all she gets. Then the video ends.'

DCI Stephens steepled her fingers and bowed her head. 'Well, that'll do wonders for public sympathy.'

Murphy said nothing, still remembering the venom in Greg's voice. He wondered if there was anything Sarah could say that could provoke the same reaction from him. He hoped he would never have to find out.

'We'll get this taken down, even if we have to go to a higher level to do so,' DCI Stephens said, placing her hands flat on her desk. 'I'm sure it'll still be out there, if you look hard enough, but we'll make sure it becomes a lot more difficult to find. Have we found out the first account who shared it yet?'

'Anonymous account called "themaninblack80". We're getting more detail on that as well.'

'Good. Let's hope he's made his first mistake.'

Murphy left the office, eschewing his normal path back to his desk and walking out through the incident room to the corridors. His phone had been buzzing away in his pocket for the previous few minutes, vibrating against his leg.

He pulled out his phone once he was in the quiet of the empty corridor by the lift area. Four missed calls and a message.

'Call me. Need to talk.'

DS Ayris from Liverpool South. His heart began to race a little as he thumbed the screen to dial the number.

'Just give me a minute,' Ayris said, the noise in the background growing quieter as Murphy heard him move away. 'Thanks for calling me back.'

'What's going on?'

'It's just a courtesy call about the Amy Maguire case,' Ayris said. 'We've cleared Keith Hudson for now. Nothing else we could do but release him.'

Murphy's grip on his phone grew tighter. 'Did you get anything more out of him at least? The little bastard knows something.'

'Nothing, sorry. I'm not sure he knows anything. The guy has some mental health issues and is known for making false claims. Probably heard the story about Amy from someone and got lucky with some details.'

'What's next then? Do you have anything else?'

'We'll keep going, but you know the score, Murphy. Mispers are the bloody worst cases to try and get info on. Far too many of them for us to make a dent. We'll keep her name out there, but she's eighteen. Could have had a secret boyfriend and buggered off somewhere with him. Not much else we can do really. If anything comes up, I'll let you know.'

'Yeah, cheers,' Murphy said, ending the call and catching himself before he launched the phone down the corridor. He settled on saying, 'Fucking idiots,' under his breath and instead finding another number in his contacts.

'Hey, it's David Murphy from Liverpool North. I need a favour ... just an address, please ... yeah, it's Keith Hudson. Lives in Speke. He was questioned in Admiral Street station by Liverpool South division this week, if that narrows it down some? Cheers ...'

Chapter Twenty-One

Sky News had been left on the television in the office, a distraction to take people's attention every now and again. The Chloe and Joe saga had lost its 'breaking news' and 'live updates' tags at that point, waiting to be resurrected once the police confirmed that the couple found that morning were linked to the story.

Then, the second video appeared on screen.

It was a passing DS from the robbery team who noticed it first, saw it appear on the mid-afternoon news bulletin as Murphy, Rossi, and DC Harris continued to discuss the first video and its implications for the case.

'Have you seen this?' the DS said, turning to a DC on Murphy's team. 'Something about your case by the looks of it.'

Murphy, overhearing, half turned towards the TV, expecting to see the video of Greg and Hannah from that morning.

'Fuck's sake, I thought they weren't going to show it?'

'That's what I was told, sir,' DC Harris replied, wheeling round his desk to get a better look. 'Duck out the way, can't see the screen from here.'

'Wait . . . that doesn't look right,' Rossi said from beside Murphy. 'The room's different. What's going on . . .'

'Shit. That's not the video we've seen. This is a new one. Stupid bloody press team can't even get this right . . .' Murphy said under his breath, lifting his phone up from his desk. 'This is DI Murphy from the Major Crime Unit . . . Yes, hello. Why the hell are *Sky News* showing a video of my murder victims before we've seen it ourselves . . . no, not the one from this morning, Chloe Morrison and Joe Hooper . . . well, sort yourselves out and stop them broadcasting it. Now.'

'That's them?' Rossi shouted, tearing her eyes away from the TV screen and facing Murphy.

'Yeah,' Murphy said, moving off his desk and pacing over to the screen. 'You can see Joe's tattoos there. What the . . . someone turn the volume up.'

'*Merda*. Well, we're for it now. What are they thinking showing this before giving it to us?'

Murphy didn't reply, waiting for the footage to end and the cameras to cut back to the newsreaders in the studio.

'Someone's getting a bollocking,' DC Harris said. 'That's for sure.'

'I want that video,' Murphy said. 'And I want it now.'

*   *   *

'They didn't play the audio live, so that's something. Hardly matters, though, as the *Daily Mail* have just published it in full. *Huff Post* will be next, then the *Mirror*. They're just waiting to see if the *Mail* has it pulled first.'

'And what do we do?' Murphy said, swiping a hand through his diminishing hairline. 'Can we stop it?'

'It's been on every news channel in the past fifteen minutes, but that's not all. They may not be showing the video in full, or playing the audio, but they are publishing the message attached.'

'What's the message?'

Rossi scrolled down on her computer screen to a highlighted block of text. 'Here we go.'

Murphy leaned over and read the message.

NOTHING STAYS SECRET

There are many secrets people keep to themselves and away from significant others. Lies, that if they were revealed, would destroy those relationships. These secrets are kept for selfish reasons. The fear of being discovered, found out for who they really are. Maybe you're the one being lied to and just don't know it yet. Lies have no place in a loving and committed relationship and I am showing the consequences of keeping secrets. It is a lesson that needs to be taught to so many. I want to make the world a better place. I want people to atone and for us all to move forward to a new understanding of Love.

I can help people.

If you know of someone who is lying to their partner, feel free to contact me.

They could be next.

The Man in Black – themaninblack80@gmail.com

Murphy stopped reading, he stood up and stretched his back. 'The Man in Black ... who does he think he is? Johnny bloody Cash?'

'Who?' DC Harris said, giving Murphy a blank stare.

Murphy gave DC Harris a perplexed look. 'You don't know who Johnny Cash is? Bloody hell. I am getting old.'

'He was a country singer years ago,' Rossi said, rolling her eyes at DC Harris. 'Before even our DI's time. Can we focus now?'

'Go ahead.'

'He wants people to get in contact with him,' Rossi said, writing in her notepad. 'Wants them to give him names of people to kill, because they're cheating or whatever.'

'Surely no one is going to do that?' Murphy said, sitting back at his own desk.

'You'd be surprised at what people will do to others on the internet. It's all pretend. They won't believe it's real. You'll have people doing it for a laugh, as a wind-up, that sort of thing. They won't believe anything will actually happen.'

'We need to release a statement now,' Murphy said, lifting his phone again. 'I'll get the press team to put something together.'

'Here's the boss as well.'

DCI Stephens left her office, the door banging against the wall as she walked towards Murphy. 'Want to tell me why I'm getting down the banks for something I've not even heard about?'

'Sorry, I came over to tell you but . . .'

'I'm not interested in apologies, David. Tell me what the hell is going on?'

Murphy took a deep breath and began updating DCI Stephens on what had occurred in the previous hour. He paused at one point to allow her to vent her spleen about the idiots who had put the video on live news.

'We've got calls in now to make them stop showing it. It'll be part of a potential prosecution, so we're hoping they see sense.'

'Good,' DCI Stephens said, shifting on her feet. 'This message as well, can we get that taken down?'

'That might be a bit trickier,' DC Kirkham said, joining their bank of desks. 'The email address is everywhere online now. Loads of people discussing it on social media.'

'Twitter, you mean?'

'Erm . . . yeah. There's a hashtag for it and everything.'

'Great,' DCI Stephens said, turning her back on DC Kirkham and facing Murphy again. 'We'll do press asap. We've got to get a handle on this. Where are we with possible leads?'

'We've got in touch with Twitter to let them know we want the details of the account that was set up to post the video. They've already suspended the account, but that's not really stopped anything. Once it got out there, it was game over for us. It was set up with dummy details, but we're hoping for a hit on the IP address.'

'There's one more thing,' DC Kirkham said, everyone turning to look at him again. 'LiveLeak are showing the whole video uncut. Audio, everything.'

Murphy pointed to Rossi who was already spinning in her chair to get the website up. 'What's it under,' she said, not looking away from her screen. 'Don't worry, I've found it. Hottest video right now, apparently.'

The noise of the video filled the room; conversations ended and other detectives in the office began peering over desks to get a better view. Murphy bowed his head, having already seen enough of the images. This time, it was the words he was most interested in.

'I don't love you, Chloe. I never have. It was all for the money and the fame. Once we'd got married, had a couple of kids, made an absolute fortune, I was going to tell you, honest. I thought we would have made enough for it not to matter too much. You could make a ton of money on the divorce as well, from all the magazines and that.'

'Did you sleep with other girls?'

'I . . . I did. But I kept it really quiet. No one knew.'

'I think it's too late for that. You evil bastard . . .'

'Hey! That's not fair. You knew the score, surely? This is how it all works. You got famous for doing fuck all and made a shit ton of money out of it.'

'Like that matters now.'

'Did you expect me to just put up with it all or something? I couldn't stay with just you. I don't like you that way. You're all right, I suppose, but not for me. I am sorry. Honest.'

'You're a fucking bastard, is what you are. If I could, I'd break your fucking neck right now.'

The camera position changed again, the same as in the first video.

'Do it. Kill him. He deserves to die. He's . . . let me do it. I want to do it . . .'

The screen cut to black. A collective gasp went around the office before muted conversation started up again.

'What are we dealing with here, David?'

'Someone getting payback for something. Killing cheating partners? Probably got rejected and took it much harder than most of us do. He'll screw up soon enough. Probably already has. We'll have him in an interview room within hours, I reckon.'

'There's more to it than that,' Rossi said, leaning back in her chair. 'This is about love. A twisted form of it, but it's there.'

'Laura, I don't know what the hell you mean.'

'*Mannaggia* ... There's something happening here. Something more than a vigilante cupid. We should be working out what that is.'

'Great,' Murphy said, as he clapped his hands together. 'You sort out the love stuff. Kirkham, you come with me.'

'Where are you going, David?' DCI Stephens said, stepping back as Murphy walked past her.

'Well, I'm not just sitting here whilst all this is going on. We've got stuff we can be doing. There must be something linking one of the people who knew about Hannah's secret to whoever killed her and Greg. We need to work that out. And fast, before the whole country has emailed a serial killer asking him to bump off their next-door neighbours.'

Murphy left the office, Kirkham scurrying behind him.

'Where *are* we going, sir?'

'To speak to someone who knew about Hannah and her secret.'

*   *   *

Rossi watched Murphy walk off and waited for DCI Stephens to do the same. She turned back to her desk after risking another look to see if Murphy was going to come back and tell her what the hell he was doing. She wasn't surprised when he didn't. With Murphy, she would just wait him out.

'You all right?' DC Harris said, not looking over at her. Still squinting at his computer screen.

'Why wouldn't I be?'

'Just seemed like you got blown off there.'

'If that sort of thing bothered me, I would have quit the job years ago. I'm quite used to you men sticking together.'

DC Harris pursed his lips, looking towards Rossi. 'Whatever, Laura. For what it's worth, I agree with you. There's something darker going on with this one.'

'Good to know,' Rossi said, pulling her phone out of her bag. 'If you have any more thoughts on things, don't be afraid to voice them. You know . . . when it's not just me sitting here. Now, I'm going to the "little girls' room". See if I can find your bollocks in there, shall I?'

Rossi walked off before DC Harris could reply. Instead of going into the Ladies, she walked past them, carrying on down the corridor and heading to a different floor altogether. Satisfied she had complete privacy, she looked through her phone and, finding the number she wanted, pressed it and dialled.

When the answer service kicked in, she considered hanging up and sending a text instead, but decided against it. She had to do things differently to the way she would normally.

'Hi, it's Laura. Just got your text. Hope work isn't too manic. I know mine is. Anyway, I had a great time the other night, so yeah, let me know when you're free again soon, I'd be up for that . . .'

Up for that . . . Christ, Laura.

'So ... yeah, just give me a call. Or a text. Whatever. Speak to you soon.'

She ended the call and rested the back of her head against the wall.

'*Liscio*, Laura Rossi. Very smooth.'

Normality

He was starting to lose his grip on reality. He could feel it. The ridiculous name he had come up with for his other self – The Man in Black. As if he could divorce himself from what he had been doing. What he was doing. It needled at him. He liked to believe his life looked normal. Ordinary. Not that it was anything like *ordinary,* but appearances had to be deceiving. He hadn't really missed much work but his absence had been noted. He could tell from the extended looks from certain people, the barbed comments as he walked down the corridors.

He wished he could tell them. Shout it into every room, every office. Proudly announce that he was the man everyone was afraid of. His heart hammered against his chest as he imagined the looks on their faces. The disbelief and shock it would create. That he was someone, something, they could never imagine.

That he wasn't what they thought he was.

The man he was at work was someone else. Another character he had to assume. He saw everything as a stage, an act. He was beginning to accept that there was no real person behind the mask he wore. It had disappeared. Now there were only roles he played.

Always too awkward, too weird to be friends with. He'd always felt like an outsider, the person no one wanted to be around. That was all he had heard throughout his life. He had worked on an act, so that he would fit in better. Honed it over the years, until now, when no one would be able to tell he had ever been that type of man.

He'd gone through university, moved away from the city and explored a different place. Then he'd worked his way round the country before returning almost ten years later.

Not that much had changed in Liverpool in that time. Those without still had nothing, those with everything still ruled. The waterfront was a changed place now, more buildings springing up across the city almost constantly, but the people were much the same. A few more foreigners, but that was the same everywhere in England.

He had changed. Over that time, moving about, never really having anywhere to call home, he had become different. He lamented not doing things he should have done when he was younger. Regretted not standing up for himself – publicly – and shaming those who had tried to keep him down. The girls who had strung him along, the lads who had bullied him; they were to blame.

He had wanted love, but it was never going to be the right kind. Not the real love that he could show someone.

There was a girl. One without a number. It was her fault. She was also to blame. Now he was stuck, using her as a veneer of normality.

He spoke to Number Four. Told the story again and again so he could make her understand that this other woman meant nothing to him. That it was her – Number Four – who was his real love.

'She loves me, I can see that, but I know it's a lie. She could never love me. I don't know if anyone ever could. Not the way you will.'

He felt the anger rise as he thought of those people he had visited in the previous weeks. The ones he had placed in the chairs. How they had lied and kept things hidden away. Pretended to love, whilst doing everything to protect themselves above all else.

'They will never realise what they have. They will never know love. I see that, at the end. When I give them every opportunity to show it. It's never enough.'

He blinked away the emotion, sending it back into memory. Shivered as it became colder in the room.

'They'll say things about me, I know they will. That I probably tortured animals as a child. Maybe they'll drag up someone I've never met to talk about me putting bees in a jar and watching them suffocate. I couldn't do that. I remember wanting to be God. As a teenager, probably even younger than that, I wanted the ability to decide everything. I wanted to control fate, people's actions and decisions. To control everything around me. What am I?'

He waited for an answer that was never going to come. Pulled his coat around him tighter, blowing into his hands to warm them up.

'It's cold in here, I know. It's supposed to be spring and most people probably still have their heating on. I should do something about that.'

He watched Number Four shiver and pull herself tighter into a ball – the clank of the chains on her wrists and ankles echoing round the room as she moved.

The Man in Black. Something he had heard his dad call

an old singer he couldn't recall. He was another character. Someone to hide behind.

'I've played the games and lost every time. Read advice, but still got nowhere. And then I'm forced to watch these people, hear their stories and do nothing. Why should I?'

There was no win to be had for him. He knew he wasn't the only one. That there were millions of men out there who suffered just as he had.

'I don't think I have a future, Number Four. You're my last hope. If I can't make you see, then I don't know what I will do.'

He wanted to accept normality. To be like everyone else. Have a family, work hard and provide. Settle down and embrace life instead of death.

'There will be a choice. I can feel it. What if they finally discover me, what will I do? What will I do with you? What if they never find out who I really am, then what do I do? Will you ever be ready? Will you ever love me the right way? What if I don't show you enough?'

His phone buzzed in his pocket. He reached for it, still staring at the wall above Number Four's head. The yellowed wallpaper, peeling away. Layers of the past lying underneath. He looked down at his phone, focusing his eyes on reality once more.

He thumbed his phone, then smiled.

Adam

If he had thought things through a little more – given an equal weight to what would happen if he went through with it – he might not have sent the email. He would have decided against it, thinking of a better way to do what needed to be done. Chosen a different path to destroy what looked, on the surface at least, to be indestructible.

Adam knew that if the truth was put in front of her, so she couldn't deny it, hide from it, things would have to be different.

He had met Carly three years earlier, although it seemed like much less than that. They were both starting a job at the same place, a month-long training session being their introduction to the company. The training was a pointless exercise, but a necessary evil if you wanted to work for the company. It was a requirement, no matter how much he'd argued the point with the two pseudo-teachers delivering the training course.

He had become aware of Carly early on. There were around twenty people on the course, but his gregarious personality and ability to talk to anyone meant he had became friendly with many within in the group quickly.

Carly was quiet at first, watching everyone during breaks in the canteen, sitting on the outside, taking it all in.

She was attractive, there was no doubt about that. Not someone you'd notice in a crowd, but in an environment such as the one they'd found themselves in, it was more obvious. He'd guessed most of the other women there to be in their mid-forties, with some even older. He was just into his twenties and he imagined Carly was of a similar age.

They'd shared a few conversations as the week went on and she came out of her shell a little more. Soon, this had progressed to emailing each other during the classes, peering over computer screens at each other, smiling at a shared joke.

It could have been a perfect romance. A tale to tell grandchildren one day.

The emails had given them a chance to open up, without the worry of being judged face to face. They'd talked about hidden feelings, the past, their hopes for the future. All laid out in black and white.

It should have been a perfect romance.

The problem was her boyfriend of eight years.

Over those first few weeks, and the months following, they'd grown closer. They would meet up, just for a few minutes sometimes. They'd walk to the coffee machine together, just to get away from the desks they were forced to sit at for eight hours a day. Away from the endless telephone calls. Carly had rarely mentioned her partner, preferring instead to laugh at Adam's jokes, to be complimented, made to feel special. It was something he always did well.

The emails had continued. Became text messaging. An almost constant line of conversation throughout the days, only going silent for the few hours Carly's boyfriend took her attention.

She had been with him since the age of fifteen. Didn't know any different. They had drifted through their teenage years, moving in together once they were both working. The boyfriend had been worried when she'd lost her last job, but was happy she had walked into a new one quickly.

Adam wondered if he would have been as happy if he'd known Carly was also walking into his life.

Months had passed, Adam had been convinced that Carly was beginning to share the same feelings he had. His focus on anything else had gone now. His personality was eroding, he was becoming slowly obsessed with Carly. With her life, her dreams. With what he could provide for her, if only she would realise.

The first rejection had been in month four. A works night out, which had ended with him walking her to the taxi rank in town. He had a fantasy that too much alcohol would loosen her tongue and she'd reveal her true feelings for him. They'd ride off into the sunset and a future for the two of them would begin.

She'd rejected that opportunity.

It had continued for months in the same vein. They did everything together during work hours – spent time with each other outside work sometimes – but nothing happened physically. The emails and texts became more sexual, more explicit, but still unrealised. Then, a year after they had first met, another works night out had ended with a kiss in an alleyway in town. A few months of similar contact followed, kisses exchanged, gropes in secret. Then, it all came to an end, Carly deciding that, given the ultimatum, she would choose what she was comfortable with. What she had known all her life.

Adam couldn't let go. He'd followed her, to see what her life was like. Then he'd followed the boyfriend, to see what he had that Adam didn't. That's how he'd discovered the things he did behind Carly's back.

His name was Will. Worked for a solicitor's firm, but Adam was unsure what he did. Had never asked Carly for more information. Following Carly's boyfriend was a thrill for Adam, watching him as he went about his normal life, not knowing the man who had turned his girlfriend's head was shadowing him.

What he'd discovered hadn't really shocked him. He'd expected to find out that Will was unfaithful to Carly.

Carly and Will had been thrust into adulthood with no outside experience, desperate to discover if there was something better out there for them.

All they had known was each other. No one can survive that.

Adam had never told Carly what he'd found out. Months later, he was still talking to her every day, as if nothing had happened between them. The flirtations and explicit conversations continued, but Carly kept him at arm's length. Reading the words on a screen was enough for her.

He could sense himself changing. Becoming a different person. He began snapping at people in work if they did something he deemed to be wrong. He would walk through crowds, deliberately pushing his shoulder into people. He knew she had changed him, but couldn't let go of her.

Adam blamed Carly. He couldn't tell her what her boyfriend was doing to her; he needed Carly to want to be with him without that.

He hadn't meant to read the article, sitting there in the canteen waiting to see if Carly would appear. He was just scrolling through the news app on his phone, seeing if there was anything of interest. It was only because Liverpool was mentioned in the headline that he clicked on the link.

Another couple of murders. Some video or something. It wasn't until he read the words further down the page that he began to take notice, found himself taking note of the email address provided by the apparent serial killer. A fleeting thought flashed across his mind. He dismissed it, turning his phone off as Carly approached his table with a smile.

He listened for an hour as she complained about her boyfriend and how bad her life was with him. Adam told her, once again, to leave him. To come with him. To change her life. But her eyes told him all he needed to know.

It was never going to happen.

That's all it took. The straw that broke him. On the way back to the office, where hundreds of other workers sat staring at computer screens every day, Adam made a decision.

His voice had shaken as he'd spoken to her earlier. He'd pleaded with her, was more accusatory than he'd ever been. Why not him? Why did she carry on with someone she didn't love? Why, why, why?

She had simply shaken her head, given him a look, and walked away. Sent him an email when she'd got back to her desk.

He wouldn't open it. Refused to.

Instead, Adam opened a new message. Took his phone out and checked the email address again.

He typed out a message, hovering the cursor over the send button for a second or two before clicking.

Chapter Twenty-Two

The rain had stopped. That was one for the plus column, Murphy thought, driving to yet another grieving relative. Another house where death would be the main conversational piece for months, years to come. At least he could drive there without the windscreen wipers on.

You look for the little victories.

DC Kirkham was playing the dutiful passenger. Eyes locked ahead, hands clasped together in his lap. Murphy was waiting for some spark, some semblance of personality to appear, but nothing had turned up yet. Every now and again, Kirkham would take out his mobile phone, look at it for a few seconds, then return it to his pocket.

'Why do you keep looking at that?' Murphy said, after the fifth or sixth time. 'If you're worried, I don't mind you taking it out, you know?'

'I get car sick if I look at it for too long.'

'Ah,' Murphy replied, checking the satnav on his dashboard to make sure he was going the right way. 'You don't mind the music, do you?'

'No, not at all. Quite good actually.'

Murphy accepted the lie and continued driving, lowering the volume a little as the song changed. 'Pink Floyd isn't to everyone's taste, but it's the first time in a while I haven't had Laura in the car with me. Making the most of it.'

'My dad likes them,' Kirkham replied. 'Not that I'm saying you're old or anything.'

Murphy turned, raised his eyebrows at DC Kirkham. 'I didn't think you were. I do now, of course.'

'Erm ... no, not at all. You're only a few years older than me.'

'You could probably add a couple more on to that few.'

Murphy thought he'd grow to like DC Kirkham over time. He knew when to be quiet and not make things worse. They drove on in silence, save for Roger Waters's pained vocals and Gilmour's wailing guitars, entering the town of Stoneycroft where Hannah Flynn's sister lived. Murphy parked the car before taking note of the address once more.

'Always check the address before ringing the doorbell,' he said, switching off the engine and unbuckling his seat belt. 'I once sat in the wrong house for half an hour before realising. Saves awkward conversations.'

'I'll make a note of that,' DC Kirkham replied, pulling out his notebook. Murphy waited for him to finish writing, unable to keep a bemused smirk off his face.

They didn't need to wait long after knocking, the door was almost swung off its hinges by the family liaison officer posted at the house. Murphy introduced himself and Kirkham to a blank stare, producing his ID when there was no movement from the officer.

'These new ones never recognise me,' Murphy muttered under his breath. 'Not sure if I like it or not.'

The house was well kept, but small. A terraced house on a nice street; one Murphy wasn't that familiar with, which meant it didn't see a lot of trouble. The carpets were a bit thin, but the furnishings all seemed to be made of a good quality dark wood, packed into the small space of the living room where they'd been left alone with Hannah's sister. Nicola Flynn was a brunette version of the blonde Hannah. A little softer in the face, but the resemblance was uncanny.

'Nicola, we just have a few questions, if that's okay?'

As Murphy was about to introduce himself Nicola burst into tears. He hadn't expected her to get upset straight away but it was as if she'd been waiting for him to arrive before opening the floodgates.

'I'm . . . I'm sorry. I, I just couldn't hold it in any more.'

'It's okay,' Murphy said, moving towards where she was sitting on the sofa. He sat beside her, his hand hovering in the air, before resting on his own knee. 'I'm Detective Inspector David Murphy, this is Detective Constable Jack Kirkham. We're very sorry about Hannah and Greg. Take your time.'

'Thank you,' Nicola replied, her crying easing off. 'It's all just so unreal. I've been sitting here since me mum left with Millie, just watching the news.' She pointed to the TV displaying *BBC News*, its red banner crawling across the screen. 'I wasn't expecting the video of Chloe and Joe to come on. That woman you sent here told me to turn it off, but I couldn't. It just doesn't seem real.'

'I'm sorry you had to see that,' Murphy said. 'We're working to get the news channels not to show it.'

'It hardly matters now, does it? It'll be everywhere. And that's the same thing that happened to Hannah and Greg. I refuse to watch that one. Don't make me.'

'We'll try to make sure that doesn't happen,' Murphy said, turning to DC Kirkham and motioning at him to sit down. 'Your mum told us earlier that Hannah only told you and her about what happened with Millie—'

'That's not really true,' Nicola interrupted. 'That's just what me mum thinks. There were a couple of other people who knew. Just Hannah's close friends though. And not the whole story. What's happening? Have you found out who did this yet?'

'We're working on it, Nicola. We just need to ask a few questions, get a fuller picture of Hannah and Greg.'

'But there's nothing to tell,' Nicola said, staring at the now-muted television. 'They were just . . . normal. Apart from the Millie thing, but even that wasn't a big deal.'

Murphy shifted in his seat; his view of a 'big deal' was obviously very different from Nicola's. 'Who knew of Hannah's secret?'

Nicola gave a couple of names, which Murphy made sure DC Kirkham wrote down. 'That was it though, no one else. We were all sworn to secrecy. It was really difficult for her, but she decided not to tell Greg. It would have destroyed him . . . I guess in the end, it did.'

Murphy waited for the tears to start falling again, but it looked like he was safe. 'Did they have any arguments, or fallings out, that sort of thing?'

'Not that I know of,' Nicola replied, flopping back into the sofa and running both of her hands through her hair. 'This is all just so weird.'

'I know, but we're going to find out what's happened, okay?'

Nicola nodded, leaving one hand in her hair to play with it. 'They had a couple of tiffs, but nothing major at all. Hannah used to say it was the most normal relation-ship she'd ever had. She was devastated when she made that one mistake. Millie is just gorgeous, though, and Greg was so good with her. No one needed to know the truth. It wouldn't have helped anyone.'

'Do you know who the father is?'

Nicola shook her head firmly. 'Hannah didn't even know. It was some bloke in a club she went off with. Absolutely stupid of her, but then, she did do some stupid stuff. She wasn't sure if she was going to stay with Greg at the time, so some bloke said all the right things to her and got her on her own. She never did anything like that again.'

'They didn't have any contact at all afterwards?'

'She never said they did. She just wanted to put the whole thing behind her.'

'Her and Greg were having problems at one point then?' DC Kirkham said from the other side of the room.

'Oh, that was just silly shite. Hannah was getting a bit fed up with the way he was. Greg was a good guy, but he could be a bit boring. She wasn't sure he was totally committed to her. It wasn't his fault, but Hannah just wanted something more out of life. When she got preg-nant, she grew up a bit. Decided things weren't that bad after all. That being content was much better. She loved him.'

Murphy glanced at the TV screen, its presence making him a little nervous, given the events of the day. 'So, they were happy, but this secret Hannah was keeping must have been difficult?'

'Not really,' Nicola replied, sitting forward and clasp-ing her hands together. 'She just got on with it. It was for the best. She told us late on in the pregnancy, when she was working out dates and stuff. I always thought that's how Greg would find out, but he never questioned it. Just got on with it and never said a word.'

Murphy asked a few more questions about the relationship, but received much the same responses. 'What about from the outside, did they have any issues with anyone, any confrontations or arguments?'

Nicola thought for a few seconds before replying. 'No, not that I know of. She left that for me.'

'Why do you say that?' Murphy said, glancing at the time on the TV screen, noticing it was later than he'd thought.

'Oh, just some problems at work. Some bloke who is a bit weird, that's all. Nothing I can't handle. Thankfully, they've given me some time off, after what happened this morning. Not that I would have gone in anyway.'

'Okay,' Murphy said, lifting himself off the sofa and producing a card from his pocket. 'If you think of anything else, this is the direct number for our team. Call any time, okay?'

'Yeah, great. Do you think we'll be able to see her soon? Mum is a bit anxious to say goodbye . . .'

The tears were threatening to start up again. 'It won't be too long,' Murphy said. 'We're going as fast we possibly can for you all.'

Once outside, Murphy turned to DC Kirkham. 'How many death knocks and interviews with relatives have you done?'

'Too many,' DC Kirkham said, waiting for Murphy to key the central locking so he could open his door. 'Always different, aren't they?'

'Like you wouldn't believe. They don't get any easier, either. That's just a lie. You learn to get used to them though.'

'I think I'm halfway there.'

Murphy opened his door and got into the car, shoving his paperwork onto the back seat. 'I'm going to drop you back the station and nip off for an hour.'

'Okay . . . no problem. Anything I can help with?'

Murphy thought about the man he was going to see. A foot shorter and heavier by at least five stone.

'No, it's fine,' Murphy replied, shifting the car into gear and driving away. 'Nothing I can't handle.'

Chapter Twenty-Three

There was a time Murphy could have ended up somewhere like this. A dingy little ground-floor flat in a converted building in Speke, round the corner from where he'd grown up. Graffiti covered the brick outside, and an overflowing bin sat next to the front door – the smell of rotting rubbish becoming the stench of desperation. The drawn faces of the few people walking through to the main road were grey and resigned.

There was barely any upward mobility to be seen here, Murphy thought. No chance of escape, a path to a better life. It was why he didn't live here now. The sentimental feelings outweighed by the knowledge of what the place stood for.

The people were good, but driven into the ground by the lack of support. Things hadn't changed enough over the years.

Jess had felt the same way. She'd also moved away and built a life for her and her son. Peter.

Murphy shook the memory from his mind, attempting to focus on the matter at hand. He thought about Amy Maguire and what he could do for her. Imagined she was someone he could save.

He knocked on the door with a closed fist, rattling the old wood in its frame. Banged again when a few seconds had passed without a response. He heard footsteps clattering from within and thought he heard Keith Hudson almost falling over his feet as he ran to answer the door.

'Who's there?'

Murphy hadn't expected that. Usually people just answered the door.

'Delivery,' Murphy said, hoping Keith didn't recognise his voice.

'Not expecting anything.'.

'Is it Mr K Hudson?'

'What is it?'

Murphy was becoming bored already. He wondered if one kick would be enough to put the door through. Judging by the cracks in the wooden frame, it probably wouldn't take much. 'No idea, mate.'

'Just leave it there,' Keith said from behind the door, with an attempt at sounding gruff, Murphy thought. 'I'll get it later.'

'Need you to sign for it, mate.'

'Fuck's sake . . .' Murphy heard before a bolt was pulled back from the inside. Maybe more than one kick then. The door opened slowly, half a face appearing in the crack. 'Wait . . .'

That was all Keith had a chance to say before Murphy stuck a foot in the gap and pushed the door back with one hand. Keith was knocked back into the wall and to his knees, as Murphy entered, closing the door behind him.

'Sorry about that, Keith,' Murphy said, offering him a hand. 'Didn't think you'd want to talk to me if I just announced myself.'

Keith ignored the proffered hand and lifted himself to his feet, brushing off the dust from his torn jeans. 'Yeah, you're right. My brief said I'm not to talk to any of you lot without her. She made me promise . . .'

'Well, she's not here right now. And I'm not here to start anything. I just want a word, that's all.'

'I've got nothing to say.'

Murphy looked to his left and at the open door leading from the communal hall into Keith's flat. 'Through here, are you?' he said, walking in.

'Hey, you can't do that,' Keith said from behind Murphy as he entered. The smell of damp and dust hit him as he walked into what passed as a living room doubling as a kitchen–diner. He looked round the small area, noting the familiar black mould in the corners of the room and the dust motes floating in the air, waiting to enter your throat and settle in. The curtains were drawn so only a pale light illuminated the room.

'Nice place,' Murphy said.

'You have to leave,' Keith said, standing in the doorway. 'Or I'm going to call the . . . erm . . .'

'Me?'

'She'll have your job for this. She's good is my brief. Doesn't take any shit.'

'Oh, I know. She's great. You should try and find some money so you always have her around. She won't always be the one appointed to you.'

Keith shifted on his feet, arms crossed over his body. 'What do you want?'

'Just to talk,' Murphy replied, finishing with the niceties. 'About why you came into my life the other day, confessing to that murder.'

'It was all a mistake,' Keith said, raising a hand and scratching at his head. Dandruff flew into the air. 'I was confused, that's all.'

'And you're not now?'

'No, I'm not.'

'Good. I'm glad to hear that. The only thing is, I'm not completely satisfied with that. I think there is more to it.'

Keith shook his head, Murphy wondering if his brain was about to spill out of his ears with the vigorousness of the action. 'Definitely not. I was just having a bad time of it. Felt a bit ill. Not right in the head and that. It was all just made up.'

'Are you sure about that? Only there were some things that you said that made sense. Did you kill the girl, Keith?'

'I didn't, honest. I . . . I just made a mistake. I'm all right now, though. Saw the doctor and everything.'

Murphy thought back to what DS Ayris from Liverpool South had said about Keith having mental health issues. The way the flat looked made him feel no better. In the kitchen was an overflowing open-topped bin, frozen meal wrappers and cartons perched on top. A microwave, which might have been considered new when Murphy was still a teenager, was the only thing on the counter apart from a kettle with a frayed power lead. Evidence of someone who couldn't look after himself, never mind anything else.

Still, he couldn't be certain. And he had to be.

'That's not good enough for me, Keith. See the thing is, I have a thing about girls just up and disappearing. Get's right on my wick. So, I'm not going to just accept your word for it.'

'I've got nothing else to say,' Keith replied. 'Please, I want you to go.'

Murphy stood still for a second, weighing up what to do next. 'So, you just knew Amy from where she worked?'

'That's all. When she disappeared, I missed her. She used to talk to me nicely when I went into the shop. One of the only ones who did. Always smiled at me. Treated me well. Everyone else around here just thinks I'm the local nutter, but I'm not. I've just been unlucky, that's all.'

'So why would you say you killed her?'

Keith looked down at the torn carpet at his feet. 'I was worried.'

'Worried about what?'

'That I had. That I'd done something to her. To make her disappear. I didn't want her to go away, but sometimes I do things and don't remember them. I heard her voice and thought it was my head telling me I'd done something. That's sometimes how it happens. I'm not well, I told you.'

Murphy crossed the space between them in two strides, his long legs covering the short distance with ease. Keith jumped back, but Murphy grabbed him by his crumbling T-shirt, forcing him against the wall.

'Tell me the truth,' Murphy said, a globule of saliva spraying from his mouth and hitting the now cowering Keith on the cheek. 'What did you do? Tell me what you did, right fucking now, or I swear to God I'm going to bash your fucking head into this wall. Tell me.'

A door opened and closed somewhere out in the corridor, Keith's head snapping towards the noise and then back to Murphy. 'I don't . . . I didn't do anything.'

'You're a liar,' Murphy said, grabbing Keith's jaw with one hand and squeezing. 'Tell me the truth.'

'I have,' Keith replied, tears springing from his eyes. 'Don't hurt me. Please.'

Murphy hesitated, seeing himself and what he was doing for a second. Then an image of Amy Maguire replaced the one of him and he gripped tighter.

'If you don't tell me everything you know now, that's it, Keith. I won't even kill you. Just leave you a fucking vegetable, do you understand? Just enough so you understand what's going on. All those thoughts and voices in your head and you won't be able to fucking move. You won't be able to make them go away.'

'Please,' Keith said, now sobbing and trying to prise Murphy's hands off him. 'Somebody help me, please.'

Murphy hesitated again, loosening his grip on Keith. 'You don't know anything, do you?'

The crying was louder now. It was like a drill in Murphy's ears as he stepped back and let go of the shivering and shaking man in front of him. 'I'm sorry. I . . . I just need to find her.'

'Go away,' Keith said, his arms crossed over himself again. 'Leave me alone.'

Murphy walked out, leaving the door open behind him as he left the flat and stepped onto the street outside. A tracksuit-wearing lad who couldn't be out of his teens skirted round him pushing a buggy. The man-boy adjusted his baseball cap with one hand, muttering something under his breath as he turned the corner.

Murphy reached into his pocket, took his car keys out and, after a few attempts, managed to push the button on the fob. His hands shook as he crossed the street and walked to the car.

Once inside, he gripped the steering wheel, his knuckles going white. He bent his head towards it, swearing to himself in a whisper. He looked up, expecting the street to suddenly fill with police cars, ready to arrest one of their own for assault, but it remained empty.

Murphy turned the key and put his foot down, tyres squealing as he tore out of there.

* * *

Sarah's hands were shaking as well. Not that she had any idea that back in her home city her husband's were doing the same.

She refused to shed a tear. She could feel that familiar lump at the back of her throat, but tried to ignore it. She wasn't going to let it happen.

He wasn't going to win.

She hadn't known what to expect. Not really. When the letter had arrived, letting her know she'd been asked to visit, everything within her said to just throw it away. Move past it and try to drive the memories back down.

Another voice had piped up. One which wouldn't be silenced.

What if she could get some closure? Something to tell David, so he could also move on. Something that could remove a barrier.

Instead, she had got lies from that piece of shit, who was currently residing within the prison walls behind her. She banged the steering wheel in frustration, swearing loudly enough for someone walking past to give her a glance and then quickly scurry off.

Sarah calmed down a little, taking her phone out of her bag and looking at it. She went through her call list, found

David's number and hovered a thumb over the call button.
She pressed the message button instead and started typing.

I miss you. Hope you get home for an early night ;-) xx

She shook her head, turned the ignition and pointed
the car towards home. Tried to forget what she had just
heard and lock it away.

Resolved never to tell anyone else about what she had
done that day.

Chapter Twenty-Four

The sense of frenetic activity was beginning to wane as the day grew longer. Murphy had arrived back a few hours earlier. He'd sat in the car park, trying to work out what had just happened. What had caused him to snap so easily? Amy Maguire was missing, but it wasn't his case. There was a chance she was his daughter, yes, but he didn't really believe it. He knew what her mother, Stacey, was doing. If he was in her position, he didn't think there would be much he wouldn't do either.

After a few minutes, he'd calmed down enough to get out of his car and concentrate on what he was supposed to be doing.

Whilst the news channels breathlessly discussed what had happened so far that day, the detectives working in Major Crime were beginning to yawn and stretch in unison. Huddled round desks they were looking at new images and information which seemed to be doubling by the second.

'You all right?' Rossi said, as Murphy dropped into his chair and looked over at the murder board at the end of the room.

'Yeah, sound as a bloody pound, Laura. Anything happen whilst I was gone?'

Rossi didn't say anything at first, staring at him with those dark Mediterranean eyes of hers.

'Nothing much. Let's go for a walk.'

Rossi was out of her chair and walking away before Murphy had a chance to argue. She stood waiting near the door for him as he looked round the office for a distraction, finding none.

'What's going on?' Murphy said, once they had walked down the corridor a few steps. 'Something happened or what?'

Rossi turned on him, making him put his back to the wall. 'What's going on with you now?'

Murphy looked away. 'Nothing, Laura. Everything's fine.'

'No, it's not,' Rossi said, looking left and right to make sure no one was sharing the corridor with them. 'I've seen you like this before. Remember?'

'That was a long time ago. Everything's different now.'

'Is it? Only I seem to recall you saying much the same thing to me a few years back. Right before you were almost killed. Something is going on that you're not telling me about. I've been watching you, you know? The same distracted looks, having to repeat myself because you're not listening . . . I remember this, Murphy.'

Murphy leaned against the wall, looking down at Rossi. 'There's nothing to worry about, I'm good. There's a lot of pressure on us with this case and that . . .'

'It's not about this case.'

Murphy looked round him, trying to find an escape. Failed to do so. 'Fine. I was chasing something up.'

'To do with this?'

'No,' Murphy said, still not meeting Rossi's eyes. 'Amy Maguire.'

Rossi sighed and shook her head. 'What is it with you and that bloody case? I don't get it. It's not ours. It's some missing girl from South Liverpool that we have nothing to do with. Why do you keep going back to it?'

Murphy hesitated, realising he'd already said more than he'd wanted to. He finally looked at Rossi, sizing her up anew. Thought about trust and how it was earned.

'There's a possibility she's my daughter. A very small possibility, but one all the same.'

Murphy waited for a flinch or an admonishment. Rossi didn't move. He continued, giving her a little more of the history he had with Stacey. Still Rossi made no move. He waited a few seconds and was about to speak again, when she finally gave him a response.

'You know what's going on here, don't you?'

'Of course,' Murphy replied. 'I know the odds are massively against it being true. I'm 99 per cent sure that her mother is just desperate and trying to use me. But, I can't just ignore it.'

Rossi stared at him, Murphy holding her gaze. It became uncomfortable after approximately two seconds.

'You can't do this now,' Rossi said, finally looking away and taking a step back. 'You know it's bullshit. What can you really do on your own, anyway? You're not Liam bloody Neeson.'

'I need to leave it for them to sort out . . .?'

'Exactly. We've got six people dead and the killer is releasing videos to the media. We need to get this guy now, before we all look like *cazzos*.'

'Is that Italian for idiots?'

'Something like that. I'm serious, we're screwed at the moment. We've got next to nothing on this guy and I'm not sure what we're supposed to do, other than wait for him to make a mistake.'

Murphy put his hand on Rossi's shoulder. 'We'll find a way. We always do. Don't worry, I'll let Liverpool South sort the Amy Maguire case. There's nothing I can do, so I promise, this has got my undivided attention from now on. Let's go back in there and get everyone together.'

Rossi murmured her agreement and walked away, Murphy following behind her after a second or two. He hoped Rossi believed his lie. He took a deep breath and entered the office.

'Right everyone,' he said, his voice loud enough to make a young DC who was sitting nearest to the door jump in her chair. 'Meeting room now.'

Murphy waited for everyone to scramble from their desks, picking up various notepads and files along the way. He stood to the side as they hurried past, whispered conversations coming to a halt. DC Harris waited at the end of his desk for everyone to go past before wheeling himself along behind them.

'I've missed these gatherings,' DC Harris said, as he went past Murphy.

'We can have them hourly if you'd like, Graham?'

DC Harris snorted and carried on into the room. Murphy shared a look with Rossi at the door, then followed her inside.

It was always a little jolt when he realised the number of people now working under his command in Major Crime. Once, there had been himself and Rossi, along with a couple of DCs on a rotating basis, investigating things as they came in. Now, staff numbers were in double figures, with more working in different places in uniform waiting to be called upon. All waiting for him to speak, to lead.

It was equal parts fun and daunting.

'Okay,' Murphy said, quietening down the room in an instant. 'Things are moving along but we need to find this guy soon. What's the current situation on the videos, Harris?'

DC Harris produced a piece of paper from somewhere in his chair. 'Sky and BBC have agreed to only show stills from the videos, but they're refusing to stop talking about them constantly. Nothing we can do there. ITV will be doing their own thing later, our press team are in contact with them over that. The websites are all showing the video in its entirety, linking to the sites we can't control. YouTube have taken down a few videos now. That may become a losing battle.'

'They're out there now, I suppose. Nothing we can do. And no way of tracking them either, I'm guessing?'

'Not entirely,' DC Harris replied. 'We've spoken to Twitter, which is where the video was originally posted. They've suspended the account and sent us the details of where it was created and accessed from.'

'That's good,' Murphy said, breaking into a smile. 'We've got him then. All that technological stuff means we can track him to house, right?'

'Not really,' DS Rossi said, looking towards DC Harris who shook his head. 'Tell him where the trace came back to.'

Murphy turned back towards DC Harris, his smile gone as quickly as it had appeared.

'Some café in Bootle that has free Wi-Fi. We can't even trace the phone as it was a pre-pay one.'

'CCTV?'

'The account was created months ago and the café only has one camera. They delete the footage after a couple of weeks. Nothing doing there.'

'Is there any good news?'

DC Kirkham cleared his throat. 'I think I might have something,' he said.

'Go on,' Murphy replied, hoping he was right.

'Well, the email address the killer provided was with a major provider. We've asked for records and such like. Taking a bit longer, but we should be able to find out where he was when he accessed the email account.'

'Isn't that going to lead us to the same thing as the Twitter account though?'

DC Kirkham didn't shake his head, but he did look down. 'He'll . . . he'll have to look at them again, though. Today. You know . . .'

'To choose his next couple,' a voice said from behind the DC. 'How can he follow through on his promise unless he checks?'

There was silence in the room, before someone near the back muttered under his breath. Within seconds the noise level had increased.

'All right, everyone, that's enough,' Murphy said, his hands raised in the air. 'Kirkham, you get in contact with those email people again. Throw everything we have at them and get the information as soon as you bloody can, okay?'

Murphy looked towards Rossi who stepped forwards. 'Post-mortem on the third couple – Greg and Hannah

– will be happening in about an hour. Hale, you're with me on that one.'

DC Hale turned a shade of grey for a second, before slowly nodding.

'We're waiting on the drug reports for Chloe and Joe to come in any second. Everyone is working to get this sorted out as soon as possible, so that should help for any requests you have of other departments. With the first couple, some type of anaesthetic drug was used, so we need to look into possible places the killer could have got that from.'

Murphy kept the wince on the inside. That wasn't proving to be a simple task. 'I want people chasing up reports of thefts at hospitals, doctors' surgeries, pharmacies, everywhere you can think of on that one.' He pointed at a couple of people and assigned the task to them. 'Good, now we're getting somewhere.'

'Who's been going through CCTV?' Rossi said, scanning the room.

'That'll be me.' A DC near the back raised her hand. 'Got nothing suspicious at the moment. Two cars, but both came back as taxis . . .'

'Check them out,' Rossi said, Murphy giving her a quick look as they both remembered a case from a few years earlier.

The meeting didn't last much longer, but Murphy could already tell that it had had an effect. He was always good at galvanising other people. Rossi smiled at him as everyone filed back to their desks.

'Better?' Murphy said, once everyone had left.

'Much. Looks like we've got more than we thought. He'll have screwed up at some point. We'll have him soon enough.'

'Let's hope so. I really don't want a fourth couple. I can't be dealing with any more of these secrets.'

Rossi began to speak, then stopped herself.

'What, go on, say what you were going to say,' Murphy said, folding his arms across himself.

'It's nothing,' Rossi said, gathering up the files she'd brought into the room with her.

'No, it is. I'm listening now, okay?'

'It's just, I think there's more to it than just exposing secrets.'

Murphy scratched at his elbow and began to stand up straight from where he had been leaning against a desk. 'Does it matter, really?'

'It could do,' Rossi replied, standing in front of him, files in the crook of her arm. 'I'm just saying it could be something more than just a random guy playing games.'

Murphy sighed, uncrossed his arms and gave Rossi a withering look. 'I'm sure he has all kinds of reasons for doing what he's doing, but for now, I just want to catch him and get him off my streets. Sound fair?'

Rossi didn't answer. She nodded and began walking out of the door. As she was about to open it and leave she turned back round. 'I just don't want to miss anything important, you know? Something that might help us catch him sooner.'

'I know, Laura,' Murphy replied, walking towards her. 'But sometimes we've just got to concentrate on what's in front of us. Send a report of what we have so far to the profiling team – for all the good that will be – but let's get on with what we have and then see where we are, okay?'

Murphy followed Rossi out of the room before returning to his desk and going through the information he'd just been told minutes earlier. A raft of messages, all concerning different aspects of the case, were waiting for him to read and discard.

The phone on his desk began to ring. Murphy picked it up as he continued to read.

'Murphy,' he said, still scanning the papers in front of him.

Ten seconds later the person on the other end of the line had his full attention. A minute later Murphy slammed down the phone and began clicking on his computer.

'Stupid piece of shite,' he said, louder than he'd wanted.

'What's going on?' Rossi said from opposite him.

'Come over here. Graham, you as well.'

DC Harris and Rossi made their way over as Murphy began to talk, struggling to keep up with Murphy as he spoke.

'Say that again,' Rossi said. 'He's sent us what?'

'He's sent us his password. We have access to the emails. People are sending him all kinds of stuff.'

DC Harris came round to Murphy's desk and placed himself next to him. 'Want me to do it?'

Murphy nodded and passed him the details he'd scribbled down on a piece of paper. 'The press team got the email from him. They've already checked the password works properly.'

'Here we go,' DC Harris said, swinging the monitor round for Murphy and Rossi to see. 'Over a thousand emails in there already.'

'*Mio dio . . .*'

'They can't all be sending him people to kill, surely?'

Murphy said, peering at the screen and waiting for DC Harris to start opening the messages.

'You can already tell from the subject lines that they're not.'

There was a sound from behind the three of them, making them all jump back a little.

'I think I have something,' DC Kirkham said, a grin on his face. 'He accessed the email address an hour ago. With a bit of digging, I've got an address.'

Murphy matched his grin. 'Let's go get the bastard.'

Chapter Twenty-Five

The house didn't feel right from the start. Murphy ignored that feeling, imagining a quick end to what felt like an unending investigation. Never mind that it had only been a few days; the fact that they had six bodies cooling in the morgue was enough. That was before he considered the media's twenty-four-hour coverage.

'Press is here already,' Murphy said to Rossi, pointing towards the end of the street which had been blocked off. 'Who the hell is telling them?'

'If this is the right place, they'll have a new story by tomorrow morning. Other people to piss off.'

Uniforms were stationed at both ends of the street, blocking access to enterprising news people who wanted to be as close to the action as possible. Every officer had been briefed about the case and told what to say, and what not to say, if asked questions.

Murphy just hoped that whoever was in the house wasn't watching the news and preparing to hop over the garden wall.

'Do we just knock?'

'Let firearms go in first,' Murphy said into the radio. 'We'll follow when everything is cleared.'

He and Rossi were sitting up front in the marked van, a few doors down from the house they had all converged on.

'Amazing how many people we can rustle up when there's something major going down. We ask for more money for stuff and get knocked back though.'

Rossi forced out a laugh beside him. 'Does this house strike you as the right place?'

Murphy shrugged. 'Takes all kinds,' he said, turning up the radio as the firearms officers approached the house. 'They can't all live up in Formby in big houses like our last one. Sometimes our serial killers live in two-bedroom terraces in Walton.'

'Suppose so.'

The light had faded fast outside, the dark clouds above them painting the scene in a dingy glow. 'At least it's not raining.'

Rossi didn't say anything, leaning forward against the dashboard to see more clearly what was happening ahead.

The house was on a street that branched off Long Lane, which ran alongside Everton Cemetery and playing fields. From halfway up the road, where they were parked, you couldn't see the green patch of land at the bottom of the road, just the houses which ran along each side. Two-bedroom terraces most of them, small houses for older couples and new families.

'*Back is secure.*'

Murphy turned the radio down a touch, the chatter a little loud for a small van. 'You're a red, right, Laura?'

'Yeah,' Rossi replied. 'But I don't really follow it.'

'*House seems quiet.*'

Murphy lifted up the radio and held it in mid-air. Kirkham and Hale, seated behind them in the back of the van, leaned forwards to listen. 'I got into it a bit more last season, but it's hard to watch every week.'

'It's weird not seeing Gerrard in a Liverpool shirt.'

'Yeah, he's been there so long he's part of the furniture. It was weirder when Carra left though.'

'Put the door in.'

'You're a blue, aren't you, Hale?'

'Yeah,' Hale said from the back of the van. 'Staunch Evertonian me.'

'Well, as long as you're not a bitter one, I don't mind.'

'On three . . .'

'What about you, Kirkham? Red or blue?'

'Neither. I support Tranmere Rovers.'

'One of the remaining few,' Murphy said, laughing as he turned back to look at him. 'Only joking. I'm sure there's more than a few left, even after being relegated. At least a thousand. You should tell your fellow wools that they need to get behind their team, rather than picking up ours over here.'

'Yeah, yeah.'

'Looks like movement,' Murphy said, moving forward. 'Wait a second.'

They went quiet in the van, listening to the radio as the chatter went silent, before voices broke in.

'Hallway clear . . . stairs clear . . . get down on the floor now. Get down on the fucking floor.'

Murphy opened the van door. 'Looks like someone's home,' he said, getting out.

*   *   *

The elderly woman was still shaking half an hour later, every now and then almost convulsing. If there wasn't a recent picture of her on the mantelpiece – a child under each arm – Murphy would have thought they had just turned her hair white. The hunched-over look was probably new, he thought.

'I'll be okay,' Joyce Langdon said, bony hands cupped round a hot cup of tea someone had made for her. 'Just a shock to have you storm in like that. You could have knocked, you know. I would have answered.'

'We're sorry, Mrs Langdon,' Murphy said, surveying the room. 'We can't be too careful. You understand? We'll have someone fix the door for you.'

Murphy looked towards Rossi who came over and sat next to Joyce. 'You're going to have to come down to the station with us, but I'm sure we'll have you back here in no time.'

'Fine, fine,' Joyce said, lifting the cup up to her mouth. 'I don't have to wear handcuffs or anything, do I? Only the neighbours will think I've done something wrong.'

Murphy thought that was already going to be the case. 'I think we can skip those for now.'

They had known that they didn't have their man pretty much as soon as they'd walked in. The firearms officers had done their work leaving Joyce Langdon face down on her mottled red carpet, arms up her back and pinned to the floor. A quick search of the property had yielded enough evidence to suggest they weren't in the right place.

You could never be too careful though.

'Can we just ask you a few questions, Joyce?' Murphy said, needing to know for sure.

'Yeah, of course. What's this all about?'

Murphy turned and looked at the Blaupunkt flat screen TV in the corner. He picked up the remote. 'Do you mind?' Murphy said, keying the buttons before Joyce had the chance to answer.

The now familiar scrolling black text on yellow background appeared on the screen. Along with a view which Joyce recognised.

'That's the bottom of this road!' she said, a high-pitched exclamation escaping her mouth. 'What are they doin' – Oh, no.'

Across the bottom of the screen, words appeared.

ARMED POLICE RAID HOUSE: IN CONNECTION
WITH 'CHLOJOE' MURDERS

Murphy pressed mute on the remote and placed it down on the mantelpiece. 'Joyce, have you got anything to say?'

'I . . . I have nothing to do with anything like that. Honest, you've got to believe me. I'm a pensioner. I'm seventy-nine years old, for Christ's sake. I couldn't do anything like that even if I wanted to. Didn't you see the Stannah on the stairs?'

Murphy had, which had been the first indication that something wasn't right.

'Is there anyone else who lives here with you, Joyce?'

'No, just me now. Gerry passed away three years ago, God rest his soul. This would have killed him off if he hadn't already gone to the other side. Always had a dodgy ticker.'

'So, there's no children, grandchildren?'

'We only had the one. My Barbara. She's got two kids. Both girls.'

Murphy was beginning to wonder whether technology was all it was cracked up to be.

'Did we get the wrong house?' he whispered to Rossi.

'No,' she said, writing something down in her note-book and then scanning the room. 'Do you have a computer at all, Joyce?'

'Oh, yes, but I never use it. Barbara gave me her old laptoppy thing, but I can't work it. Told me I could be one of those golden surfers . . .'

'Silver surfers,' Rossi said.

'Yes, that's right,' Joyce said, perking up slowly. 'That's what she said. Truth is, I haven't had it out for months. It's in the cupboard, next to the good plates, in the back room, if you want to see it.'

'Do you have internet here, Joyce?' Murphy said, look-ing for a router. 'A box that lets you connect to the internet?'

'Yes, it's behind the telly. The cable people told me I needed it to watch all the old programmes they have on the planner thing. I've never touched it. I leave all that to Barbara to sort out for me.'

'Can you just excuse us for a moment, Mrs Langdon?' Murphy inclined his head to one side at Rossi and walked away into the hallway. 'She doesn't have a clue what the internet is,' he said, once they were out of earshot. 'Never mind how to use the thing for posting videos and that. There must be someone who comes here.'

'Maybe,' Rossi said, digging around in her pocket and

producing her work phone. 'I'm just thinking there might be something else.'

'Because technology has done well for us so far . . .'

'Shush a second, Grandad.'

'I'm hurt by that comment,' Murphy said under his breath. 'Not even forty yet.'

'Just give me a second.'

Murphy held up his hands, shaking his head.

'Here we go,' Rossi said a minute or so later, turning the phone to face Murphy. 'Her Wi-Fi is unlocked.'

'Shit . . .'

'Anyone parked on the street could hook up to it and then everything traces back to here. That's why we've got this address.'

'That's if she's sure there's no one else who has access to this house,' Murphy said, rubbing his temples. 'What if it's her daughter, or her son-in-law? It could be anyone.'

'I think my idea makes more sense than the suggestion that this woman has forgotten about a load of visitors.'

'How would our guy know the internet wasn't protected here? Tell me that then.'

Rossi went silent for a few moments, before raising a finger in the air. 'He was looking for one. He knew if he did anything online, we'd eventually trace him. He could have an untraceable phone for all we know. Chuck a pay-as-you-go SIM card in it and it's job done.'

Murphy mused for a few seconds. 'Okay, if we can really prove that there isn't anyone else with access to this house, then fine, I'll go along with it. Still seems a bit strange that he could drive here and use Wi-Fi like that.'

'That's modern technology for you,' Rossi said, putting the phone back in her pocket and walking towards the living room. 'Unless you know how it works, it's all so confusing.'

Murphy aimed a push towards Rossi's back, but she skipped away with a smirk.

Media

He was transfixed by the television as shifting graphics ran across the screen and collided with the edge. Images flashed up on one side of the screen while an impossibly dapper man with a suitably serious face talked from the other. The images were repeated over and over; the same faces and same voices, saying the same things. Nothing new being reported, nothing new being spoken.

It was all because of him.

He was expecting a live interview with Kay Burley and him sitting in his home to appear at any point. Always at hand to appear at any tragic event or ongoing incident.

That was how it was now – the same faces at every tragedy, ready with a microphone and a po-faced look.

The way it all worked sickened him.

He remembered how he'd watched two buildings collapse on the other side of the Atlantic on a balmy September day. It was an aberration; their destruction something that united people across the world as they watched it unfold. An event unlike anything they had seen before; the mass killing of thousands of people live on television.

He had watched it, almost hypnotised by the images: planes slamming into buildings, scared New Yorkers running through dust-cloud-ridden streets, flailing bodies disappearing into nothingness.

Since then, violence had become prevalent on news channels, he thought. Beamed into living rooms, all for the viewers' pleasure. The Iraq war, dead civilians piled up on streets, suspected terrorists tortured and humiliated. Hostage situations in Sydney and Paris. The London bombings, the armed sieges. The Boston Marathon bombing and its subsequent man hunt.

Raoul Moat, Derrick Bird. Mass killings as entertainment.

All shown live on a flat screen television or an electronic device of your choice. Twenty-four hours a day.

He had watched all these events. Looked up videos on the internet when the TV channels decided not to show them live. Beheadings and executions. He wanted to experience them all.

Society loved violence. It was everywhere, on every TV, inside every newspaper, at football matches, nightclubs – every event with more than one person. It lurked beneath the surface, just waiting to be examined, enacted. Love was the ultimate violence. He believed that with everything he had to give. Now, he was giving them what they wanted. Violence.

He thought back to a couple of years previously, when Liverpool had gained notoriety with the man who called himself Alan Bimpson. The image of him walking down the streets of the city with an automatic rifle, gunning people down, teenagers and elderly alike, had been burned into viewers' minds.

The same detective who'd failed to save that final victim now hunting him.

Society had changed. Violence was the new norm, making them all so different.

Today he was responsible for the latest story which was keeping people riveted and engrossed.

* * *

Later, back in that room he was now so familiar with, his voice spoke into the shadows. 'I'm not sure when things changed. When this became entertainment for so many of us. I think it might be twenty-four-hour news. Now we have the ability to change channel at any point and ingest a small morsel before moving on. Or there's the invention of the internet, imparted to the masses to consume and enjoy. With that comes social media, the new conduit of society, the way in which conversation and argument is held. Offence given and taken. What do you think, Number Four?'

He didn't wait for an answer.

'I consume it all. I'll read and watch everything I can manage.'

He allowed it to fuel him, scrolling through comments on the various websites which were all talking about him and his actions. The account he had created to post the video online had been taken down in the hours since, but there were still comments naming him by that stupid moniker he had chosen.

'I'm trending on Twitter,' he said with a chortle. 'I never expected that to happen.'

He had needed only one email. Somewhere local, so he didn't have to travel. The emails he had received had reached the hundreds within an hour. Most were calling him every insult imaginable, listing the violence that should be inflicted upon him. The things he should do to himself, before he was caught and cost them money by being imprisoned.

SUBJECT – KILL YOURSELF
SUBJECT – FUCK YOU!!!!
SUBJECT – YOUR DEAD
SUBJECT – THIS COUPLE SHOULD BE NEXT

One email was all he required.

It had come an hour or so after the address had been posted online. A Liverpool-based couple, with a secret held on each side. He had noted down the details after accessing the email account via an open Wi-Fi spot he had found at a house near where he worked. He'd discovered that lots of people were still not up to speed with current technology and left their internet open to anyone passing, unprotected by a password.

The easiest way for him to stay under the radar.

They could trace the IP address, he guessed, but all they would find was a confused silver surfer in a two-bedroomed terraced house.

Not enough.

He had opened a few other emails but there was something about the first story that he had been attracted to. Concise and explicit. He had deleted the emails he had looked at, emptying the trash folder so no one else would see them. He left the rest there unread.

'This is the new couple. What do you think?'

He sat beside Number Four, leaning into her as she

shifted. He laid his head on her shoulder and moved the mobile phone into her eye line. 'It's the same story you always hear. Someone trapped in a lie. Choosing what they know and are comfortable with, rather than what could be. That's not how it should be. I can save them. This couple will be the ones. They'll see what I'm trying to do. I can feel it.'

Back at that anonymous street, he had sent one final email, hoping it would be all that was needed to make his point. He'd found the email address easily enough. Typed out a one-line message and clicked the send button, before logging off the free Wi-Fi and returning back to Number Four.

To Merseyside Police. The password for this account is loveisviolence.

Chapter Twenty-Six

It was a few hours later when Murphy finally left the station. The clock in his car announced he'd been at work for almost fourteen hours, which wasn't a record, but it had been a while since that had happened. His phone had been buzzing in his pocket periodically for a few hours. Murphy knew who it was so he hadn't even bothered to look.

He drove away from the station and down St Anne Street, waiting until he was a good distance from it before turning down a side street and pulling out his phone.

Stacey Maguire – six missed calls.

Murphy keyed the call back button and lifted the phone to his ear.

Stacey answered after only one ring. 'I've been trying to get hold of you for ages,' she said, without a greeting.

'I've been busy,' Murphy said, suppressing a yawn. 'You know I'm involved in the other case.'

'Yeah, that bloody ChloJoe one. How could I forget? Now my Amy doesn't have a chance of anyone doing anything, does she?'

'That's not true, Stacey . . .'

'Of course it is. I know the score. Tell me you're still trying to find out where she is, David. They're not telling me anything down here. Just putting me through to some kid who doesn't know his arse from his elbow.'

Murphy rubbed the bridge of his nose with his free hand. 'The guy who came in at the beginning of the week . . .'

'I still can't believe they let him out. He must know something. Why would he just confess like that and then say he was lying?'

'Listen, Stace, what I'm about to tell you stays between us, okay? I'm serious, if this got back to anyone, I wouldn't be able to help any more.'

'No problem. I won't say anything.'

Murphy paused, still unsure if it was a good idea to tell her or not. Decided it wouldn't come back on him and would save the detectives in Liverpool South any more questions. 'I went to see him.'

'The guy who confessed? What did he say? Did you find out where she is? Oh my God, oh my God . . .'

'Calm down,' Murphy said, immediately regretting saying anything. 'I would have led with that if it was good news.'

There was silence over the phone for a second. 'What happened then?'

'I asked him a few questions. Made sure he was telling the truth . . .'

'He could be lying still.'

'No, he's definitely not. He had nothing to do with this. He doesn't know where Amy is, Stacey. I'm sorry.'

'Are you sure?'

Murphy felt a growing pain behind his eyes. The start of one of his oh-so-bloody-wonderful tired headaches. 'I'm sure. We're no closer, I'm sorry.'

'What am I supposed to do now, David? I thought you were going to help me. Help us both. You haven't been there for her for almost nineteen years, you should be doing more.'

'Why haven't I been there for nineteen years? Because I didn't know she existed until a week ago.'

'There's no need to shout,' Stacey replied, huffing down the line at him. 'I need someone in the police to help me find my daughter. That's all.'

'I'm doing all I can. I think it's best that we leave it to CID near you now. If I get involved any more, they're going to start asking more questions. I'll keep in touch with them, though. Make sure they know the importance of it. And I'll do the best I can to ask more questions around the place. Make sure every copper in the city knows to be on the lookout for her.'

Murphy listened as Stacey Maguire berated him for a few more minutes, accepting the insults and heartbreak.

'Please, please keep trying. I need someone to help us. You could be her dad. Doesn't that mean anything?'

'Of course it does,' Murphy said, trying to keep the venom out of his voice. The certainty that he wasn't Amy's father had risen to 99.5 per cent over the course of the conversation. 'I will try my best.'

Murphy hung up and pointed his car towards home and drove away.

* * *

Rossi was expecting an easy evening. A couple of hours in front of the latest box set she was catching up with, then an early night. Ready to get back to work the next day, fresh and revitalised. The night shift would have messages to pass on to her and the rest of the team, but until then, she could just switch off.

That was until she spotted the figure on her doorstep.

She stopped dead at the entrance to her path. Tried to decide whether to confront or run. The street lights weren't making a dent into the darkness of her doorway, all she could see was a shadow in human form.

'Laura?'

Her heart didn't stop thumping, but it began to calm from the jackhammer it had been moments earlier. She took her hand away from her back pocket where it had been resting – the weapon inside it unused once more – and swallowed. '*Vaffanculo*. You scared the life out of me.'

'I'm sorry,' Darren said, stepping away from the door. 'I just had to see you. I tried ringing, but it was going straight to voicemail.'

Rossi remembered turning her phone off when they had begun the house raid on what had turned out to be an old woman, with an almost as ancient laptop. She hadn't switched it back on again. She lifted it out of her pocket. 'Had to switch it off. Work stuff.'

'You going to invite me in?'

Rossi walked towards Darren, shrugging him off as he went to plant a kiss on her. 'Not out here. My neighbours are prudes.'

Darren laughed and placed his hands on her shoulders as she opened the door. 'Let them see. About time they had something to talk about around here.'

'*Stai zitto!* Be quiet. Just get in, will you.'

An hour later, lying in bed next to Darren, Rossi could feel her eyes closing. 'If you don't want to stay, I suggest going now. I'm going to be asleep any second.'

'I'll have to go,' Darren said. 'I've got an early shift in the morning and I don't want to wake you. Looks like you're dead on your feet.'

'I am now, thanks to you.'

Darren touched a palm to his chest. 'I am honoured to make you feel that way.'

Rossi sometimes didn't know if he was joking or being serious. That was the only thing that made her pause. If he was kidding, all was good. If not, then some of the things he said were slightly . . . weird.

The sex was good though. Very good, she thought. Best she'd had for a long time and that was saying something.

'You're best going then,' Rossi said, turning over onto her side. 'Do us a favour, lock the door on your way out and post the keys.'

'No problem,' Darren said, sitting on the edge of her bed and pulling on his trousers.

Rossi was almost asleep when she became aware of him standing over her.

'I'll speak to you tomorrow or something,' she said, half into the pillow.

'Okay,' Darren said, leaning down to lay a kiss on the top of her head. 'Speak later.'

She was never sure if he was joking or being serious. That's why she didn't respond when he stood at her bedroom doorway and whispered, 'I love you.'

Rossi let sleep consume her instead.

*   *   *

He saw her car as he pulled into the driveway – she'd parked a bit further down the road, her licence plate briefly illuminated in his headlights. Murphy frowned as he snapped off The Who mid-squeal and got out of the car. He let himself into the house, waiting to hear voices but instead was greeted only by silence.

'Hello?'

There was a murmur from behind the living-room door as he removed his coat and hung it up. 'Through here,' he heard Sarah say.

Murphy took a deep breath and pushed open the living-room door.

He was transported back a couple of years, before anything terrible had happened. He would return home to find his wife Sarah taking up one side of the sofa, her legs tucked up underneath her and a glass of wine half full on the small table in front of her, Jess sitting next to her. The sound of laughter and chatter emanating from the room, before he'd even entered. Two, three times a week this would be what greeted him when he came home.

Now, the scene was similar, but so different in many ways. Sarah was in her usual place, but she was sitting upright, her feet on the floor, a half-empty cup of tea in front of her. Jess was perched next to her, ready to stand up at any second, still wearing her coat.

'Hey,' Murphy said, not sure what was going on. 'Everything okay?' Sarah turned to him with puffy, red eyes. Not a great sign, he thought. 'What's going on?'

'I think you know, David,' Sarah said, looking away from him. 'Do you want to tell me what's been going on?'

Murphy locked eyes with Jess who returned his stare.

'What's been going on? What are you talking about?'

'Sit down, David,' Jess said, her voice calm and so unlike the angry tone he'd received before. 'Let's discuss this.'

Murphy perched on the arm of his chair, trying to run through excuses as to why he hadn't told Sarah the truth about what was going on. Trying to come up with lies he could tell, just so she wouldn't think badly of him. But his mind wasn't playing. Nothing coming to him easily.

'My client, Keith Hudson, called the office this afternoon,' Jess said, once she'd paused a few seconds to make Murphy sweat more. 'Said he'd had a visitor to his house.'

Murphy wanted to scratch his beard, play with an earlobe, anything. Instead, he kept his hands still, clasped together on his lap. 'Yeah, go on.'

'He said the big detective who had first interviewed him had come to his house, walked inside when he wasn't invited and then physically threatened him. Pushed him up against a wall and hurt him by grabbing him by the throat.'

Murphy didn't say anything, wondering when the actual body blow of Amy Maguire and her mother was going to appear.

'Why would you do that, David?' Sarah said, sitting forward on the sofa. 'You could be sacked for something like that.'

Murphy shook his head. 'No, that wouldn't happen.'

'Are you sure about that?' Jess said, raising an arched eyebrow. 'I've heard of people getting demoted for much less. You don't think a detective going round to an innocent man's house and assaulting him wouldn't result in a tribunal?'

'Assaulting him?' Murphy said, standing up and pacing towards the mantelpiece. 'It wasn't anything like that. I just thought he had more questions to answer and that's it. I had a bit of time, so I went over there.'

'Surely you can see that's not right?'

'Well, if you hadn't come along, Jess, and stopped him talking, maybe I wouldn't have had to do that, would I? There's a poor girl somewhere out there, waiting for someone to help her. What was I supposed to do?'

'You really think Keith Hudson had anything to do with it? You've met him, spent time with him. He's not well, David. It was bloody obvious to me. You're a detective and you couldn't work that one out?'

'You can never be too careful.'

'I think in this instance you ought to be,' Jess said, standing up and pulling her coat tighter across her body. 'He's not going to say anything for now, but that's only because I've convinced him not to. But you've got to sort yourself out.'

'Thanks, Jess,' Murphy said, attempting a smile as he gripped hold of the mantelpiece. 'I appreciate it.'

'I didn't do it for you,' Jess replied, turning away from him. 'I did it for Sarah. That's why she had to know, to make sure you don't make any more mistakes by hiding things away from her. She doesn't deserve to go through any of that. She's done nothing wrong. I won't do it again, though. Believe me. You mess up again and I won't be here warning you off.'

Murphy gazed down at the carpet, the edge of the rug he had never wanted to buy jutting out from underneath the coffee table. 'Okay.'

Jess headed for the door, Sarah jumping up as she did so and following her out of the room.

Murphy considered going after her, making another attempt at reconciliation, but knew it wasn't worth it. It still wasn't time.

He heard the door close and waited with his eyes still down. All thoughts of an early night now washed away as his mind clicked into gear.

'You want to tell me what's going on?' Sarah said as she entered the room.

Murphy lifted his head to look at Sarah, wanting to tell her so much. Everything that had happened in the previous few days. Why he was becoming slowly obsessed with the case of a missing girl he knew wasn't anything to do with him.

'It's nothing,' he said, putting one foot in front of the other and walking past her. 'Just work stuff. There's nothing to worry about. Just went a little bit too Gene Hunt, that's all. Won't happen again.'

He watched as Sarah took in what he said, waiting for her not to accept the lie. A look passed over her face, gone in an instant.

'Okay, fine. I've missed you today.'

Murphy smiled, glad the conversation was over. 'Well, I'm home now.'

Part Three

Will and Carly

There was a time when Will hadn't hated Carly. There must have been. A time when all he felt for her was love and nothing else. Now, he was used to her. He knew his life wouldn't be the same without her, but the love he'd originally felt was gone. He was stuck with her. That was all.

They had met at fifteen, when all he'd wanted to do was finally lose his virginity. To anyone, at that point. It didn't matter. All his mates had shagged someone, so it was his turn.

Carly just happened to be that someone.

Once that was out the way, they'd fallen into a relationship. It was just how things went. One day, Carly was some girl in his year at school, with tits bigger than most of the other girls'. Not one of the nicest looking in the year, but he had spent a few weeks chasing after her anyway. They'd finally had sex on the living-room floor of her auntie's house whilst Carly was meant to be babysitting.

Both of them couldn't wait to leave school, as if they had something to look forward to after it. They'd worked a few different jobs, leeched off parents for a bit, then moved in together. It seemed the done thing.

It hadn't taken long for Will to cheat for the first time. Since then, he'd lost count of how many other girls he'd been with. He'd grown into adulthood, looking better than Carly would have normally deserved, he thought. He knew he was out of her league, but that was just the way things went. She had problems keeping her weight down – he had problems keeping track of who he was fucking that weekend. Now, she was in bed early every night. Watching the same shit programmes on TV, then yawning and going off upstairs, leaving him to it. Making him smoke outside, rather than inside where he should have been able to.

He stepped out onto the step. It was pitch black out there; no neighbouring houses had their back lights on. He'd installed a light a year before, which turned on when something moved, but the bulb needed replacing. Another job he couldn't be arsed sorting.

'Night then,' Carly said from the kitchen door. 'See you in the morning.'

'Yeah, night, babe,' Will said, closing the door a little more behind him. 'Fucking bitch,' he then muttered under his breath. They'd argued again, her wanting to go out and see that sister of hers. He knew she only went round there to complain about him. She'd given up eventually, knowing she wouldn't win the argument.

He waited a few seconds, lit a cigarette, and then pulled his phone out. It was permanently in his pocket, so there was no chance of Carly finding anything on it. He always had to text first. Those were the rules.

The red glow from the end of his cigarette illuminated the smoke as it drifted away into the dark sky. He took another drag and started messaging the other girl in his life. The new one.

The only light in the yard was from his phone as his thumb danced across the screen. He got an instant response, smiled and messaged back. It wouldn't be long until the pictures started coming. He could already feel himself stirring at the thought of what he would soon see. What he could get her to send him.

He loved modern technology.

He sent another message, then locked the phone and put it back in his pocket. He threw the cigarette down and watched it float away. Then looked up.

Two eyes from behind a ski mask looked back at him.

* * *

There was a knife to his throat. The blade pressed against his skin, sharp and painful even without it piercing his neck. His breathing had slowed to an almost imperceptible amount, his fear of moving even an inch taking over. There was a smell above him, sweat and fast food. A hand was on his opposite shoulder to the knife, pressing into him, fingers digging into flesh.

'You can't forgive him, can you?'

The voice was hard, gritty. Spoken through clenched teeth, spittle flying onto the dining-room floor.

'He has lied and lied and there's nothing he can say to make that better. I can't help you, can I?'

Will knew who the man was, and what he had done. It was the talk of the city, so it wasn't as if he could have missed it. Everyone was talking about what had happened to ChloJoe, then that second couple. Then there was that couple from the Wirral.

And now them. Him and Carly were next.

A blade against his throat.

He was going to die, and it wasn't right.

*   *   *

Carly knew Will cheated on her. Well, knew as in suspected strongly. There were things that didn't add up, things he said and things he did. Sometimes you just know. That was why she didn't feel any guilt over what she had done with Adam. She wondered then if he was the man behind the mask, but only for a second. The body shape was wrong, the height different. The smell of his aftershave wasn't the same.

She had listened as Will was forced to confess what he'd been up to. Heard the stories of other women and what he had done. She wondered why she didn't feel anything. No hurt, no betrayal. Just a nothingness.

There was no love between them.

She thought there had been, back at the beginning. She had thought there was something special about meeting one another at such a young age, then staying together for all that time. Despite all the things people had said to her over the years, how it would never last, how they would eventually want something else, they had stayed the course. They had just gone on and on. Stuck with each other.

Carly had been scared about what single life would actually be like. She couldn't remember a time when she hadn't had someone at home, late at night. She was never alone. Not really. It didn't matter that she knew he no longer fancied her, never mind loved her. He preferred a skinny, platinum blonde on his arm, not the size twelve-fourteen she was, dark roots showing through her badly dyed hair.

She knew she was attractive, just not to Will any more. Yet, she couldn't make the break. Couldn't make the change she needed to.

Strapped to the chair, she knew she should have made different choices. Tried to do something other than settle. She should have allowed this relationship to fester and die.

Stubbornness had overruled self-preservation. She could have been happier. She could have had a better life than the one she'd settled for. That's what she thought now.

Now.

Now, all she could do was sit and watch as a man dressed in black began to cut into Will's throat with a sharp blade.

* * *

This wasn't love.

There was something there, he thought. Something underneath the surface. They weren't begging for their lives like the others had. They just sat there, waiting. They knew who he was, what he had come to do. They weren't prepared to fight for themselves or each other.

He didn't understand it.

He had waited a day, after driving to the house the night before and deciding against doing anything so rash as not planning it further. It was now Thursday night, only two days on from Greg and Hannah. Six days after Chloe and Joe.

He could feel sweat gathering underneath the ski mask, the heat under his dark clothes increasing by the second. He blinked away moisture, held the blade in trembling hands and prepared to begin.

'Finding you didn't take long. Although being given your address was a nice head start. See, someone wanted me to come here.'

He looked from face to face. 'I went online and trawled through what info I could find on you both. Facebook, etcetera. Yours was private, wasn't it, Carly?'

He traced a finger across her face, enjoying the flinch she gave in response. 'Could only see your profile picture and that was it. Will's, on the other hand, is open and easy to look at.'

He crouched in front of Carly, staring into her blue-green eyes and then giving her a wink. 'You know, when I first started out doing this, I would spend hours following people around, learning as much as I possibly could about them. The first couple I had in chairs facing each other, I didn't have the luxury of being told what they had done. I had to find information on them first. On him. I knew he had been lying but I wasn't sure what it was about.'

He crossed the room and rested an elbow on Will's head, facing Carly. Will bucked underneath his weight, so he pressed harder.

'I became a third member of that relationship, without them even realising it. I was a part of them. I heard conversations they had, listening for something underneath the surface. I wanted to find out if the lie was already known, if it was no longer hidden. They're no longer with us, so I think you can guess at the answer to that. She knew at the end. I made sure of that.'

He grabbed Will's jaw, forcing him to look up, and Will screamed behind the tape across his mouth.

'You're a bit of a fool, Will. An idiot. I sent you a friend request but it was a fake profile. You accepted instantly.

All I needed was a few pictures of a blonde hairdresser, which I plucked from another profile. It's easy enough to do. Do you remember the message you sent her?'

He tightened his grip on Will's jaw. 'Naughty, naughty boy, Will.'

He forced Will's head back even further, before letting go and giggling to himself as he crossed back to Carly.

'I wanted to find out as much as possible about you both, before it became time for me to show myself. I wanted to understand you and become a part of your lives. You look less plastic in real life, Carly. And are you really a Man United fan, Will? You're brave, being that in this city. Although, I do know you weren't born in Liverpool, so that probably explains it.'

He moved to the side, facing both of them.

'I read through all your posts, Will. All your laddish bullshit, your right-wing idiocy. The way you talk about women, like they're objects. Quite the catch you have here, Carly.'

He studied her once more, trying to see what was behind those eyes.

'I don't understand you, Carly. Why do you allow him to treat you this way? People notice, you know. They must wonder how he gets away with it. You didn't accept my request, so I don't know much of anything about you. I bet you dote on him though. That's what I think. There to answer to his every beck and call. Dye job, and tan from a bottle. All to make him happy, I bet. But it makes no difference, does it? You mould yourself to be better for him, to make him happy, yet nothing changes.'

He stared at Carly, waiting for a response, but received nothing. As Will bucked in his chair and shouted behind his tape, Carly remained stock still. It was as if she were watching something being acted out in front of her, rather than being a part of it.

'This . . . this is what happens when you can't change. Which you both evidently can't. You're stuck together. There is no love here. No real love. You don't deserve it. Carly, I'm going to make everything better for you. I'm going to get rid of him.'

He waited to see if anything changed, but there was only silence. Carly stared back at him, watery blue-green eyes almost glowing. The duct tape across her mouth remained tight and she made no attempt to say anything.

'This is it.'

He could feel himself wavering, not knowing what to do. Then he felt the anger swelling inside him. How could these two people be given everything and not him? It wasn't fair. They had every chance to love, they had found each other, and now sat there waiting for him to do something, rather than fighting for it.

It wasn't right.

He slid the blade of his knife into the neck, holding the head steady as it rocked about, the noise increasing from behind the duct tape. He saw the blood begin to flow, and kept going. Not a clean cut this time. Not for this person.

He kept cutting. Blood pouring over his gloves as he continued. He could hear the noise from the woman on the other side of the room, her muffled screams filling the room.

He could hear himself talking over the gurgling noise which emanated from the man strapped to the chair, the sound slowing down as he cut further and further into his neck.

'Not good enough. This isn't good enough. This isn't what you're supposed to be.'

@EchoNews
BREAKING – Police say a Manhunt
is under way. More news here – bit.ly
#BreakingNews #LiverpoolMurders

@SteffJelling1
Did anyone email that guy? #ManInBlack

@RockoGym99
I sent him a message. Told him to come to
Liverpool if he thinks he's hard. #ManInBlack

@ChloeFanGroup
Feel sorry for Chloe now. He never loved
her. She should of just got rid. #RIPChloe

@WilkosMaxi
Only good thing about being made
an idiot of is that she wasn't around
to see it. #ManInBlack #ChloJoe

@SteveHewson94
Can't watch the news. Just keeps going
on and on about Liverpool. #Whocares

@Pundertaker_12
I emailed that account. Told them to kill
#ChloJoe again. #annoyingscousers

@UndercoverMother
Why is this even happening? Bet we're
not being told the whole story . . .

Chapter Twenty-Seven

From the outside, it was just another normal semi-detached house in one of the better areas of Liverpool – Litherland, just past Bootle as you headed north from the city centre. The more affluent areas of Crosby and Formby were a little further up the road. 'Not many cars about,' Murphy said as he suited up next to Rossi. 'Most of the drives are empty.

'All out at work, I imagine. Ten in the morning on a Friday, it figures. Probably not expecting to come home to this.'

'You're joking, aren't you? They'll know what's happened here before lunchtime.'

Rossi tied her hair up and pulled the cap over her head. 'I thought we wouldn't be doing this again. He's moving quicker.'

Thursday had been quiet, but the storm was simply resting. 'Three days since we found Greg and Hannah. He's definitely not hanging around.'

An ordinary house, in an ordinary street, full of ordinary people going about their ordinary lives, now surrounded by uniformed officers and white-suited SOCOs. People in neighbouring houses tapping out messages to people they didn't really know, updating their

Facebook page before ringing a parent or partner. Retweeting the latest comment from the *Liverpool Echo* account. Never believing that something like that could happen to them. Scarcely believing it could have happened in the same street, never mind the same city. That was the thought that picked at Murphy late at night, when he closed his eyes and sleep evaded him. The idea that it could happen to anyone, at any time.

Rossi let Murphy go in first, the smell inside not as bad as the first house in Anfield. The curtains were still closed across the windows in the living room, but it wasn't in there that most of the activity was taking place.

'I'm guessing through here,' Rossi said, taking the lead.

Murphy knew what to expect now and wasn't disappointed. The small dining table, which he assumed would have usually taken up residence in the middle of the room, had been pushed back and replaced with two chairs facing each other.

'He didn't remove the duct tape this time,' Murphy said, his voice muffled behind his mask. The mouths of both victims were still blocked by the tape, one bloodied and almost torn away, the other untouched.

'This took some force,' Dr Houghton said from near the male victim. 'He was well on the way to decapitation here.'

Murphy had deliberately chosen not to look at the male victim too closely, but now he allowed his gaze to drift over to where Dr Houghton's gloved finger was pointing. 'Bloody hell . . .'

Houghton was right. The wound was wider and deeper than Hannah's had been, evidence that a significant effort had been made to increase the torture.

'Those last moments ... I don't even want to think about them.'

'More violence used this time around,' Houghton said, moving round the body. 'Numerous contusions and bruise marks. Slash marks on the victim's face and back. Looks like he was beaten with something round, if you look at the bruising.'

Murphy moved closer, looking at the circular marks on the back of the male victim. 'Hammer?'

'Possibly,' Houghton replied. 'This is a bad one, David. I'd prefer it if these were the last ones, if that's okay with you?'

'Yeah, yeah. We're working on it.'

Murphy muttered something under his breath, catching the doctor's eyes and then averting his gaze.

Houghton moved towards the female victim opposite, examining her as best he could without moving her body too much. Murphy stepped to the side to allow more photographs to be taken, ducking out of the way as someone swept past filming the scene.

'Needle mark in the same place as the other victims,' Houghton said, pointing towards the right arm. 'He's consistent at least.'

'How long have they been here?' Murphy said, looking towards the patio doors, the floor-length blinds blocking his view to the outside.

'Hours. Around twelve, I think. I'll be able to tell you more later, of course. I'll make this top priority.'

Murphy thanked the doctor and left the room, Rossi following behind him. He stood in the hallway for a second, looking at the walls.

'What are you thinking?' Rossi said, closing her notebook.

'Marks on the walls,' Murphy replied, pointing to where he was looking. 'Where the colour doesn't match.'

'He's taken photographs off the walls again. Created his collage from the personal photos.'

Murphy moved closer to the wall, above a radiator with fading enamel paint. 'Look though,' he said, his finger brushing against the wallpaper. 'The pictures have been ripped off the wall this time. The picture hooks have been torn, taking half the plaster with them.'

'I don't understand,' Rossi said, peering over his shoulder. 'He took them off the walls last time.'

'It's not that. Think back to that scene with the third couple. There was nothing like this. The hooks were still on the wall. These have been ripped from the wall with force.'

Rossi was silent for a second, then began doing her best Bobblehead doll impression.

'He's angrier, that's what's happened here. He's not keeping control of his emotions. That's why the male victim has more injuries, why he's doing things like this.'

Murphy pointed to the wall and then turned to Rossi. 'If he's angry, he'll make mistakes. Come on.'

Murphy took the stairs two at a time, not feeling out of breath as he reached the top for a change.

'Not using the lift in work is starting to kick in,' he said to Rossi, once she'd joined him on the landing. 'Feeling the effects already.'

Murphy kept on walking, ignoring the two bigger rooms upstairs and making his way to the smallest bedroom at the end of the landing. The door was open but it was empty inside, low voices coming from the other two rooms. He slowed as he reached the doorway, spotting the empty picture frames discarded on the floor.

'Not very big in here,' Rossi said, standing in the doorway as Murphy stepped into the room.

'He's used that Pritt Stick stuff again, by the looks of it,' Murphy said, studying the photographs on the wall. 'The photo frames have been smashed.'

Rossi leaned further into the room, looking to the floor past Murphy. 'It could have been that he was in a rush, maybe? Worried about being disturbed?'

'No,' Murphy said, reading the words inked across several of the photographs. 'It's not that.'

WE CAN'T ALLOW THE LIARS TO WIN

'Look at some of these photos, Laura,' Murphy said, sweeping a gloved finger across them. 'They've been torn and damaged. Slashes right through some of them.'

'We're back to angry then. Although, I have to say the other scenes weren't exactly a picture of calm.'

'No, this one is very different. He's losing it, Laura.' Murphy turned to her with a grin, which faded when he remembered what was downstairs.

'Wonder what the secret was between them,' Rossi said, leaving the room and standing out on the landing.

'I'm sure we'll find out soon enough,' Murphy replied, calling one of the techs from the main bedroom and pointing towards the box room. 'Get that photographed and printed. I want full forensics done as soon as possible. There'll be something in there.'

Murphy headed past Rossi after having a quick look in the other two bedrooms. Nothing leapt out at him: small main room with a double bed, a couple of wardrobes and a flat screen TV fixed to the wall. The other was quite plainly used as a spare bedroom for visitors, doubling as a home gym, with a weights bench and exercise bike taking up the rest of the space within.

'I want the list of people who were named in those emails,' Murphy said as he made his way down the stairs. 'We need to see if Carly and Will were on that list and not informed. If someone's screwed up, I won't be happy.'

'No problem,' Rossi replied, walking past Murphy and out the front door, removing her gloves as she left the house.

Murphy padded into the living room. He couldn't see anything out of the ordinary. There were more faded marks on the walls where pictures had been removed. A glass picture frame lay smashed on the floor, the photo had not been removed.

'Sir,' a voice said from behind him. 'You got a second?'

Murphy turned slowly, finding it difficult to tear his gaze away from the jagged image of the couple. The photo had once sat in the middle of the mantelpiece; an A4-sized, happy, smiling vision of the pair. They were dressed up and looked content, his arms wrapped around her as she stood in front of him, facing the camera.

'What is it, Hale?' Murphy said, once he'd stopped looking.

'We've got names for the two of them,' Hale said, holding on to his notepad as if he were worried about dropping it. 'Will Callaghan and Carly Roberts. Lived here for about three years.'

'Who found them?'

'Carly's sister. They were supposed to meet, but Carly didn't show up. She gave it until this morning then came round. Had a spare key. She's outside in the van, but I wouldn't advise talking to her just yet. Think they're going to take her to the station and try and calm her down. She's trying to beat up anyone and everyone.'

'Okay,' Murphy said, leaning against the cold radiator on the nearest wall to the doorway. 'Did you give Laura the names?'

DC Hale nodded, his head dipping low enough for Murphy to see the white of his scalp showing through his over-gelled hair.

He wondered if anyone was willing to take a bet on Hale losing his hair before him.

'Right, well, let's hope our killer didn't find these two from one of the emails. Or we'll look pretty stupid.'

Murphy left the house, finding Rossi sitting in the car outside, talking on her phone. He slipped into the driver's seat, waiting for her to finish.

'Okay, cheers,' Rossi said, ending the call. 'Names don't match any of the emails we went through.'

'How long was that email address running for before we started monitoring it?'

'Only a few hours,' Rossi replied, loosening her hair before retying it. 'All the messages were unread though. I think he was just messing with us.'

'Possibly,' Murphy said, rubbing the palm of his hand across his cheek. 'Could be that I was right and he deleted some before sending us the password. How many emails have come in so far?'

'Thousands.'

Murphy shook his head. Despite releasing a press

statement asking people not to send anything to the email address and convincing the newspapers and news programmes not to publish the address, there were still messages trickling in.

'We could have blocked it,' Rossi said. 'Taken it down.'

'It's the only thing we can link to him, though,' Murphy replied, taking in the scene through the windscreen. A helicopter flew overhead, the noise making some officers look skywards. 'We had to keep it up. I didn't think so many people would actually send messages to it.'

'That's the world we live in.'

They'd had to contact fifty people in the city the previous day, warning them to take extra precautions for their safety. There had been conversations about whether they should tell the people why they were getting in contact. However, Murphy had known it wouldn't have taken them long to work out why, even if they'd kept the reason quiet. The headline in the late edition of the *Echo* had made it crystal clear. The story had run without many details, but there was enough to make readers understand what had happened.

All over the world, people had sent in emails detailing the lives of couples who they thought deserved to die. Murphy was still trying to wrap his head round that.

'If we don't find him soon, we could be in for a busy few days.'

Chapter Twenty-Eight

Murphy stared at the murder board, as if he were waiting for the photographs of the dead to begin speaking to him. Six faces and now two new names to add. People gone in an instant, leaving behind only grieving relatives and friends and a sense of loss which couldn't be described.

'We're back,' Rossi said, sidling up next to him. 'Cause of death the same as Greg and Hannah. Only the other way round. Hannah had her throat cut, as did Will in this case. Drug overdoses for their partners.'

'The first two male victims were different,' Murphy said, continuing to study the photographs, reading the sparse notes next to each face. 'Both strangled. Why are they different?'

'I hate to be so blunt . . .'

'Since when?' Murphy said, turning to face Rossi.

'Shut up. Can I finish? Thank you. It's probably a time thing.'

Murphy arched an eyebrow. 'As in . . .'

'Think about how long it takes to strangle someone to death. He's doing it in front of the partner, we assume, after they ask him to hurt them. That gives the partner too much time to change their minds maybe.'

'Almost as if he doesn't want to be responsible.'

'The Man in Black character he's created is purely a vehicle for the hate from one partner to another after the secret is revealed. He's carrying out their wishes. If he's hearing nothing but the person who initially has given their approval telling him to stop, it has an effect. On him, I mean. He doesn't want to hear that. He wants the person to wish harm on the other, so he can feel less guilty.'

'Why does he kill the other person?'

'I don't think he sees it like that,' Rossi said, turning her back on the murder board and leaning against the wall beside it. 'Think of the method. Overdose on some kind of anaesthetic drug? It'd be like going to sleep. He knows that. For him, it's probably like he's putting them out of their misery.'

'Nice of him. This would be four deaths by the same drug. It's not like he just has a stockpile of drugs lying around. If he's been planning this for a while, or just started up on the spur of the moment, he will have had to get it from somewhere. We need to clear hospitals in the area. Anywhere he could have got this from. What's the latest on that?'

Rossi wrote 'Drugs' on the murder board, adding a question mark to the word after staring at it for a second or two. 'We've heard that there's been a few missing bits and pieces here and there, but we haven't narrowed it down much. There are just too many hospitals in the area, before we get on to any other possible places. Plus, we're asking for any drugs being misplaced. We can't even tell them which actual drug it is being used, only the type of drug.'

Murphy swore under his breath. 'There must be something we're missing. Some kind of connection that we can use.'

'Is the sister calmer now?'

'Not sure. Do you want to go and find out?'

Murphy watched Rossi leave before walking over to DC Harris's desk. 'You got anything from the emails, Graham?'

DC Harris tapped away on his keyboard, holding up one finger for an instant before finishing. 'Sorry, had to send that. No, to answer your question. New messages are still coming in, but not at the rate they were. Most are just threats against the guy. Still a few names coming in, but nothing from Liverpool.'

'You're still forwarding them to the relevant forces around the country though?'

'Of course. Celebrities have been the most popular, you know. Loads of people asking for various famous couples to be killed. It really doesn't make sense to be well-known these days. Too much hassle.'

Murphy leant a hand on Harris's desk, looking at the various subject lines on the emails. 'If this case has taught me anything, it's that as a species, we're pretty much screwed.'

'This is a minority,' DC Harris said, sitting back in his chair. 'A vocal minority, I'll give you that, but mostly people just want to get on with others and keep their heads down. Look at what happened to me. I could have concentrated on the bastard who did this to me, or the things I read afterwards online . . .'

'Online?'

'Yeah, there's always people talking about coppers and that. I stupidly looked after what happened to me. There were people who were actually annoyed I wasn't killed. Although a lot of them were happy I was paralysed, I'll give them that. You want to look at the hashtag ACAB on Twitter once in a while.'

Murphy straightened up, feeling nauseous suddenly.

'But, that wasn't all,' DC Harris continued. 'There were also hundreds of people who sent nice messages and best wishes. I had to concentrate on them instead. Otherwise, I would never have come back.'

Murphy let out a short laugh. 'So what you're saying is, we should concentrate on all the good, rather than the bad, and life would be so much better?'

'Precisely.'

'I think that shotgun unlocked your inner Buddha, Graham. You should do talks.'

'I do as a matter of fact,' DC Harris said, barely above a whisper. 'To the cadets and stuff.'

'Good,' Murphy said, moving round to his desk. 'I honestly couldn't think of anyone better to do something like that. They should all know what it takes to be a good copper. But also, what can happen on the job.'

There was an uneasy silence between the two of them, broken by Rossi coming back and announcing that the sister was ready. Murphy gave DC Harris a nod, not checking to see if he got one in return, and followed Rossi out of the office.

'She's calmed down a bit now,' Rossi said, as they reached the family room one floor below. 'Her name is Kim. She's the older of the two.'

'Okay, any other family?'

'Yeah, but I think it's a little complicated. Listen, I can do this if . . . you know . . .'

'Why? Am I giving you any reason to think I can't do this stuff?'

Rossi shifted on the spot, swiping a foot across the carpet. 'No, I was just thinking ... about what you told me the other day.'

'What about it?'

'I just hope you didn't think I was out of line. You know, for suggesting it was all make-believe about Amy.'

Murphy breathed noisily, a deep breath in and out. 'I'm pretty sure it is.'

'What if it's not though?' Rossi replied, looking up at him, an inscrutable expression plastered across her face, which Murphy couldn't work out. 'I don't want you complaining that no one believed you. That's why I'm asking if you want me to interview this girl. Give you a bit of time to yourself.'

'First off,' Murphy said, leaning closer as a couple of constables walked past them. 'You're one of only a couple of people who know about this. So, don't go thinking I've been canvassing opinion. I trust you not to say anything. Secondly, I know what's going on, I know why Amy's mother is saying this now. Not saying there's no chance it's true, I'm just saying it's remote. And thirdly, and most importantly, she's an eighteen-year-old girl, living in Speke, working in a shop. Odds are, she had an argument with her mum and has had a better offer elsewhere. She'll be back in a month or two, with her tail between her legs, a sad love story to tell, and a great tan. Whereas we ... we have eight dead people and a serial killer we can't find. I know where my priorities lie here.'

Rossi weighed up his words, staring at him before tearing her gaze away. 'Fine, there's no need to make a speech about it. Just checking, that's all.'

'Course you were,' Murphy replied, as a smirk appeared on his face. 'We're a team. Don't forget that. That's why I tell you shit you don't want to hear. Same goes both ways. *Capisce?*'

'Ugh, you sound like a reject from *The Godfather* now. Let's get on with this.'

Murphy's smirk turned to a smile, which he promptly wiped off his face as Rossi opened the door into the family room. They waited for the family liaison officer to leave before sitting down opposite Kim and introducing themselves. There was a slight resemblance to the pictures he had seen of Carly, but there was a more wearied look to the older sister. Murphy wasn't sure if that was due to the fact she'd found her murdered sister – or if there was something else. Maybe it was just the morning's events, he thought, but there was something about her eyes. She looked as if she was about to jump out of the chair at any moment, her eyes darting round the room.

'Do you need anything, Kim?' Murphy said, placing down the cup of coffee he had brought with him. 'Drink or something?'

'I need you to find out who did this so I can kill him. Can you do that for me?'

Murphy glanced at Rossi who had her eyes fixed on Kim's. He waited a second to see if she was going to answer, but she kept her mouth closed.

'We'll certainly do everything we can to find out who did this, Kim,' Murphy said, attempting his soothing voice. 'We just need to ask a few questions.'

'Is it the same one? The guy who killed those other couples and ChloJoe?'

Murphy internally shuddered at the use of the abbreviation. Everything he had learned about the pair in the previous week made the name even more ridiculous. 'We're not ruling anything out at the moment, Kim. We just want to know a bit more about Carly and Will at this point.'

Kim straightened up in the chair and performed some kind of breathing exercise. Murphy was aware of Rossi shifting in her seat next to him, but he waited Kim out.

'Carly was twenty-four years of age,' Kim said eventually, the words coming out staccato-like, as if she were reading from a script. 'She has worked for one of the big banks for the last three years, dealing with payment protection refunds, out in the business park in Speke. Earned a good wage. No children, but she told me she wanted them someday. She was concentrating on her career for now. We grew up in Fazakerley, both went to primary and high school there. She's three years younger than me and we have a younger brother who is twenty. Our mum and dad live in Spain, where Dad bought a property a year ago. Retired in his mid-fifties, after making his money early.'

Murphy listened to Kim recite their family's history, as if it were something she was used to doing. He wondered if she'd been through this before and no one had thought to ask, before admonishing himself quietly.

'She had a few friends, but no one as close to her as I was,' Kim continued. 'She rarely went on nights out, preferring to stay at home after work.'

Rossi was making a note of everything Kim was saying, her pen flying across the pages of her notebook as Murphy glanced towards her.

'Carly met Will while they were still in school. Both fifteen. They moved in together when they were both eighteen.'

There was silence in the room as Kim's stilted voice stopped. Murphy wondered if she had finished or if she was just taking a breath. As the pause grew longer, became more uncomfortable, Murphy decided it was the former.

'How was the relationship between Carly and Will?'

'I don't know. I never asked, not once. Carly was a very private person and wouldn't have told anyone about that kind of thing.'

Will had told someone something, however, Murphy thought. The fact that it was Carly who had received the drug overdose meant it must have been Will who had the secret. Something came to him then, a thought, but it was gone as quickly as it had arrived.

'He's been around the family a while though,' Rossi said, taking over from Murphy. 'What did you think of him?'

'Will wasn't the one for Carly, but I don't think she ever realised that,' Kim replied, her voice softening a touch. 'If you were around them, it was almost like they didn't know how to be with anyone else, so had just settled for each other. Does that make sense? I can try it again if not.'

'That's fine, Kim,' Rossi said, her soothing voice much better than his, Murphy thought. 'Is there anything that Carly may have said recently, anything she was worried about?'

'No, there's been nothing. We weren't those type of sisters really. We didn't discuss our private lives. It was more about what we were watching on telly, or which film we were looking forward to seeing. That sort of thing. She was more into fashion than I was, so she'd talk about a bag or a dress she'd seen in some shop. I'd talk about how quick I'd run 5K in the gym that day. We didn't talk about our other halves.'

Murphy was beginning to see the mask slip a little. Kim was putting on a good show, but he could tell underneath the surface there was a multitude of emotions going on.

'When was the last time you spoke to her?' Murphy said, a question which had burned him in the past, but seemed to make no impression on Kim. It was the word 'last' which usually struck home. No one wanted to remember those final words spoken to their loved one.

Kim breathed in for a few seconds, let a long breath out. 'I spoke to her Wednesday at around eight or nine p.m. We arranged for her to come to mine last night, but she didn't show up. I texted her, but didn't get a reply. That's unlike her, but I gave her until this morning. I texted, rang, sent an email, all before ten a.m. I couldn't just sit there and not know, so I went to the house. All the curtains were drawn, so I let myself in. I thought I may have been interrupting something between her and Will, until I saw the photographs had all been removed from the wall. It didn't make sense. Of course, that was until I walked into the dining room.'

Murphy watched as Kim wavered slightly before composing herself once more. He looked towards Rossi who shaped to say something more, but was interrupted by a knock at the door. Another knock came a second later, louder and more insistent.

'Excuse me a second,' Murphy said, walking over to the door, ready to fire a volley of words at whoever was knocking. He opened the door and slipped out in one movement.

'What the hell is it?' Murphy hissed at DC Kirkham, who took a step back and shrunk an inch or two smaller. 'We've got a family member in there, or have you forgotten that?'

'Sorry, I wouldn't have interrupted, but it's urgent.'

'It best bloody had be.'

'It's him, sir,' DC Kirkham said, still trying to catch his breath. 'He's sent us a message.'

Left Behind

It had been five days since Karen Morrison's life had been upended and changed irrevocably. Beyond repair, she thought. Nothing would ever be the same again. Her entire existence would come down to the moment she watched her daughter eventually be lowered into a grave.

She wasn't meant to go first. That wasn't the way it was supposed to happen. Chloe was expected to look after her, when she finally allowed the ageing process to take hold. That was the correct way of things. Not this.

'Don't you dare touch that remote.'

Neil moved his hand back slowly, still not willing to look at her. Karen knew he was taking it hard, but was too focused to take into account his feelings as Chloe's stepfather.

Karen couldn't bear to have anything but the news on the television now. Waiting for any kind of update, not wanting to miss a thing. Watching the same faces, listening to the same voices over and over. The same news, again and again. Hating the dispassionate way they spoke of her daughter as a 'victim'.

When they had shown the video a couple of days previously, of her daughter in darkness in her final moments,

Karen had sat transfixed, listening to her speak. It didn't matter what she said, she just wanted to hear her voice.

The girl they had portrayed on that reality show wasn't the one Karen knew. It was a caricature of the real person. Chewed up and spat out for entertainment purposes. They didn't know the girl who had played on Moreton Shore as a five-year-old. The eight-year-old Chloe who had cried all the way home from New Brighton because the 2p machines had 'eaten all her money'. The fifteen-year-old who had come into Karen's bedroom at midnight, crying over the loss of a first love.

All they knew was the Chloe who had gone on some stupid reality show and become the twenty-first-century version of famous. The Chloe who modelled for lads' mags and was never seen in the same outfit twice. The Chloe who was followed around by pre-arranged paparazzi so she could be pictured shopping or visiting fellow celeb friends.

They would never know the girl Karen had.

Neil had sent away the woman who had been with them for the first couple of days. Family liaison officer or something. She'd been cluttering up the place anyway. Always there, waiting for Karen to break down so she could offer platitudes and a soothing voice. Just like she'd been trained to do.

Karen didn't want that. She'd begged Neil to send the woman away. She didn't want to worry about a stranger in the house on top of everything else. There were only so many times she could see that stark reminder of what had happened, sitting at her dining-room table, or in her living room. Eating her biscuits and drinking her tea.

On the television, it was less real. Chloe would now forever be just what she'd always wanted. Famous. Infamous. No one would ever forget her now.

All the news channels were full of the story, the coverage increasing as the week had gone on. Two more people found that morning, unnamed at that moment, but Karen knew their stories would be coming soon enough.

'I can't keep watching this, Karen. It's the same thing over and over. It's not healthy.'

Neil didn't understand. How could he? He didn't know the bond a mother and daughter have. How that never disappears, even as that daughter grows up and becomes an adult. The link between Chloe and Karen had never been broken.

Chloe had always been her favourite.

Karen detested the way, even in death, Chloe was still not recognised for who she was as a person. Every news programme, every newspaper, all lumping her together with the man who had caused her death.

ChloJoe.

They didn't see her as a person in her own right. She wasn't good enough to be spoken of as a single entity. She was bonded forever with the man whose actions had led Chloe to her fate.

Now they couldn't have a funeral until they *released her body*. Her daughter was lying all alone in a morgue drawer somewhere in Liverpool. Karen just wanted her home, to see her walk through the door as if nothing had happened. Eleven years old, on the cusp of transition, still a small happy child. Or fourteen years old and in the throes of puberty and teenage angst.

Karen wanted to be sitting up in a hospital bed, her new baby in her arms, the feelings of exhaustion and relief washing over her. Thinking she could never love anyone as much as she loved that newborn lying in her arms.

Karen refused to cry now. She had got it all out of her system on that first day, leaving nothing for afterwards. It wasn't about her now. She just had to get through each day, waiting for the news to change.

'I'm going out for a walk.'

Karen didn't move her eyes away from the television. Another couple found that morning. More death, more drama for the news to keep the interest going.

She didn't move as she heard the door slam.

The scrolling news ticker remained unchanged; the new couple found in Liverpool now included with the other victims.

'*Get out of my way.*'

Karen could hear Neil's raised voice coming from outside, but ignored it at first. There were still people camped outside their house, cluttering up the pavement so you couldn't get past them. She knew the neighbours would be complaining behind closed doors, wondering how long it was going to go on for. How long they were going to have to suffer through it.

'*I said get out of my fucking way! Let me just have five minutes alone!*'

Karen had the volume on the television turned down low, but now she muted it as she walked over to the window to look out. She pulled back the closed blinds, peering out through the gap.

Neil had his hands clasped around the collar of a short

balding man who still held on to his camera as Neil got in his face.

'This is what you want, isn't it? Keep pointing that thing at me, I'll rip your fucking head off, you understand?'

Karen sped to the front door, tearing it open and leaving it to bang against the wall inside. She ran down the path, cameras and microphones turning in her direction as she opened the gate.

'Neil,' she shouted over the voices of so many others. 'Come inside, now.'

Neil turned to look at her and she saw him for the first time in days. The dark rings under his eyes, the way he seemed to have aged ten years in less than a week. He let go of the photographer, who fell to the floor.

'You all killed her,' Neil said, looking towards the multitude of photographers and journalists standing on the pavement outside their home. 'You understand that? It was all of you. You're the reason she's dead.'

Karen went to his side. She put an arm around him and dragged him back towards their house.

'There's blood on your hands,' Neil shouted at them as they walked back up the path. 'And now you're after us. I hope you're all proud of yourselves. You sick bastards.'

Karen ignored the questions still being shouted at them as she closed the front door, the noise finally quietening a little.

'You shouldn't have done that,' Karen said in a low voice. 'That's not the way we're supposed to deal with this.'

'I can't take this any more,' Neil replied, pacing up and down the hallway, hands clenched into fists. 'They're making us prisoners in our own home. They just can't leave us alone. How are we supposed to deal with any of this, if they're out there waiting for us to make one move?'

'That's just the way it is. Let me get past. I might have missed something.'

'You're just going to go back to watching the shit them out there produce?'

Karen slid past Neil, taking up her familiar position on the sofa opposite the television. She picked up the remote and turned up the volume, drowning out the voices from outside.

'We can't go on like this, Karen. You need to speak to me. We need to talk about all this. I'm hurting too, love. I'm really fucking struggling here.'

Karen continued to watch the news, turning up the volume a little more.

So many things that needed sorting out, she thought. So little time.

*   *   *

There were fewer reporters camped outside Emily Flynn's house, but they were there all the same. Waiting to ask her a multitude of questions every time she tried to leave the house.

Since the video had been released, showing Hannah confessing to Greg of her *transgression*, the questions had been different.

Now, they were all geared towards Hannah's infidelity, the choices she had made and how she'd lived her life following them. They didn't know how good a mother she was day to day; they were judging her on that single decision.

Emily didn't understand how anyone could do that, ignoring the fact that she might have made similar judgements if she'd had no connection to Hannah.

She had the news channels on constantly, waiting for a mere mention of Hannah, but any time the story appeared, it was behind the cloak of celebrity. ChloJoe and that circus. Hannah was a side story. Something which was connected, but only in passing. Since the video, she could be even further dismissed. A harlot, a bad mother, a slag. Words Emily knew were being used about her daughter in death.

Flowers had arrived the day before from Chloe Morrison's mother. They were currently filling an overflowing bin in her kitchen. She didn't want anything from her. Didn't want her daughter to be connected to someone like that.

She didn't want to leave the house any more. Didn't want anyone visiting either. She wanted to wallow, wait the whole thing out and hope for the day to end. To wake up the next day and for everything to be normal again. Yet, she found herself preparing to go out in front of those cameras to appeal for help. To find the man who had destroyed her family. To get justice. To get closure.

Emily knew it wasn't going to be enough. Nothing would ever be the same, no matter what happened next. Never again. Her life, Hannah's life, Greg's life, everyone connected to them. They would all be defined by this. She would be forever known as the mother of the murdered woman. The mother of the woman who got pregnant by another man and never told her partner. The mother of the woman who had to reveal that secret to her partner and then be killed for it.

There was no normal now.

There was only Emily, her other children and a little girl called Millie, who didn't understand that her parents were never coming home.

That was all that was left.

Chapter Twenty-Nine

The email was short, but to the point. Addressed to no one in particular, which was a blessing of sorts.

No one wanted to be in his sights.

Dear Merseyside Police from ME,
I'm sure you'll be getting a lot of messages from people who say they're me, HOAX emails and messages, that sort of thing. I'm sure there are very few people who you told about my last message, so here is the password again.
Loveisviolence
Now you know it's me. I am the so-called MAN IN BLACK. I am the man people are SCARED of. They SHOULD be. I don't care who you are, I am coming for you. I am going to HELP you all. I am the man who is fixing it all. I am LOVE. I am VIOLENCE.
There are so many LIES out there. Everyone seems to have them. I have watched you all, keeping SECRETS and lying to your partners. It must stop now.
I am not done. I am only just starting. There are SO MANY people who need my help. Judging by the amount of emails I got I think everyone is behind ME. Even if they

don't know it yet. They are all talking about ME and what I can do for them.

EVERYONE will learn to LOVE again. The RIGHT way. No LIES, no SECRETS.

I CAN'T STOP NOW. DON'T TRY TO STOP ME. I'M DOING THE BEST FOR EVERYONE. YOU WILL ALL LEARN THIS.

I WILL DO IT AGAIN, TO MAKE THINGS BETTER. TO STOP THE LIES, THE SECRETS. NO ONE SHOULD LOVE LIKE THIS. I'M MAKING IT ALL BETTER.

ME

P.S. – You won't find WILL and CARLY on the emails. I deleted it, along with some others, so you wouldn't know they had been chosen.

ASK ADAM EVANS. HE KNOWS WHY IT HAD TO BE THEM.

Murphy stopped reading and waited for Rossi to finish. He read the last few lines again, shuddering at the block capitals on the page and the sentiment behind them.

'This guy is on the way down,' Rossi said, placing the paper carefully on her desk, as if it were the only copy. 'He's struggling.'

'You think so?' Murphy said, screwing his copy into a ball and missing the bin as he threw it. 'There doesn't seem to be any struggle there at all. It's like he's getting stronger. He's enjoying himself.'

'I don't think so. He's becoming more desperate for attention . . . no, not attention. Gratitude. He wants to be thought of as doing something good. That what he's doing is somehow right.'

'You know,' Murphy said with a growing smirk. 'We could both be right here.'

'How so?'

'Think about it. He could be getting stronger in one way, in that his convictions are clearer, he knows what he wants to do. He wants to "fix" as many people as possible, those he thinks are deserving of his particular brand of justice—'

'Alongside that though,' Rossi said, taking over from Murphy's thought, 'he's also becoming weaker, as he is also killing what he thinks of as the innocent party as well. This is the fourth time he's killed someone who perhaps hasn't done anything wrong in his eyes.'

'The other part of the couple.'

'Exactly.'

'So, he has to carry on,' Murphy said, spying DC Harris out of the corner of his eye, listening to their conversation. 'Because he doesn't know any other way to justify his actions other than to keep going. He is struggling to keep a lid on how strong he is becoming.'

'He's going to make a mistake. Or he already has.'

Murphy leaned back in his chair. 'And that's our job now. Find his mistake.'

DC Harris loudly cleared his throat. Murphy turned his head towards him. 'Bit dramatic that, Graham?'

'Wasn't sure you were both finished with your psychology session.'

Rossi grabbed the ball of paper Murphy had thrown at the bin off the floor and launched it at DC Harris's head.

'Shit,' Harris said, rubbing the side of his head. 'You've got some arm on you.'

'Don't take the piss out of Italian women. Or Scouse ones while you're at it.'

DC Harris shook his head and wheeled himself round to Murphy and Rossi's bank of desks. 'I just thought you'd like to know about something mentioned in the email, that's all.'

'Go on, Graham. We're listening.'

'I know who Adam Evans is.'

*   *   *

It was one of the things about Speke that Murphy was pleased to see whenever he returned: the new business park and retail centre, built adjacent to the airport. What was once a run-down area had been regenerated over a decade into something that looked half-decent, and the hotels dotted around the place helped to bring in more people.

All the buildings on the business park looked the same, so it took a few minutes – and a map – to find the correct place. The guy on reception gave them the floor details, once he'd made himself feel important by inspecting their warrant cards. He picked up his mobile phone as soon as they had moved away, tapping away at the screen, every now and again looking up and catching Murphy's eye.

'Probably already texting people upstairs,' Murphy said, as they waited for the lift to arrive. 'I imagine we're about to get a welcoming party.'

It seemed as if there was a call centre on every floor. He imagined most of the cold calls and the multitude of spam email he received came from a place like this.

The lift doors opened up onto an almost identical

reception area to the one in the lobby of the building. The name of the company Adam Evans worked for was emblazoned across glass behind a high-fronted desk.

'Can I help you?' the sharp-suited young man behind the desk said, all teeth and cheekbones, while his slicked-over hair was thrust into a parting he'd probably battled his mum not to have as a child. How fashion changes, Murphy thought.

'We're here to speak to Adam Evans,' Rossi said, moving in front of Murphy and DC Kirkham.

'Do you have an appointment?'

Murphy was already annoyed. He held up his warrant card. 'Do we need one? He's a call centre worker not the bloody director of the whole bank. Tell him to get out here, or we'll make him look a right dick in front of his co-workers by going in and getting him ourselves.'

The guy lost his smile, his cheekbones fading alongside it. His hands began to shake as he picked up the phone and spoke into it.

A minute later, Adam Evans walked out of the office. He was a three-stone-heavier version of reception guy, but much more scared.

'I'm Detective Sergeant Laura Rossi, this is Detective Inspector Murphy and Detective Constable Kirkham. If you'd like to come with us, Adam we just want to have a little chat.'

'Erm . . . what's this about?'

'We can talk about that in private, Adam, if you'll just come with us.'

Adam's eyes shifted left, then right. He started bouncing on the balls of his feet. 'Do I have to? Don't you have to arrest me or something?'

'Do we need to arrest you?' Murphy said, widening his stance.

'No . . . I mean . . . I don't know. Why do you need to speak to me?'

Murphy took a step forward, standing next to Rossi and blocking Adam's one path of escape. 'Would you prefer to talk about this here, Adam? Would that be more comfortable?'

Adam's forehead creased in confusion, making him look as if he were squinting. 'What, here?' he said, pointing to the floor of the reception area.

'Yeah,' Murphy replied. 'You don't seem to want to come with us, so why don't we do it right here. How about we start asking questions about Carly, where anyone could walk past and hear?'

Adam turned a shade of white Murphy thought would look good on his landing walls. 'I . . . I'll come. I haven't done anything, though.'

'We'll see about that,' Murphy said, nodding to Kirkham who pressed the lift call button and stood off to the side. 'Cheers, lad,' Murphy said to the reception guy as he stepped into the lift with Rossi and an increasingly ashen-faced Adam. 'DC Kirkham is going to stick around, speak to a few more people. And tell you what we need. I think it's time you got your manager, don't you?'

The reception guy looked around, perplexed at the events that were unfolding.

'I . . . What's going on?'

Murphy didn't answer, but smiled as Kirkham radioed down to the uniforms waiting outside.

*   *   *

Murphy had chosen to take Adam Evans to interview room two. Not for any reason other than it was the coldest room out of the lot. The radiator on the wall needed bleeding, Murphy thought, but no one had done anything about it.

'Do you understand the caution, Adam?'

Adam Evans had shrunk since arriving at the station, the media scrum around their vehicle as they'd pulled up to the station having had a major effect on him. They had decided to arrest him on suspicion of perverting the course of justice, once they had arrived back at the station. Murphy was prepared to upgrade that within minutes.

'Yes.'

'I'll ask again if you're happy to proceed without a solicitor?'

'It's okay. I . . . I just want to tell the truth.'

'Good,' Murphy said, opening the murder file up and laying it flat on the desk. 'So, we just want to ask a few questions, that's all.'

Murphy asked the standard opening questions. Easy ones, about Adam's life and work. The answers coming quick and easy.

Rossi then took over.

'Can you tell us about your relationship with Carly Roberts?'

Adam scratched at his arm, his eyes shifting. 'We . . . erm . . . work together.'

'How long have you known her for?'

'About two, three years. We started at the same time.'

'Were you friends?'

'Yeah, kind of.'

Rossi leaned forward, trying to catch Adam's gaze. 'Were you more than friends, Adam?'

'It . . . it was complicated.'

'Complicated how?'

'We were close, at one point. But she has a boyfriend, so I backed off. Nothing more than that.'

There were a few more questions to which Adam gave non-committal answers. Murphy broke in. 'What do you know of the murders that have happened this week?'

'Only what I've seen on the news.'

'You've watched the news, read the papers, that sort of thing?'

'Yeah,' Adam replied, sinking into his chair. 'Nothing much other than that.'

'Did you read about the message which came from the so-called Man in Black, Adam?'

'I . . . I don't remember.'

'Of course you do, Adam. Because you saw the email address, didn't you?'

Adam stayed silent. Murphy waited for an answer, but realised none was forthcoming. 'You were more than close to Carly, weren't you?'

'Yes.'

'You loved her, didn't you?'

Adam nodded, his lip began to tremble slightly. 'We loved each other.'

'But she rejected you, didn't she?'

'She had to,' Adam replied, suddenly staring at Murphy with watery eyes. 'Because of him.'

'Who?'

'That boyfriend of hers. We were . . . seeing each other. For a while. We talked all the time, really became close.

Closer than he ever was to her. I know her better than him, that's for sure. He treats her like she's nothing. I can be there for her. She just doesn't realise that. We barely talk any more. I just can't do it. Every time we start trying to be friends, it just ends in me getting my heart broken again when she doesn't leave him.'

'What about her boyfriend? What do you really know about him, other than what you were told by Carly?'

'I know enough.'

'Like what?' Rossi said, turning over a new page in her notebook and continuing to write.

'I followed him for a bit. To see what he did. What made him so special that she couldn't leave him for me. I am the better option. I make sense. He doesn't.' Adam wiped his mouth with the back of his hand. 'He cheats on her. I've seen him with these girls when he's pretending to be working. He goes on work calls in his car, but makes them longer than they really are and visits these girls.'

'How many other girls?' Murphy said, beginning to realise the secret Will had been hiding.

'I've seen three different ones in the past year.'

'So, you've been following him for a while then?'

Adam nodded. 'I wanted something to happen to him, to show what he's been doing to Carly. I could never tell her though. I didn't want her to blame me for finding out.'

Murphy rubbed his palms together, his fingers cold to the touch.

'Am I in trouble for sending the email?'

'What email, Adam?'

A couple of tears dribbled down Adam's cheek. 'I didn't mean to send it. I was just angry. I tried to take it back but I couldn't. I'm sorry.'

'What did your email say, Adam?'

Adam lowered his head into his crossed arms on the table. 'I didn't want anything to happen to her. Either of them. Not really. I'm so sorry. I can say sorry to Carly, she'll understand. I know she's not in work today, is this why? It was just a stupid mistake.'

'Did you get any response to your email, Adam?' Murphy said.

'No. I was reading that loads of people were emailing it, so I thought it was just some mad thing that no one would ever read. Did I break the law sending it or something? I'm really so sorry. I didn't really mean it.'

Murphy glanced at Rossi who slowly nodded her head at him.

'Adam ... Carly and Will were found dead this morning.'

Chapter Thirty

Murphy was surrounded by tired faces, tired minds. The week's events were beginning to catch up on many of them. Not least himself. Every now and again, the face of Amy Maguire – still missing after all this time – would enter his mind, and shake him. He knew she wasn't his daughter. Almost knew. There was something there, however, something that kept dragging his thoughts back to her.

The chance to save her.

Instead of which, he was listening to Rossi talk about her weekend plans. She was speaking directly to him, which made tuning her out more difficult.

'So, I think everyone on his team will be there,' Rossi said, her hands moving round in the air. 'Which will be a bit weird. I bet he'll bloody introduce me as his girlfriend or some such shit. I don't know why I agreed to go. It starts at five, but I've told him I'll be late if I'm there at all. What do you think?'

'When is this again?' Murphy replied, knowing the moving hands meant she was either excited or nervous. 'Did you say?'

'Yes, I did, when you obviously weren't listening.

Tomorrow night. Darren wants me to go for this meal with his workmates.'

'The doctors?'

'I don't know, do I? Doctors, nurses, that sort of thing.'

'What's the problem again?'

Rossi sighed and ran a hand through her hair. 'With everything that's going on ... you know, I didn't think it was a good idea.'

'This is meeting his friends, isn't it? People he works with every day at least?'

'Well, yeah.'

'That sounds pretty important to me. You should be there. It's not until tomorrow, so you never know. Maybe the whole case will be solved by then. Hey, it's anaesthetic drugs being used ... maybe it's him and you'll wake up on Sunday not knowing what happened.'

Rossi raised her voice. 'Don't even joke about that. He's not that type of guy. He's ... he's good. He's not a killer or anything like that. Be very careful about what you say, you hear me?'

'I'm sorry,' Murphy said, holding his hands up in surrender as he noticed Rossi's hands shake a little. Her jaw clenched as she waited for him to continue. 'Just a joke, honest. He seems cool. I didn't realise it was that serious ...'

'Neither did I,' Rossi said, lowering her voice. 'Guess I'm a bit protective. You don't think that joke's being made by some other people round here? They all know who he is and where he works. It's just getting on my nerves.'

'Look, Laura, we can't ever let these types of things interfere with our lives. We have to keep going as if every-thing is normal ...'

'You're one to talk.'

'I know,' Murphy said, holding his hands up. 'But, I am trying to get better at that type of thing. If we let cases like this one, or the next, or the next ... if they get to you, they win. You'll end up resenting your job and that'll make you a worse detective. You're already getting better than me.'

'*Vaffanculo.*'

'Well, you're a better swearer than any of us, at least.'

Rossi smiled at him. Murphy looked across at her, seeing the effects of the previous few years on her. When he began working with her almost three years ago, she had just turned thirty, a smooth-faced, Mediterranean-featured young woman. Now, the darkness was under her eyes, the lines creeping in. Murphy didn't want her to end up like him. When he looked in the mirror now, he saw a reflection of all the horrors he had seen in the previous decade. The scars and lines well earned. He'd been handsome once, he thought, but it was beginning to catch up on him.

'Go,' Murphy said. 'Have a good time and make me jealous. You deserve it after this week. I'll be making sure you're out of here tomorrow in time to meet them.'

'Fine,' Rossi replied, still smiling. 'What are we going to do with our new friend in there?'

Murphy considered the broken man they had left in the interview room. 'It's obvious he had no idea it was Carly and Will who were killed overnight. So, unless we're being played by the greatest actor alive, I don't think we have our man yet.'

'Agreed, but he deserves something.'

'Conspiracy? I'm not sure it would stick.'

'He can't just get away with it, though,' Rossi said, her smile now gone. 'It's because of him they're both dead. And for what? Because she didn't go running to him when he showed up on his horse like a good white knight? He deserves to take some responsibility here.'

Murphy suppressed a yawn, tired of standing in the hallway, a little way down the corridor from the interview room. 'I understand, I just don't know what CPS are going to say. If you want to try, I'm willing to back you on it.'

'Thank you. We can't just have men like him out there.'

'I get it, I do,' Murphy replied, looking at his phone and tutting under his breath when he saw the time. 'Listen, I'll send Kirkham down to help you sort him out. I've got to go and show my face at this bloody press conference now.'

'Go, I'll be fine. Don't let Butler get to you if he tries anything on.'

Murphy left Rossi in the corridor, almost jogging up the flight of stairs to his office. He sent Kirkham down to meet Rossi, checked he didn't look like a crumpled mess and made his way to the press room.

He was late. DCI Stephens shook her head at him, pointing at her bare wrist as he made his way up the corridor to meet them. DSI Butler was smoothing down his hair, the strip lighting reflecting off the flecks of grey.

'Glad you could make it, David,' DSI Butler said, his assistant straightening his tie for him. 'Now, is there anything you can tell me about the man we've arrested today?'

'He's under caution, but he only sent an email,' Murphy replied. 'We've just finished interviewing him now. He emailed the Man in Black address, but it looks like whoever our guy is deleted it before we even saw. Along with God knows how many others. We have arrested him on suspicion of perverting the course of justice. We're going to approach CPS with a possible conspiracy charge for this lad, but I'm not sure it'll stick.'

'He is a person of interest at the moment,' DSI Butler said. 'Sounds better. Helping us with our enquiries?'

'Yes, use both,' DCI Stephens replied. 'It will keep them off our back a little.'

'I'm not so sure about that,' DSI Butler said, smoothing out his jacket. 'There is significant interest in this case. The coverage is non-stop and we look like a bunch of bloody amateurs at the moment. Eight murders. Six in one week. What am I supposed to tell them, David? Please tell me we're getting closer to an actual arrest.'

'We're working on it,' Murphy said, wondering if the superintendent had any clue what was going on. 'It's a very complicated case, with very few leads . . .'

'I don't care about that. Just find the guy, before we have even more problems with this lot to deal with. Every day this goes unsolved, it's more pressure on us all. This new unit was set up so things like this didn't happen. Certainly not for this long. Get out there and find out who this bloody nutcase is and get him off my streets.'

The media was king, Murphy thought. He was surprised he hadn't been thrown under the bus and made to go out and face them by himself.

They filed in and headed to the table at the front of the room. Murphy noticed the number of people in attendance was almost double the amount of the previous press conference. On the other side of the room he saw the mother of Hannah Flynn being prepped to join them and make her own statement.

'Did you see Chloe's stepdad blow up earlier?' DCI Stephens said to Murphy behind a cupped hand. 'Not sure that's helping at all.'

'Didn't see it,' Murphy replied, looking out into a mass of faces. 'I'm surprised it hasn't happened sooner. I'm betting the press has been camped outside their house all week.'

'We've had a word and sent the family liaison officer back there.'

Murphy sat down to the left of DCI Stephens, with DSI Butler on her right.

The preamble went without a hitch. DSI Butler made an impassioned speech, which even Murphy began to believe by the end. As he spoke about the hard work and man hours being put in by his staff, Murphy began to tune out and list the things that could actually catch the 'Man in Black'. He winced to himself when he thought of the ridiculous moniker once more.

The list was short. They were down to trawling the archives online, checking IP addresses provided by large service providers. CCTV had turned up nothing of use.

The drugs were a possibility if they ever got an actual name, but the time taken to get any answers was just an opportunity for more victims to appear. Forensics on the scene had turned up nothing. It was one dead end after another.

'A man in his early twenties was identified as a person of interest earlier today and is helping police with their enquiries,' DSI Butler continued in a low voice. 'We will give you more information on this in due course.'

Murphy knew the name would be common knowledge within an hour. That's just how these things worked. Adam's life would be shattered, once it became known what he had done. Even if he was never charged for an offence, his life was about to change overnight.

Good, Murphy thought.

Murphy waited for Hannah's mother to begin speaking, feeling like a spare part. Someone to make up the numbers behind the panel of microphones.

'Hannah was just starting her life,' Emily Flynn said, looking very different from how Murphy had seen her a few days previously. 'She didn't deserve for this to happen to her.'

Someone coughed in the audience of journalists, which seemed to start a chain reaction of people clearing their throats.

'Hannah and Greg's daughter, Millie, is about to turn two. She doesn't understand what has happened to her mummy and daddy . . .'

Murphy waited for any sign of emotion to appear, but Emily Flynn was in determined mode. He'd seen it with other grieving relatives when they were in front of cameras. Their nerves kept their emotions in check. He knew five minutes after the press conference had ended, she would be a wreck.

'I'd ask anyone who has any information to please get in touch with the police. Someone, somewhere will know the person who has done this. Someone who has been acting strangely in the past few days. Please, please help my granddaughter and come forward.'

'Any questions?' DCI Stephens said beside him. 'We're able to take a few.'

Hands shot up round the room.

'Yes,' DCI Stephens said, pointing to someone on the front row.

'Emily, can we ask if you've spoken to the parents of Chloe Morrison and whether you're supporting each other through this.'

Emily Flynn picked up a glass of water in front of her with shaking hands. 'No, I haven't. We're very different people. I don't imagine they're taking many calls from people right now.'

'You've got that right,' the man asking the question said under his breath. A low laugh spread through the room.

'You think this is funny?' Emily said, water spilling over the sides as she slammed the glass back down on the desk. 'Is this a joke to you?'

There was silence in the room, the reporter who had made the comment now finding the floor of much interest to him.

'This isn't just words, or stories. This is real life. My granddaughter has lost her parents to some crazy bastard, and you lot aren't interested in that. No one has asked me anything about my daughter. All you're interested in is some celebrities and what happened to them. We're a sideshow to you lot. I've seen what you've been saying about Hannah, relegating her to a non-victim, just because of one mistake . . .'

'I think we should move . . .'

'No,' Emily said, holding up a hand to the press officer who had tried to intervene. 'They need to hear this. It's because of you lot that this sort of thing goes on. You're getting messages and videos from the sick individual who did this and showing them on television, printing them in your newspapers. Do you not think that's helping him, rather than helping us? Giving him a thrill. Making him do it again, and probably again soon enough . . .'

'We're just reporting the news,' a voice from the back shouted. Murphy, who had been watching Emily with a growing respect, scanned the crowd for the source. He wanted to remember the face, just to make a note of it.

'That's enough,' DSI Butler said, cutting in. 'This is obviously an emotional time for Emily. Are we . . . are we going to end?'

DSI Butler looked towards the press officer for help, before a cacophony erupted as the reporters in the room began to rise to their feet and voice their dismay.

'Hey, quieten down,' Murphy said, standing up and shouting over them. 'Have a bit of respect.'

DCI Stephens stood up next to him, placing a hand on his elbow. 'Let's just go,' she said, trying to lead him away. 'They're not going to listen.'

Murphy allowed himself to be led away, looking back to make sure Emily Flynn was being cared for.

Outside the room – noise still growing inside the press room as the occupants became more indignant – Murphy stood off to the side as DCI Stephens and DSI Butler argued in what they thought were quiet voices.

Once it started going round in circles, each accusing the other of perceived transgressions, Murphy became bored.

'That's enough,' Murphy said, taking a step towards them. 'Who cares what went wrong in there? You ask me, that's the best thing that could have happened.'

'How is that, Detective Inspector Murphy?' DSI Butler said, turning to him with a wearied face.

'Well, that'll be all over the news for hours now. And they'll have to include what Hannah's mother said. If someone, somewhere knows anything, they're going to be moved by that. That was real. Everything we do in those things isn't. It's always the same spiel that people just tune out. Emily Flynn has just done us a favour. Now, I'm going back to work. You two can sort this out between you.'

Murphy turned and didn't wait for a response. He walked away up the corridor, expecting to be called back, but the order didn't arrive.

He smiled to himself as he turned the corner, pleased that Emily Flynn had been the one to argue with reporters and not him this time.

It worked so much better coming from a relative than a detective.

Truth

He was normal again, but the time between the two parts of him colliding was becoming shorter. He wanted to switch off from it all. Stay in normality for a while longer, where his thoughts didn't overpower him.

There was a truth that he couldn't face. That he didn't want to voice, for fear of it taking over and consuming him. Allowing one part of himself to become dominant.

He wasn't sorry for what he had done.

There was no conscience, no worry that he was going to hell or anything like that.

That was what bothered him. What he had become, killing not only the liars and those who held secrets, but also the innocent. After the fourth of those *innocents* he thought it would begin to have some effect on him, but he went to sleep not thinking of their last moments. Of their relatives left behind. He thought of nothing. Other than who would be next.

That was part of his truth and it scared him.

The celebrity couple had been a mistake. He saw that now. It had focused people's attention away from his message and onto them. The truth was he had been given a gift and couldn't pass it up. Inside information about someone high-profile, from a drug-induced friend of the liar. A patient, who had thought his tale could be kept secret.

There were no secrets in that hospital. He knew everything that was going on with everyone in the place. Gossip was the sole source of trade within those walls.

He was in the break room when the press conference came on the TV in the corner. The sound was turned down, so he had to wait for the subtitles to catch up with the voices on the screen. The police all serious and dressed smartly. The mother of one of his victims sitting close by, waiting for her turn to speak. He was glad to see the big detective sitting there and that he looked even more tired with each passing day.

So he should, he thought. Lies have a way of catching up with you.

It was almost interesting, watching them talk about what he had done, the panic he had created. The lives he had changed forever. There was more interest in it than anything else he could remember happening in the city. Liverpool was now a base camp for what seemed like every member of the media in the country.

He felt a sense of pride for that.

He was tired. That was also his truth. Tired of having to split his life into two compartments. Normality and the man he became when he tried to help these people. When he'd read about serial killers, they hadn't mentioned the way it took up so much of your time.

'You still coming tomorrow?'

There were always people wanting to speak to him, interrupting him whilst he was thinking or trying to pay attention to something. On the television screen, the mother of one of the liars was becoming more agitated as she spoke at length. He saw misspelled words appear across the screen, which seemed to be blaming the press for what had happened.

'I wouldn't miss it, mate. Still at five?'

'Yeah, we're meeting in Flanno's first. Are you bringing someone?'

He looked at the interrupter finally, giving them a smile he'd practised in the mirror a number of times.

'Think so. Just waiting for her to say it's okay.'

How could she blame them? It was he who had taken her daughter. It was he who had orphaned her grand-daughter. How dare she try to take credit away from him. For all he had worked hard for, what he had created. It wasn't the media to blame for her daughter's lies.

She was going on his list. He'd get round to her one day.

He continued to watch the screen, hoping to catch a glimpse of someone. A familiar face. Disappointment grew by the second as the face didn't appear.

Then, the camera panned across and the big detective filled the screen. On his feet, pointing at some-one in the . . . audience? He wasn't sure what to call them.

The press conference finished then and the programme cut back to the studio; his interest disappeared.

He was tired. There was something missing. When he had killed the first couple, there was a buzz which lasted for days. He had trashed their house when they were both dead, just to do something with all the pent-up excitement he had felt once the two people sitting in their chairs no longer drew breath.

The pair he had killed the previous night had brought no excitement. Only anger. They didn't understand. Hadn't wanted to be helped.

The gaping wound in the male's neck reminded him of videos he had watched on the internet, of men in the Middle East, killing for their own reasons, just like him. The woman had died with no sounds, slumped over in seconds, just like the rest of them.

Walking round the house, seeing the happy and smiling vision of the pair beaming from every photograph ... it sickened him. He couldn't get out of there quickly enough after tearing the photos off the walls and creating the flawed masterpiece.

He had made a mistake. He knew it now. The truth was that he thought he'd done it on purpose. That somewhere, deep down, he wanted to be found out and stopped. He was sick, he knew that. He just couldn't help himself.

He wanted to make things better. For everyone. He wanted to be told that he had done a good thing. That the things he had said and thought were correct. That he wasn't crazy or deserving of derision. That everything he did for Number Four meant something.

When he looked into the eyes of the innocent party, he saw no love. Only hatred and a desire for violence. The rational part of them overridden with jealousy and hurt. He had done that to them. Brought them to that place. He was doing right. He had to remember that. They deserved to know the truth. To know what they had signed up for when getting into that relationship.

There were voices now, with no distinction between what was real and what was false. His thoughts were taking over, making it difficult for him to tell what he had imagined or what had happened.

He was tired. Not exhausted, but close to it. He wanted to take someone else. Another couple. To show the world that he would continue to do his work. To do the thing he was best at. Not leave a trace of himself behind.

Except his mistake.

The drug which made them go to sleep. To move on and never know they had. Not kicking and screaming behind a gag, as he cut their throat or their air supply. The girl from the previous night, he thought. She'd had too much.

He wanted to see if she would suffer.

There would have to be changes. He would have to kill the innocent in the same way as the guilty.

Normal. He just wanted to be normal. To love someone and be loved back. To consume someone's life and allow them the same luxury with him. To be entwined with someone and never to let go.

He hated as well. Hated the way love had been distorted and moulded into something it was never meant to be. Hated those who lied and kept secrets, destroying the love from within.

He hated them.

There was someone speaking to him, standing in the doorway of the break room, saying his name, trying to get his attention, but he didn't want to look over. He was scared what he would do. Whether normality would finally slip away and all that would be left was the side of him he couldn't control.

374   LUCA VESTE

He turned his head and smiled. Wondered if the woman standing there knew there was a possibility she could be part of his next project.

Wondered if he could control himself until the time was right to do so.

Chapter Thirty-One

DC Hale felt good about himself. He'd worked his way up, starting as a uniformed copper and putting in for promotions, eventually making it into CID. Now, he was a detective constable, which had proven to be a title he could use to his advantage. When the new command had been established, he'd made sure he was involved.

Now, he was in the middle of a big case. A serial murder. All his friends were jealous, he knew it. Spotting him on TV, as he strode into crime scenes. All of them ringing him for the latest gossip, wanting to know all the juicy details. Stuff he wasn't supposed to reveal, but that didn't really stop him.

DC Hale opened the door to the family room, putting on his best sombre face as he walked in. 'Kim, do you need anything? Tea, coffee, water?'

He waited for her to turn towards him. She looked him up and down, appraising him in a second.

'No, I'm fine.'

DC Hale slipped into the room proper, feeling a little frisson of excitement as he thought about who Kim was. The sister of an actual murder victim. A very high-profile case and he got to spend time with her.

'Who is the person they've arrested?' Kim said, nonchalantly as if it didn't really matter. 'Is it Carly's killer?'

DC Hale didn't hesitate. 'No, it's some bloke who sent an email to the guy. Apparently it named your sister and her boyfriend. We're not sure of all the details yet . . .'

'So, this guy emails the murderer and what? Asks him to kill my sister?'

DC Hale felt the ground slip away from him a little. He'd already said too much. 'We're not sure that's exactly what happened . . .'

'Who is he?'

'I'm afraid I can't give you that information at the moment, but if you give me some time, I'll get someone in to talk to you about it.'

'Is he here?'

This time, DC Hale did hesitate. 'I . . .'

'He is, isn't he?'

*　　*　　*

Adam didn't know what was going to happen next, but he didn't think it would be anything good. He'd screwed up. He had made one single stupid decision, and his life was never going to be the same again. Not that it had amounted to much anyway, but it was still his.

He couldn't believe Carly was gone.

He allowed himself to be led out of the interview room, towards the cells at the other end of the station. Passing people in the corridor, all staring and judging him. They all knew what he'd done. He may not have been in that room, but he might as well have been.

He'd killed Carly.

The thought brought on a fresh bout of sobs, as the uniformed officer gripped his arm harder, pulling him along the corridor.

'What have I done?'

It wasn't supposed to end this way, he thought. Not like this. Through a film of tears, he saw something ahead. A blonde version of Carly, walking towards him, shouting.

'There he is. You little prick, I'm going to kill you.'

*　　*　　*

Murphy was heading back to the main office when he heard the commotion coming from one of the corridors leading off the stairs. He assumed it was some rowdy prisoner who wasn't taking kindly to being held.

'An email?'

The shouted accusation made him stop in his tracks. Murphy shook his head and was about to move on, when he placed the voice he'd heard.

He started running.

In less than a minute, he reached the confrontation. DC Hale was trying to hold back Carly's sister from a cowering Adam Evans, the volume of noise all coming from one direction.

'You as good as killed them, you piece of shit,' Kim said, baring her teeth at Adam. She was almost out of DC Hale's grip, only a uniformed officer standing between her and Adam.

'Get him out of here,' Murphy shouted, sprinting towards the group. 'Move him now.'

The uniformed officer came to life, grabbing Adam by the shoulders and lifting him to his feet. Kim was almost away from DC Hale, slashing at the air between her and Adam with one hand as Murphy shoved DC Hale to one side and grabbed hold of Kim himself, his arms locked around her waist so she could no longer move.

'Let me go. Let me get at him. I'll kill you. You hear me? You killed my sister. I'm going to end you. They can't keep you here forever.'

'I'm sorry . . . I'm sorry,' Adam muttered through tears, as he was led away. He ducked his head, but not quick enough to dodge the glob of saliva as it flew from Kim's mouth.

'Keep your fucking sorries. I'm going to find you.'

'That's enough,' Murphy said, still holding on to Kim. He walked her across the corridor and shoved his way through the nearest door. Thankfully, the office inside was empty.

'What the hell is going on?' Murphy said, once he'd placed Kim into a chair, standing between her and the door. He turned to DC Hale who had followed them in. 'Wait here, Kim.'

Murphy gripped Hale's arm, leading him out of the office and closing the door behind him. He glanced to his left, saw Adam Evans being led round the corner, still crying uncontrollably.

'Start talking.'

'I . . . I . . .'

'Did I say start stuttering? No, I don't think I did. You've got precisely three seconds to tell me what the hell is going on, or I'm going to tell her you're the one who killed her sister and leave you alone in there with her for a while.'

'I wasn't thinking,' DC Hale said, lifting a shaking hand to his hair and trying to smooth it out. 'It just came out.'

'What did?'

'What Adam Evans was arrested for. About the email and that. I wasn't thinking. That's all. It was a mistake.'

Murphy puffed out a breath and stared at the top of Hale's head as he lowered it to his chest. 'You stupid little dickhead. You could have screwed us all up, do you know that? We're at a very critical stage right now and the last thing we need is for one of our victim's relatives to be arrested for assault, or worse. Do you understand that?'

'I was just trying . . .'

'I don't care what you were "just trying",' Murphy said, banging his fist into the wall beside Hale's body. 'All I want to hear is, "Yes, sir, it won't happen again." Got it?'

'Yes, sir,' DC Hale said, six inches shorter than when the conversation had begun. 'It won't happen again.'

'Good. Now piss off and stay out of my sight for the foreseeable future.'

Murphy turned and entered the office behind him without looking back. Kim was sitting on the chair next to the desk, swivelling it from side to side.

'You shouldn't have a go at him, he did me a favour.'

'That's not the point, Kim,' Murphy said, leaning against a filing cabinet opposite her. 'I know you're angry. Trust me, I've been there. But this type of thing won't help us find your sister's killer. I need you to be cool and calm. I don't care what happens after all this is over, but for now, I need everyone on side. Understand?'

Kim looked at him with dark eyes, peering at him as if she were looking at him for the first time. Her brow knitted together, the lines fading as she processed what he'd said.

'Yes. I can wait.'

Murphy nodded and stood upright. 'Good. Now, I should get back. Stay here, I'll have someone come get you and take you to the family room again.'

Murphy left the office, stood outside for a few seconds and breathed in deep. What had been a long week, was becoming even longer.

Chapter Thirty-Two

There was no feeling of being refreshed; no one had been revitalised by the night's sleep. It was Saturday afternoon and everybody at the station wanted to be anywhere but there. Murphy almost had to drag himself into the station that morning, kicked out of bed by Sarah after his alarm had gone off more than three times. He had taken one look at himself in the mirror and decided when the case was over, he was going on holiday.

The image of Amy Maguire appeared in his mind and he decided a holiday may not be the best option.

'Have we got anything on forensics?' DCI Stephens said to him, sitting out in the incident room now. She'd moved from her quiet office into the area where the 'magic' happened. Of which there was none to be found at that moment.

'Not a thing,' Murphy replied. 'Just who we've ruled out from family members and friends. There's nothing else we can find there.'

'Not even off the photo collages he does?'

Murphy shook his head. 'He's careful. Bloody television has made our lives so much more difficult. Given away all our secrets.'

'We must have something, David?'

Murphy saw DC Harris smirk over DCI Stephens's shoulder at the use of his first name. 'We should have a drug report on Carly coming in soon which may hold more information.'

'We can't wait around for that. Damn things always take too long. Speak to Dr Houghton and see if he can shed any more light on this thing.'

'We did speak to an anaesthetics guy in the Royal a few days ago, but he couldn't really tell us much at all.'

'Tell the doc *I* want to know the information. He'll listen to that. CCTV of the ChloJoe apartment turn up anything?'

Even the DCI had taken to merging their names, Murphy thought. There was no hope for any of them. 'We went through what we could get for last Friday night, but all we saw was Chloe entering and then leaving the apartment half an hour later. There's a number of people who arrive and leave before her, but we're still working on ruling those people out.'

'Do we know when Joe was taken?'

'No,' Murphy replied, giving Rossi a nod as she left the office without saying anything. He glanced at the clock, glad to have got her out of there early enough to make it to her night out. He almost smiled. 'He had footy training, but we don't think he made it home.'

'Our guy was waiting for him. Which means he'd planned this out. Makes sense, given the profile of them both. Just snatching them off the street wouldn't have worked.'

'I'll ring Dr Houghton then,' Murphy said, wanting to move past the questions focusing on everything they didn't know. 'See if he has anything of use to say.'

Murphy waited for DCI Stephens to walk away and speak to one of the other detectives in the office, then picked up his phone. After a few minutes of being on hold, transferred, then transferred to the right place, Houghton's dulcet tones eventually came over the phone.

'David.'

'Yeah, you got a minute?'

A moist breath came over the earpiece. 'I suppose so. What do you need?'

'We're talking about the drug that was given to one part of each couple as an overdose . . .'

'The opioid? Used in anaesthetics. What about it?'

'Well, how easy would that be to get, really? And is there any way of finding out what it actually is?'

'Have you not had the drug report back yet on the latest pair? Buggers always take their time. I bet it's Propofol. There's very little else it could be really. Nothing that you could get easily in this country anyway.'

'The report is due back any second, but DCI Stephens said she needed to know more about it and that you would help.'

'Not sure how much help I can be. Didn't you talk to that anaesthetist?'

'Yes, but he wasn't much help regarding how it could be traced . . .'

'Really? I suppose that's true. Unless something is left behind, like a vial of some sort. Or it's a new type of drug used.'

Murphy sat forward in his chair, almost knocking into his desk. 'What do you mean?'

'Well, let's for argument's sake say it is Propofol.

That isn't something you can just find in a chemist's, David. As I'm sure you already know, it's a well-regulated drug, only for use during general anaesthetic procedures in this country – although in the States, they're using it for executions now – so there are things you should know.'

'Like what?'

'Like how it doesn't just disappear without anyone noticing. We've had a few instances in the hospital over the years of some doctors using it recreationally to get "high", as the kids say. Although that happened more in the past than it does now.'

'We've already gone over this, but the boss wants me to check again. Does every hospital keep a record of any drugs that might go missing?'

'Of course, but it's only if large amounts over a long period go missing that something would be done.'

Murphy rolled his eyes, knowing the answer already. 'Only when they start actually losing money?'

'Exactly. Look, here's something they don't really like to tell people . . . drugs go missing all the time. Just little things, here and there. You can't keep track of it all. We talk about having very strict protocols over drug care, but sometimes it's impossible to do. Something like Propofol or the like, if it was only small amounts, it could be chalked up to an administrative error, or perhaps someone dropped some and didn't want to come clean. It happens. But that's not the only way to trace it anyway.'

'Enlighten me, Doc.'

'I really don't appreciate that term. Makes me feel old, David.'

'Would you prefer I call you Stuart?'

There was a pause over the line. Murphy smiled, knowing he'd won a point for once.

Houghton continued. 'Never mind. Each drug is made up of different properties. If this isn't just Propofol and something different, you may be able to work out where it came from that way. I assume you're looking at local hospitals?'

'It makes the most sense,' Murphy said, making notes on the lined paper on his desk. 'The victims are local, so if it's a new drug, for argument's sake, that can only be found in hospitals, it's likely to have come from one in this area.'

'Merseyside is a big area though,' Houghton said. 'I'll do some chasing up of my own. See if I can find out if anything has been flagged up yet.'

Murphy thanked the doctor and then called over DCI Stephens.

'I don't care who you have to call, or what favours you need to pull in, but we need that drugs report in now.'

Murphy leaned back in his chair. There was something else, something he wasn't considering.

He glanced at the clock, wondering if Rossi was already out with Darren's workmates, having a good time whilst he was stuck in the office. He hoped so, otherwise he would have to have another word with her. She deserved it, he decided. Even if it was something she thought she didn't really need, like a partner or the dreaded 'boyfriend' – a word she so detested. He thought back to the joke he'd made about the possibility the killer could be Darren, and Rossi's reaction to it. There was something real there, with that relationship, he thought. He was glad of it.

He went through some messages left on his desk, discarding ones which were from days before, or just weren't that urgent or interesting. Then he looked through his emails, doing the same thing. He pulled up the crime scene photographs, looking through them to make sure there was nothing he had missed. The images offered no clues, the only thing that stood out was how similar each scene looked.

But there was something about the picture collages that held Murphy's attention; it was as if a life was being put back together, after being destroyed. It was not the work of someone who understood the nature of relationships. It was someone who fetishised them. Made them into something that didn't actually exist.

'He's a loner,' Murphy said, voicing his thoughts. DC Harris who was sitting at his desk near him lifted his head. 'Or someone who has been in almost no relationships at all.'

'What makes you say that?' DC Harris replied.

'He's creating something with the photographs. Trying to portray an image of what he thinks a relationship should look like, then desecrating it with his words. He's saying what is normal and what isn't. Which means, to me, that he has no concept of normal relationships at all.'

'Aren't they always loners? Serial killers, I mean.'

'Not always. Not even often. There've been loads who have had families, friends, all of whom had no idea about this other part of their loved one's life. This guy, though, I can't see that being the case.'

'Unless his wife did something that led him down this path? Lied, cheated, whatever.'

'Possibly, but I'm not so sure,' Murphy said, tapping his pen against the desk. 'It's too perfect. He killed Joe Hooper based on the fact he was cheating on Chloe and that the whole relationship was a lie. He killed Will based on a stranger's email telling him that Will had cheated on Carly. Will and Joe's infidelities are minor compared to something like the secret Hannah Flynn kept from her partner, or the secret Stuart kept from Jane.'

'To him they're not minor, though. He sees them as all the same.'

'Exactly. I don't think it would matter what the transgression was if he couldn't make it fit into his view of what a relationship should be. Which means any relationship he's had wouldn't have lasted long, surely?'

'I don't know, sir,' DC Harris said, wheeling his chair back and forth. 'Are you saying we should be looking at all the loners in the city?'

'Scour the lonely hearts column in the *Echo*, you mean?'

'Something like that.' DC Harris smiled and crunched up a piece of paper on his desk, throwing it in the bin. 'Could take a while.'

'I'm just thinking out loud more than anything else.'

Something else came to Murphy then.

'Where did the first victims work?' Murphy asked DC Harris over the desk. 'Can't remember seeing that information.'

'Erm, not sure now,' DC Harris replied, shuffling paper

round his desk. 'Here we go. He worked for a cleaning firm, some place over the water. She was a nurse in the Royal.'

Murphy sat forward. 'The hospital?'

'Do you know any other places we call the Royal?'

Murphy ignored the sarcasm. 'That's one.' He picked up the phone whilst still scrolling through the system on his computer for the number he needed. A few minutes later he put the phone down again.

'That's another one.'

DC Harris came round to his side of the desk. 'Who was that?'

'Joe Hooper's friend Charlie Smith who was in here the other day. Told us about Joe's indiscretions. Turns out Charlie had surgery on his knee at the Royal.'

'Could be a coincidence?'

Murphy shook his head. 'Think about it. Our murderer needs to get these drugs from somewhere, but not only them. Maybe he also chose his victims from the place. Maybe it's somewhere he works?'

DC Harris didn't answer, just wheeled himself back to his desk.

'What are you doing?' Murphy said, as DC Harris began going through a multitude of paperwork.

'Something has just come to me. Hang on a minute.'

Murphy waited, as he tried to work out what the new information could mean.

'Here we go,' DC Harris said after a minute. 'Another one.'

'The sister? She said she had problems in work with someone . . .'

'No, not her. She works in some car place on the front. No, Hannah Flynn told two people outside of her family about the fact she didn't think the child was Greg's.'

'That's right,' Murphy said, already starting to feel the excitement wash over him, ridding him of the tiredness. 'Friends or something?'

'Exactly. I remembered something from Laura's notes from their interviews. One of them was recovering from hernia surgery. She wrote down the hospital she'd just been discharged from.'

'The Royal.'

'In one,' DC Harris replied, a wide smile on his face. 'This is it, don't you think?'

Murphy didn't reply at first. Ignoring the emails, Murphy thought about the previous victims. Will and Carly were an aberration. A way of throwing a whole toolbox in the works. If he played six degrees of separation starting with each couple, everything came back to the same hospital. Then the drugs angle played its own role also.

'We need more, but this could be the answer. We need the latest drugs report.'

Within an hour, they had it.

*　　*　　*

Murphy read the report again, his forehead creasing up as he tried to make sense of it. 'And this is ... what is it I'm looking at?'

'The name of the drug,' DC Harris said, shaking his head. 'A heavier dose was used with Carly, so we have it now.'

Murphy wrote down the serial number next to the drug and called back Dr Houghton.

'It was Propofol,' Houghton said by way of greeting. 'I'm guessing that's why you're calling me back.'

'No. And no,' Murphy said, rubbing his forehead, trying to ease a little of the tension stuck there. 'That's not the drug.'

'Really? Now that's interesting.'

'It may not have been Propofol, but apparently it shares a lot of its make-up with it. Not a lot of this makes sense to me . . .'

'What's it called?'

Murphy spelled out the name of the drug, which had been found in Carly's system.

'Doesn't sound like anything I've heard of before. Let me check this out.'

Murphy listened as Houghton typed on his keyboard, imagining the pathologist leaning over his ever-expanding waistline to reach his desk. The thought made him smirk, earning a frown from a waiting DC Harris.

'Here we go,' Houghton said finally. 'It's a trial drug, created by the lovely people over at the City of Liverpool University. It's supposed to work like Propofol, but have fewer side effects. Only three hospitals in the country have taken the trial on.'

'The Royal is one of them, isn't it?'

'As much as I'm pleased to say it is, I'm also dreading what's about to happen. The other two are further south in the country – one in Birmingham and one in Surrey. I bloody knew it. I'm telling you, the things that get over-looked in hospitals at the moment. All down to government cuts. They couldn't give two bloody shites about what's going on in the NHS at the moment. People getting away with murder. Quite literally, by the sounds of it. Who do you think it could be? It must be someone in a certain department, given it's a trial drug.'

'I was hoping you would be able to help with that. I don't want this guy tipped off . . .'

'How do you know it wasn't me?' Houghton said, the mocking tone of his voice raising Murphy's blood pressure a few levels.

'Because you'd be out of breath just getting into the house in the first place.'

'Touché, David. okay, what do you need?'

Murphy pulled the sheet of paper closer to him. 'I know you said there were drugs going missing in small quantities more than we realised, but do you think this could be different?

'I would imagine so. It's a trial drug, so there'll be much tighter controls on it than others. Possibly. I'm guessing more than anything here.'

'If there are tighter controls, do you have access to a log of dates and times, for when drugs have been reported missing?'

'I don't,' Houghton replied, his voice dropping a level. 'But I can definitely find out anything you need to know. Just give me the details and I'll call you back.'

Murphy read Houghton the information and then put the phone down. He waited, counting down the seconds on the clock hanging on the wall. Finally the phone rang on his desk. Murphy snatched it up, dragging the base over the desk as he did so, clattering it against his coffee cup.

'Murphy,' he said, mopping up the resulting little spillage with the back of his tie.

'It's Houghton. I've got three names for you ... you're probably not going to like one of them. Is young Ms Rossi in earshot?'

Chapter Thirty-Three

Rossi really didn't want to leave. Not then, in the middle of everything that had been going on. Yet, she knew Murphy was right. There was nothing that couldn't be done if she wasn't there. And she deserved this.

It wasn't like they were close to a result anyway. She was growing tired of investigating possibilities which never amounted to anything. The case was going to be lost to a bigger taskforce at some point soon, she decided. With absolutely zero leads, it was always going to be the way.

She wanted a night off before all that began, and Darren had given her the best excuse to have one.

It didn't take long for her to get ready. Home by quarter past four, she had a quick shower then changed into the clothes she'd already set aside. She was just applying the third lipstick she'd picked out – the first two discarded when they didn't look right – when there was a knock at the door.

Rossi rushed down the stairs, thinking that she really should have gone with her second choice on the lipstick, and maybe even done something more with her hair. She opened the door. Darren stood there with a grin and a single rose.

'Evening, you look great,' Darren said, handing her the rosè and then planting a kiss on her forehead.

'You don't look so bad yourself,' Rossi replied, stepping back so he could come into the house. 'You scrub up well when needs be. Had a haircut or had your ears lowered?'

'Bit of both,' Darren replied, the wide grin she had noticed on the first date making an appearance. It was a notch below the Joker, which made it endearing rather than worrying.

'Just give me two seconds.'

Rossi grabbed her jacket off the banister and went into her living room to find her handbag.

'Everyone's meeting at five,' Darren said from the hallway. 'But we're not eating until later, so we've got plenty of time.'

'Good, I'll need a drink before we sit down anyway. Let me just find my smokes.'

'What did I say about all the diseases those things can give you? Hope you're not going to get addicted.'

'I'll only do it when I have a drink. Besides, I've heard it's people who work in hospitals who smoke more than any other profession anyway.'

'I can't see that being true.'

'Oh, I definitely can,' Rossi replied, finding an unopened packet of Lambert & Butler and shoving them in her handbag. She came out into the hallway again. 'I still can't believe I agreed to this. Meeting your workmates . . . must have been mad to say yes.'

'Mad about me, I imagine . . .'

'Oh, don't start getting soppy on me. I can still drop you so fast, you'll be wondering what happened a week later.'

'You'd never do anything so silly,' Darren said, looping an arm around her and pulling her in for a kiss.

'Come on,' Rossi said, breaking away before she had to consider getting ready all over again. 'Let's get going. We'll be late.'

'So we're late. Sod them.'

'No, you can wait until later,' Rossi said with a smile, walking towards her front door. 'Let's get going. After the week I've had, I'd prefer a drink first anyway.'

'That almost hurt my ego,' Darren said, following her outside, pouting for effect.

It was easier than she had expected. She'd fallen into a relationship almost overnight. Quicker than she had thought was possible. She had spent years actively avoiding them, thinking the reality never matched up to what was imagined. It was still not even close to being perfect, but she could, for the first time, actually see further than a month or so with this one.

Darren began speaking to her in the car as he drove. Rossi was distracted by thoughts of the week's events, which crept back in and pushed aside the better ones being created now. Always the way.

'Are you somewhere else?' Darren said, giving her a quick glance.

'A bit. As I said, I need that drink.'

'Don't tell me I've got myself an alcoholic. The prettiest ones always have these problems . . .'

'Shut up. I'm definitely not an alcoholic. I just know what will help and that's a large glass of red wine.'

'*Italiano?*'

'Of course,' Rossi replied, smiling again. 'Nice accent by the way. Could almost be mistaken for a native.'

'Thanks, I've been working on it.'

They lapsed into a comfortable silence, the journey taking only ten or fifteen minutes. The roads weren't as busy as she'd been expecting for a Saturday evening.

'I think this week's news has put people off coming into town,' Rossi said, as she spied the entrance to the Liverpool One car park coming up.

'I didn't think anything could put people off going out in Liverpool. Shows you how wrong I can be.'

They parked up, walking the short distance to the pub on Hanover Street where they were meeting up. Rossi began to feel her heart pumping a little more as they got closer. They passed Waterstones, Rossi fighting the urge to go in and sit amongst the books and lose herself in fiction. Anything to get away from the nervousness that had annoyingly appeared.

Why did she care so much what these people thought of her?

Darren slipped an arm around her shoulders and she fought the urge to shrug him off. Accept this new normal life, she told herself.

A few minutes later, they passed the old Irish bar which was loud and rocking despite the almost empty streets and entered the quieter pub opposite it. A shout went up from the corner, marking their arrival.

'I'll get us drinks,' Darren said, giving the loud group a wave and taking his wallet out of his back pocket. 'You can stay and give me a hand.'

Rossi breathed a sigh of relief, glad that he hadn't suggested she go over and introduce herself. It was bright in the pub, an old-style place, which was desperately clinging on to its history, even though a chain had quite plainly taken it over. There were flat screen TVs on every wall, all showing *Sky Sports News*, which made a change for her. It was nice to see news which she wasn't involved in for a change.

She thought she may have been in here when she was a student and had tried to visit every alcohol-selling establishment in the city centre, but she had no more than a vague memory of that. It had grown darker outside, the coolness of the approaching evening becoming more noticeable as she'd entered into the warmth of the pub.

She had a quick glance at the group who had taken over the corner of the bar. It seemed evenly spread, gender wise, which brought another sigh of relief. There was a moment when she'd wondered if she would be the only partner to turn up. From the way people were sitting, the body language on show from some of them, there were definitely a few couples in the group.

Oh God, she thought. I'm part of a couple.

Darren turned to her, handing her something which looked like a fishbowl, full to the top with red wine. He grabbed his own drink and lead the way to the table.

She was glad she was still smoking. It would give her an excuse to walk away from the table and take a breather if needs be.

It was a little uncomfortable at first. Rossi kept catching people glancing at her. After the first few gulps of her drink, she began to relax a little more.

She pulled Darren closer to her and whispered in his ear, 'I'm glad I came.'

* * *

Murphy slammed the phone down and grabbed his jacket from the back of his chair.

'What's going on?' DC Harris said, the smile on his face now replaced by a look of genuine concern. 'Have we got him?'

Murphy swore to himself under his breath as he tried to find his car keys. 'Yes ... no ... I don't know. Has anyone seen my bloody keys?'

'They're on your desk where you left them, sir,' DC Harris said, wheeling himself across to Murphy. 'Is it the drugs? Do we know where they came from?'

'The Royal,' Murphy replied, snatching up his keys and looking round the office. 'The bloody surgical department.'

'Slow down,' DCI Stephens said, coming into view from round her office door where she'd been listening. 'Do we have a possible name?'

'We have three of them,' Murphy said, handing over his notes containing the three names. 'The drugs were from a trial of a new type of anaesthetic and the Royal was one of those taking part in the trial. We've also nailed down our first six victims as having links to the hospital. Our guy was clever. He stole just small amounts over the course of around three months ...'

'He'd been planning this for a while,' DCI Stephens said, as everyone in the office began to listen in. 'All those links ... it's how he found them.'

'Enough of the drug to cause someone to overdose, but not enough to begin a major investigation in the hospital, it seems.'

'These three names – Ben Flanagan, Sam Bishop, and Darren Logan – they all work in the same department?'

'Yes, two anaesthetists and a nurse. There are three people who were working at the time the drug has been used, each time. Only three, as it was only a a few occasions it was actually used with patients. There were strict protocols around it, given it's a trial drug. There are four instances of small quantities going missing following procedures. Three people had access to it at those times. It doesn't matter though, I know who it is. It's Logan.'

'Who?'

'Darren Logan,' Murphy replied. 'We met with him and there was something about him. It fits. Why he's suddenly on the scene. I'm sure of it. It all makes too much sense, the way he's got himself in there. Could be a problem with that though.'

Murphy became aware of the number of eyes and ears on him at that moment. He stopped, thinking of Rossi and how closely she guarded her life outside work. 'Can we talk in your office?'

DCI Stephens extended a hand towards her office, following Murphy as he walked over quickly, closing the door after her. 'What's going on, David?'

'It's Laura,' Murphy said, his stomach turning as he thought about her. 'She's been dating Logan for a few weeks now.'

'I know that, David. We all know that. Gossip travels fast round here. But, I see your point. It started about the same time of the first couple's murder ...'

'The best time to have someone in the police on your side, perhaps? I don't know. All I do know is that she could be in trouble.'

'She's here, isn't she?'

Murphy shifted on his feet and looked down at the worn-looking carpet. 'I let her go early. She's meeting with Logan, to meet the people he works with for a drink and a meal. I thought she deserved it.'

'And now she might be in harm's way.'

Murphy's shoulders slumped a little as he thought about the situation.

'It could be any of the three names.'

'Are you joking, boss? With our luck around here?

Murphy fixed his boss with a stare.

Stephens sighed. 'It's a huge leap to believe it's him in particular.' Another sigh. 'Okay, here's what we're going to do. We're bringing all three in for questioning, now. Let's get out there and find them.'

Chapter Thirty-Four

Murphy's plan was to walk straight into the pub, grab Rossi and then let everyone sort themselves out with whatever else needed doing. Unfortunately, that wasn't what DCI Stephens wanted to do, and instead she called in Authorised Firearm Officers to deal with the situation.

'Do you really think this is wise?'

'Yes,' DCI Stephens replied, tapping the radio in her hand against one leg. 'We have no idea what this man is actually capable of. If Rossi is with the guy, we neutralise him fast and work all that out later.'

It had taken Harris a few phone calls to find out where Rossi and Logan had gone. It was a departmental night out, with only those on shift at the hospital not in attendance. After twenty minutes of holding and being transferred to various wards Harris had managed to get the name of the pub on Hanover Street.

All three people mentioned by Houghton were inside, but Murphy had made sure everyone knew what the main objective was.

Remove Rossi from the situation and take down anyone who stopped that happening.

Murphy sat in his car, watching the entrance to the pub through the windscreen, waiting for the advance to begin. He crossed his fingers, looked across at DC Kirkham who was sitting beside him.

'We go in straight after. Get Laura away and deal with her. Okay?'

DC Kirkham looked back at him, a shade or three lighter than his normal complexion. 'She's one of ours, sir.'

Murphy gave him a nod and turned back to the pub entrance. Placed his hand on the car-door handle and waited.

*   *   *

Rossi wasn't sure if she was having a good time, or if the wine had gone to her head quicker than she'd realised. She hadn't eaten yet, which was probably a bad idea, she thought, but she was already on her second glass. At that point, it wouldn't really matter anyway, she decided.

Darren's work friends were all welcoming, attempting to include her in conversations she was unable to contribute to. Mostly work stories – patients who had done strange things whilst coming out of anaesthetic, the sights they had seen. Nothing compared with what Rossi could tell them from her own work life, but it was nice to just be a part of it.

'Before he'd even gone under he was being a pain,' Ben said from the other side of the table, a childish grin on his face. His partner moved a little further towards him, her face upturned in a way which made Rossi want to roll her eyes. Utter devotion, hanging on every word. Rossi didn't want to become *that* type. 'It was all right until we were trying to wake him up. He's trying to roll round and that, but can't. And then he tries to grab me, right, and I'm like, shit, what do I do now? He looks me right in the eye and says, "Someone did something to my arse, didn't they? I know they did. It's doesn't feel the same." '

Everyone round the table laughed, some louder than others. The girl he was with laughed longest, stroking his arm as she did so.

'I had to spend ten minutes with him, telling him over and over that nothing had gone on with his arse. He was convinced of it though. You've got a similar one, haven't you, Sam?'

Rossi laughed along, as Sam began to tell his story. Every now and again she would glance towards the door, wondering if escape was still an option.

'Does this kind of thing happen a lot?' Rossi said, turning to Darren and lowering her voice. 'Getting together like this, I mean?'

'Yeah, we try and do it once every couple of months or so. First time I've been able to bring someone in a while.'

'So, there hasn't been a string of women behind me to be judged against? I feel so special.'

Darren was stone-faced for a second, then smiled. 'Yeah, you are.'

'I wasn't being serious,' Rossi replied, unsure what to make of the conversation. 'We're being rude anyway, turn round.' She flashed a smile, which disappeared as she faced back to the group, catching sight of a couple of people at their table glancing away, as if they had been listening to the conversation.

'I'm going outside for a second,' Rossi said, standing up and taking her bag. 'Won't be long.' She stopped for a moment, then bent down and kissed Darren on the top of his head.

'Hey, wait, you going *outside*?' Ben said, making a smoking gesture with his fingers. 'I'll go with you.'

Rossi smiled and nodded, wondering what the hell she was going to say to Ben once outside.

'We may as well go out on the terrace,' Ben said, tucking his shirt back into his trousers. He bent down and kissed his partner's forehead. 'Be back in a minute. Yeah, the terrace is closer . . .'

Rossi followed Ben as he walked ahead, continuing to talk. She turned back to the table and saw Darren staring after her, his face blank until he realised she was looking at him. The smile was instant, but it didn't reach his eyes.

'Enjoying yourself?' Ben said, lighting up a cigarette with a practised hand. 'They can get a bit rowdy, this lot.'

'Sounds like you're one of the rowdy ones,' Rossi replied, taking a drag on her cigarette and waiting for the whirly feeling to arrive, the result of only smoking every now and again.

'Oh, I just tell the stories. Everyone in there knows them really. Just a way of being normal. Some of the stuff people say when they're coming out of anaesthesia is just amazing. You learn all kinds of secrets.'

'I bet. I'm also betting that it gets even louder as the night goes on. Not sure I can keep up. I think I should slow down. Wine isn't the best thing to drink before eating.'

Ben gave a short laugh. 'We usually end up grabbing something to eat in the pub eventually. Everyone gets to drinking and talking and they suddenly don't want to move on.'

Rossi tried to look through the doors to their table, but the view was blocked by a couple of pillars. 'Well, I don't mind leading the charge for food.'

Ben laughed again, taking another drag on his cigarette. 'How's it going anyway? Any closer to catching the guy you were talking about the other day?'

Rossi wasted a few seconds smoking. 'I can't really talk about it. Enquiries are ongoing, as we say. We'll have him soon enough.'

'I'm sure you will,' Ben replied, stubbing his cigarette out in the upright ashtray on the deck, then lighting another. 'Always end up smoking two.'

Rossi's head turned as she heard noise from inside, carrying over the music and voices. 'Did you hear that?'

Ben moved forward, standing at the doors and peering into the pub. 'Oh, no.'

*   *   *

Murphy waited a minute before moving out of the car and towards the pub. The noise over the radio was sporadic and unintelligible for the most part, voices banging into each other as people talked over one another, the chatter constant.

'Table secure.'

That was all he was waiting for. Outside, other vehicle doors opened and shut, echoing in the now busy street. People holding shopping bags crowded round to see what was going on, a few uniforms keeping them from getting closer.

Murphy entered the pub, DCs Kirkham and Hale close on his heels. He stopped near the bar, waiting for the sergeant in charge of the AFOs to wave him over.

Ten to fifteen people were sitting at a table in the corner, AFOs surrounding them. As Murphy got closer, he saw the occupants with their hands interlocked behind their heads. There was a sudden shift in movement, as two officers all in black took down two people and forced them to the floor.

'This isn't right,' screamed one, moving his head back as hands grabbed him. 'You can't just do this.'

Murphy looked round, trying to spot Rossi, but failing. 'Where is she?' He turned back to Kirkham and Hale who were also searching the room. Kirkham shook his head.

Murphy saw Darren Logan on the floor, his face pushed against the wooden boards, sticky with spilled drinks and God knows what else. Murphy suppressed a smirk as he saw the sight.

'Got him,' he said under his breath. He got a wave from the sergeant and walked directly to Darren who was being pulled to his feet. 'Kirkham, take the other two. This one's mine.'

Murphy faced Logan and almost smiled. 'Darren Logan, I'm arresting you on suspicion of murder . . .'

'What the hell is going on?'

'You don't have to say anything . . .'

'I've got no idea what you're talking about. Where's Laura?'

Murphy stopped giving the caution and moved closer to Darren. 'What did you say?'

'Where's Laura? She'll tell you. This is all a mistake.'

'Isn't she here with you?' Murphy said, looking round, making sure he hadn't missed her.

'No, she went outside with Ben for a smoke a few minutes ago. Please, I haven't done anything wrong.'

Murphy's stomach fell. 'Ben Flanagan?'

Darren saw the change on Murphy's face and began to nod his head. 'Yes,' he replied, a panicked tone to his voice now. 'What's happened? Why are you all doing this?'

*   *   *

Outside on the terrace, Rossi could hear that the noise inside the pub had increased, causing her to move closer to Ben to see if she could see what was going on. The music stopped; she heard familiar voices.

'That sounds like . . .'

Ben stepped backwards onto the terrace, almost bumping into Rossi as he did so. He closed the doors, looking round for something.

'What's going on?' Rossi said, seeing sweat appear on Ben's face as he dragged a table in front of the doors. She saw his strength, until then hidden behind a boyish-looking body, now suddenly very worrying. 'Tell me now, Ben.'

'Just be quiet for a second. Let me think.'

Rossi began to back away. 'Wait . . . *merda.*'

They're here for a reason, Rossi thought. They've found something out.

'No . . . no,' Ben said, shifting the weighty table with little problem. 'It's not the time.'

'They've worked out where the drugs came from. They're from your hospital, aren't they?'

People revealing things when they're under the influence of anaesthetic. The way Ben was now acting. Rossi felt her stomach drop a few floors. 'It's you, isn't it?'

'Stop talking . . .'

'Ben, listen to me,' Rossi said, the shouts from inside the pub muffled now the doors were closed. 'We can talk through this, okay? Get you out of here safely. You just have to listen to me.'

'No, it's too late for that. I can't go anywhere yet. It's not time. It's not time.'

Rossi glanced round the terrace for something she could use. Her handbag was now on the floor, dropped from the table Ben had been trying to move.

'I know it looks bad now, Ben, but trust me. We can get you through this, right? You just need to calm down and listen to me.'

'Trust you?' Ben said, turning on her. 'You're one of them. I know all about you and that bloke you work with. I know all your secrets. You lie to Darren. I know it. I can see it in you. And that big bastard you work with . . . I know everything about him. I've seen him.'

Rossi's feet bumped into the wall behind her, she was unable to back away from him. 'Ben, listen, we just have to be calm and work through this.'

'Oh, "we" don't need to do anything,' Ben replied, walking towards Rossi and putting his hand into the inside pocket of his jacket. 'I just need to get out of here so I can finish what I started.'

Chapter Thirty-Five

Murphy had a familiar feeling of dread as he let go of Darren Logan and walked up the steps which led to the terrace at the side of the pub.

'What's going on?' DC Kirkham said, rushing to catch up with him as he quickened his pace. 'Where's Laura?'

'She's with Ben Flanagan, outside.'

'Wait, I thought we wanted Darren Logan, haven't we got him?'

Murphy kept going towards the terrace doors, his brow furrowing as he saw they were closed. 'I think we got it wrong. I don't know.'

Once he reached the closed doors, he realised they had.

He didn't say anything, just put his boot against the door, sending it into the table which was blocking the entrance. Murphy used his shoulder to open the door more and pushed through the opening.

He held up a hand behind him. 'Wait,' Murphy said to DC Kirkham who was shoving the door next to him.

'Stay back,' Ben Flanagan said. 'Don't move another step.'

Murphy took in the scene in front of him. Ben Flanagan – now a different animal from the one they'd met a few days previously. The way a face could change always astounded Murphy. The convivial smile, the boyish charm had now disappeared, replaced with a creased frown of concentration. Sweat poured down Ben's face as his fist gripped the knife which was pressing against Rossi's neck. Murphy locked eyes with Rossi, wanting to make sure she knew he was there.

'Ben, you're going to make this even worse,' Murphy said, his hands outstretched. 'Just put that down and talk to us.'

'I don't want to do that. I need to get away.'

'I understand that, Ben, but I can't talk about that whilst you're still holding that knife against Laura's throat.'

'No, don't speak. I have to think.'

Murphy risked edging a little closer, ten feet away from the pair, as Ben looked behind him.

'I can let her go,' Ben said, turning back to face Murphy. 'But you have to do something for me.'

Murphy stepped closer, his vision full of Ben, the knife, and Rossi's throat. 'What do you want, Ben?'

'I want you to tell the truth. For once. I know what you've been doing.'

Murphy frowned, then seeing red appear on Rossi's neck, he rushed towards the pair. Ben shoved Rossi forward into Murphy's arms.

There was blood on the floor, dripping from Rossi's neck as he caught her. Rossi's hand flew to her neck as she lost her footing and fell into Murphy. There was a shout from behind them as more officers entered the terrace.

'We need a paramedic here, now,' Murphy shouted back behind him. 'Get someone in here for fuck's sake. Laura, speak to me.'

'*Cazzo!* I'm fine,' Rossi said, lying across Murphy as they sank to the floor. 'It's nothing.'

'Don't let him get away,' Murphy shouted as he looked up quickly, the terrace now full of bodies, getting in the way of each other. 'He went over the wall.'

'It was him,' Rossi said, pulling her hand away from her neck and looking at the red it left behind. '*Figlio di troia.* The bastard was talking to me like he was normal.'

'You're going to be okay, Laura,' Murphy said, looking at the wound on Rossi's neck. 'He didn't do anything more than break the skin.'

'Feels worse than that. My neck is on fire. Have they got him yet?'

Murphy looked up at the wall Ben Flanagan had leaped over after he'd pushed Rossi towards him, now surrounded by officers peering over and climbing it themselves. He heard a shout from beyond it, DC Kirkham's voice travelling back to him.

'Don't worry,' Murphy said, spying two paramedics getting the okay to enter the terrace. 'They'll find him. He won't get far.'

'I should have done something . . .'

'Don't be stupid, Laura. What were you supposed to have done.'

'Anything other than what I did.'

Murphy moved aside and allowed the paramedics to take over, remembering a similar scene a couple of years earlier, when Rossi had been injured but not as seriously as she could have been. He wondered exactly how many lives Rossi had left.

Pushing aside anyone in the way, Murphy moved towards the wall, his height allowing him a better view.

'You got him yet?' he asked, receiving blank looks in return. 'What's keeping you all?'

'We've got people moving towards his last position,' one of the AFOs said, avoiding Murphy's eye contact. 'He moved quick, sir.'

Murphy turned away, walking past the paramedics tending to Rossi and out through the pub. Inside, the medical workers were still sitting round the table, drinks in front of them now standing untouched and unwanted. Darren Logan was still on the floor, handcuffed arms behind him, looking towards Murphy with pleading eyes.

'Is she okay?' Darren said, trying to get up from his position on the floor, but being pushed back by an AFO. 'What's happened out there?'

'Let him up,' Murphy said, helping Darren to his feet. 'She's going to be fine. You can see her in a little while. What do you know about Ben Flanagan?'

'Nothing much,' Darren replied, still trying to look past Murphy and towards the terrace. 'He started working with us a few months ago. What's happened?'

'Do you know anything about him . . . where he lives, what he does outside work, anything?'

'I don't know, honestly. I just know him through work. That's all.'

Murphy turned to the rest of the table. 'Does anyone here know anything about Ben Flanagan at all?'

The table was silent. Shock had kicked in, and Murphy shouting at them did little to help.

'Christ,' DCI Stephens said, as Murphy made his way to the pub entrance. 'What the hell went wrong?'

'They were outside when the AFOs went in,' Murphy said, pacing in front of DCI Stephens. 'Did they not check that everyone was there before storming in?'

'I don't know, I would imagine so. Mistakes happen . . .'

'Well, that mistake almost cost Laura her life and now Ben Flanagan has got away.'

'Wait . . . Ben? I thought you were sure it was this Darren Logan?'

'We got it wrong,' Murphy said, coming to a stop by the side of DCI Stephens. 'If we'd have checked before storming in, he'd still have been sitting at that table. He looks like a little kid, honestly. I didn't think it would be him at all. He can't be more than thirty . . .'

'I don't think that matters,' DCI Stephens replied, placing a hand on Murphy's elbow to stop him pacing again. 'We'll catch him, don't worry. There was nothing else we could have done.'

'There was plenty.'

'He won't get far,' DCI Stephens continued, ignoring Murphy's comment. 'The area is going into lockdown. Did he have a car or anything here?'

'I don't know,' Murphy said, spotting DC Kirkham outside the pub, pointing towards the top end of Hanover Street and Liverpool Central train station.

'We'll ask the people left in there.'

Murphy walked past DCI Stephens and went outside to talk to DC Kirkham. 'You got him yet?'

'I almost did,' DC Kirkham replied, out of breath and red-faced. He stopped and placed his hands on his knees, gulping in air. 'Bastard was fast. Ran down School Lane behind the shops. I lost him. There were others coming from the opposite side, so they'll pen him in.'

Murphy turned to the uniform standing close by. 'Get on to CCTV and track him down. The place is crawling with cameras.'

The uniform rushed off, shouting into his radio as he did so. 'Did you get close to him at all?'

'Not really,' DC Kirkham replied, standing upright once more. 'He was too quick even for me. Is that really our guy?'

'It definitely looks that way.'

'Shit,' DC Kirkham said. His face then turned a darker shade of red. 'Is Laura . . .?'

'She's fine,' Murphy said, placing a hand on Kirkham's shoulder and turning back to the pub. 'Barely broke the skin. It was just a distraction. Worked as well.'

'Any of us would have gone for her, rather than him.'

Murphy murmured in response and walked back into the pub. The medical workers were still sitting in chairs round the same table they'd been drinking at only minutes before. Darren Logan sat at the end of the row, ashen-faced and shaking. Murphy saw him casting glances behind him towards the terrace every few seconds.

'His arse hasn't even touched the seat,' Murphy said under his breath. 'He cares.'

There were more voices and a group of paramedics and AFOs crowded round something.

'Just let me walk, for Christ's sake.'

Murphy smiled and strode over. 'All right, let her walk without you all getting in her way,' he said, placing himself between a few of the officers there.

Rossi was moving slowly, one hand against a white bandage on her neck. 'Didn't even lose that much blood. Don't know what all the fuss is about.'

'You know how it is,' Murphy said, brushing aside another officer who was determined to keep a steadying hand on Rossi. 'You're one of us.'

Rossi looked up at him, her complexion whiter than he'd ever seen it before. 'Is Darren okay?'

Murphy hesitated as they reached the steps which led down to where the table was. 'He's fine, just worried about you.'

Rossi saw him before Murphy had a chance to signal to the officer standing by the table. 'Get those bloody cuffs off him now,' she said, one hand still up to her neck, the other pointing at the uniform's chest. 'He's with me.'

'Laura . . .' Murphy began to say, walking across to her. 'We can't just . . .'

'No, Murphy,' Rossi said, shrugging him off. 'He's got nothing to do with this. Arrest her, though,' she said, pointing towards a cowering brunette, attempting to hide behind another man. 'She was with Ben. She'll know something, I'll bet.'

Murphy looked towards the uniform and gave him the nod, before leaving Rossi to it and walking back to DCI Stephens at the entrance.

'Looks like she got away without anything major happening,' DCI Stephens said, a smirk appearing across her harried face. 'Good news at least.'

'Any word?'

'Nothing yet, but he can't have got far. We've got a perimeter set up around the whole of town. He's not getting through.'

'He was with someone here,' Murphy said, gesturing back towards the table. 'Laura has pointed her out. We'll need to question her.'

'Good,' DCI Stephens replied, tucking a stray strand of hair behind her ear. 'Hopefully she knows something.'

Murphy nodded, checking the time and rubbing a hand across his face. 'What do we need to do?'

'Set up a command post and monitor the situation. That's all we can do really.'

Murphy took a look outside, past DCI Stephens, and rolled his eyes. 'Press are here.'

'Surprised it took this long,' DCI Stephens said, glancing back to where Murphy was looking. 'Hopefully we'll have good news for them soon.'

Murphy tried to be optimistic, but failed.

* * *

It was ten p.m. by the time Murphy decided to call it a night. There was little he could do. He had traipsed the length of town, made sure that all the shops in the vicinity were closed for the evening and that the area had been evacuated. Safety had triumphed over profit.

There was a helicopter circling above and cars on the ground, all failing to report the one thing Murphy wanted to hear.

It seemed as if Ben Flanagan had disappeared.

The woman who had accompanied him to the pub was still being questioned, but Murphy doubted anything substantial was going to come from that. She'd said it was a new relationship, only a month or so old. It was clear she had fallen for him, but Murphy doubted those feelings were mutual.

The hospital had provided them with Flanagan's address, but when they had stormed it, they'd found only an empty bedsit, save for a few bills in his name.

No clues as to where he actually lived.

Murphy wasn't looking forward to the fallout, especially if they didn't catch him within hours. He'd called Sarah early on, just to put her mind at ease. His phone had buzzed at nine thirty.

Are you coming home yet? Thought I'd make the effort to give you something to relax . . . ;-) xx

Murphy had smiled at that. Normality. It was exactly what he needed after the week he'd had. There wasn't much he could do now, but still felt like he should stay.

Almost an hour later, he'd been ordered home and hadn't put up much of a fight. He was almost dead on his feet. He'd caught a lift back to the station so he could pick up his car and then he'd driven home on automatic pilot.

Murphy parked up, leaving the radio on as he switched off the engine. It was the local call-in show, hosted by Pete Price, talking about the manhunt. Callers moaning about how their kids weren't safe because the police weren't doing their jobs properly.

'Yet, the first people you'd ring in an emergency is us . . .' Murphy muttered in his empty car.

Then a voice came over the speakers, one he knew.

'*You probably don't even remember my name, Pete, never mind my daughter's. My daughter is Amy Maguire . . .*'

Murphy turned the radio up a touch, shaking his head as his heart began to hammer in his chest.

'No one cares about her, do they? She's been missing for weeks, and all anyone can talk about is these celebrities and stuff. Some guy giving them the run around in town now. My daughter is still out there and no one is looking for her, are they?'

'Now come on, Stacey, there's something more important going on at the moment . . .'

'More important than my daughter's safety?'

'She's eighteen, isn't she? We've got a murderer loose in Liverpool right now – how are we supposed to be looking for an eighteen-year-old while that's going on, love?'

'Don't "love" me, Pete, my daughter matters. She's out there, God knows where, and no one cares. She didn't get her face plastered over the Echo all week, or on Sky News twenty-four hours a day. No one cared when she went missing—'

'Sorry, Stacey, but we've got lots to get through tonight . . .'

Murphy switched the radio off and rubbed a hand over the rough skin on his face. He made a promise to himself. Once this was all over, he would find Amy.

Show that someone cared.

The house looked dark from the outside, only a pale light coming through the curtains in the living room. He let himself in, closing the door behind him.

'Hello?'

Candles where laid out in the hallway, leading into the dining room at the back, past the living room.

Murphy grinned, rubbed the tiredness out of his neck and took off his jacket. 'Now this was a very good idea, babe. I'm sorry I'm so late in now. I'm sure you've seen the news and know why.'

Murphy shook his shoes off and padded through into the dining room, flickering tea lights leading the way. 'Not much else I can do out there, so I'm not even going to feel guilty about this.'

He pushed open the dining-room door, saw more candles laid out on the floor and on every surface. He smiled, walking into the room.

Murphy froze as the familiar scene hit him.

Two chairs. Facing each other. One unoccupied. One not.

Sarah, looking at him, duct tape across her face. Bound to the chair so she couldn't move or make a sound. Shaking her head as her eyes widened.

Seconds. Not even that. To process what was in front of him, his feet still stuck to the floor. The whole of his insides dropping a few millimetres, the breath sucked from his body.

His feet began to move finally, but didn't get far. A noise behind him made him turn round, just as something struck him in the temple.

As Murphy fell to the floor, darkness already descending upon him, he saw his wife Sarah scream silently behind her gag.

And a man dressed in black, standing over him.

Number Four

There was somewhere he had to go, before reaching the home of the lying detective and his wife. One last place to visit.

That room and the place he could talk freely. Without judgement or interruption.

The room which contained Number Four.

'I have to go now,' Ben said, the smell within the room overpowering him. 'I don't know if I'll be back. They're trying to stop me, but you can tell them. You can tell them that I was right. That you love me now.'

He waited for an answer that wasn't going to come, then carried on speaking regardless.

'I did this for you. For us. I had to prove that there was a chance for us to love each other and do it right. All of those people – liars and enablers – they meant nothing. They're not as strong as we're going to be. You can tell them. If something happens to me. You can tell them that I was just proving my love, our love, was stronger. One last time. Tell them I had to bring you here, so no one could get in the way of that.'

Ben crouched down next to Number Four. 'We'll have new names. You won't be a number any more. Okay?

We'll be together, just you and me. No one will get in our way. It can still happen. I just have to finish this. Stop the lies one last time. Then, it'll just be me and you, right?'

He raised his hand to her face, stroking away tears which rolled down her cheeks. 'You're so like her, just like Number One. This time, everything will be the way it was supposed to be.'

*   *   *

The pain was unlike anything Amy had experienced before. The hunger was not the issue any longer. It was the agony of being chained to a radiator, her limbs cramping, twisted into awkward angles. The pain increasing if she tried to break free.

Her voice had gone hoarse from shouting, now barely a whimper escaped from her throat. Not that it mattered anyway, with the tape across her mouth. She couldn't remember the last time she'd had even a sip of water.

He was going to kill her. She didn't know when, but that was what was going to happen. Everything screamed this fact at her. She had tried to escape, tried to talk her way out of the situation. It didn't matter.

But he wasn't going to break her. She wasn't going to die the way he wanted her to.

The clothes she was wearing hadn't been changed since she'd been captured. They now hung off her, her already small frame now emaciated.

He wanted love from her. That's all he asked for. He would talk about things they could do together, places they could go.

He would talk about the things he would do for her. The things he had been doing to prove to her that love could be the way he imagined. Amy didn't want to listen, but there was no choice. He talked about the people he had murdered. In her name.

The love they shared would be different. She was going to see that, he'd said. He was going to change it all, across the world. Everyone would soon think the way he thought, he'd explained to her. He was going to show them.

She just wanted to go home.

There was a moment, a couple of days before that night, when she'd hoped it was over. He had arrived late at night, dressed in black and still sweating. He had removed the tape covering her mouth and poured water into her. He'd even given her a few bites of a sandwich.

She'd asked to be let go, but he hadn't listened. He'd cut off a new piece of tape, placing it over her mouth as she'd bucked and tried to move away from him.

It's not working. There's too many of them. They're all sick. You're the only one who can understand. This is what love can do. I have you here, with me, that means something. But them out there, they don't care. They don't get it. I can't make you see, can I? I can't do enough to show you.

She was going to die. He was going to finally do it. As he'd paced round the room in front of her, the echo of his footsteps had made her flinch and she'd closed her eyes.

I'm sorry.

He'd left her there. He hadn't been back in the room since then, although she'd heard him in one of the other rooms in the flat. Now he'd returned. He was in the room that had become her tomb.

There was something different about the way he spoke, the way he moved. He seemed misty-eyed as he looked down at her.

When he started speaking, she wished for silence.

She hoped he would never return.

Hoped that she wasn't going to be left there to die.

Chapter Thirty-Six

In and out of darkness, flashes of light, consciousness, confusion. His body being moved, lifted, something going around his wrists. The sound of breathing, close by, wet exhalation on his neck. The smell of sweat, musty and cloying, hitting the back of his throat.

The room spun out of control before slowly righting itself. His head felt heavy on his neck, as if it had been replaced by something too big, too cumbersome to be normal. Murphy squinted against brightness shined into his eyes, then the light was snapped off.

Candles. He remembered them dotted round the hallway. Into his dining room.

His eyes began to focus, blurred visions of what was familiar. The display unit against one wall, the photographs on the wall, his wife sitting opposite him. Only an outline of her body, the features still not coming into focus.

Murphy tried to move, his hands resting against the base of his spine, bound together. He was unable to stir his feet into action, there was a restraint around them too.

He tried to speak, the sound nonsensical to his ears. He felt the tape across his mouth, stopping him from talking aloud. He shook his head, trying to clear his vision. The room spun once more, the pain in his head growing each time he moved. Feelings of nausea hitting him like a wave.

'You with us, Detective?'

A voice in the shadows. Permeating the thickness of the atmosphere surrounding him. Each second becoming more and more clear. His eyes opening and closing of their own accord.

Murphy remembered in stages. The text message from Sarah. Walking into the house, the sight of candles, the smell of wax burning. The tea lights Sarah had bought months before, laid out along the laminate flooring in the hallway. Taking off his jacket and shoes.

Walking into the dining room.

He remembered the view in front of him as he'd walked in. Sarah, bound to one of the chairs they had picked out in a furniture shop a year earlier. Duct tape across her mouth, shaking her head, trying to speak to him.

'You're really heavy, took all my strength to lift you onto that chair. Almost didn't think I'd make it.'

He wanted to answer, but couldn't. Cramp hit his legs, the pain causing him to convulse and attempt to stretch out. But there was no give in the ties binding him to the chair, only his fingers able to move.

'I had to do this, I really did. I'm sorry it's not my usual well-thought-out way of doing things. I don't like to hit people in the head before we start. Everything can go wrong straight away with head injuries. I've seen them in my line of work. One punch can destroy a life. One unnoticed kerbstone, or missed stair, sending you over. A slip is enough.'

Murphy looked towards the shadow where the voice was coming from. The unmoving figure blending into the walls.

'This doesn't work if you can't speak to each other, so I'm going to remove the tape covering your mouth, David. Do you mind me calling you David?'

Murphy stared into the darkness, calculating his next move. His mind was still not firing correctly, thoughts colliding with each other. He shook his head slowly, expecting another wave of nausea to hit him. His body had settled a little, only his heart hammering against his chest gave him the sense something was happening inside.

'If you shout or scream, David, I'm going to start slicing into your lovely wife. Do you understand that?'

Murphy nodded a little more forcefully, turning his gaze back to Sarah. Her head was down, her shoulders hitching every few seconds. His heart rate increased, every fibre within his body on alert, wanting to cross that room and hold her.

'Good, I can do that then.'

The slight figure emerged from the shadows, crossing the short space between them and appearing in front of Murphy. The baby-faced form of Ben Flanagan, standing a foot away, looked down on him with an expression of interest. His face lit up by candlelight.

A hand gripped the side of his head, whilst the other tore away the tape covering his mouth. Murphy sucked in air, his breaths shallow and quick. He looked up to see Ben now standing close to Sarah, his empty hands now holding something against her face. It shimmered in the light and he saw the silver of a blade.

'What do you want?' Murphy said, coughing as he reached the last word.

'I want to go back,' Ben replied, smoothing down the hair on Sarah's head as she continued to look down. 'To not make the mistakes I made last time. It was the drug, wasn't it?'

'That's something we can talk about later. You just have to let us go.'

'I thought it was. I didn't have a choice really. Once the drug had been decided on, I had to use it. I thought I'd given just enough so it wouldn't show up afterwards. I guess I gave that last girl too much, didn't I? Didn't cover my tracks well enough, obviously.'

'Why . . . why are you doing this?'

'When you all turned up at the pub earlier, I was ready to hand myself in. End this whole thing. It's been difficult this past week . . . but I can't leave Number Four now. Not after everything we've been through. Then I remembered you. I know you, Detective. I've seen you. There was one last game I could play and stop you in the process. I can show Number Four that I was right.'

'Number Four?'

'She doesn't understand. None of them did. They don't listen to me. I only wanted to show them all that I was the better choice all along. That if they'd given me the chance, I could have shown them that.'

Murphy's eyes were becoming more used to the darkness within the room, the outline of the room clearing. 'This isn't the way, Ben.'

'Don't use my name,' Ben said, his voice echoing back from the walls. 'That's a trick. I've seen it on telly. I'm the one in control here.'

'Of course you are, I'm sorry,' Murphy replied, hoping his voice sounded sincere. He couldn't take his eyes off the blade held against Sarah's throat, pressing closer as Ben had shouted back at him. 'You're the Man in Black.'

Ben giggled, a high-pitched noise which made Sarah flinch. 'Ridiculous, I know, but I didn't know what to call myself. I needed something, though. I needed people to listen. I needed to show you all. Teach you about love. You're not doing it right. You know that, I hope? All the mistakes you've been making. You're corrupting it. Defiling it with your lies and your secrets. It's wrong. You're all wrong.'

'What do you want?'

'I've been following you, David. I wanted to see what you did when you weren't trying to find me. I've seen what you've been doing. Your little journeys. You came close to finding me just from those. So close.'

'What are you talking about?' Murphy said, his hands beginning to shake behind his back. He felt the familiar weight against his lower back for an instant. A reminder.

'Don't you think it's best you tell your *wife* about this? What you've been doing? What secrets you've been keeping?'

Murphy lowered his head. 'There isn't anything you know about. Nothing you would understand.'

'It's not for me to understand, is it? I've been here a few hours now, speaking to little Sarah here. She doesn't know anything about what you've been keeping from her. She's totally in the dark. Doesn't that mean anything to you?'

'I was going to tell her,' Murphy said, looking across at Sarah who was now staring at him. He couldn't tell what she was thinking, which scared him. 'It's nothing that deserves this.'

'Why hide it at all then? Why not tell her what you've been doing? You were supposed to be concentrating on me and my work, but instead you're driving round the city talking to people left, right, and centre.'

'You want me to tell Sarah? I'll tell her. No problem at all . . .'

'No, that's not the way . . .'

'I don't need to be tortured,' Murphy said, looking at Ben now. 'I can tell her anything. I know she'll understand. That's what love is, Ben. You have it wrong. You mistake it for power, when it's nothing like that.'

'You have no clue, do you?' Ben said, the knife in his hand pressing further into Sarah's throat. 'You don't know what real love is.'

'I know it better than you. You've never experienced it in return, have you? You don't know what it's like to have someone love you back. How can you do this, not knowing that feeling? How can you take that away from people?'

Ben's hands began to shake, the knife in his hand slipping away from Sarah's neck, before being pushed back against. Murphy strained at the bonds tying him to the chair as he heard Sarah moan against the tape across her mouth.

'No. You're wrong.'

'Okay, okay. Don't hurt her. Just keep talking to me.'

'You need to tell her now. The truth. Or I start cutting her.'

Murphy breathed in, his mind now almost as clear as it had been when he'd first entered the room. He shifted in the chair, just a little further forward. 'There's a girl I used to know,' he began, looking at Sarah, who was fitfully blinking as he held her stare. 'Back where I grew up. She lived round the corner from me. She got in touch recently, as her daughter has gone missing. Amy Maguire. Just about to turn nineteen. You know who I mean?'

There was a slight nod from Sarah.

'The case was with Liverpool South, but it got shunted across to us. When it did, I met with Stacey, Amy's mum. She told me something . . .'

Murphy hesitated, unsure how to continue.

'Keep talking,' Ben said, his childish tone sounding odd in that room. 'Tell her everything.'

'When we were about seventeen, eighteen, we slept together. One night, that's all it was. She thinks Amy might be the result of that one time. I don't believe it's true. Stacey's desperate to find her daughter, but with her being missing, I can't be absolutely certain. When the bodies of Chloe Morrison and Joe Hooper were discovered, the case went back to Liverpool South. I was keeping an eye on it, speaking to people and that.'

'I was keeping an eye on it,' Ben said, mocking Murphy's voice. 'You kept the possibility that you had a daughter from your wife. That's not good, David. Who's saying that's all that happened? Maybe old flames were rekindled when this mother came back on the scene.'

'There was nothing like that going on,' Murphy said, his jaw clenched, teeth grinding against one another.

'We'll never know, will we? That's the problem with keeping secrets and lying. How can we ever really know the truth. What do you think about that, Sarah? Do you still trust him? How could you? He's lied to you. Kept things from you. Is that the sign of someone committed to the relationship?'

'Look at her. Look in her eyes. She still loves me. I can see that, because we have history. You don't know us. You've got what you wanted from me. Let's talk about this.'

'No,' Ben replied, moving towards Murphy, the knife held up in front of him. 'I haven't got what I wanted yet. It doesn't work like that. You're not giving me what I need . . .'

'What do you need?'

'You'll find out.'

'What are you going to do? You need to work with me here. I can help you.'

'You can do nothing but listen,' Ben said, moving directly in front of him, blocking his view of Sarah. He replaced the duct tape across Murphy's mouth.

'You're not the only one who has been lying.'

Chapter Thirty-Seven

His voice was cut off, his words silenced. All he had was the vision of his wife sitting a few feet away, her eyes locked with his. He tried to communicate with her, not knowing if his unspoken message was getting through.

We're going to be okay. We're going to get out of this.

Ben Flanagan glanced Murphy's way before stepping forward and placing a hand on Sarah's face.

'Remember,' Ben said, holding the knife up to Sarah's face making her flinch back. 'I'll slit his throat if you scream. Okay?'

Sarah nodded, then closed her eyes as Ben tore away the tape covering her mouth. She gulped in breaths; Murphy remembered how she hated things covering her mouth.

'Please don't put that back on me,' Sarah said, looking up at Ben. 'I can't breathe properly with it on.'

'Don't you have more important things to think about, Sarah?'

Sarah went silent, looking across at Murphy as he slowly inched forward once more.

'While we were waiting for you to come back, I had a bit of a look round your house. You don't mind, do you?'

Murphy stopped moving and shook his head.

'That's good,' Ben replied, standing closer to Murphy now. 'Anyway, Sarah here was safe and sound, so I took the chance to search a real-life copper's house. Bit boring really. Couldn't find anything of interest at all. You must have a really dull life, outside of the big cases you always seem to find yourself involved with that is.'

Murphy continued to stare at Sarah, listening to Ben's words but not reacting.

'I started digging round a little more. I knew you would be back late, given what happened earlier . . . by the way, is Laura doing okay? She seems nice. Her and Darren may have a future, as long as they don't lie to each other.'

Murphy didn't respond; instead he raised his hands up a little more, resting them on the waistband of his trousers.

'I only gave her a little scratch,' Ben continued, as if Murphy had replied to him. 'Just enough to make you go towards her rather than me. Almost didn't get away either. But it's amazing how quickly you can blend in when you're in the city centre. All the rat-runs, the alleyways. Almost too easy to disappear. Anyway, I'm getting away from the point. I had a bit of a snoop, but didn't find anything. That was until I persuaded Sarah to help me out and I found this.'

Ben moved something into Murphy's line of sight. An envelope, with Sarah's name and their address scrawled across the front. Ben turned the envelope round, displaying the return address.

HMP Manchester.

Murphy frowned for a second. Sarah was looking away from him now.

'Don't . . .' Sarah said, her voice barely travelling across the room to Murphy.

'I thought, we're in the house of a copper,' Ben said, ignoring Sarah's interruption. 'What's a letter from a prison doing here? It's not right. It doesn't make sense. And it wasn't even addressed to you, it was to her. So, I asked her about it.'

Sarah looked up towards Murphy, tears now falling down her face. 'I'm sorry—'

'That's not the way we do it,' Ben said, crossing the space to Sarah and grabbing her by the hair and pushing her head backwards. Murphy bucked in the chair, but couldn't move any further. 'Wait until I've finished.'

Murphy gripped the waistband of his trousers and moved his shirt tail aside.

'I asked if I could read it, but she didn't want me to. Said it was private. I came here because I thought you had the secret. I thought it was you who was lying, but it wasn't. It was her, David. She's been lying to you. Tell him. Now.'

There was silence for a few seconds. Murphy kept his eyes on Sarah, the effort to remain still causing him to perspire a little more.

'I didn't really want to go,' Sarah said, normality gone. Her voice somehow different from how Murphy remembered it. 'Not at first. He writes to me sometimes, but I always throw them away. I didn't think you'd want to know, so I don't tell you about them.'

Murphy thought about the only person he and Sarah knew in prison in Manchester. The man who had almost destroyed his life.

'He said he had things to tell me. Things that I needed to know. I thought it was just another game to him.

Another way to get back at me. But I wanted to know. Needed to know—'

'I hope you're listening to this, David,' Ben said, cutting over Sarah's words. 'She's been lying to you.'

'Please, let me speak.'

'Of course,' Ben replied, his boyish features turning into a sick grin. 'Your turn.'

'He put my name down for visiting and I spent a couple of months thinking about it . . .'

Murphy's hand rested on the case attached to the top of his trousers.

'I'm so sorry, I should have told you . . .'

'She went to see him,' Ben said, almost jumping round the room. 'She told me all about it. How this man had beaten her half to death while they were together. How she found the courage to get away from him and then find love with you. Then, the revenge he took on you both. Killing your parents in their own homes. He ruined your life, I remember it. I read about you back then, years ago. I was working away at the time, but used to read about stuff that happened in Liverpool. Sarah told me you spent almost a year apart, before getting back together. You forgave her, and now she does this to you?'

'It wasn't like that—'

'Can you believe anything she has to say now? She's a liar. Who knows what really happened. Maybe she put him up to it. Thought that killing your parents would be enough to make you disappear. Didn't want to kill a copper, so went for the next best thing. His only mistake was in going too far and he got caught. But they still love each other, so she agrees to wait for him. It's almost like a fairy tale romance . . .'

'It wasn't like that, you sick bastard.'

Ben turned on Sarah, as if he were shocked she was still there. 'How would we ever know? You brought lies here. You kept secrets. You don't love this man, how could you?'

'You don't know anything about love,' Sarah said with an edge to her voice. 'David knows how I feel.'

Sarah looked across at him, her breathing wavering. Murphy stared back, thinking about nothing other than the fact that his wife had recently sat opposite the man who had killed his parents. The man who had also destroyed his marriage.

'Love isn't this,' Ben said, stepping between Murphy and Sarah. 'It's not sneaking around behind each other's backs. It's not hurting each other with lies and secrets. You need to understand it shouldn't be this way. It's supposed to be about being truthful and loyal. Becoming one person, together.'

'I walked out, David,' Sarah said, Murphy not looking at her now. 'It was just a game to him. He had nothing to say. I thought I could find out a reason for it, something, but he didn't have anything. He disgusts me. I told him that. Please believe me.'

'Now she begs to be believed. It's not right. What you have here is not right. You don't deserve this of each other. It has to be stopped.'

Ben crossed the room towards Murphy, ripping off the duct tape from his mouth. 'Speak to me, Detective. Tell me how hurt you are, how much she disgusts you.'

'I understand,' Murphy said, staring at Ben whilst he spoke to Sarah. 'I know why you did it. You don't need to explain yourself to me.' He turned towards Sarah.

'I love you.'

'No. This isn't right,' Ben said, beginning to pace up and down between them. 'She betrayed you. I need to stop this . . .'

'Ben, we're stronger than you think we are. We love each other, more than you could ever know.'

'That's right,' Sarah said, her voice stronger now.

'No. I can't have this,' Ben said, coming towards Murphy again. He replaced the duct tape across his mouth. 'You're lying. Both of you.'

Murphy stiffened in the chair as Ben walked back towards Sarah.

'I can stop all this now. I can make it all better. You want me to hurt her, don't you, David? I can see it in your eyes. No matter what you say, you're broken now. Both of you. Nothing will repair this relationship. I have to stop it. You need me to hurt her.'

Murphy strained violently against the tape binding his hands and feet and shook his head.

'You want to do it yourself. I see that. Don't worry, David, I can do it for you.'

Murphy straightened up and sat back into the chair. He snapped open the case tucked in the waistband of his trousers and, with shaking fingertips, removed the short-handled knife within.

Ben moved closer to Sarah, looked down at her and then replaced the tape across her mouth as she screamed.

'This is it. The best way, the only way. I'm helping you get out of this. I can show her what real love is. I can do this and then she'll know. Number Four will know. So much better than the other three. She'll know why I took her away from that place. Working where she was, no future, only dirty old men leering over her as she served them. It's better this way. You'll see. You'll understand. You will, won't you? She'll love me. She will.'

Murphy held the knife behind his back. He pictured the duct tape binding his hands together and knew he would only get one shot.

'Watch this, David,' Ben said, pulling back Sarah's head to expose her throat. 'This is what lies bring.'

Murphy didn't feel time slow down. He felt every moment. The glint of the knife pressed against Sarah's throat, the feel of escape in his fingertips. He jerked upwards with his blade, praying in an instant that it would work. He sliced through the duct tape binding his wrists, freeing his hands. He watched as Ben turned his face away from his, the look of concentration and disgust the last thing Murphy saw of him.

His legs were still bound to the chair legs, but it was a short distance to the chair holding Sarah.

It took just seconds. It was all one motion. After the blade sliced through the tape, freeing his hands, he planted his feet and dived across at the man who was about to cut into the throat of his wife.

He knew he would only have one shot. Once chance to stop what was about to happen.

Murphy jumped, the chair coming with him, still attached to his legs.

All one movement. One last hope.

Chapter Thirty-Eight

There was a moment when he thought he hadn't made it. That he had not thought things through well enough. That the extra weight would be too much. That he would fall at the last, never reaching his target.

He thought he saw blood, dripping then gushing onto the carpet as the knife went across her neck. He couldn't have, not in those final few seconds, but that was what his mind told him.

All that worry ended in the instant he crashed into Ben Flanagan.

Murphy's leg came free from the chair, the other, still taped to it, bent awkwardly, sending a shockwave of pain through to his upper thigh.

Murphy brought Ben down, landing on top of him as they fell to the floor. The short-handled knife he was holding fell from his grip as he pulled his hands free. Ben landed on his side, candles going out round the room as they struggled on the floor.

Ben was stronger than Murphy had been expecting, but there was something he had on his side.

The will to live.

Murphy grabbed Ben's left arm, twisted it up hard behind his back and pulled, causing the man beneath him to scream. As he gained the upper hand, he glanced up at Sarah and tore off the duct tape across his mouth.

'Are you okay?'

Sarah nodded slowly, lifting her head up towards Murphy.

Her neck was clean, no blood.

'Get off me,' Ben said, his words muffled as Murphy used his other arm to force Ben's face into the floor. 'I'll kill you.'

'Don't move,' Murphy replied, keeping his full weight on Flanagan's back, tugging his arm further up, almost willing it to snap.

Ben bucked beneath him, tipping Murphy to one side as the chair still attached to him affected his balance. He clung on, lessening the grip on Ben's arm as they struggled with each other.

Murphy brought his free leg up, placing his knee in the middle of Ben's back as he turned on his side. He looked round the floor for the knife Ben had been holding, but couldn't see it.

'Drop the knife now,' Murphy said, unable to see Ben's right hand. 'I said drop it.'

'Don't do this. I have to finish. Let me go.'

Murphy continued to hold Ben's arm as he tried to free his other leg from the chair.

'Stop moving,' Murphy said, finally pulling the tightly wrapped tape away from his leg.

Ben struggled beneath him, pushing Murphy backwards. The younger man was on all fours, about to get to his feet. Murphy moved quickly, scrabbling across to reach him as Ben turned round.

The knife was still in his hand.

Murphy grabbed for Ben's wrist as he moved towards him, squeezing in the hope he would have to let go. He brought them to their feet, still gripping Ben's wrist with both hands, forcing him backwards.

Ben used his free hand, punching and slapping at Murphy, hitting him across the head and shoulder as Murphy pushed him further back into the wall, crashing him against it.

Murphy attempted to sweep Ben's legs from underneath him, but Ben was still fighting. Murphy began to lose his grip on the other man's wrist.

'Let go,' Murphy said, trying to think of options but failing to come up with any. 'Let go of it now.'

Murphy could see the younger man's eyes now, black in the pale light and shadows. Ben's teeth bared back at him as he squeezed his wrist tighter. Murphy drew back his head and aimed a headbutt at Ben, missing his target by an inch as the other man moved at the last second. His forehead smashed into the side of Ben's head, a wave of dizziness crashing over him.

What should have broken his nose instead galvanised Ben. Murphy lost his grip with his left hand, leaving only his right holding Ben's wrist. He didn't pause, he threw a left hook to Ben's side, into the space his old boxing trainer had drummed into him to aim for. Underneath the ribs, taking any air Ben had left in his body.

Ben began to weaken, his legs losing the will to carry his weight, as Murphy kept a tight grip on Ben's wrist.

Then there was a noise Murphy hadn't heard before. A wild, guttural sound which blared into his face. Murphy finally lost his grip as Ben pushed back, the knife coming towards him.

Murphy stepped away and allowed the knife to follow its own trajectory.

Ben looked down. He was still holding onto the knife. He looked back up and grinned at Murphy.

He couldn't see the blood through the black clothing, but Murphy thought it was there. The knife was buried in Ben's midsection, only he no longer looked like Ben. Or The Man in Black. He'd become a child almost. The boyish features, unlined and untouched, turned into a grin which was rapidly fading as he crumpled to the floor.

Murphy turned and went to Sarah, carefully taking off the duct tape across her mouth.

'Are you okay?' Murphy said, brushing a hand across her face. 'Did he hurt you?'

'I'm fine, I'm all right,' Sarah said, leaning her face against his. 'Are you?'

'Yes. Let me get this off you.'

Murphy went round to stand behind Sarah. Taking a grip on the duct tape he ripped it free. He moved to the front and did the same for her legs. Sarah came slowly to her feet.

'Is he . . .'

'I don't know,' Murphy replied, looking over to the shadow where Ben had fallen. 'I don't care. As long as you're okay, I don't care.'

They embraced, Murphy holding on to his wife, her shoulders beginning to hitch as she buried her face in his chest.

He heard movement from the shadows, turned but couldn't see anything.

'Right,' Murphy said, lifting Sarah's face away from him. 'Go upstairs, lock yourself in the bathroom and wait. I'll stay with him until people get here.'

'I'm not leaving you . . .'

'You're not leaving me, you're being safe. Go upstairs, take the phone with you. They'll be here within seconds, honestly.'

Sarah nodded, kissed him on the mouth and then left the room through the open doorway.

Murphy watched her go, frowning as she left.

'Wait, no,' Murphy shouted, bounding across the room and reaching the door, spinning into an empty hallway.

'What? What's the matter?'

Murphy walked back into the dining room, switching on the light on the wall as he did so. He looked to the spot where Ben had fallen.

'Shit,' Murphy said, his voice echoing back at him. 'Sarah, don't move.'

Murphy went back into the hallway, switching on the light as he went. As Murphy moved closer to the front door, he realised it had been opened and not shut properly.

'Do what I told you to,' Murphy said. 'No, wait . . . I'll go with you first.'

Murphy walked Sarah up the stairs, waiting for Ben to jump out at them, before hurrying her into the bathroom and waiting for the lock to click.

'I'll be back soon,' Murphy said. He took the stairs two at a time, bursting into his living room, seeing it was empty. He went back into the hallway and grabbed his jacket as he opened the front door with his foot.

Outside, it was dark, the street lights not giving much illumination. He heard a car on the street rev its engine. Murphy slipped his feet into his almost new walking boots, used once and then left in the hallway. He didn't bother with the laces, instead he walked through the doorway and out, checking either side of him as he paced quickly to the end of the front path and leaned on the gate.

A car sped past him, a figure in black at the wheel.

Murphy rummaged in the inside pocket of his jacket, producing his keys and phone. He dropped his jacket to the floor and within seconds was starting his own car up and backing out of his drive.

'This is Detective Inspector David Murphy with Liverpool North,' he shouted into his phone, cradling it on his shoulder as he placed both hands on the wheel. 'I'm in pursuit of Ben Flanagan ... Yes, that one, don't you think it'd be big a coincidence if it was a different one? ... He's travelling in a black Ford Fiesta towards Melling Road, past the golf course.'

Murphy saw the car up ahead weaving across the road, attempting to right itself. 'He's wearing all-black clothing and a black ski mask over his head ... he has an injury ... a knife wound to his abdomen. He assaulted two people at their home before escaping.'

He rattled off his home address, shifting into fourth gear and speeding up.

'He is struggling to keep his car on the road ... how long until air support can get here?'

Murphy watched as the car in front slowed down, twisted to the right, then straightened up and sped off again.

'I'm right behind him ... who do we have in the area?'

Murphy lifted his foot off the accelerator as Ben slowed down once again.

'Where the hell are you going to go?' Murphy muttered to himself, his eyes never leaving the road in front of him. The streets were quiet, which was at least something in his favour. 'Continuing down towards Fazakerley train station. Longmoor Lane,' he shouted into his phone.

The car in front approached the traffic lights just as they turned to amber; instead of stopping the car veered to the right and turned off.

'Onto Lower Lane,' Murphy said, turning the car. As he shaped to put his foot down, another car coming from the opposite direction blared its horn.

'Shit.'

Murphy slammed on the brakes, turning the wheel back as the car whipped round. His mobile phone slipped from the crook of his shoulder and bounced out of sight. His car came to a stop in the middle of the junction, more traffic appearing, almost trapping him there. 'Bollocks. I don't know if you can still hear me, but I'll keep a running commentary.'

He shifted into gear and accelerated again. He peered into the distance, hoping to see Ben's car in front appear once more. There were no street lights on the tree-lined road of Lower Lane, his own headlights the only illumination. He spied a car ahead, dim lights shining as it dipped behind a small hill in the road.

'Got you,' Murphy said, slowing up as he approached. He wasn't going to play his game, he decided. 'Still on

Lower Lane, reduced speed to make him think he's lost me.'

Murphy kept the car in front in sight, but followed at a distance. 'Where are you going?'

Ten minutes later, he had his answer.

* * *

Ben almost pounded the wheel with excitement. He'd felt for sure it was over, once when that detective had over-powered him in the house, and again when he had caught up with him in the car. Now, looking in the rear-view mirror at nothing but empty road, it looked as if a simple right turn had been enough.

He laughed, quietly at first, before the inside of the car rocked with his laughter. He simply couldn't believe it was as simple as that to outmanoeuvre a copper in a chase.

He felt invincible.

Ben took one hand off the steering wheel, eyes locked forward. He peeled away his jacket and rolled up the layers so he could feel the damage to his midsection. It was sore to the touch, a definite wound opening up there. He quickly calculated how long the journey back to the flat – and Number Four – would take, he decided it was enough time. There was a first aid kit there; he could patch himself up and make a move.

He thought of Number Four. Imagined the delight on her face when he walked back through the door, ready to take her away, far from this place. The knowledge that this final act proved that he had been right and true all along. The wound he had suffered was testimony to the fact he was worthy of her love.

The thought of it brought a wider smile to his face. The

fact that there was nothing that would hold her back now.

Ben kept checking the rear-view mirror, waiting for it to fill with blue flashing lights, and for his pathway to salvation to be blocked. But despite some minor traffic here and there, there was no sign of anything.

He was going to make it, he thought. As he took a few turns here and there, just in case he was being followed, he opened the window and listened over the engine noise for the sounds of a helicopter above, but received only silence, save for his own car.

He allowed himself to smile once again. He was safe. As he reached Speke Hall Road he began to think of the future. Where they would go, what they would do. He had been stashing money away for months, almost as if he knew something like this was going to happen. The sale of his dad's house had gone through six months earlier, which with a fully paid-off mortgage meant a nice profit had been made. The reason he had come back to Liverpool.

Bury his father   find Number Four.

Ben knew they would be freezing his accounts, but they wouldn't find the money. He was too clever for them, he thought. Even when overpowered by their best detective, he had escaped. And now he was going to be with Number Four for ever. Comfortable and in love.

He reached Western Avenue and pulled the car to a stop behind the row of buildings where the flat was located. He waited a few seconds to see if anyone was there watching out for him.

Ben slipped out of the car, looked round the quiet street, his shadow bouncing off the pavement, and began to walk quickly to the flat entrance.

All he had to do was get Number Four and start driving. He was going to be free. They were going to be free.

No one was going to get in their way. He wasn't going to let anyone come between them any more.

Chapter Thirty-Nine

Keith Hudson heard the voice again. Through the walls. Like they were talking to him when he knew they weren't. He turned up his television but it made no difference. They were in there now. In his head. In the hallway. In the way.

He had tried to be normal like everyone else, but it hadn't worked. The girl had gone and it had been his fault. He wanted them to know that he was sorry, but they never listened.

He had seen it all. The man they were all talking about on TV. In front of his window, in his hallway, in his head. Banging around in the top flat.

It was his fault, Keith's fault, his fault. He'd written it down somewhere, but had forgotten where he'd put it. He made lists. That's what he did. Of things he could and couldn't do. Could and couldn't say.

The big detective's voice was out there now. Shouting his name. He didn't like him. He was the reason he wasn't getting better. Only worse.

'Go away,' Keith shouted, wanting everyone to leave. 'You're not here.'

Real life was getting harder and harder to cling on to. 'Leave me alone.'

Keith put his hands over his ears and stared at the window as the noise banged on and on.

'I'll make you go away,' Keith said, standing up with his hands still over his ears. 'I'll open the door and it'll stop. Then what will you do?'

Keith crossed the room, almost falling over a bin bag full of clothes, and gripped the Yale lock on the door, but didn't open it straight away. 'I'm opening the door and you'll disappear.'

The voice continued, so Keith opened the door and then crossed to the outer door and opened that as well.

'Oh, you're real.'

'Yes, I am,' the big detective said, looking past Keith and into his home. Keith shrank back.

'Have you come to try it on with me again, ya big knobhead?'

'No, Keith, I need you to help me . . .'

*   *   *

Murphy began to put it together as he followed Ben onto Western Avenue in Speke. His old home town, the familiarity bleeding from every street light and paving stone.

From a hundred or so yards away, Murphy watched Ben pull his car to a stop. With his headlights switched off so he blended into the darkness, Murphy waited a few seconds, his car idling at the side of the road as he watched Ben slip out onto the street.

Murphy risked moving his car closer, just as Ben disappeared into an alleyway behind a row of buildings.

Opposite the shop Amy Maguire worked at. The same row of buildings which housed Keith Hudson – the man who had confessed to murder.

The man who said he heard Amy's voice.

'You took her,' Murphy whispered into the silence of his car. 'She's Number Four.'

Murphy waited a minute or so more before pulling the car closer. Once he was stationary, he searched the passenger footwell, finally locating his phone. When he hadn't been joined by a fleet of marked cars, he suspected the call had been lost. He checked the screen and his fears were confirmed. All his shouted directions had been in vain.

He quickly dialled and waited for a connection.

'Detective Inspector David Murphy from Liverpool North,' Murphy said into the phone, his voice still barely above a whisper as he rattled off his ID. 'Bottom of Western Avenue in Speke, the flats opposite the shops ... The buildings there are flats ... No, I don't know the fucking number, just get down here ... Everyone, get everyone.'

Murphy placed the phone down on the passenger seat, without ending the call, then checked the pocket at the side of his seat. He pulled out the telescopic baton he kept there, before opening the glove compartment and moving aside the few papers stuffed in there. He pulled out the pepper spray and tucked it into his trouser pocket. He picked up his phone again and spoke into it.

'They need to get here now. Is someone at my house?'

He waited for an answer in the affirmative and then placed the phone into his other pocket and pulled on the door handle. There was a brief second when he stilled himself, asking himself if what he was doing was the right thing. Then the image of Amy Maguire came to his mind, and it drove him forward.

He left the car, blinking into the dark ahead of him as droplets of rain started to drift down onto him. Stilted illumination came from the occasional street light that still worked, making the path ahead even less inviting. He made his way across to the front entrance of the buildings, knocking as softly as he could, before moving across to the window at the side.

'Keith, let me in,' Murphy said, cupping his hands around his mouth and getting closer to the windowpane. 'It's important. I have to get Amy.'

There was silence for a while, so he tried again. Then again. Finally, he crossed back to the door and began to put his shoulder to it. Attempting to break in without making too much noise, hoping Ben wasn't taking Amy out the back door while he was stuck at the front.

'Keith, let me in, please.'

Murphy banged on the window again, risking the noise it generated. 'If I have to, I'm going to put my fucking fist through this window. Open the door, now.'

He heard the rattle of a lock within the flat and breathed a sigh of relief. He crossed back to the outer door and waited for it to be unlocked. A crack appeared, a face peering back at him.

'Oh, you're real.'

'Yes, I am,' Murphy said, looking past Keith and into the hallway.

'Have you come to try it on with me again, ya big knobhead?'

Murphy shook his head, already pushing past him. 'No, Keith, I need you to help me . . .'

*   *   *

Ben gathered up the few possessions he wanted to keep and moved quickly. He knew there would be an entire police force looking for him now, especially since he'd attacked one of their own. He was reasonably sure he had some time left, just not much of it.

He went back into the room which contained Number Four, the smell knocking him back. He placed a hand over his nose and mouth.

'I'm sorry,' Ben said, moving towards her. 'I should have taken better care with the waste.'

Number Four looked up at him, something intangible in her eyes. Something he thought was love.

'We have to go now. Everything's going to be okay. I couldn't do the final ones. I took a knife for you, getting away from them. Stabbed me right in the stomach, but don't worry, it's just a flesh wound. I've already patched it up. They couldn't stop us being together. It doesn't matter that they're still alive, does it?'

He waited for her to answer, but didn't get a response.

'It doesn't, does it? Answer me?'

She shook her head, causing Ben to breathe a sigh of relief. 'Good. We can go then. I've proven myself, haven't I?'

She nodded, then tried to motion to her mouth.

'The tape,' Ben said, smacking his forehead. 'I'm sorry. I didn't even think. Yes, I can take it off, but first we have to go.'

She shook her head harder now, the chains rattling against themselves.

'Okay, you need water?'

Number Four paused for a moment, then nodded vigorously. Ben tried to recall the last time he'd given her something to eat or drink, but couldn't. 'I'm sorry, you can drink, but we have to be quick.'

*   *   *

Amy waited for him to remove the duct tape, knowing that even though every ounce of her wanted to scream at that point, she had to wait. The situation was still too volatile, she could see that. Every motion he made was jittery, stuttering along like someone on drugs.

She had to wait for him to lead her to wherever they were going, and then try something. Screaming, shouting ... if she got enough freedom, she would rip him apart with her bare hands.

'Come on,' he said to her, gripping her by the arm. 'Drink up, we have to go.'

Amy drank greedily from the cup of lukewarm water which was tipped into her mouth. She still didn't speak, just waited for her moment.

When he grabbed her again, a gloved hand slipping into her armpit and pulling her up, she realised the futility of it all.

'Seems like you've been lying around for too long. You can't even stand up.'

He stood over her, grunting with the effort of forcing her to her feet. Her legs were useless, though, weeks of inactivity had left them numb.

'Come on, we have to g—'

Both of their heads snapped towards the hallway, as they heard banging. One shouted word which made Amy almost cry out with relief.

'Police.'

*   *   *

Murphy crept up the staircase, ears straining to hear any sound from above him. The stairs creaked as he made his way upwards, the only light being provided by the open door to Keith's flat. As he got further up, the light failed him and he walked into the shadows which surrounded the door at the top.

He wasn't sure what he was going to do once he reached it.

Murphy stood for a few seconds at the top of the stairs, working out his options, wishing he'd thought of this sooner. He'd made no plans for once he got inside, other than to make sure he had a weapon of some sort, but even that wouldn't get him very far.

There was a young girl inside, Murphy thought. And she needed to be safe.

He was thrown back two years, to a time when he stood in front of a very different door, someone else inside who he needed to keep safe. Murphy hadn't been able to save that person.

The door was older than the one downstairs, wooden and cracked in places. It matched the run-down feeling within the place – almost as if the whole building was just waiting for its inevitable demise. It would soon be demolished to make way for progress, like so many other places in the area.

Murphy raised a fist and banged against the door. 'Police.'

He didn't pause. Stepped backwards with a raised boot and drove his foot into the centre of the door. It didn't do much other than warp backwards, but he followed up quickly by banging his shoulder into the frame. He felt some give, but it was going to take more than one go.

'Police,' Murphy shouted again, his breathing becoming harder as he strained against the weight of the door. 'Open up.'

He heard a crack in the frame finally and geared up for one last effort.

There was the sound of a cry, then silence. Murphy stepped back, a snarl erupting from him as he crashed through the door.

He could hear a hushed voice coming from down the hallway, then another cry. Murphy moved quickly, his back against the wall as he came to a stop.

'Ben, it's me. It's David Murphy. Come out here, we'll talk.'

There was no response, so Murphy moved closer to the room, his eyes now fully adjusted to the dim light. Opposite, in another room, Murphy spied a mattress on the floor and a lamp next to it. A holdall lay nearby, half full with items.

'Don't come in here.'

Murphy heard Ben's voice, but it was different to the one he had heard previously in his house. Gone was the confidence, replaced by fear and panic.

'I'm going to come in, Ben, and we're going to talk.'

'No, don't.'

Murphy didn't wait any longer, slipping round the corner and raising his arm up, holding the baton in front of him. The room was bare from what he could see. No carpets, just exposed wooden floorboards. Faded light entered from the window opposite the doorway, giving the room a ghostly glow.

'I told you not to come in here.'

Murphy made his way along the wall, the baton still in his hand as he did so, one hand poised at his pocket. Ben came into view, standing against the opposite wall.

'You know I had to come in,' Murphy said, stepping into the centre of the room. 'I have to take her with me. You understand.'

Murphy glanced at the woman Ben was standing over. He recognised her from the photograph which adorned her mother's living room. It was Amy Maguire and she was alive.

Her hands and feet had been chained together, as if she were about to be led into an American prison. She was slumped at Ben's feet, leaning into his leg. Her clothes were tattered and dirty, her hair matted with weeks of neglect, her face a mask of browns and red. Dried blood had crusted on her cheek and jawline. The smell was worse than Murphy had been expecting; he spied a bucket in the corner of the room.

'It's all right, Amy. It's going to be fine.'

He had said similar words before and been wrong, but as Murphy locked eyes with Ben, he had a feeling he was right this time.

Not a feeling. A knowing.

'This is it, Ben. It's done. Let her go and we can get her out of here.'

'No, no, that's not going to work,' Ben said as his eyes darted round the room. 'You're going to let us past. We have to go. We have to be together.'

'That's not going to happen and you know that. Just step away from her and this'll all be over.'

Murphy glanced across to the window, hoping to see blue lights flashing, but saw nothing. He looked towards Amy instead, saw a familiar glint in her eye.

'But, you don't understand,' Ben said, stuttering. 'She's not a number any more. She's really mine. She knows what I've done. She knows what this is all about. Everything I've done is for us. So we can be free.'

Murphy inched towards Ben. 'In a few minutes, this building will be surrounded by the entirety of the Merseyside Police. Officers with firearms, itchy fingers and all. Is this how you want it to end? Or do you want to walk out, still alive, with me?'

There was silence for a second, then a gasp from Amy. She felt the knife at her neck before Murphy saw it, twisting her head closer to Ben's leg in an attempt to get away from the blade. Ben was almost at a crouch now as he lifted her head up by her hair.

'If I can't have her now, then that's it for me anyway.'

Murphy controlled his breathing and took another step. 'No, Ben, that's not what's going to happen. I'm not going to let you do this.'

'Then let us walk out of here.'

Murphy shook his head. 'I can't let you do that.'

Ben's voice filled the room, echoing as it bounced off the walls. 'Leave us alone. It's just me and her now. She's Number Four. I'm not starting again.'

Amy murmured under her breath, Murphy hearing only a few words. He tried to catch her eye, but she had her head buried in Ben's thigh. The blade glinted as it caught a snatch of a street light from outside. It was pressed into her neck, closer and closer to breaking the skin.

'We need to talk about what you're doing,' Murphy said, blinking and being momentarily thrown into an entirely different room, with a different man holding a weapon against someone's head. 'This isn't what you want, Ben.'

'What I want is to be left alone.'

Amy lifted her head towards Murphy. He glanced down at her and tried to communicate something with his eyes. He wasn't sure what.

'Why this? Why end her life over this?'

'I should have known,' Ben said, his shoulders slumping down. 'It was never going to be right. They're all the same. It's her fault, isn't it? That's why you're here. That's why you won't let us go. My dad was right . . . they're all the same.'

Ben raised the hand holding the knife as he spoke. That was all that was needed.

Murphy crossed the room at speed, just as Amy clamped onto Ben's leg with her mouth, tearing into the flesh of his thigh with her teeth. She snarled as she bit through the fabric of the black combat pants he was wearing. Murphy was on Ben at the same time, an arm locked around his neck, pulling him backwards to the floor. Blue lights cascaded across the room as he dragged him down, cutting off the air supply to Ben's throat.

'It's over,' he heard himself say.

He turned to Amy, now curled in a ball on the floor, saw the knife glinting in the light six feet away. 'You're safe.'

*　　*　　*

Keith answered the big detective's questions, then walked back into his flat, leaving the main door open. He waited at the entrance to his home, listening for any noise from upstairs.

He was the last line of defence. That was what he was. He couldn't let the man leave with the girl.

After a few minutes, he heard voices from upstairs; the deep sounds from the detective, a higher pitch from the man who lived there. He strained to hear a woman's voice, but couldn't make any out. Then he heard a crash and his breathing began to increase. He heard sirens getting closer. At first, he thought they weren't real, but then lights surrounded him and he ran back into his flat.

He walked over to the window which faced out into the street and pulled the curtains back. He didn't need to defend anything now. There were people outside for that. Blue lights flashing across the road. People all there, crowding round looking up at the flat above.

Keith waited for them to come and get him, but that didn't happen. He watched and counted out seconds.

After he'd lost count, he saw the big detective again. He was carrying someone in his arms, someone sprinted over from the ambulance parked across the street and took over from him.

Keith saw only a whisper of the blonde hair, the shape of a leg, the glimpse of cheek, but he knew.

They'd found her.

Amy was safe. She was real. She was back.

After

The room fell silent as she began to speak.

She was still surprised that she had a voice.

Almost three years since she'd been freed from hell, this was the culmination of long therapy sessions and a nice amount of compensation. Not bad for a year spent in a psychopath's basement.

She'd rented a few rooms in a small building away from the bustle and noise of town, in a nice spot on the Wirral side of the Mersey. The building was anonymous-looking, with no signs outside proclaiming who they were, or what they did. Jemma shared it with some media group, all black jackets and big ideas. They thankfully left her alone to get on with things, too involved in their own business to be interested in what she was doing.

'Hello, everyone,' she said, looking round the room at the different faces filling the space. 'My name is Jemma Barnes, and I'm a survivor. I'm here to talk about my experiences, but also to hopefully help you as you talk about yours. We're all here for a reason – because we made it through something. Now, I'm sure you know my story – the bloody *Liverpool Echo* won't leave me alone . . .'

That always got a polite laugh.

'But what you won't know is what I talk about in here. To you people. Because no matter what you think, we all share a common bond. We all survived something. It doesn't matter how long, or how bad we think the situation was, we're all survivors. And that means something.'

Jemma went on, talking about her experience in the year she'd been locked away. How she'd felt during that time, the long road she'd had to travel to get to the point she was at now. Then, she went round the room, listening to others talk about their own experiences.

An hour later, she gave them all a break and walked down the steps to the outside of the building. Breathed in fresh air, like it was her first time, then lit up a cigarette.

'I don't know. I save your life and now you're smoking?'

Jemma shielded her eyes with one hand, saw the figure at the end of the gravel path and smiled. 'That's the thing about getting a second chance. You get to make your own stupid decisions.'

She walked towards the bulking figure of David Murphy and stopped in front of him. 'Besides, I'm down to five a day now.'

'You can do whatever you like, Jemma, that's the beauty of life. How are you?'

'Getting there. Still having the dreams, but they're not as frequent as they used to be. I've stopped seeing things that aren't there, all that sort of thing.'

'I'm glad you're doing this.'

'You come to see the new place? Only, I've got people in there at the moment . . .'

'That can wait,' Murphy replied, looking over at the building past her shoulder. 'I've come about something else.'

'The girl ...'

'Amy Maguire.'

'I read about that. Granted it wasn't quite as long as me, but a few weeks is plenty.'

Jemma looked away as Murphy scuffed at a piece of gravel.

'She needs to talk to someone. I think it would be best if it was someone she could relate to.'

Jemma breathed in, turning her gaze back to Murphy. 'You still have my number?'

'Of course.'

'You give it to her. Tell her I'm ready when she is.'

*   *   *

It had been two weeks since Murphy and Sarah had been sitting in those chairs in their dining room. Facing each other, as secrets and lies they had kept from each other were forced out of them. At first, they had just been happy to be alive. Glad to be with each other and have another chance.

Then came relief, as they both realised how strong they were. That even the secrets they'd held from each other hadn't damaged their relationship even a little.

Murphy felt safe. Comfortable. Ready. He drummed his fingers on his knee, sitting in his chair in the living room of a house now up for sale. It would never feel the same again, not after what had happened. The decision to move was the easiest one they'd made.

What to do after that had been a more difficult decision. One that Murphy had been avoiding for a long time, but now he was starting to feel differently.

It was time.

His knee bobbed up and down of its own accord, Murphy chewed on the corner of his lip, waiting for blood to burst out if he bit too hard.

'She's here.'

Murphy didn't know what to do. Whether to stand, or stay in his seat. In the end, he settled for perching on the edge.

'Hey, Sarah,' Jess's voice drifted in from the hallway. 'How are you?'

'Can't complain. He's through there. I'm going in the other room to get on with some packing.'

The living-room door opened a little more. Murphy waited a second before turning.

'Hi,' Murphy said, wishing he'd thought of something better to say. 'You coming in?'

'I suppose,' Jess replied, unbuttoning her coat, hesitating, then leaving it on. 'I'm only here because she made me feel guilty. If something had happened that night . . .'

'I know.'

'So, you still off work?'

Murphy waited for Jess to sit down on the couch opposite, then sat back in his chair. 'Going back in tomorrow. Two weeks was enough.'

'Everything cleared?'

'Just about. The investigation will continue, but given what he'd already done that week, I think they just want it over. They're not going to do anything about the injuries he sustained during arrest. Not that there was much anyway. Laura Rossi is fine, although her fella is facing an investigation at the hospital. They want to know why the disappearance of the drugs wasn't looked into properly. He'll get a slap on the wrist and that'll be it. Hopefully.'

'The girl . . .'

'Stacey lied.'

Jess lowered her head, nodding slowly into her chest. 'I knew it was rubbish. She was always making up stuff. Even when we were younger.'

'I never believed her anyway.'

Murphy picked at a bit of fluff on the arm of his chair, rolling it into a ball between his fingers.

Jess filled the silence. 'Did you find out why he killed those people?'

'He's refusing to talk in interview. His solicitor is almost as terrier-like as you are.'

'I'll take that as a compliment,' Jess said, a smile forming which almost reached her eyes. 'Do you have enough?'

'Yeah, pretty much. We know what he's said to Amy. He'd spoken about someone he called "Number One". Met her back at school, stalked her, was warned off. We've looked into it and found out who she was. There's a possibility he had something to do with the death of that girl's boyfriend at the time, but we're not sure. The mixture of rejection and seeing what those who rejected him put up with. He could never work out why they didn't want him. We think he tried to get with the first female victim – Jane – and when she turned him down, he became obsessed with her. Once he found out her partner's secret, well . . . something sent him over the edge. He came back to Liverpool when his dad died. His mum was found dead when he was only a baby. Suicide, with a suspicion on the father. He had a very warped view of women and relationships. Power and control. The usual.'

Jess nodded, silence growing around them as the real reason she was there began to fill the room.

'When I look at you, I see him. That's why.'

'I'm sorry,' Murphy said, not letting his gaze slip from hers. 'I wish I'd done a million things differently that night. That week.'

'I know you're not to blame. Not really. It just makes it easier if the one person who was in that room, who is still alive, was to blame. That's all.'

'I miss you, Jess. Twenty years. I can't walk away from that.'

'Every time I see you, I'm reminded of that night. I go back to those feelings. When that evil bastard was killing people in the street. When my son, who was just with his friends, out having a laugh, ran into his path.'

'What do you want me to do?'

Jess sniffed, wiped at her face and shook her head. 'There's nothing you can do. It's just the way things are.'

'I tried to save him . . .'

'I know you did.'

Murphy didn't speak for a while, the ticking of the clock on the wall breaking the silence.

'I see you and I get all those feelings back. I see you and I see Peter. My son, killed before his life had begun.'

Murphy closed his eyes, seeing the moment instantly.

'But, maybe I need that reminder. Maybe I need to see those things. To know that my boy didn't die alone. That

his uncle David was right there with him. Trying to save
him.'

Murphy opened his eyes and looked across at Jess.
What he saw gave him something.

It gave him hope.

Acknowledgements

The words may start with one person in a darkened room, but getting them into *your* hands requires a whole number of people. These are just a few of them.

Firstly, Eva Dolan, Nick Quantrill, Steve Mosby, Craig Robertson, and Pete Sortwell. You're all fine and excellent people, I am incredibly lucky to know you.

Mel Sherratt and Mark Edwards, for your continued support and inspiration.

Sarah Hughes, Linda Moore, Liz Barnsley, Keith Nixon, Paul D. Brazill, and Jan Russell, for all the support on and offline.

Jo Dickinson, my incredible editor, who has improved this book immeasurably. Emma Capron, Louise Davies, Elizabeth Preston, and all the rest of the Simon & Schuster team – I am beyond pleased to be starting this journey with you all.

My agent Phil Patterson – your continued determination and ambition in the face of personal adversity is astounding. You're a good man. A very good man. Also to Sandra Sawicka and Luke Speed, for being ace agents in foreign rights and TV.

My parents, my grandparents. My siblings and in-laws. Uncles, aunts, cousins, next-door neighbours, etc. There's a whole bunch of Vestes and Woodlands, and Kirkhams and Hales, and Robertsons and Smiths, who all contribute to me being who I am, and buying the books in great quantities. Never stop.

Special thanks to Andrea Robertson, for all her medical advice. All mistakes are my own and intentional. Honest.

Thank you to Uncle John 'Murphy' Kirkham and Gina Kirkham.

Finally, my wife, Emma Veste, and daughters Abigail and Megan. Abs and Migs – fist bump, balalalala. Thank you for being two of the best and brightest daughters a dad could ever hope for. Emma – not many people know how much work goes into being a writer's partner. Thank you for taking on that burden. *Ti amo, bella.* Thank you for everything you do and everything you are.

LIKE YOUR FICTION A LITTLE ON THE DARK SIDE?

Like to curl up in a darkened room all alone, with the doors bolted and the windows locked and slip into something cold and terrifying...half hoping something goes bump in the night?

Me too.

That's why you'll find me at The Dark Pages - the home of crooks and villains, mobsters and terrorists, spies and private eyes; where the plots are twistier than a knotted noose and the pacing tighter than Marlon Brando's braces.

Beneath the city's glitz, down a litter-strewn alley, behind venetian blinds where neon slices the smoke-filled gloom, reading the dark pages.

Join me: **WWW.THEDARKPAGES.CO.UK**

AGENT X

@dark_pages